The Plainsmen Series by Terry C. Johnston
from St. Martin's Paperbacks

BLOOD SONG

THE BATTLE OF POWDER RIVER AND THE BEGINNING OF THE GREAT SIOUX WAR OF 1876

TERRY C. JOHNSTON

St. Martin's Paperbacks

BLOOD SONG

Copyright © 1993 by Terry C. Johnston.

Cover art by Jim Carson.

All rights reserved. No part of this book may be used or reproduced in any manner whatsoever without written permission except in the case of brief quotations embodied in critical articles or reviews. For information address St. Martin's Press, 175 Fifth Avenue, New York, N.Y. 10010.

ISBN: 0-312-92921-8

Printed in the United States of America

St. Martin's Paperbacks edition/January 1993

10   9   8   7   6   5   4   3

*for the charming little lady
who has brought such tremendous joy
to her daddy,
I lovingly dedicate this book
to my daughter,
Erinn Noel*

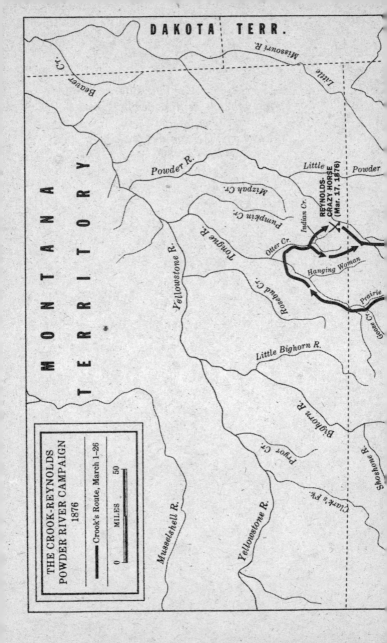

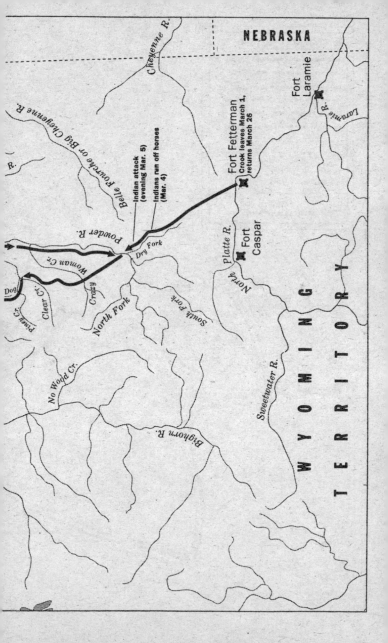

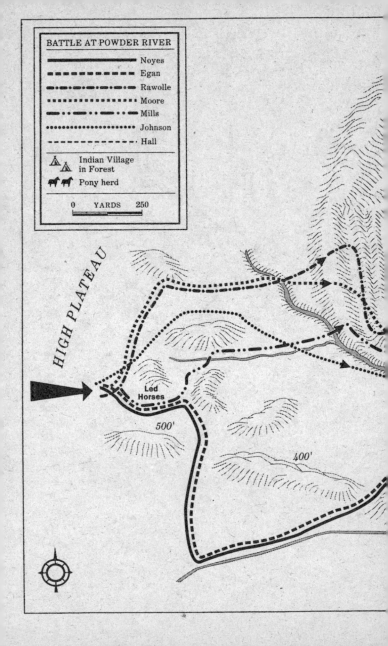

BATTLE AT POWDER RIVER

————————	Noyes
— — — — —	Egan
—·—·—·—·—	Rawolle
················	Moore
—··—··—··—	Mills
··············	Johnson
– – – – – –	Hall

⚠ ⚠ Indian Village in Forest

🐎 🐎 Pony herd

0   YARDS   250

HIGH PLATEAU

Led Horses

500'

400'

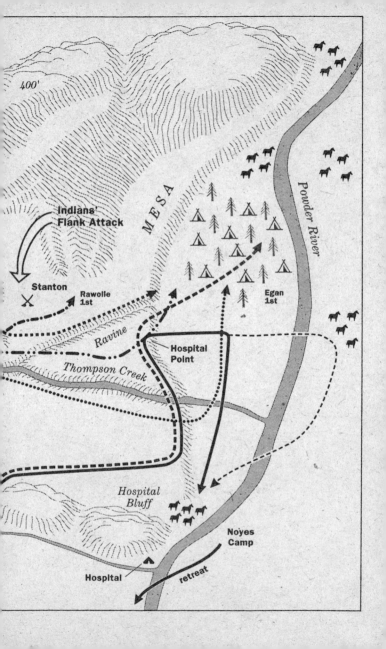

But war must be justified—by illusion, if reality will not do. Behind the scenes the props had all been marshalled to set the stage for a grand illusion. When the time came, a benevolent government would be able to show the people that it had given the nation's openly rebellious wards still another gracious chance to become peace-loving, Christian farmers. It was only their defiant rejection of this handsome offer that compelled a sympathetic Indian Office to request disciplinary action from a reluctant army. The nobility of the charade almost brings tears to white eyes!

—John S. Gray
Centennial Campaign: The Sioux War of 1876

The overwhelming disaster at the Little Bighorn was merely the unplanned and undesired climax of the U.S. Army's ill-starred 1876 campaign against Sioux and Cheyenne hostiles on the northern Plains. It was a campaign whose opening action, only months before the George Armstrong Custer debacle, left another cavalry commander's career in ruins as he, like Custer, made the mistake of underestimating the tenacity and aggressiveness of his Indian opponents. An attack launched in ignorance against the wrong target, it set in motion the train of events that led inevitably to the 7th Cavalry's martyrdom on the banks of the Little Bighorn.

—Wayne R. Austerman
"Debacle on Powder River"
Wild West magazine

General, these winter campaigns in these latitudes should be prohibited . . . The month of March has told on me more than five years of my life.

—Colonel Joseph J. Reynolds
to General William T. Sherman,
April 11, 1876

I'd like to be a packer
And pack with George C. Crook
And dressed up in my canvas suit
To be for him mistook.
I'd braid my beard in two long tails,
And idle all the day
In whittling sticks and wondering
What the New York papers say.

Popular soldier's doggerel
during the 1870s

Most important of all, the Indians were aroused by this failure of the troops, their old feeling of superiority to the white man was reawakened, and they became convinced that they not only could elude the white soldiers but could also defeat them on a battlefield of their own choosing . . . Accordingly, the extent of Crook's failure is to be measured not so much by what he failed to do as by the increased confidence that that failure gave to the hostiles; and the task faced by the army, never an easy one, was now rendered much more difficult and formidable, a fact of which its leaders themselves seemed to be supremely unaware.

—Edgar I. Stewart
Custer's Luck

Cast of Characters

Seamus Donegan

Civilians

*Samantha (Pike) Donegan
*Rebecca (Pike) Grover
Sharp Grover
*Lucy Maynadier
Zachariah Chandler—Interior Secretary
Benjamin R. Cowen—Assistant Interior Secretary
Jeff/Jefferson—Crook's personal cook/butler
Robert E. Strahorn—correspondent for the *Rocky Mountain News*
Thomas Moore—master of the mule train
mule skinners' crew chiefs:
   Tom McAuliffe

Richard "Uncle Dick" Closter
—— Foster
—— Young
Edward DeLaney
   packers:
      Hans ——
      Pat ——
+Jim Wright—herder
Kid Slaymaker—owner of the Hog Ranch, near Fort Fetterman
Eugene Tillottson—contract sutler, Fort Fetterman

* fictional characters

Military

General William Tecumseh Sherman—Commander of the Army
Lieutenant General Philip H. Sheridan—Commander, Military Division of the Missouri
General George C. Crook—Commander, Department of the Platte

Colonel Henry E. Maynadier—Post Commander, Fort Laramie
Colonel Joseph J. Reynolds—Commander, Third U.S. Cavalry
Lieutenant Colonel John S. Mason
Major Alex Chambers—Fourth Infantry, Post

Commander, Fort Fetterman

Major T. B. Dewees—Commander, Fourth Battalion: Companies A and B, Second Cavalry

Major E. M. Coates—Commander, Sixth Battalion: Companies C and I, Fourth Infantry

Major Samuel P. Ferris

Captain Anson Mills—Third Cavalry/Commander, First Battalion: Companies M and E, Third Cavalry

Captain William Hawley—Commander, Second Battalion: Companies A and D, Third Cavalry

Captain Thaddeus H. Stanton—Army paymaster, Department of the Platte, Omaha (Crook's chief of scouts)

Captain James ("Teddy") Egan—Company K, Second Cavalry

Captain Alex Moore—Third Cavalry/Commander, Fifth Battalion: F Company, Third Cavalry; E Company, Second Cavalry

Captain Henry E. Noyes—Commander, Third Battalion: Companies I and K, Second Cavalry

Lieutenant John G. Bourke —aide-de-camp to General Crook

Lieutenant Charles Morton —adjutant to General Crook

*Lieutenant August C. Paul —Company M, Third Cavalry

Lieutenant Christopher T. Hall—Company I, Second Cavalry

Lieutenant J. B. Johnson—Company E, Third Cavalry

Lieutenant George A. Drew —Third Cavalry, Quartermaster for the Big Horn Expedition

^First Lieutenant William C. Rawolle—E Company, Second Cavalry

First Sergeant Frank S. Rittel—M Company, Third Cavalry

^Sergeant Charles Kaminski —M Company, Third Cavalry

Sergeant Frank V. Erhard—M Company, Third Cavalry

Sergeant Henry Prescott—M Company, Third Cavalry

Sergeant Franklin B. Robinson—M Company, Third Cavalry

Sergeant Alexander B. Ballard—M Company, Third Cavalry

Sergeant John Gleuson—K Company, Second Cavalry

Corporal John A. Kirkwood —M Company, Third Cavalry

^Corporal John Lang—
E Company, Second
Cavalry

+Corporal—Slavey

Private Andrew Peiser—
Crook's striker

Private Augustus E. Bellows
—trumpeter, K Company,
Second Cavalry

Private Jeremiah J. Murphy
—M Company, Third
Cavalry

^Private John Droege—
K Company, Second
Cavalry

^Private Edward Eagan—
K Company, Second
Cavalry

+Private Peter Dowdy—
E Company, Third
Cavalry

+Private Michael McCannon
—F Company, Third
Cavalry

+Private Lorenzo E. Ayers—
M Company, Third
Cavalry

+Private George Schneider—
K Company, Second
Cavalry

^Farrier Patrick Goings—
K Company, Second
Cavalry

Blacksmith Albert Glavinski
—M Company, Third
Cavalry

Dr. Curtis E. Munn—Chief
Medical Officer, Big Horn
Expedition

Dr. John Ridgely—Acting
Assistant Surgeon

Dr. C. R. Stevens—Acting
Assistant Surgeon

William C. Bryan—Hospital
Steward

* fictional characters
^ killed in the Battle of Powder River
+ wounded in the Battle of Powder River

Scouts and Interpreters

Frank Grouard
Baptiste Garnier (Little Bat)
Baptiste Pourrier (Big Bat)
Ben Clark
Jules Ecofee
Charles Richard
Joe Eldridge
Mitch Shimmeno
John Farnham
Louis Reshaw/Richaud/
Richard

Louis Shangrau
Speed Stagner
Charlie Jennesse
(LaJeunesse)
John Shangrau
Tom Red
John Provost
Buckskin Jack Russell
Louis Gringos

Cheyenne

Old Bear	Two Moon
Monaseetah	Yellow Bird
Sees Red	Scabby
Rolls Down	Wooden Leg
Little Wolf	Big Head Woman

Sioux

He Dog—Hunkpatila warrior	Black Buffalo Woman—wife of No Water
Lame Dog Woman—He Dog's wife	No Water
Crazy Horse—Oglalla war chief	Hump
	White Cow Bull
Black Shawl—wife to Crazy Horse	Little Hawk
	Lone Bear

Author's Foreword

There are few imperatives in my life, and most of those I have discovered are of emotional, deeply sentimental importance. Among the highest of those imperatives are maintaining the continuity I began with the first book in this series, *Sioux Dawn,* wherein I gave the reader either a foreword or an afterword to explain historical and social context of the "novel" they held in their hands.

In this case, with *Blood Song,* volume 8 of the Plainsmen Series, you will find both.

The reason for that turned out to be a complicated, infuriating and ultimately saddening thing: with its multihued characters and varied locales, *Dying Thunder* as written was simply too long for the publisher's requirements. So be it. In our discussions and eventual settlement on what to do to make of that novel something they could live with and I could be proud to have my name on, I consented not only to dropping the Prologue from *Blood Song,* but also to dropping the extensive "Afterword" from that story of Seamus Donegan and the last days of the Buffalo War on the southern plains as told in *Dying Thunder.*

Yet, doing so did not absolve me of what I feel to be a very great responsibility to you, my reader. What was begun seven novels ago should not be discarded out of hand—no matter the amount of consideration given. Therefore, I offer you this foreword as a bridge between the story and characters and place in time you read in *Dying Thunder,* and that story and those characters you will now find to thrill you in *Blood Song*.

I hope this foreword, and its placement here, will be as meaningful to you as it has to friends who have agreed that it should find its proper home here—before you begin this eighth volume in the farflung travels and adventures of Seamus Donegan.

Then too, I hope my readers are as thrilled as I am to see the fantastic job in what the publisher has done to enhance the covers on these two volumes. Let everyone know I am well-pleased, and hope that you, my readers, will find these great new covers as stunning and dynamic as I do.

"The Old Mackenzie Trail"
by William Lawrence Chittenden

Where are now the scouts and soldiers
And those wagon-trains of care,
Those grim men and haggard women?
And the echoes whisper—Where?

Ah, what tales of joys and sorrows
Could that silent trail relate:
Tales of loss, and wrecked ambitions,
Tales of hope, of love, and hate;
Tales of hunger, thirst, and anguish,
Tales of fear, and death, and danger,
Tales of lonely prairie graves.

Nevermore shall bold Mackenzie
With his brave and dauntless band,
Guide the restless, roving settlers
Through the Texas borderland.

Yes! that soldier's work is over,
And the dim trail rests at last;
But his name and trail still lead us
Through the borders of the past.

As I have done before in all the previous novels in this series, I feel again the need of offering you something in way of an historical explanation before riding with Seamus

Donegan through the pages of this new novel. In this case, it is my hope to tie up any narrative and historical loose ends for my readers—something I believe is required of me because this was a story that encompassed two novels, *Shadow Riders* and *Dying Thunder,* dealing with the frontier army conquering the southern plains.

I sit here now in the late June sunshine beside the Prairie Dog Town Fork of the Red River, this alkali-laced, muddy creek, looking to me like coffee laced with milk as it races noisily over a rocky bottom, dragonflies suspended over every streamside rock, while I begin listening to the ghosts of the Kiowa and Cheyenne and Comanche caught here by Mackenzie's Fourth Cavalry some 117 years ago. The flies torment the air, then are gone on the hot breeze as I cool my overheated white man's feet in the muddy water and wait to understand those whispered voices. That revelation comes only when one uses all one's senses, experiencing this place of a bygone time both magical and protective to the tribes whose trails haunted the trackless Staked Plain.

The ultimate importance of this often little-known Red River or Buffalo War to the history of our nation is undisputed among American frontier historians: through it, we saw the final subjugation of three of America's most powerful tribes brought about by employing the most massive use of troops ever pitted against Indians to that time. The very same period witnessed the extermination of the buffalo from the southern plains, while the closing of the Buffalo War brought about a greater awareness in the hearts of a few the inhuman cruelty of the government's treatment of her Indian wards, imprisoned on bleak reservations ever since.

It is therefore perhaps ironic that we find General Nelson A. Miles, the commander of the combined campaign to take the field later that same year, writing with heartfelt sentiment during the early days of 1874 that:

> One of the strongest causes of unrest among [the Indians] . . . was the fact that the promises made to induce them to go on to reservations were not always carried

out by the government authorities. They had been removed from . . . the ranges of the buffalo, but under
distinct treaty stipulation that they were to be provided
with shelter, clothing, and sustenance . . . They were
sometimes for weeks without their rations. Their annual
allowance of food was usually exhausted in six or seven
months.

Yet it was official Washington's position, in a city too far
removed from the frontier and the lives of both white and
red who clashed there, that the government refuse any sympathy for the passing of the Quaker's "Peace Policy." Perhaps Interior Secretary Columbus Delano set the stage for
the outbreak of warfare, from the southern plains to the
Dakotas of Sitting Bull and Crazy Horse, when he ex-
pressed the government's official position in early 1874:

In our intercourse with the Indians it must always be
borne in mind that we are the most powerful party . . .
We are assuming, and I think with propriety, that our
civilization ought to take the place of their barbarous
habits. We therefore claim the right to control the soil
they occupy, and we assume it is our duty to coerce
them, if necessary, into the adoption and practice of our
habits and customs . . . I would not seriously regret the
total disappearance of the buffalo from our western
prairies, in its effect upon the Indians, regarding it
rather as a means of hastening their sense of depen-
dence upon the products of the soil.

For some reason, there might be those who would find
fault with me for telling the story of this war in the manner
I have herein chosen. I could have written as well of the
autumn and winter campaign of General Nelson A. Miles.
Too, I could have chosen to include the campaign movements of Buell and Price, and told the reader of what tran-
spired during Colonel Black Jack Davidson's "Wrinkled-
Hand Chase." But none of those stories, none of those
troop movements, even the campaign of Mackenzie after

he had driven the tribes out of the Palo Duro, was near as dramatic as telling you the history of the Buffalo War through the eyes of those common folk who fought at Adobe Walls, suffered the siege of the Lyman wagon train, survived the Lost Valley fight of Major Jones's Texas Rangers, lived through the slaughter of the German family in Kansas or the Lone Tree Massacre of Oliver Short's survey party, not to mention surviving the high tension of the little-known Buffalo Wallow Fight.

In the end it was my story alone to marshal and to tell you in some sensible, orderly, yet emotionally-charged manner. Rather than treating novelistically solely with what I have come to believe was mostly an ineffectual maneuvering of troops back and forth across the Texas Panhandle, I wanted to bring the conflict down to its most basic element: the individual himself (and sometimes herself), the individual caught up in the drama. By now you readers of the Plainsmen Series have already come to know other heroes and heroines. In *Dying Thunder* you met that many more—of their quiet dignity, real flesh and blood—who came and bled and sometimes died to bring peace to that land once ruled by the red lords of the southern plains.

Mystically, the tribes of the southern prairie came to believe that one final, dramatic war could push the white man far from the buffalo country, once and for all. The Buffalo War of 1874 began at that quiet meadow we have come to call Adobe Walls.

But in order to keep this high drama on the far frontier in proper historical perspective, one must remember that less than a week after the battle at Adobe Walls, Alexander Graham Bell was demonstrating for a wondering and admiring public back east his newest invention: the electric telephone. Quite a stark contrast with the bloody vignettes then unfolding in the Texas Panhandle, where buffalo hunters and buffalo soldiers, settler families and captive children, civilian scouts and surveyors were all caught in a war against a primitive, stone-age people.

Although in the weeks, months and years following that fight at Adobe Walls many men came forward to falsely claim they were there at the battle, both the popular and historical literature shows the number of white men at the meadow on the order of twenty-nine men, two of whom (Ike and Shorty Scheidler) were killed in the first moments of the attack. While giving us what will perhaps remain as the best accounting of those who were there versus those who clearly were not, however, the supreme authorities on the battle, Baker and Harrison, nonetheless state:

> It is not known how many white men took part in the fight. Probably the smallest estimate to come from a battle participant is fifteen; other white participants in the fight remembered as many as twenty-eight defenders.

Likewise, Indian strength has been variously noted; Lieutenant Baldwin's conservative estimate was two hundred warriors, the same number accounted for by A. C. Myers and General Nelson A. Miles; Dixon reported to journalists and others that he remembered between three hundred and five hundred attackers. And as high as fifteen hundred was the number quoted by Willis Skelton Glenn, a hide man who was not in the fight but who knew many of the men who were, men who ought to know. So from all the reading I have done, I've come to accept the opinion of some of the finest writers on the subject, believing that there was something on the order of seven hundred warriors charging into that meadow, attacking the hide men that hot June day.

The preeminent importance of the fight at Adobe Walls is not only that it marked the first time the warrior bands had attacked a commercial center populated by nonarmy personnel, it as well marked "the beginning of the end." This end as well spelled the demise of the buffalo hunters, the end of the buffalo itself—not only an eclipse of the power held by the Kiowa, Comanche and Cheyenne.

Yet I would be remiss if I did not mention that although the Indians lost the fight at Adobe Walls (in that they failed to wipe out the settlement as originally planned), they nonetheless did achieve their objective in that traditional buffalo country they had roamed for so long. For some time following the fight, they did indeed drive the hide men back across the Cimarron River. In fact, Billy Dixon himself never hunted buffalo after Adobe Walls. And veteran Jim Hanrahan lost his whole business by staking it all in buffalo country, quitting the hide game and coming back north to begin a political career in Dodge City.

In the first days following the fight, the count of Indian dead was said to range from thirteen to fifteen. It appears the count actually went much higher—likely something on the order of at least seventy killed and wounded. Two years after Adobe Walls, Chief Whirlwind of the Southern Cheyenne accounted for 115 dead. A few weeks after the skirmish an army scout with Lieutenant Baldwin's group (the first to see how the hide men had cut the heads off the thirteen Indian bodies and stuck those grisly trophies high atop the spikes on the Myers and Leonard stockade) reported at least thirty Indian graves dotting the buttes surrounding the meadow at Adobe Walls. The reader must remember that Cheyenne invariably did bury their dead in the rocks.

Charles E. Jones in 1876 learned from Spotted Wolf, an Arapaho chief, who counted the dead by raising "fingers on both hands three times and then five fingers on one hand," that there were thirty-five braves killed.

The true figure will never be known.

But for a long, long time following that bloody battle with the hide men, the Indians refused to visit the meadow. Among the tribes, it was known as an evil place. One has only to imagine the sight of those thirteen heads impaled on those stockade spikes, where the crows and magpies and robber jays sat picking eyes from their sockets and bits of flesh from the skulls to find your own hair rising at the back of your neck. Truly, the meadow had proved to be an evil place where Isatai's medicine turned sour in the mouths of all.

Billy Dixon did in fact make that famous "mile-long" shot of his, in just the manner as I have written it in *Dying Thunder*. Afterward, Dixon and others measured the exact distance of his shot at that far hillside: 1538 yards, just shy of a mile. As it has been stated by historians, if any one bullet did more than other bullets to end the southwestern buffalo war, it was that one bullet fired from Dixon's borrowed .50-caliber Sharps rifle.

Even as the buffalo men were packing up to light out for the relative safety of Dodge City, the controversy of where they had built their settlement and what it meant to the overall war effort was only beginning. In the battle's aftermath, General John Pope, commander of the Military Department of the Missouri, publicly justified why he was refusing to send troops to lift the siege at Adobe Walls, why he wouldn't in any way aid the hide men trapped there. He said:

> A trading post [without] any permit or license from . . . any United States authority, was established by some persons doing business in Dodge City, at Adobe Walls, in the Pan-Handle of Texas, and far beyond the limits of this department . . . mainly to supply the buffalo hunters, whose continuous pursuit and wholesale slaughter of the buffalo . . . had driven the great herds down into the Indian Reservations . . . When the Cheyennes made their attack upon this trading post . . . the proprietors made an application, through the governor of Kansas, not for the protection of life, but to enable them to keep up their trading post and the illicit traffic. I declined to send a force for any such purpose . . .

Learning of Pope's refusal of support, General Philip H. Sheridan, commanding the entire Military Division of the Missouri, publicly chastised his general:

> Regardless of the character of these men . . . you should have used the troops for the protection of life and property, wherever it might have been.

As things began to quiet down in Texas following the end of the Buffalo War in the spring of 1875, Charlie Rath himself later established another trading post in the Panhandle on Sweetwater Creek. This new Rath enterprise flourished, drawing in more and more businessmen, who together formed quite a little settlement complete with saloons, dance halls, whorehouses and two restaurants. But Rath's new endeavor was to put itself out of business, although not as quickly as his store at Adobe Walls had closed its doors on that hot summer morning in June of 1874.

What began in 1872 as the hunters fanned out from Dodge City along the Arkansas River, was brought to a speedy completion before 1878. The buffalo were gone and the hide men had worked themselves out of a job. In less than half a dozen years these hunters—surprisingly few in number—had shot their way through the herds that had once blanketed the southern plains. The last band, numbering only fifty, was slaughtered by a sporting party from back east in 1887.

In 1924, fifty years after the battle at Adobe Walls, the site was presented to the Panhandle Plains Historical Society by Mr. and Mrs. W. T. Coble, owners of the Turkey Track Ranch. Another fifty-one years passed until the first of five archeological seasons, beginning in 1975, were spent excavating the site that is now listed on the National Register of Historic Places.

Besides fine examples of period clothing, weapons and accouterments, precise scale models of the buildings at Adobe Walls in June of 1874 may be viewed from all angles at the Hutchinson County Museum in Borger, Texas. It was there I finally met the man who had taken countless hours of his time to talk with me on the phone, discussing both the battle and its participants, before I was able to finally travel south to walk that ground myself. Ed Benz spent the better part of a long June day at my side there in his museum, answering even more questions and dealing in speculations with this author, seated in his office poring over his personal library on the battle and the overall Panhandle War, in addition to eventually walking over every yard of that now-quiet meadow with me.

Uncannily, Ed knew when to talk and when to stay quiet and follow along as I knelt here and there, placing my hands along the rain-washed remnants of the stockade walls, those of the Rath store and saloon, the privy and O'Keefe's blacksmith shop. I could not have reached an understanding of the fight and its place in the broader Red River War had it not been for Ed Benz, director of the Hutchinson County Museum.

I saw for myself where Isatai, the yellow-painted Kwahadi shaman, sat naked atop his pony during the day-long battle. Fully disgraced, he returned to his band and eventually surrendered. Isatai lived out the rest of his life in shame among his people on the reservation. He was still living as late as 1912 near Fort Sill, and by the late 1940s the Indians in the area remembered him to tribal and historical researchers as "that comical fellow."

Indeed, the inability of hundreds of the finest warriors on the southern plains to defeat two dozen buffalo hunters symbolized the beginning of the end for the tribes that had long ruled the Panhandle buffalo country of Texas.

Ultimately, in 1929, Olive K. Dixon succeeded in her own private battle—bringing her husband to be reburied with full military honors at a spot that for the rest of the old scout's life remained central to every story of his exploits on the southern plains, tales most central to the history of West Texas. The bones of Billy Dixon now rest in that whisper-quiet meadow at Adobe Walls.

After the troops from General Miles's base camp arrived to rescue the defenders of the Buffalo Wallow, Billy Dixon and Private Rath dragged Private Smith's body into that bloody wallow once more, the wallow that Dixon had believed would prove to be his own grave. Again the survivors scooped out the soil with their knives and bare hands, this time to dig a grave for one of their own. After saying a few words over the last resting place of Private George W. Smith, they limped down to the creek where Miles's soldiers prepared a much-awaited meal for the five. The following morning, the wounded were transported to Camp Supply, where the surgeons amputated Amos Chapman's leg below the knee. Dixon goes on to write:

> Amos was as tough as second growth hickory and was soon out of the hospital and in the saddle . . . Chapman could handle a gun and ride as well as ever, the only difference being that he had to mount his horse from the right side, Indian fashion.

General Miles severely censured Major William R. Price for his callous treatment of the five men when Price passed them by at the Buffalo Wallow—leaving them no food, no medical care beyond Surgeon Fouts's cursory examination, much less any weapons and ammunition. In a matter of days Miles recommended that all six of those men from the Buffalo Wallow receive the country's highest commendation, the Congressional Medal of Honor. Indeed, all six medals were awarded, but in the case of Dixon and Chapman, the commendations were revoked years later because the War Department determined the two scouts "were not officially enlisted in the army." It turned out to be a tragic and unnecessarily shameful epilogue on the part of the government, which had required the utmost in loyalty to it, even to the point of demanding one's life in service to the Red River War—yet in return for that loyalty, the government refused to award its highest honor to those who willingly had given such selfless service to the war effort.

The four cowboys who were chased by the warriors riding under Lone Wolf and Mamanti in the Lost Valley of north-central Texas were James C. Loving, owner of the famous ranch himself, along with W. C. Hunt, I. G. Newcomb and Shad Damron—otherwise nameless men who disappear into history, although they had momentarily taken center stage in the first act of one of the most dramatic vignettes of this border war. I felt this story of that war would not be complete without the telling of Jones's Texas Rangers and their fight against those Kiowa warriors who successfully ambushed the major's detachment, another in the long recitation of citizen law enforcement that was ultimately required to subdue the far frontier throughout the West.

Colonel Ranald S. Mackenzie's slaughter of the 1100 ponies and mules at Tule Canyon left a prominent landmark that was to stand for many years to come, a mountain of bones viewed by cattlemen and settlers alike when passing through the area. The destruction of those animals also provided grist for a supernatural-legend still popular in the Panhandle: reports of folks witnessing a ghostly herd of riderless steeds seen galloping on bright, moonlit nights along the rim of Tule Canyon, their nostrils flaring, manes whipped by prairie winds.

So I had the tale complete, from Dixon's mile-long shot ending the fight at Adobe Walls, to Mackenzie's putting an end to the battle of Palo Duro Canyon, bringing ruin to the tribes by slaughtering their wealth in ponies. Both acts together brought a close to the Buffalo War, and in so doing cleared the way for establishment in 1876 of the first cattle ranch in the Texas Panhandle, known as the J A and founded by Charles Goodnight (who acquired fame for blazing the Goodnight-Loving cattle trail north to the Kansas railheads).

On the fateful day that the Kiowa, Cheyenne and Comanche prisoners were being loaded aboard wagons to begin their long trip to Florida's Fort Marion prison, the owl shaman Mamanti looked up to find the peace chief, Kicking Bird, sitting atop his tall gray horse, an animal that had been given him by the Fort Sill soldiers.

The warrior medicine man cried out to the peace chief, "You remain free, a big man with the whites. But you will not live long, Kicking Bird. I will see to that!"

Two days later, while drinking a cup of coffee in his lodge near Fort Sill, Kicking Bird died mysteriously. Just as he had been cursed. Every tongue on the reservation wagged that it was the doing of the powerful shaman taken far away in iron chains.

And only three months later, when he finally learned of the death of Kicking Bird some two thousand miles away back on the reservation, Mamanti also died suddenly himself—yet died among strangers at Fort Marion. The Kiowas believed that the shaman had willed his own death as the ultimate atonement because he had summoned all his powers to destroy a fellow tribesman.

The rest of the seventy-four prisoners, chiefs and war

chiefs alike, continued making palm-frond hats and polishing alligator teeth for St. Augustine visitors through the years. One by one they sickened and died over the endless seasons of their captivity in those ruins of the ancient Spanish fort.

Ironic that it was the Spanish legions of Coronado who had penetrated to the very heart of the Staked Plain in the 1540s.

Lieutenant Pratt, in charge of the military detachment escorting the prisoners to Florida, tells us something of the conditions these proud men had to endure in their final days, when he wrote of his disgust upon seeing where these brave but defeated warriors were to be incarcerated: "The roofs and walls of every casement are dripping with water, and in places covered with a green scum, while all the cells have a musty, sickening odor."

The mighty White Bear, Satanta of the Kiowa, had turned back to the reservation after lifting the siege of Captain Wyllys Lyman's wagon train, subsequently surrendering to Colonel Neill's infantry on October 4, 1874. Two days later, on 6 October, President Grant approved of returning the aging chief to the Huntsville Penitentiary, just as Commissioner Hoag and Agent Haworth were attempting to pull strings in Washington to get Satanta released. General Philip H. Sheridan himself had seen to it that White Bear would never again roam the plains.

As his people gathered around him for the last time before their chief was taken back to prison in Texas, Satanta pointed to the soldiers and said, "The white men are as numerous as the sands in these hills. We may kill these, but others will come. The Indians' days are over."

For some four years Satanta endured in that prison. Then, in the fall of 1878, other prisoners recalled how the old chief finally seemed to accept that he was never going to be released this time. And how in despair he spent most of his final days staring out at the trees clothed in the fire of the changing season, when the air cooled and the great animals put on their winter coats for the coming time of cold and snow. Inside the soul of White Bear the memories still lived, while his body (and in those final days his spirit as well) became a prisoner to the great white tide sweeping over the southern prairie.

There from his barred window he stared to the northwest —to the land of his youth and his people's greatness.

On the morning of 10 October 1878, a prison guard found Satanta near death. Below his cot lay two puddles of blood. He had slashed at his neck and leg arteries in an ugly attempt to free himself from the prison and the white world that had brought ruin to his people.

Guards carried White Bear across the prison yard to infirmary which was located on the second floor at Huntsville. It was there that the chief was given emergency treatment to stop the blood flow, then was left lying on a cot near an unbarred window, alone. Sometime later in the morning Satanta staggered to that second-story window in his weakened state. Opening it as he sang his death song, White Bear folded his arms across his chest and plunged head first to the ground and died—a scene that reminds us of the suicide of Blue Duck, Larry McMurtry's fictional renegade in *Lonesome Dove*.

It would not be until 1963, however, that Satanta's relatives won their long court battle with the Texas government to have White Bear's bones brought from that Texas prison cemetery back to the reservation in Oklahoma and laid to rest.

With that leap from the window, Satanta had seized his freedom after years of enslavement. According to the ancient Kiowa beliefs, White Bear's spirit arose from his crushed and battered body, then traveled into the west, hurrying to overtake the sunset. His soul had first to cross the far Rockies before coming to the shore of the seemingly endless ocean.

After crossing, his soul would find waiting on the far side the spirits of friends and relatives who had died before White Bear, now welcoming the chief to that distant land of joy, where there was no pain of body nor of spirit—where Satanta would again find buffalo aplenty, grazing on the green grass as once more he leaped atop a favorite war pony and took up the chase.

About the same time, in late 1878, the government decided to return the Fort Marion prisoners to their reservations in Oklahoma. Of the original seventy-five, only seven Comanches and thirteen Kiowas had not died in the heat and disease of Florida during those three years. One of the survivors, the once mighty Lone Wolf, had already contracted malaria while at Fort Marion by the time he was carried home to the reservation at Fort Sill, a mere shadow of his former vitality. The following year he died of his untreatable fever at the young age of fifty-six, and was secretly buried somewhere on the north shoulder of Mount Scott.

Five years later, in 1884, an outfit of cowboys from the Box K Ranch drove up a herd of steers from Texas, under contract to feed the dwindling numbers of Kiowa and Comanche now consolidated with the Cheyenne at Anadarko. Cowboy Jim Williams wrote of the tragic scene of seeing a once proud people:

> There were about 6,000 of both tribes, both Kiowas and Comanches, and everyone had a pack of dogs but few papooses . . . the agent had his warriors . . . at the corral gate on their ponies with their shooting irons. They were bare-backed on their horses and them just as poor as they could be . . . When they came out of that pen the wild riding and high shooting would come off. Sometimes they would kill their steer in just a short while, and again they might empty their sixshooter into a steer and not have him down—maybe kill him two miles from camp . . .
>
> The old buck wouldn't turn his hand at anything, the old squaws did the work—what little there was to do. And when they cleaned up a carcass there wasn't anything left but a pile of grass.

Then, in 1887, a Kiowa medicine man on the Kiowa-Comanche Reservation revived an old doctrine espousing the return of the buffalo and bygone times of warrior glory. He said the Spirit Above demanded that all whites and any nonbelievers among the reservation bands would be swept off the earth by consuming fire and furious whirlwinds. This last great excitement overwhelmed the reservation as the prophet claimed the ability to raise the dead and kill his enemies with a withering glance. At the western end of the reservation on Elk Creek, the prophet set up a base camp where he soon drew a growing and fanatical following as year after year of drought brought ruin to the crops.

The following year the agent prohibited the sun dance at last. Angry, the Kiowas refused to plant their seed in the flaky, unforgiving ground that next spring, and pulled their children out of the agency's missionary schools.

Yet they never arose in force as did the Lakotas to the north, precipitating both the murder of Sitting Bull and the massacre of Big Foot's band at Wounded Knee.

Eventually realizing the shaman's prophecy would not be coming true, the Kiowa and the few Comanche who had joined them wandered back to their Cache Creek settlements near Fort Sill in the spring of 1891, and once more attempted to walk the white man's road.

As well as any part of this story, it is my hope that you found stirring the tragic vignettes involving Sophia German and her sisters. Again, these four girls were very real people; their story told not only with what I hope was electrifying emotion, but also with authenticity, a fidelity to the facts.

After their release by their captors, Colonel Nelson A. Miles himself, along with his wife, became guardians of the four German sisters. For a while they were given quarters in a large home at Fort Leavenworth. In addition, to assure the girls' continued support, Congress authorized that an amount sufficient to take care of the German sisters be withheld from the annuities of the Southern Cheyennes. As late as 1934 all four of the former captives were still alive— two living in California, one in Nebraska, and the fourth (unnamed in contemporary accounts) had raised a family, surrounded by children and grandchildren, in that rolling country of Kansas, the land her father, John German, had so desperately sought to escape in the bloody summer of 1874.

As I write these words concerning the German girls, I see

among my papers their dark eyes staring back at me from the photographs taken only days following their release from Stone Calf's band. Piercing my soul are the serious countenances of the young Sophia and Catherine German —faces that should otherwise exhibit the brightness of their youth. Instead, the chromos show clearly what horror they had already endured in their short, tragic lives.

I move the copy of their photographs aside and find beneath it the small daguerreotype of little Adelaide and Julia German—the same photo that I wrote about General Miles sending with the half-breed to Stone Calf's band, his handwritten note to the older girls scrawled on the back.

Now for those of you who, like me, wish to read everything you can get your hands on regarding a specific campaign, I would recommend not only those titles I listed for you in the foreword to *Shadow Riders*, vol. 6, of this Plainsman Series, but the following as well:

The Long Death—The Last Days of the Plains Indian, by Ralph K. Andrist

War Cries on Horseback—The Story of the Indian Wars of the Great Plains, by Stephen Longstreet

The Texas Panhandle Frontier, by Fred Rathjen

Adobe Walls Bride, by Olive K. Dixon

Bat Masterson—The Man and The Legend, by Robert K. DeArment

Men of Fiber, by J. Evetts Haley

Great Western Indian Fights (two articles written by J. C. Dykes on the Fight at Adobe Walls and the Battle of Palo Duro Canyon)

Five Years a Cavalryman, by H. H. McConnell

Indian Wars of Texas, by Mildred P. Mayhall

In Search of the Buffalo: The Story of J. Wright Mooar, by Charles G. Anderson

Quanah, Eagle of the Comanches, by Zoe A. Tilghman

The Indian Campaign on the Staked Plain, 1874–1875, by Joe F. Taylor

Quanah Parker—Last Chief of the Comanche, by Clyde L. Jackson and Grace Jackson

In attempting to find an appropriate way of bringing to a close this afterword, I wanted to draw upon the tragic story of the last great chief of the Comanche nation, who, on 2 June 1875, led his starving band of holdouts onto the parade at Fort Sill in a heart-wrenching scene of surrender.

I want you to understand that those who accompanied Quanah into Fort Sill that summer day accounted for only one in every twelve of the Kwahadi at their greatest. Only one in twelve had survived a quarter century of incessant warfare and loss of the buffalo, the rigors of pursuit, along with the devastation of the white man's diseases.

Quanah's surrender in the final chapter of *Dying Thunder* gives one the image of thunder rumbling off into the distance across the far prairie—the final act in the last red storm to batter the southern plains. That surrender opened up the ancient land of the Kwahadi to white settlement. Over the next five years, the white man advanced more into West Texas and the Panhandle than he had in the previous forty years, when the red raiders stood between the white man and the buffalo.

And with that surrender, Three-Finger Kinzie kept his word to Quanah. The leader of the Kwahadis was neither punished nor was he imprisoned with the others in that unfinished stone icehouse where the soldiers threw raw meat over the walls. Neither was Quanah forced to join the prisoners hauled down to die in the swamps of Florida.

Still, what he was forced to do was perhaps all the more painful: forced to watch his people struggle to survive on the reservation, walking the white man's road. They were given flour with stones in the bottom of the sacks, kegs of salt pork half filled with lumps of coal. More times than not their beef allotments never arrived.

Upon surrender, Quanah's Kwahadi were instructed to erect their lodges west of Cache Creek, where the water was polluted after passing through Fort Sill. There, in the swamps of the fort's making, the Comanche children suffered and died of malaria every bit as voracious in its hunger as was the malaria ravaging the prisoners in Florida. Quanah himself caught the fever in 1875. Perhaps only his strong constitution kept him from succumbing as did the weak and the old, and the very young.

After recovering enough of his strength, Quanah requested permission to go in search of his white relatives. More than anything, he told the agent, he wanted to see where his mother had lived out the last few years of her life, back among the Parker clan.

Clothed in beaded buckskins and a red blanket befitting a Kwahadi warrior, able to utter few words in English, and, as author Lucia St. Clair Robson states, "armed only with a letter of introduction from the Indian agent, he set out through Texas to find the Parkers." That letter, written by the reservation agent, said in English: "This young man is the son of Cynthia Ann Parker, and he is going to visit his mother's people. Please show him the road and help him as you can."

The Parker clan did indeed make their dark-skinned relative welcome. Quanah paid close attention to the teachings of his great-uncle Issac, learning as much as possible about the white man's ways while he visited among his mother's people.

Nonetheless, Quanah had to return to his own people, and to the despair of their lives on the reservation. The tiny clapboard houses that the government built for the Indians meant that the camp circles were broken up. Now the families were forced to live apart and isolated from one other. The houses were not of much use anyway, according to Quanah—perhaps only for storage or as barns for their few prized horses. He said there were too many snakes in those wooden lodges. However, children and adults alike did enjoy going inside to whoop and holler, if only to hear their echoes bouncing off the walls of each empty room. Quanah even liked to tell the story of a Comanche child who asked his mother to place his bed in the fireplace so that he had only to gaze up the chimney at the stars.

Three years later, in the late spring of 1878, the Kwahadi appealed to their agent for passes to hunt buffalo. The agent agreed and arranged for a small military escort to go along to be sure that no cattle nor horses were stolen in Texas.

More than 1500 people joyously prepared to follow Quanah once more to the western prairie, hopefully to relive some of their former glory. The old men told the little ones of the stories dating back to the old days of the coup and the hunt. With dances and feasts and much singing, the Kwahadis prepared to enjoy the journey, stalking after brother buffalo.

As he had done so often in years past, Quanah dispatched scouts to search for the great shaggy beasts while the rest of the band waited, watching for the signal fires the scouts would light along the horizon. There were no fires that year. In this direction, then in that, the hunting parties rode for days at a time, seeing nothing but the empty-eyed skulls and the bleaching bones that marked this land where once the buffalo had numbered in the millions.

The air grew cold, while the leaves, like so many orange and red arrow points, blew along the dry arroyos of the Staked Plain. Still, the resolute among them vowed they would find the buffalo soon. The old men danced the traditional steps, the women sang the old songs, and without stop they beat their rawhide drums and shook their bladder rattles.

But at long last those Kwahadi who could no longer stand the crying of the children with the empty bellies packed up their canvas lodges and trudged wearily back to the reservation beside Cache Creek. While it was a place of sickness and despair, at least the agent would likely have rations waiting for them there.

When the stubborn few refused to come back, even the army couldn't find it in their hearts to press the point and inform the holdouts that their passes had expired. But when the first snows drove icy flakes into life-robbing snowdrifts, the agent sent wagons of food to Quanah's people, who huddled starving and freezing in their canvas lodges far out on the Staked Plain. In the end, Quanah was once more persuaded to return to the reservation. This time for good. Sick with resignation, he abandoned the killing ground that had been home to his father and mother, to generations of his people.

His was the last to roam free.

In 1884 the federal government appointed him chief. Quanah was destined to be the last chief of the Comanches.

Two years later, while in Fort Worth for the annual Fat Stock Show, he placed an advertisement in the local newspaper, asking for a photograph of his mother. The Texas Ranger who had himself led the raid on Cynthia's village in 1864 and now lived in Waco, Sul Ross, had acquired a copy of the daguerreotype that was made a few days after that successful recapture. Ross sent the small chromo to Cynthia Ann Parker's son. It must surely have stunned him to see his mother dressed in the clothes of a white woman, her hair cropped at her ears.

Indeed, it is a sad photograph that I look at now— Naduah of the Kwahadi tribe shown as she is—her blond hair shorn off above the collar, nursing her daughter named Prairie Flower, those pleading crystal-blue eyes staring at the camera, evoking such immense melancholy in me.

Quanah had a large painting made from this photograph, which he hung in his house, where it was pointed out to every visitor.

At long last, as an aging man in 1910, Quanah wrote to the Parker clan of Anderson County in East Texas, asking that his mother's bones be sent to him. The family sternly refused. After several more attempts, Quanah's final plea to the Parkers was read to them from the pulpit one Sunday morning:

My mother, she fed me, carry me in her arms, pat me to sleep. I play, she happy. I cry, she sad. She love her boy. They took my mother away, kept her. Took her away to Texas. Not let boy see her. Now she dead. Her boy want to bury her. Sit by her mound. My people, her people. Our people.

Lonesome. Boy bury mother. She mine. Me bury her. Her dust, my dust. I sit on her mound. Love mother. Boy plead. My mother. We now all one people.

In the face of her son's eloquent plea, the bones of Cynthia Ann Parker, Naduah of the Kwahadi band, were raised from the ground at the Old Fosterville Cemetery in Anderson County, Texas, then carried by one of Quanah's most trusted white friends to Oklahoma, where the last chief of the Comanche hacked off his long braids in mourning over the bones of his beloved mother.

In reburying her remains in the Post Oak Cemetery near his Cache, Oklahoma, home, Quanah requested two friends to read special words over the grave—both preachers, one a Baptist and the other a Mennonite. The U.S. government even allocated one thousand dollars to pay for the removal and reburial of Quanah's mother, along with money for a monument.

At graveside, Quanah said,

> Forty years ago my mother died. She captured by Comanche nine years old. Love Indian and wild life so well no want to go back to white folks. All same people anyway, God say. I love my mother. I like white people . . . I want my people to follow after white way, get educated, know work, make living when payments stop. I tell um know white man's God. Comanche may die tomorrow or ten years. When end come they all be together again. I want to see my mother again, that's why when Government U.S. gave money for new grave, I have this funeral and ask white folks to help bury. Glad to see so many my people here at funeral. That is all.

A short time later, in February of 1911, he became seriously ill while on a journey that had taken him far from the reservation. Quanah told his friends he wished to return home to die.

There in Oklahoma on 23 February, his wives summoned a medicine man, though they did not call on the old shaman Isatai. The medicine man burned white sage over the last chief of the Comanche and prayed, "Father in heaven, this, our brother, is coming." He then wrapped his arms around the dying chief, after which he stood and flapped his hands, with a wing-bone whistle imitating an eagle's plaintive call.

In that ancient prayer the great war bird still drifted on

the warm air currents rising from the Palo Duro Canyon, freeing Quanah's spirit to rise on the wind.

Across the next few minutes, Quanah's breathing grew easier and he drifted peacefully into death. Gone now, this man who so often had taunted death itself, daring it to take him as he rode headlong into the jaws of the white man's guns. Now he belonged to those who had gone before.

Quanah's wives removed every stitch of white man's clothing so that the last chief of the Comanche could be buried in full Kwahadi costume, once more in the clothing he had worn while freely roaming the wildness of the Staked Plain. In 1911, when he passed on to the ages, there were even fewer Comanches in Oklahoma than when Quanah had laid his rifle at the feet of Colonel Ranald Mackenzie that summer day thirty-five years earlier.

By spring of the next year the U.S. government erected a red-granite marker over his grave that by his request was dug next to the resting place of his mother's bones. On that monument are found the words:

Resting here until day breaks and shadows
fall, and darkness disappears is
QUANAH PARKER
Last chief of the Comanches.

So it was that it took many years for the last curtain of the Red River War to close. For some, the struggle was over in 1875. Others would not see the end until the last chief of the Comanche was laid to rest in the ground.

All around their dwindling numbers the war bands had only to look at the writing on the wall in that summer of 1875 as *Dying Thunder* closes. The great Indian leaders were dead or in chains like animals. The buffalo were not to be found. The former might of the red raiders of the southern plains was gone the way of winter breath smoke, forever. An ancient, once-powerful way of life was over. In waging a total war against the Indians, the army had totally defeated the Indian.

The glory days of the war pony and the buffalo lance, the Osage-orange bow and rawhide shield, had come to an end. The sun had finally set on the southern plains.

Terry C. Johnston

Palo Duro Canyon   Adobe Walls
June 20, 1991   June 21, 1991

Prologue

Late June 1875

*F*or months now she had been growing accustomed to riding astride a horse. It had taken some getting used to, but Samantha had done it.

No longer did she have to ride sidesaddle. It was something he had asked of her. Time and again he remembered how she had giggled so easily and told him, "Of course, I'll learn to ride like a man if that's what you want me to do, Seamus."

He was truly in awe of her as she struggled longer and harder every day through the spring, learning to ride like a man, working shoulder to shoulder with him to saddle and unsaddle the animals.

Even more in awe of how she had learned to handle a gun, where a year ago she had refused to even touch one. Now she could hit even a man-sized target at twenty paces three out of five shots. Always—he had taught her—without fail, leave that last bullet in her gun until the target got close enough that she did not have to leave a thing to chance. But three out of five at twenty yards wasn't bad shooting for anyone—much less a girl raised as Samantha Pike had been.

But there he went again—thinking of her as Samantha Pike still, even though a week back he had seen to it she took a new name. His.

"Now, you promised you'd write me at every stop along your way, Sam," Rebecca was saying again for the hundredth time in the last week, her eyes redder than ever, dabbing them with that corner of her apron the way she did.

"I will write you constantly, Becky," Samantha vowed. Then she flashed her straight-toothed smile at Seamus. "But I don't know how much time Mr. Donegan is going to give me to write, really. With the way Sharp says this big Irishman climbs in the saddle before sunup and rides until well past sundown—why, I don't know if I'll have time for much else besides keeping up with him and sleeping."

"You'll have plenty of time for writing, Sam," Rebecca chided her younger sister. "For writing . . . and anything else you put your mind to," she said, winking now.

They giggled as Sharp strode out of the shadows onto a porch all butterscotch in color, drenched with early light. He carried the last of the canvas-wrapped bundles, which he tossed down to Donegan, who laid it into the final, un-used crevice on the sawbuck and began lashing the dia-mond hitch over whole load. They were taking three extra mounts; a sturdy, big-legged one for packing, and two extra for breaking up the riding chores. It wasn't as if the couple were merely traveling up to Dallas, Grover had told the Irishman. Seamus Donegan was, after all, intent on taking his new wife all the way to, by God, Montana.

"You'll be back here . . . someday, won't you?" Grover asked again as he came up to Seamus.

Pulling the last half-hitch tight, Donegan turned, looping his big arm around the older man's shoulders. "I'll be back. It's plain to see that Sam and Rebecca can't live for long without one another. And I figure I'll have a story or two to tell you when it's time I come wandering on back to visit Texas again."

Grover wagged his head as they moved over to unhitch the saddle horses. "Still don't know what it is that pulls you up that way. A damned cold country."

"Maybe when I get to be your age, I'll see things through the same keyhole, Sharp. An old man's bones don't take the cold the way a young man's can, eh?"

Grover laughed as he strung the first spare mount out and lashed it to the sawbuck pack frame. Seamus tied the other spare mount in the same fashion.

"Been some time since you've heard from this Sam Marr, ain't it?"

The Irishman nodded, staring off into the distance as the Texas landscape shimmered under another summer's heat. "Last word I had, Sam was still up near the diggings around Helena. Wrote me after I sent him a letter from Oregon—out there finding Ian."

"And nearly getting yourself separated arm from asshole by Captain Jack's Modocs, I hear."*

He stopped and dragged Grover toward him, glancing over his shoulder to be sure the women did not overhear. "There's been some of the finest try to do just that to Seamus Donegan, I want you to know—using Toledo steel forged into a Confederate cavalry saber, or simply a lead ball fired from some old Injin musket. I didn't come this far, carrying this many scars in my life, to of a sudden go under easy now."

With a grin, Grover threw a punch at the Irishman's midsection. "Just make sure if you don't write, that Samantha will. Tell Becky and me what you both are up to. What you see on that long ride north."

"Long ride is right. And if I stand here gabbing any more with you, we won't get started in time to make Montana before the snow flies."

"When is that—August?"

He clamped his arm around Grover's head as Sharp went to laughing, then rubbed his knuckles through the older man's hair. "What you got against snow anyway?"

"Nothing. Not a damned thing," Sharp answered. "Think I like it, in fact. It's just fine . . . up in Montana!"

"Are you two little boys done playing, so Mr. Donegan can get his new wife down the road this morning and on her way to her new home?" Samantha asked, that disapproving look on her face betrayed by her eyes, twinkling with devilment.

Sweeping the slouch hat off his long hair, Seamus dragged it across the yard as he swept low in a graceful bow.

"Mr. Seamus Donegan, late of Mackenzie's Fourth Cavalry, ma'am.* At your service."

"You're really ready, Seamus?" she asked, her question a little more quiet, her face a bit more serious of a sudden.

"Yes," and he nodded. "Let's be going."

Samantha sighed as she turned back to Rebecca. They fell into one another's arms, embracing as if it would have to last them a lifetime, while Sharp and Seamus looked on. Suddenly the two men were hugging as well, pounding each other on the back before they drew to arm's length and looked into one another's faces.

"I owe you, Sharp," Seamus said, eyes moistening, words coming hard.

Grover nodded. His own eyes wet now, his lips barely moving, he struggled to find the words. "I know, you bleeming Irishman. I know you owe me good."

"I'll pay you back one of these days," Seamus said, letting go of Grover's shoulder as he turned toward Rebecca.

"Make sure you do," Sharp replied as he in turn held his arms out for Samantha. She hurried into them, laying her cheek against her brother-in-law's chest, sobbing her farewell.

"You'll take good care of her for me, won't you, Seamus?" Rebecca raised herself up on tiptoes to whisper into the Irishman's ear. "I'm counting on you."

He nodded, bending down now to kiss Rebecca on the cheek, squeezing her shoulders as she dabbed the corner of that apron to her reddened eyes once again.

Seamus pulled away, untied Samantha's horse and held a hand out for her to step into. Instead she pushed his hand aside and drove her boot into the stirrup, rising gracefully, then settled atop the saddle, spreading the special skirt she and Rebecca had made for riding astride a horse, slit and sewn up the middle to make long, flowing pantaloons. There were three more like it back there on the packhorse among her dowry.

"You'll watch after this crazy, moonstruck Irishman for

me, won't you, Samantha?" Grover asked, coming over to her stirrup.

She nodded, grinning that impish smile that animated her whole face. "Someone has to, don't they, Sharp? If you're not going to be around—it's for goddamned certain someone has to!"

"Samantha!" exclaimed Rebecca. "I never—"

"No, I suppose you never in your life did," Samantha interrupted, turning to flick those impish eyes at Donegan. His face wore an expression of genuine surprise. "And I suppose it won't be the last bad habit I pick up from my husband, will it be?"

He gulped, then turned and rose to the saddle. "Never bet against a sure thing, I always say. Never bet against a sure thing."

Grover stepped to Donegan's mount. "You're still going up through the Territories?"

He nodded. "Cross the Red River. Fort Sill. Camp Supply. On to Dodge City and then west to Fort Lyon. North from there to Denver City, where we'll celebrate and hurraw a little—spend a week or so sleeping in a real feather bed and drinking champagne."

"Every new bride deserves some champagne and a feather bed, don't you think, sister?" Samantha asked of Rebecca.

Rebecca blushed, grinning. "My, how you have already changed my little sister, Mr. Donegan."

"I'm not just your little sister now, Becky," she replied. "I'm Mrs. Seamus Donegan."

"North to Laramie from Denver City?" Grover asked.

"Yeah, and then up the Bozeman Road if the way's safe. Bridger's Bighorn Basin route, if the Sioux and Cheyenne are of a mind to make things tough on travelers. But I'm going over ground I've pushed a horse across before. None of it's new to me, Sharp. Nothing to worry yourself about."

Grover's eyes flicked over to Samantha, then back to the Irishman's face. "Rebecca will worry, you understand."

"She has no reason to worry at all, Sharp," Samantha told him. "Now, if you'll give us your blessings, we can be on our way before I get a year older and Mr. Donegan becomes any crankier about our late start."

"You . . . you both have my blessings," Grover said, hurrying to her side.

Samantha leaned down and gave him another kiss. "Thank you, Sharp. For everything. But most especially for fetching this big, handsome Irishman down to Texas for me."

"And you have our prayers too," Rebecca said, waving as the pair of riders urged their animals into motion.

"Get that roan mare bred before August," Seamus shouted back over his shoulder at Grover, suddenly remembering something that he felt vitally important in that moment.

"You watch your backtrail, Seamus Donegan!" Sharp hollered as he ran forward a few steps then stopped, his arm held high as he waved.

"By the saints, I will, Sharp Grover!" Donegan's words came hard, thickened as they were and hard to spit out around the sob clamped in the back of his throat.

"And don't forget to keep your eye on the skyline!"

Chapter 1

Late November 1875

*T*he streets below their room in the Inter-Ocean Hotel were gummy from yesterday's snow, slicked this morning to a pale pink with a rime of ice. It would all begin melting again today beneath the late autumn sun, then freeze as quickly when that bright disk ducked its head beyond those mountains far to the west of Cheyenne City.

Samantha Donegan shuddered. Just the thought of those mountains made her all the colder.

Her husband ushered her into the warmth of the fragrant café amingle with the smells of hardworking men and tobacco smoke, coffee brewing and wood smoke seeping in whispery trails from the chimneys on those three glowing stoves that heated this leaky clapboard building. Most of the eyes in the lamplit interior raised like window shades upon her entrance, instantly appraising her before flicking over to take the measure of her husband. Every man of them quickly went back to their cup or their plates or just about anywhere but be caught staring at the attractive light-haired woman on the arm of that tall, gray-eyed Irishman.

Samantha squeezed his arm and nodded to a table in the corner near one of the smoky windows badly in need of some soap and water. There she settled, her back to the room, remembering to leave Seamus the chair that would allow him a full view of the smoky café. It was something she had found amusing that first night they had arrived in Denver City. Her big, strap-jawed husband standing there at the table in the hotel's restaurant, speechless, a look of pure consternation pinching his face as he sputtered, trying mightily to explain to her why he must always have the chair facing the room. Something about that wide, wrinkled scar and its jagged path down the great muscles of his back. Something explained a bit more as she had watched his eyes that night, roaming as they did this morning, back and forth across the room, touching her face lightly, then moving on. Those gray eyes always moving.

"Coffee for you both?"

She looked up at the older man who had stopped at their table, two china mugs laced in his thin, veiny fingers, the other hand clutching a blackened coffeepot with a worn and fire-smudged scrap of towel. Samantha nodded.

"Yes, two," Seamus answered.

Her husband took a first sip of his coffee as the old man lumbered off into the smoky maze of tables and chairs, then leaned back and sighed, smiling at her. It was the first of those she had seen cross his face yet this morning.

"You sure you want to come on north with me?" he began, both his big hands cradling his china mug for warmth.

She stared at them a moment more, remembering how those hard, trail-worn hands could yet be so gentle with her, cupping her sensitive breasts, tracing each exciting tremble of her inner thighs as he tucked her legs around his waist. Just as he had last night. And kept her warm in that cold blackness of their tiny room until the faintest hint of murky light oozed through the window glazing.

"We've talked of this so many times," she started, then saw his mouth draw into a line of grim resolve.

"Yes, we have, Samantha." He sipped at his coffee. "I should have known I was not about to talk you out of this ride north—once I had talked you into it."

"I'll get used to it, this cold."

Samantha prayed she would, as cold as it was already, and they weren't even half the distance to that place high up in faraway Montana Territory where Seamus had vowed he would go. He had warned her it was bound to get a lot colder before they reached the goldfields and that gulch where her husband hoped to find an old friend.

"I never been here—Cheyenne," Seamus explained again. "Only come through Fort Laramie, north of here. First time was when me and Sam Marr rode north on that Montana Road in 'sixty-six."*

She sensed he was trying to make conversation, then his eyes went to searching out the old man, waving him over.

The waiter came to a halt at the table and ground his hands in the smudgy black towel. "What'll it be folks?"

"What does your cook do best?" Seamus asked.

He looked at Samantha before answering. "Just about anything. Got some good eggs this week. Game meat and taters. Could scare up a little bacon or salt meat if you take a shine to it."

Seamus shuddered a little. "I've had enough of army victuals to last me for a time."

Her husband looked at her across the table, and she dropped her eyes, moving them swiftly to gaze out the window as he ordered for them both.

"Bring us both some eggs. Two for my wife. A half-dozen for me. Biscuits?"

"So fluffy they'll melt on your tongue."

"A basket of them and some pan-fried potatoes."

"Onions with 'em?"

"Yes, that will do nicely."

"Care for some side meat?"

"Antelope?"

"We got it."

"Two nice steaks," Seamus ordered. "Something to stick to our ribs for the ride north."

"Going to Laramie, are you?"

"Aye, that we are."

"So, decided you'll try your luck in the Hills?"

"Hills?"

A look of confusion crossed the waiter's face. "Black Hills. Ain't you going up there to try your luck at digging up some gold?"

Seamus shook his head and grinned. "No. Montana's more to my fancy."

* The Plainsmen Series, vol. 1, *Sioux Dawn*

He shuddered. "It's cold out there," the waiter offered. "And my bunion tells me it's gonna turn miserable before it gets any warmer. A hard, hundred-year winter coming, this one, my friend." Then he glanced quickly at the woman, as if he had forgotten himself. "I'll see to packing you something to carry along with you. Biscuits and boiled potatoes. Some more of that antelope."

"I'm sure you'll do us fine," Seamus replied. "Thanks."

She had watched the old man's reflection in the window glass, its smoky surface more of a mirror than a clear glazing that allowed her to watch the wagons and mules, men and horses and what few folks dared walk across the rutted, pockmarked street. As the waiter turned away, Samantha looked back into those smoky gray eyes across the tiny table that rocked unevenly as he reached out to snag her hands in both of his. She liked that about him. How he seemed to know when she needed his touch and his reassurance.

She needed it more than ever right now.

They were heading into more of the unknown than she had ever experienced in her life.

Denver City had been quite the place. Alive and throbbing and musical with voices and animals and clattering wagon wheels and music pouring from the open doors of every saloon and watering hole along Cherry Creek and right down to the banks of the South Platte itself. It had been hot, the first of September by the time they arrived there in the shadows of the high peaks, closer to those fabled Rockies than she ever thought she would be.

What a bustling, busy place that had been, even more than this Cheyenne City busy with the trade to Deadwood and the other Black Hills' gold camps. Women strutted about, draped in their finest, lacy parasols suspended on their shoulders, their escorts wearing plug hats and clawhammer coats. While Seamus had gone off on some of his own business to a place called the Elephant Corral, intending to see friends from years past,* Samantha had ventured out on her own, something new for her. For some time she had watched a glassblower making tiny, spindly-

* The Plainsmen Series, vol. 4, *Black Sun*

legged animals and tiny masted sailing ships in his little shop along Cherry Creek. Then she had wandered down to a druggist's store. There on that counter where she found striped candy for the wee ones, she had ordered a seltzer water, flavored as she liked it with vanilla extract, the bubbling concoction issued from a spigot shaped like a nickel-plated cow's teat. The phosphate had tickled her nose, as stout as the dose of sulfur and molasses her mama had always given her for any of the tisms.

Gazing out the window of that druggist's store at the mountains, it was the stories she remembered, stories told her in her childhood as she and sister Rebecca cuddled on their papa's lap and listened to his stories of the men and animals who crossed the great continental spine, plunging on to the California goldfields back in 1849. Her father had been a young man then, leaving his wife pregnant with a child they would name Rebecca.

Samantha had stared up at those not-too-distant peaks ignited with golden fire that first summer twilight in Denver City, remembering that the same fire had gleamed in her papa's eyes when he told his daughters of the hardship and empty belly and frostbitten toes and fingers of those two years he put in digging and panning the streams of the far West.

Without question she had recognized the same glimmer of golden fire in Seamus's eyes when first he had begun talking to her of wanting to leave Texas, to go north once more, this time all the way to Montana Territory. Her papa and her husband, so much alike—wanderers both. But Samantha had sworn that she was not about to become like her mother. No, she would not stay behind, the dutiful and pregnant wife.

And besides, Samantha wasn't even sure she was pregnant. Not just yet. It hadn't been that long since she had missed her monthly. But pregnant or not, she was not going to let Seamus go off and leave her. Even though in her soul there was no doubt that he would one day return to her, just the way her papa had come home to her mama. And promptly gotten mama with child. This one, a second daughter they had named Samantha.

If there was some new life growing in her belly at this moment, she hoped her first would be a boy. How her papa had so wanted a son. And Seamus would too.

The steamy fragrances rose to her nose as the waiter slid the plates before her, taking from the crook of his arm the basket of warm biscuits.

Surely, she must be pregnant, Samantha told herself. It seemed she was eating for at least two the past few weeks.

Back in Denver City, in that heat of summer as the high plains lay baked and sweltering beneath the last onslaught of September's swan song, she had not had much appetite. Too hot to eat until well after sundown. And much of the time she spent in their small room in the same hotel Seamus told her he and Bill Cody had waited to find some horse thieves for Major Eugene Carr of the Fifth U.S. Cavalry. Time spent in as little clothing as possible, sweating and fanning, drinking pitcher after pitcher of water.

Only in the early morning or the early evening would she dare venture out on the streets with Seamus. Stopping before every window to admire the bonnets and bustles, brocades and silks, and yard after yard of ribbon and lace to spark up a woman's wardrobe. He had bought her two new dresses, with boots and bonnets and gloves to match. Along with that god-awful heavy blanket coat he told her she would need.

Samantha remembered how she had laughed at him for being such a fool then—in the midst of all that late-summer heat. So thankful now that Seamus had thrown it in with what all he had purchased there in Denver City. That coat and those unmentionably horrible underclothes. Men's underclothes bought in something approximating her size. Men's underclothes! How she had laughed at those ugly things back in their hotel room as she held them up against her. Bright red, a coarse cloth, tailored to reach from the top button at her neck clear down to the turn of her slim ankles.

"I don't know about those now," Seamus had said to her as she held the men's underwear against her, poking fun at him. "Don't know if we got them big enough."

"Big enough?" she had clucked in disbelief.

"Yes, look at you," he had replied, in that way of his that ignited his eyes with devilment. "I don't know if you have all that much room in there without having to squeeze what all God Himself blessed you with in the way of a woman's equipment."

She blushed again, here and now in this Cheyenne City café, remembering how he had taken her breasts in his big hands, tenderly, insistently kneading her flesh as he pressed his mouth down hard on hers, then lifted her gently and ever so slightly cradled her as he pushed her back onto that feather tick, shoving those awful red men's underwear to the side to promptly unbutton her bodice so that he could fondle and lick at her breasts as they came tumbling out of her clothing.

Samantha remembered too how Seamus had gasped as she locked her fingers around his rigid flesh which she hungrily pulled from his canvas britches, her frantic fingers eager to snare him, hold him, guide him toward her moistness.

They had stayed together that afternoon as the shadows lengthened in their Denver City room, stayed together despite the way their bodies grew damp and stuck to one another as they slept, then made love a second time, and slept again before the coming of summer's twilight awoke them. That, and a hunger for supper.

Word had it that with the coming of winter, spring at the latest, Congress would be voting on that territory's admission to the Union. This hard, hot land—a new state. Colorado. Having come up through Indian Territory into Kansas, then to that frontier of hard men and a brutal existence wrenched out of the ground, whether it was gold or timber, silver or some wretched crops withering beneath the high plains sun.

As she ate ravenously of the breakfast before her, watching the wonder in her husband's eyes at her appetite, Samantha hoped Seamus would one day take her to all those cities, as he had promised. The places she so longed for—carriages and cobblestoned streets, the rustle of silk and crinoline . . .

But for now she would remain silent, as she had vowed to

herself she would. This was the high, open land her husband loved. Samantha knew this frontier was as much a mistress to Seamus Donegan as any full-bodied woman could be. For some reason she had yet to discover, this land had lured him west nine years before, then once in its clutches, this land had seduced the tall Irishman with all its magnificent distance pocked with canyons and river valleys, vaulted with cloud-scraping peaks, a land crossed by few white men, intimately known by fewer still.

Perhaps this frontier was really like a woman, she had decided after all. A place forever changing, yet exerting a power over man in such a changeless, seductive way. It lured a man here, then held only the bravest to its breast. Just as a woman would choose her own suitors.

She glanced about at the others in this smoky restaurant: a motley crew of mule whackers and miners, freighters and prospectors, soldiers and dandified gamblers. Men of all shape and color drifting through this town, Seamus had explained to her. Most not tarrying here long, but instead heading on north along the Black Hills Road.

Despite the scare that was the talk on everyone's lips. As much as Seamus had tried to prevent her from hearing some of the talk, Samantha had listened to as much as she could. No matter that the road north to the goldfields were blackened with men who, like her own papa had dreamed, were now dreaming of that one big strike . . . despite the stories and songs and even grim jokes of the Indians murdering and scalping the unwary.

In every saloon and watering hole and roadhouse, the popular song of the day, a tune Samantha thought she heard morning, noon and well into the night, was the new frontier ditty making its rounds—"The Dreary Black Hills":

The Roundhouse in Cheyenne is filled every night,
With loafers and bummers of most every plight.
On their backs is no clothes, in their pockets no bills.
Each day they keep starting for the dreary Black Hills.

Don't go away—stay at home if you can.
Stay away from that city, they call it Cheyenne.
Where the blue waters roll, and Comanche Bill,
He will lift up your hair in the dreary Black Hills.

I got to Cheyenne, no gold could I find.
I thought of that dear crowd I'd left behind.
Through rain, hail, and snow, frozen plumb to the gills,
They call me the orphan of the dreary Black Hills.

Kind friend, to conclude: My advice I'll unfold.
Don't go to the Black Hills, a'hunting for gold.
Railroad speculators, their pockets you'll fill,
By taking a trip to those dreary Black Hills.

Don't go away—stay at home if you can.
Stay away from that city, they call it Cheyenne.
Where old Sitting Bull or Comanche Bill,
They will take off your scalp in the dreary Black Hills.

Nonetheless, Samantha vowed she would continue to swallow down her fear, as she wolfed down the last of her eggs and potatoes, then drew the knife's keen edge back and forth through the thick antelope steak, still pink on the inside. She vowed she would come to like the taste of this wild meat—so much a part of the frontier her husband had come to love.

Instead of Sitting Bull and Crazy Horse and the rest . . . she forced herself to think on bonnets and silk ribbons, on bustles and those new dresses he had bought for her. And how much she now appreciated the warmth of the two pair of men's underwear she was wearing beneath her dress at this moment, one on top of the other.

Along with the wool mittens and blanket muffler and this heavy mackinaw coat Seamus had bought for her, she was staying warm.

He had warned her months ago in Denver City that one day soon the day would no longer be near so hot. One day soon, he had promised her, winter would come calling to the high plains. The old frontiersmen were telling him it had all the makings of one of those hundred-year winters, what with as thick as the critters and horses were putting on their winter coats.

The season turning already. Summer and now fall gone the way of August snow.

Chapter 2

Moon of Deer Rutting

*A*lready the Second Summer had come and gone—that time right after the first frost nipped the leaves of the willow and alder, turning them gold and bloodred, presaging the winds that would come to drive the leaves along the ground in frantic gusts. But the Second Summer always came to warm the days once more as the sun's travel grew shorter and shorter.

He Dog shuddered with the cold now that the time for Winter Man's coming was truly at hand. He was growing older, his blood thinning perhaps. And he felt the cold all too easily. For once he looked forward to this coming of Winter Man as a time when he could stay in the warmth of the lodge, telling stories to his children, cleaning his guns and smelling the bone-meal soup his wife simmered by the crackling fire pit.

Yet there was worry etched upon the Oglalla warrior's dark face. Already the bands had learned of the rumors of preparations begun at the forts housing the white soldiers. And soldiers prepared for only one thing: war.

Agency Indians like his friend Crawler brought the news as they moved back and forth between the agencies and their ancient hunting grounds along the Tongue and Rosebud and Powder rivers. Back and forth riders traveled, carrying robes and jerked buffalo to trade for guns and ammunition, powder and sugar and coffee and flour. But mostly for the guns and bullets. If the rumors proved true that the soldiers were coming, then the seven circles of the mighty Lakota bands would need many guns and many, many bullets.

He Dog was Hunkpatila Oglalla, meaning "end of the camp circle." That also meant he belonged to the "Crazy Horse people," the ones who always erected their lodges on one of the two horns of the great camp circle facing the rising sun. As a young boy he had known of Crazy Horse. But they were not childhood friends in those carefree days of games. Crazy Horse had surrounded himself with a circle that included his younger brother, Little Hawk, along with Lone Bear and High Backbone. It was this one, sometimes called Hump, who was Crazy Horse's *kola,* the one with whom he paired in young childhood.

No, He Dog and Crazy Horse had come to be friends only later in life. Companions in their youth, then comrades in their first raids, and truly brothers in their coming of age.

Yet now He Dog feared he would have to tear himself from Crazy Horse. Like flesh from flesh this pain of separating would be.

He watched now as the women of Crazy Horse's band raised the lodgepoles before the sun fell too far behind the White Mountains.* No longer was there much snow down here. Most of it up there, among the high and lofty peaks. He Dog glanced over to find Black Shawl struggling with the lifting pole to which she had tied the heavy lodge cover. Crazy Horse sat alone in front of the great skeletal network of poles, smoking and unmindful of his wife's struggle. He had been like this for more than one winter, He Dog brooded.

Whereas Crazy Horse had never been a loud one, now he rarely spoke. Always thinking, praying, looking off into the distance—if not just leaving for days without any warning, sometimes weeks at a time, by himself. Gone hunting, for meat. Perhaps for ponies and scalps.

It had not always been this way for the two friends, He Dog thought. Still, it brought no lightening to his heart to remember the seasons gone, when Crazy Horse and He Dog had first ridden together. Those happier times.

---

* Bighorn Mountains

He Dog was two winters older than young Curly, son of the one they called Crazy Horse. While Curly had light skin, He Dog was darker than most. While Curly's hair hung brown and wavy, He Dog's hung straight, and as black as the bottom of an old iron kettle. Curly's face was thin, while He Dog's was square, with a strong chin, his sharp nose like a tomahawk blade set between those high cheekbones.

But it was for Curly's bravery in battle that He Dog most admired his young friend. When they first began raiding the Sparrow Hawks and Snakes to the west and south, Curly proved himself not only courageous, but a savvy fighter as well. Whereas Little Hawk and Lone Bear and Hump would go beyond daring and become reckless in their hunger for coups, Curly never rode into battle unless he meant to win. And from the beginning he always dismounted to shoot his bow, and later his rifle. Curly always hit what he aimed at.

And long before Curly had the medicine vision that instructed him to take his father's name, young Crazy Horse had infected his friend He Dog with his own all-out fighting spirit.

The two comrades were always gathering other young warriors to ride with them into the land of the enemy for ponies and scalps and plunder. In those youthful days both friends took the no-woman vow, for it was the belief among Lakota men that copulation weakened both body and mind, sapping a young man's war energies. Both swore with their mingled blood that they would be father to none, protector of all in their band. Times were good in those summers before the white man began to fight among himself far to the east.

Then four winters before they had killed the Hundred in the Hand,* Crazy Horse had first cast his eyes on the niece of Red Cloud. Helpless Crazy Horse had been, it seemed to He Dog now. Helplessly in love while Black Buffalo Woman had been courted by many among Red Cloud's Bad Face band of Oglalla. When the young Hunkpatila warrior

* The Plainsmen Series, vol. 1, *Sioux Dawn*

returned from a long raid over the mountains, He Dog was the one who had to tell Crazy Horse of the sad news.

"While you were gone, Black Buffalo Woman married."

In that light-skinned face, the dark eyes of Crazy Horse had never been more like chips of black obsidian.

"Who?"

"No Water."

Crazy Horse had only nodded, his mouth a straight line of hate. "I know him—a leading man in Red Cloud's war council."

"You will find another woman, my friend."

"No . . . not like Black Buffalo Woman."

He Dog had watched Crazy Horse stomp off without another word. For days his friend had remained morose, sulking. Then suddenly the Horse packed up two horses, telling He Dog he was riding for Crow country, alone.

"I will go with you—"

"No! You will not. If you are truly my friend, He Dog, you will know when to leave me be."

It was the first time He Dog had heard such bite in the words of Crazy Horse.

When the Horse returned at the end of that summer, he stopped before He Dog's lodge and threw two Crow scalps to the ground.

"Are these for me, Crazy Horse?"

"They are fit only for your dogs," he replied as some camp mongrels began sniffing and growling over the scalps at He Dog's feet.

"Is your heart better for it?"

Such a look of great and sudden sadness came to the face of Crazy Horse, but no words crossed his lips as he turned his pony aside and rode off. And although three summers later both he and He Dog became revered shirt-wearers— which meant they must do nothing that would bring discord to the tribe—for those next five summers the Horse brazenly flirted and courted the wife of No Water.

Deeply saddened during that time, He Dog forsook his no-woman medicine and took a wife, beginning his own family and moving with the pulse of the seasons in the wake of the buffalo. Along with others, he watched more and more white men and wagons pushing north from the Holy Road into Red Cloud's country.

Together they had traveled south to the North Platte where the soldiers had built a long wooden bridge to span the wide river for settlers and wagon traffic headed west. There at that bridge,* the Lakota and Shahiyena together fought the soldiers for two days before drawing off, tearing down the white man's humming wire strung from the bare trees as they retreated in the face of reinforcements riding up from the fort called Laramie.

At last the Bad Face and Hunkpatila Oglalla and Shahiyena of Two Moon and Black Horse had watched with growing anger as soldiers plodded north from their old fort along the Powder and began erecting their pine fort in the shadow of the White Mountains. Time and again the warriors attacked small wood details or hay-cutting parties—but never succeeded in fully engaging the soldiers.

Until in the first winter moon Crazy Horse and He Dog and Young Man Afraid devised a plan to decoy the soldiers outside their log fortress. That had been nine winters gone now this same Moon of Deer Shedding Horns that He Dog and ten others had joined Crazy Horse as the handpicked decoys to lure the impetuous white soldiers to their deaths beyond Lodge Trail Ridge.† A glorious victory as two thousand Lakota and Shahiyena rose from the brush and overwhelmed the soldiers in less time than it took for the sun to travel from one lodgepole to the next. As the last white men fell, the victory songs rang out over that frozen, bloody ground as the warriors began smashing heads and stripping bodies, hacking limbs and tongues and manhood parts from the still-warm bodies in a frenzy of blood lust. This great victory they had come to call the Battle of the Hundred in the Hand.

But as thundering as were the hooves, the war cries like lightning striking ice, He Dog had turned from the blood madness so long pent up in so many of the warriors, and

* Battle of Platte River Bridge, July 25–26, 1865
† Fetterman Massacre, December 21, 1866

found Crazy Horse looking over the scene, as if looking for a friend.

Then with growing panic, He Dog realized. "Do you see him, Crazy Horse?"

The young warrior, only twenty-one winters old then, shook his head in dismay, concern clearly etched upon his blood-splattered face as Hump came up to join them. "No. We must look."

The three of them had found Lone Bear, the hapless, unlucky childhood friend of Crazy Horse, the man-child who always seemed to come out on the short end of things, found him down near the bottom of the ridge where a handful of soldiers and civilians had circled themselves inside a tiny ring of small boulders and held off the warriors with their guns made to shoot many times without loading.

Already the front of Lone Bear's blanket coat was slicked with frozen blood as Crazy Horse knelt beside his old friend, gently rolling him into his lap, clutching the dying warrior fiercely. Three bullet holes seeped blood that as quickly froze bright and crimson beneath the midday winter's light.

"You have been unlucky again, Lone Bear," Crazy Horse had said quietly as all around them arose the clamor of victory.

"No," Lone Bear said evenly. "I was for once as brave as you and He Dog and Hump. See here."

Lone Bear had opened his left hand to show the matted red hair in his palm, between his fingers.

"With two bullets in me, I still got close enough to the soldier to grab hold of his beard so that he could see into my eyes before I drove my war club into his face."

"You are truly brave as any Oglalla warrior," He Dog had said as Lone Bear clutched the red hair to his breast, coughed, then slowly died there in the arms of Crazy Horse.

The three friends Lone Bear left behind wept quietly while around them the butchery and mutilation went on. And when Crazy Horse arose, allowing Hump and He Dog to take the body to a waiting pony, Crazy Horse spotted a rangy dog slinking among the bodies of the dead soldiers, sniffing, whining, then turning on its heel to lope off toward the soldier fort.

Crazy Horse nocked an arrow on his bowstring.

"No," He Dog said. "Let it go back to the soldiers and tell them of what we have done here."

Angrily, the Horse had pulled away from He Dog's grip and let the arrow fly, catching the dog in mid-stride. Its legs struggled for a moment, then the animal lay still. Crazy Horse peered into He Dog's eyes.

"No, my friend. Nothing will leave this battleground alive. Not even the white man's dog."

Early the next summer when He Dog and Crazy Horse returned from a raiding trip on the Crow across the White Mountains, they rode into their camp to the cheers of man, woman and child. The old men of the band presented them both with the *akicita,* the two sacred lances of the Crow Owners Society, lances reputed to be more than four hundred years old, made long before the Lakota moved west across the Big Muddy River and onto the plains, forced to migrate with the coming of the white man. These magical symbols of warrior power were presented from the older generation to those of the younger generation who had best lived the life of a Lakota warrior.

That summer, He Dog and Crazy Horse joined Red Cloud and Black Horse's Shahiyena in their war on the two soldier forts: first, the dirt fort up on the Bighorn River where the Shahiyena fought a band of white men corralled in a hayfield; then, the following day, Red Cloud led his Oglalla warriors down on a small group of soldiers who took shelter in a ring of wagon boxes not far from the pinewood fort.

It had seemed the magic was returned to Crazy Horse's soul. And that gave He Dog much happiness across the next three winters as the soldiers surrendered their three forts and retreated back down their road to the land of Fort Laramie.

Then, in a raid on the Snakes in the summer of 1870, Crazy Horse's war party found itself outnumbered more than twelve to one. And in their retreat, He Dog saw Hump swallowed up by more than two dozen Shoshoni warriors.

There were tears in many eyes that night in their fireless camp, grief freely flowing for this childhood friend of Crazy Horse who had been his *kola* through many boyhood games and the first pony raids of youth. Together at the Platte Bridge, and the Hundred in the Hand, the Wagon Box fight, and all those raids on the Crow and Pawnee and these loathsome Snake.

Lone Bear had been taken from him. And now Hump. Ripped from the life of Crazy Horse.

That winter it seemed Crazy Horse was beginning not to care if he lived or died. As if he could not care for the vows he had taken as a shirt-wearer. Crazy Horse had once again brazenly hung close around the lodge of Black Buffalo Woman whenever No Water was gone hunting.

That following spring, as soon as the rivers broke open and the air warmed, He Dog suggested they gather a war party to plunge into Crow country once more. It had made He Dog proud to once more be riding beside Crazy Horse at the head of that great column, each of them carrying their sacred *akicita*. They found a village of Crow between the Little Bighorn and Bighorn rivers. While the other warriors chased the Crow about, He Dog and Crazy Horse rode in and out of the fray, using only those ancient, sacred lances, touching, jabbing, counting coup on the fleeing Crow who scurried right back to their agency down the Little Bighorn, where they were under the protection of soldier guns.

Yet that still did not stop He Dog's warriors. They brazenly made their camp a short distance from the Crow village, and for about two weeks the Oglalla hunted in Crow country, taunting the enemy to come out again and do battle. It was a glorious time for the two old friends who had seen too much sadness darken their days.

"This is a time we will remember," Crazy Horse had said that first night after they slowly journeyed east from Crow land.

"Yes!" He Dog had agreed. "We will call that battle the 'Fight when They Chased the Crows Back to Camp.'"

He Dog hoped it would make Crazy Horse forget Black Buffalo Woman. But it did not.

By the autumn of 1871 the Hunkpatila Oglalla were more closely associating with the two wild tribes of the northern plains who wanted no contact with the white man: the Hunkpapa of Sitting Bull, and Two Moon's Northern Cheyenne. So it was after the first frost, and in the time they called the Second Summer, that Crazy Horse devised a ruse of going on a war party to Crow country so that he could return in secret one night and run off with Black Buffalo Woman.

As He Dog recalled those dark days, he remembered the black look that crossed the face of No Water when he returned from a hunting trip to find his wife gone.

"I must do something hard to him now," No Water said with sinister determination. "Crazy Horse had paid her too much attention for too long."

"Let them go," He Dog had pleaded, trying his best to soothe the dangerous situation. With a smile he had added, "You do not want a woman who does not want you, do you?"

No Water had turned his hateful glare on He Dog. "You stand in my way, you may end up eating Crazy Horse's bullet for him."

The cuckolded husband went to Bad Heart Bull and borrowed a revolver, then hastily gathered a war party of his supporters to ride in pursuit of the eloping couple. They came upon Crazy Horse and Black Buffalo Woman the second night out. No Water fired as the Horse dove for his weapon, the avenging husband's bullet tearing along Crazy Horse's upper lip and jaw in a bloody furrow.

Yes, He Dog thought. Woman trouble is bad. Usually the worst kind of trouble within the tribe. But attempted murder was all the worst, bringing about the threat of a blood feud between Red Cloud's Bad Faces and Crazy Horse's Hunkpatilas. And because he had taken the woman and caused the turmoil among his own people, Crazy Horse could no longer be a shirt-wearer.

Black Buffalo Woman went back to her family, then eventually returned to No Water.

He Dog spat now at the thought of No Water—the

Oglalla who had hurried far to the south to escape the coming war with the white man.

But nonetheless, He Dog felt anger at Crazy Horse, anger because the Horse had broken his vows as a shirt-wearer.

Because of those woman troubles, some of the sacred magic of the Hunkpatila Oglalla was gone the way of the winds. And He Dog doubted those winds would ever return that magic to his people.

Chapter 3

26 November 1875

"*N*ice shot, General!"

With a grin, George C. Crook nodded at his aide-de-camp, Lieutenant John Bourke, setting off toward the turkey he had just brought down as it broke from its roost in a nearby tree.

On what he claimed was nothing more than a brief holiday vacation from the bitter cold and mind-numbing bustle of Chicago, Lieutenant General Philip H. Sheridan had asked Crook to join him in this turkey shoot a few leisurely miles from Omaha, Nebraska. In addition to the three military officers, there was but one civilian. Ben Clark had been wired by Division of the Missouri commander Sheridan to join him in Omaha for this outing near Crook's Department of the Platte headquarters.

"He is a big one, General," Clark said, adding his praise.

With his shotgun cradled in the crook of his right arm, Crook snagged the turkey by its wrinkled legs. In his heavily burred voice he said, "Your turn to bag one, Philip."

"But if I don't shoot as well as you, we'll just have to eat yours for supper tonight, George," Sheridan replied.

Crook's gray eyes smiled, crinkling at the corners into the deep seams of many seasons spent beneath the sun and far-reaching western sky. Well enough he knew how much better a shot was he than the little Irish banty rooster, Sheridan. And now Sheridan was in his own way acknowledging the fact as well. That admission went some distance to sooth the awkward, unspoken uneasiness existing between these two old friends, their longtime friendship turned acrimonious more than a dozen years before during Sheridan's bloody Shenandoah campaign.

Right from the start of his military career it had appeared that George Crook was clearly riding a rising star. A West Point graduate who was not only a member of the same class with Sheridan but, as well as Sheridan, had served with distinction in the Pacific Northwest, George Crook amassed battle honors early in the Civil War's eastern theater. Then in 1863 he was transferred to the war in the west as part of the Army of the Cumberland, where he ultimately came to the attention of Ulysses S. Grant, himself on a meteoric rise to fame.

From that point on it seemed no harm could come to the redheaded fireball.

As part of his overall campaign to stymie the Confederates in the Shenandoah Valley, Grant dispatched the newly promoted major general to serve under Sheridan, Crook's old classmate. Theirs soon proved to be a bitter reunion.

In battle after battle Crook's forces were the hammer of Sheridan's tenacious hammer-and-anvil plan to wear the Rebels down through bloody, nonstop attrition. It soon appeared nothing could stop the Army of the Shenandoah from driving the Confederates right out of the valley.

But on 19 October 1864, a few miles south of Winchester along Cedar Creek, Crook failed to order the posting of enough outlying pickets along that quiet country stream. Perhaps he feared little from the enemy, what with the beating he and the rest of the Union troops had been handing out over the past week. With little to lose, the Rebels moved that night in a daring raid, deeply penetrating the Federal lines, and in the gray of dawn quickly routed Crook's men. Helplessly, the general watched the frantic retreat, unable to stem that tide as the forest was shredded by Confederate canister and grapeshot, erupting with the shouts of wounded and dying soldiers abandoned by their comrades in arms, those pleas serving as the only echo for the shrill yells ringing from the throats of thousands of Confederates.

In nearby Winchester, Sheridan himself heard the distant

rattle and boom of battle, and hurried to the sound of the guns. Through nothing more than stoic discipline and his own infectious personality, Sheridan regained control of three divisions by early afternoon, and ultimately wrenched the tide of victory from Jubal Early's spirited Confederate offensive. The little Irishman had turned everything he had on the Rebels—not sparing a single company in reserve.

That near-defeat turned into a victory for Sheridan—and thereby stung Crook as nothing else would the rest of his career. But even more painful to take was what that mistake caused to his friendship with Sheridan.

"George, I am going to get much more credit for this than I deserve," Sheridan had said as the sun fell that warm autumn day and Early's troops were clearly on the run. "Had I been here in the morning, the same thing would have taken place for me."

Those words of solace did little to salve the wound Crook suffered when that very evening the press began to shower accolades on his friend's shoulders—banner headlines boldly claiming Sheridan had wrenched victory from the jaws of disaster caused by Crook's bungling. Yet all the more damning to their relationship, the Commander of the Army of the Shenandoah did very little to defer the praise and glory from himself, in the end choosing to bask in that victory in such a way that it drove a huge, granite wedge of distrust between the two old classmates, creating a chasm that would last between them the rest of their careers.

But for the moment this late autumn afternoon, itself like a crisp, multihued blessing on the central plains this day after the nation's celebration of Thanksgiving, George C. Crook saw a glimmer of his old friend.

"All right, Phil. Spit it out," Crook sighed as he glanced at the distant ambulances and squad of horsemen dressed in their heavy wool military greatcoats. "What is it you have on your mind?"

Sheridan grinned, his Irish eyes flashing with humor. "You've known me too long, haven't you, George?"

"And I figure I know you too well, General," Ben Clark said, "not to tell you're cooking something."

For a moment Crook glanced at the tall, leather-lean

civilian scout, his face sharp-stitched with its lines of hard living. Long ago he had heard mention made of Clark, one of the most trusted men to guide the army across these plains. It was said the man had saddle galluses clear up to his elbows. In addition, Crook knew that for the last seven years Clark had been one of Sheridan's favorites, ever since the scout had led George Armstrong Custer to Black Kettle's sleeping camp of Southern Cheyenne down on the Washita, on a cold November day quite unlike this one here on the plains of eastern Nebraska.

Crook turned back to Sheridan, with all the more certainty knowing there was an important reason for Sheridan bringing the scout here for this meeting. Likely it had to do with why Crook himself had been summoned to meet Sheridan and Sherman in Washington City earlier in the month. On the third of November the three generals had gone to the White House for an early breakfast with President Grant. That afternoon, the four had a secret meeting with newly-appointed Interior Secretary Zachariah Chandler and his assistant secretary, Benjamin R. Cowen.

It had been Chandler's first day at his new post, and the man had openly relished discussing the possibility of once more turning Indian Affairs back to the army.

Seeing some spark of intense fire in Sheridan's eyes at this moment, Crook asked, "This has to do with our meeting three weeks back, doesn't it?"

"Yes . . . well," and Sheridan cleared his throat.

Then of a sudden Crook felt a sinking feeling, as if his hands had just been tied and the wind had been kicked out of him. "Damn. Grant's backed out on his promise of turning us loose, hasn't he, Phil?"

Sheridan glanced once more at the distant horsemen gathered about the two ambulances, the breath smoke rising like thin gauze over their heads in the midday light. "You both know me well enough to realize there isn't much nonsense about me."

Crook grinned. "Then why the charade of this turkey shoot, Phil?"

He gazed at Crook a moment before answering, then

smiled. "We've done it, George. By bloody damned, we've done it!"

Crook felt the breath seize in his chest. "You mean—Washington is finally going to let us march?"

"There's something very big afoot right now—already it's on its way. But we need to be patient only a matter of weeks more. So, I trust only two of my closest to put some wheels in motion before we get the official go-ahead for action."

"Just how long do we have to wait?" Crook asked, dropping the butt of his shotgun so that it rested on the toe of his scuffed boot. He had never been a clothes dandy like Custer or Miles, a man worried about his appearance, concerned with the figure that he cut.

"Just after the new year."

Crook chewed on that, regarding the orange and red firelit hardwoods rimed with frost. "That long before we march, hmmm."

"Dammit, George—quit your bloody brooding. We're finally going after the wild tribes of the northern plains!"

"Son of God!" Ben Clark exclaimed quietly, as if he had just put the pieces of it together. He was as much a man of uncomplicated mind as he was of indestructible bone and sinew. "You mean the army's going to track down Sitting Bull's Hunkpapa?"

Sheridan gazed at the scout whose weathered face looked like a well-wrinkled leather valise. "Them . . . and the Oglalla of Crazy Horse."

Crook rubbed a callused finger beneath his nostrils contemplatively a moment, thinking about the commander of the Department of the Dakotas. "You told Terry?"

"He's next. You and Ben here are the only ones I'm trusting with this secret right now. Clark will help you pull together the best scouts you can muster on the northern plains—"

"All right. Spill the rest of it, Phil," Crook said in that jabbing way of his, gray eyes quickly flicking to his young aide, Lieutenant Bourke, who stood in utter shock and fascination. Yes, Crook thought—what a glorious moment indeed, to be here at this crucial crossroads in our history of the West; to be here, listening to this first discussion of putting into motion the wheels of the greatest campaign to be launched against the wild tribes of the high plains—at least the first discussion since—

"Ben," Sheridan began, laying a hand on the tall scout's forearm, "what General Crook has referred to: just a few weeks back, we met in Washington with the President."

"In total secrecy," Crook added.

"Who met?" Clark inquired.

"General Sherman, General Crook and me."

"That's all?" Clark asked.

"And the top two officials from the Interior Department." Sheridan nodded. "The new men. They share something in common with men like George and me, Ben. Every man at that meeting were men of action, not content with sitting around on our thumbs. And this business of having to stand by and watch the Indian Bureau botch things with the agents and tribes—allowing them off their reservations—"

"After your boy Custer made things difficult for everybody with his advertising the gold to be found at the grassroots in the Black Hills," Crook added quickly.

"Yes, well . . ." Sheridan replied uneasily. "But the six of us finally agreed on a plan to get Sam . . . the President, off the horns of his dilemma."

"Phil's right, Ben," Crook replied, running a gloved hand up and down the rounded barrel of his fowling piece, "Sam Grant's got himself a real bitch of a problem there. Like you said, with Custer's expedition to the Black Hills last year, the President's got white miners and settlers pouring into that country like spring runoff over a dam."

Clark snorted. "All of it contrary to the treaty of 'sixty-eight we made with the northern tribes."

"But, with your permission, sirs," John Bourke said, "ever since Custer's expedition, we've found our troops unable to stop that growing tide."

"Precisely, Mr. Bourke," Sheridan said, nodding in agreement, gracing the young lieutenant with his winning smile.

"But while we can't stop the tide of immigrants onto the

great Sioux reservation, we can't just rip the Black Hills away from the Indians either, now can we?" asked Clark.

"At the least, that would appear to be illegal, and you haven't heard the likes of the hue and cry that action would cause up on Capitol Hill," Sheridan began to explain, then stopped when Crook snorted.

"Appear to be illegal, Phil? It would be nothing less than downright underhanded jigger-poky."

"All right, George." Sheridan turned back to Clark and Bourke to continue. "You see? That's just the dilemma the President's got like a hot potato in his lap right now. He lets the white immigration continue into the Hills, it breaks that treaty, the law of the land, and goes against the grain of folks back east. But out here, gentlemen, I think these folks west of the Missouri understand a little more about the situation."

"I don't know. Things been awful quiet out here this year, Phil," Crook replied. "Tribes haven't caused much of a ruckus at all."

"Be that as it may, we both know damned good and well that they can't stay quiet for much longer."

Clark shuffled his boot through the dried grass thoughtfully. "Why do I get the feeling that I'm standing here waiting for you to drop the other foot, General Sheridan?"

Sheridan chuckled a moment. "You damned well realize we can't get the land from those savages legally. Right?"

"Yeah, I suppose. I heard that commission to buy the Hills failed pretty miserably—the leaders of the war bands scared off the commissioners and the peace chiefs," Clark said. "Besides, the only chiefs willing to deal with you are the loafers and the hangabouts. Your commissioners can't get the real chiefs to sit down and—"

"You damned well don't expect Sitting Bull and Crazy Horse to come in to talk about selling their goddamned precious Black Hills, now do you, Ben?" snapped Sheridan.

Clark rocked back on his boot heels, wagging his head. "So, I guess I'll ask the question that I figure the lieutenant here wants to ask just as bad as I do. What is it you and Sherman and Grant—along with General Crook—figure to do to take that sacred Paha Sapa from the tribes, without it looking like the army is just riding in there to steal that country from them and break our solemn oath we give in that treaty with Red Cloud back to 'sixty-eight?"

"Fair enough," Sheridan said, his grin growing in his dark, bearded face. "But before I tell you what is planned, let me read you my general order of twenty-nine June, 1869, just months after that goddamned treaty became law. I brought it along to share with General Crook here."

The commander of the Division of the Missouri pulled from his coat pocket a small sheet of foolscap that rustled quietly in the soft, autumn breeze.

"All Indians, when on their proper reservations, are under the exclusive control and jurisdiction of their agents." He paused for a moment, his dark eyes touching each of the other three in turn before he went back to reading. "Outside the well-defined limits of their reservations, they are under the original and exclusive jurisdiction of the military authority, and as a rule will be considered hostile."

Crook took a deep breath. "By damn—that's a stroke of genius, Phil. A goddamned stroke of genius!"

"Sherman reminded me of this order a few days after our meeting at the White House, George. I already have precedent."

"So this directive of yours means that even though the hostiles of Sitting Bull and Crazy Horse are roaming about on the unceded territory where they were given rights to hunt in the Treaty of 1868," Clark said, tapping an index finger against his lower lip, "the army can go after any Indians found off their reservations?"

Sheridan nodded. "Any and all, Ben."

Crook straightened his backbone. This was what he had wanted for many months since coming to Omaha. "One swift stroke, Phil?" he asked, the gray eyes twinkling.

"Damn right." Sheridan nodded again, this time grinning even bigger at Crook. "It's what you've been wanting, George."

"Yeah. Me and Terry, and especially Custer."

"They'll all play a part, you know."

That put a little cold water on Crook's ardor. "I wouldn't doubt it, Phil. But you said I was the first you've told?"

"Yes, George. I want you to put the machinery into motion now."

"But this isn't official yet?"

"No, we're waiting for something first."

"President Sam is having to dance some more with those dad-blamed Quakers and their peace policy?"

"No, not that exactly," Sheridan replied. "I think he's done with that peace nonsense for now. No, we've decided it's best if the army waits to be invited in."

"Invited?" asked Bourke.

"Yes, by the civilians. By the Indian Bureau."

"I see," Crook said, the brilliance of it bringing a wide smile to his face. "So that it doesn't look like the army is bullying anyone."

"Exactly, George. You see, the rumors are already flying in Washington. I don't know how, but some reporters are on to our trail."

"How?"

"Like that Bill Curtis, from the Chicago *Inter-Ocean*. Just five days after all of us met at the White House, that damned Curtis wrote a story that gave substance to the rumors, saying that it looks like the military is now going to be having more of a hand in Indian matters. And now in response to the Watkins report, released just the ninth of this month, the Indian Bureau has begun formulating a letter to go out to all the tribes off the reservations, to be carried by runners from the various agencies, informing them that they are to return to their designated boundaries or they will be subject to military action."

"By damn! You don't say?" Crook asked. "So, if I understand this: the bureau will give the tribes one last chance to come in. Then it will turn the warrior bands over to us?" He clapped his leather gloves together exuberantly. "By bloody damn—it's just the way we wanted it to look to those peace Quakers back in Washington."

"That's right, George. On November ninth with the release of that Watkins report, we got the ammunition we needed so that the Indian commissioner has no other choice but to request the army to step in."

"The ninth of this month?" Clark asked, scratching the

side of his bearded face. "But that means that this Watkins report you're talking about came out after the six of you decided to begin action anyway."

"That's the magic in all this, Ben—don't you see?" Crook said enthusiastically. "Less than a week after we decided to find any means necessary to exercise what we see as our legal right to drive the Indians back onto their reservations, to open up the Powder River country to settlement and take the Black Hills away from the warriors bands for all time . . . we were handed just that magic wand when Inspector Watkins turned in his report to Commissioner Smith on the situation at the agencies out west."

"I'll be bloody damned," Crook said softly, clucking his tongue in approval. "We really are going to get a crack at Sitting Bull and Crazy Horse, aren't we?"

"And likely you'll bump into the whole of the Northern Cheyenne in that country too," Clark said. He spit a stream of tobacco into the dried, red-orange leaves near his feet.

"Yes, you're right," Crook replied, eyeing the scout whom he had heard was married to a Southern Cheyenne woman. "General Sheridan's asked you. Now's time for you to tell me: you want to come along, don't you, Ben?"

Clark looked at Sheridan a moment. "I suppose that's why you called me here to this little head-to-head of yours, didn't you, General Sheridan?"

"Absolutely, Ben. I plan on sending you west with General Crook here."

"To make preparations for a winter campaign?" Crook asked eagerly.

"George, you and Ben both know how I like the idea of catching the tribes hunkered down in their lodges, hanging around their fires when the snow is deep and the winds blow cold."

Crook slowly raised his shotgun and nestled it in his left arm. "Just like Custer and the Washita?"

Sheridan nodded. "As soon as you have things in order here in Omaha, I want you to hurry west to begin amassing your forces. The Third and Second cavalries."

"Is Terry going to push down from Lincoln?"

"That's part of the plan."

"Who else?"

"Gibbon, with foot and horse from Ellis and Shaw, holding the hostiles from escaping you north across the Yellowstone."

"The northern plains in the middle of the goddamned winter," Ben Clark said, then whistled low. "That will take some doing, General Crook."

"We did it in 'sixty-eight in Indian Territory," Sheridan said, smiling effusively, like he hadn't a doubt in the world.

"That wasn't the godforsaken Tongue and Rosebud and Powder River country of Montana Territory. Why, in the middle of winter that country can be a cruel, cruel place."

Sheridan turned away from Clark to stare intently at Crook. "George, I figure you're going to be first to get your column put together out at Fetterman." He took a deep breath before he continued. "You do want the first strike, don't you, George?"

Crook felt something swell inside him as his words came out like iron. "You damned well know I want it, General."

"You did this country a damned fine job down in Apache country," Sheridan replied.

The lieutenant general yanked his glove off his right hand and presented it to his old classmate and friend, George Crook. "Now, by damned, George—we want you to go crush Sitting Bull and Crazy Horse for us."

Chapter 4

21 December 1875

*G*eneral Crook stepped to the doorway between his office and the small quarters given him here at Fort Laramie.

"Is that coffee done yet, John?"

"Pulling off the fire now, General," answered Lieutenant John Bourke. He watched the general nod in that way of his that showed something clearly upsetting the man as Crook turned back to the tiny office where he had been going over maps, transcripts and scouting reports for the past three days almost nonstop. It was Crook's way of things, especially planning a campaign. He threw himself into it totally, and wanted everyone else around him to enjoy the all-consuming excitement of the chase as much as he.

This would not be John Bourke's first campaign with the general.

After graduating in the top third of his class at West Point in 1869, Bourke had served as a line officer for two years in the Southwest before joining Crook's staff in 1871. From that point on they had been inseparable—pursuing the ghostly Apache down in Arizona. And earlier this year when Crook had been assigned to Omaha's headquarters of the Department of the Platte, Bourke clearly saw that the brass back east were bringing Crook north to settle the plains—despite his often unorthodox manner of engaging the enemy.

"Here, General."

Crook glanced up from the transcript of a report from

the agent on Spotted Tail's reservation. "Thank you, John."
He took a sip of the scalding liquid and set the china mug
down amid the scattered papers and maps, laying like autumn's dead leaves on the small desk. "When Interior Secretary Delano handed his resignation to Grant in October,
he had no idea he had handed the President a way to take
the tribes from the Indian Bureau and give all Indian matters back to the army."

"I take it that the President's new secretary, Zachariah
Chandler, thinks more like Sherman and Sheridan?"
Bourke inquired.

Crook grinned in his thick, double-tailed beard. "Does
he ever!"

For years, Zachariah Chandler never lost a chance to
speechify that the army should have control of the wild
tribes. It was his December third memo to Secretary of War
Belknap that put Grant's wheels in motion:

> Referring to my letter of transmittal on the 29th ulti-
> mate . . . requesting that steps be taken to compel the
> hostile Sioux to go upon a reservation and cease their
> depredations, I have the honor to inform you that I have
> this day directed the Commissioner of Indian Affairs to
> notify said Indians that they must remove to a reserva-
> tion before the 31st of January next; that if they neglect
> or refuse so to move, they will be reported to the War
> Department as hostile Indians and that a military force
> will be sent to compel them to obey the orders of the
> Indian Office.
>
> You will be notified of the compliance or noncompli-
> ance of the Indians with this order; and if said Indians
> shall neglect or refuse to comply with said order, I have
> the honor to request that the proper military officer be
> directed to compel their removal to and residence within
> the bounds of their reservation.

"Sounds like the new secretary is going to get along
splendidly with the President," Bourke said.

"Chandler's just the sort of thinker that Grant wants

surrounding him right now—men who feel the way he does, tightening ranks. Make no mistake about this, John. The army's going to finish what may well be the last war on this continent: We're going after the wild tribes. And this time, they'll feel the sting. Just this morning I sent Sheridan a wire, telling him that from my assessment of things here, we can commence military operations whenever in the opinion of the War Department such action becomes necessary."

"And it will be necessary, won't it, General?"

Crook smiled at his aide. "There never was any doubt of that in my mind, John."

Bourke sighed, running it around in his mind. The black, drooping mustache did not hide his sensuous Cupid-bow lips. "General, may I speak frankly?"

Crook regarded his young aide for a moment. "We've been together too long not to speak openly. What do you have on your mind?"

"This campaign—driving the wild tribes off the land granted them in 'sixty-eight, driving them back to their reservations. I know the President and the rest of you have come up with a plan that is legal. But General—is it *right?*"

Bourke watched as Crook rubbed his palms together thoughtfully, then steepled his fingers before his face. After a long time of staring at the smoky window, the general replied in a quiet voice.

"John, the way I figure it, Sam Grant—and all the rest of us to boot—decided to do the only thing we could do in all of this. We have little choice."

"But sir, neither does the Indian."

"True, John. True. Still, the circumstances at present compel Grant to act, and now."

"And by force, General. Military force."

"Yes," Crook agreed, nodding before he leaned back into his chair wearily. "The army is now forced to use its might against one of two parties. Either we must make enemies out of our own people—the white men and women who are flooding into the Black Hills illegally—or we must make enemies out of the Sioux and Cheyenne already there, the red men who bode us no good."

"Then the President—the rest of you who have advised him—you really have only one choice, don't you?"

Crook pressed his lips into a thin line, then said, "Yes. The only decision left us is what enemy we're going to fight."

Bourke cleared his throat and drew himself up. "Then, General—in finding ourselves in these circumstances, it seems there isn't much of a choice to make, is there, sir?"

The department commander wagged his head. "No, John. There is but one choice. And after you realize that you have but one choice, you resolve to go after your enemy with everything you can muster, every man and rifle and mule you can put into the field."

The lieutenant watched Crook's shoulders sag a bit. He realized the general had paid an awful toll down in Arizona, called upon to wage an unwinnable war against the Apaches. And Bourke prayed the army had not again asked the same of George C. Crook: to come to the northern plains to fight another unwinnable Indian war.

"How many warriors do you expect we'll find, General?"

"Says here the agent reports that we might encounter no more than five to eight hundred."

"Do the scouting reports confirm that, sir?"

Crook's eyes crawled across the big map laid at the center of his small, cluttered table. "Yes. And with us marching up there to track them down in the heart of winter—scouts tell us that those eight hundred warriors likely won't all be together in one place."

"Fight them piecemeal," Bourke replied, thinking back to the ghostly fighters of Apacheria.

Crook's eyes wrinkled. "If I've got to do it in winter, and on the enemy's own ground, I'd prefer one decisive battle just to get it over with. Get in quick . . . do our job . . . and get the hell out just as fast. I'll leave it to others to shepherd the survivors back to their agencies."

"Perhaps when we've got our victory, General Sheridan will have his interior post he's been championing for some time now."

"The one he wants in the Black Hills?"

"Yes, sir," Bourke replied. "As the general said, such a

fort at an interior point in the heart of Indian country could threaten the villages and stock of the Indians if they dared make raids on the settlements."

"We'll leave the fort building to others, John. You and me—we're cut of something else, a different mold. We're not engineers. We are warriors. Like this Sitting Bull. Like Crazy Horse. And the fighting bands they lead. Like them, you and me are warriors."

It was true enough, the young lieutenant felt. And that sort of praise from a man who wasn't fond of offering praise to others was enough to make Bourke smile easily, honored and proud. To have George C. Crook state that his young aide shared a trait with the general was something the Philadelphia-born son of Irish immigrants took some real pride in. After all, it was in this profession of soldiering in the west that John Bourke had found himself.

At the age of sixteen he had received his first baptism of fire. Having lied about his age to enlist in the Fifteenth Pennsylvania Volunteer Cavalry, Bourke galloped boldly into battle at Stones River in Tennessee, his first blooding, where he did no less than earn himself the Medal of Honor for gallantry in action. Two weeks after his nineteenth birthday, following the end of the war, Bourke was mustered out of volunteer service, and that very fall entered the U.S. Military Academy.

Upon arriving in New Mexico after graduation in 1869, assigned to the Third Cavalry, Bourke began what would become a lifelong practice of keeping a diary. His youthful fascination with this foreign land, its native peoples, flora and fauna soon made a respected ethnologist and folklorist of the young officer. And perhaps as important, Bourke learned from George C. Crook about Indian fighting.

"Soldiers alone can't defeat a dogged band of warriors who can cover seventy-five to a hundred miles of rough ground like a whisper of a breeze," Crook had declared many times. "Especially if that ground is as broken as the Chirichaua and the weather bakes a man's brains as it does in southern Arizona."

The general was one of the first leading army officers to come to the belief that only the Apaches themselves would be capable of following, and ultimately defeating, their hostile brethren. Crook hired scouts and guides, trackers and mercenaries from one band to hunt down and defeat those Apaches in another band. So for close to three years John Bourke found himself not only fighting the elusive Apache, but living with and learning from the Apache as well.

That time among the wild tribes of Arizona had served him well.

When Bourke had first come in the Southwest in 'sixty-nine, he gave his voice to the commonly-held opinion that "the only good Indian was a dead Indian, and that the only use to make of him was that of a fertilizer." So popular and all-pervasive was this belief that in the following year Bourke mounted an Apache scalp, complete with the warrior's ears, in a suitable frame.

Yet through the tutelage of General Crook, Bourke began to look at the savage world of the frontier West with a little different eye. Together, both men believed much of what the hard-bitten Scottish pragmatists espoused: all of human society represented progress from the state of savagery to the condition of civilization. When they spoke to an Apache, Cheyenne or Sioux warrior, both Crook and Bourke believed they were actually conversing with a living historical specimen.

So it was that John Bourke not only welcomed, but zealously relished, this opportunity to witness firsthand the warrior tribes of the central and northern plains. He therefore threw himself eagerly into the preparations for what promised to be a tough winter campaign.

"We get Sitting Bull and Crazy Horse corralled, do you think Sheridan will get his forts built up on the Yellowstone, General?" Bourke asked as he settled in the only other chair in the small room, his steaming cup cradled in his hand.

Crook stared at the map. "Here at the mouth of the Tongue, the other at the mouth of the Bighorn?"

"Yes, sir. The two that Sheridan wants on the Yellowstone."

"Maybe." Crook finally peered up at Bourke. "We are going to have to corral the war chiefs first. Subdue their bands. Indeed, things are going to have to change somewhat up in that country."

"Everyone around here claims it's the last great hunting ground of the Sioux and Cheyenne."

Crook leaned back and smiled, folding his hands across his chest, interlacing his fingers. "The army found that out back in 'sixty-six and 'sixty-seven."

"Then it sounds like it's up to us to clear the way to settling things down, General."

"Before there can be any river traffic on the Yellowstone, we're going to have to drive the hostiles back to their reservations, and make their punishment severe enough that they won't even consider jumping their boundaries for fear of the throttling the army will give them."

Crook rose and walked to the window. "You have no idea how much satisfaction it gives me to now have this sanction within my own control. After all the years of Grant's nilly-nallying back and forth with those Quakers and Indian commissioners and agents—to be given the freedom of striking first and hard and often. Washington has finally turned us loose for one final campaign."

In contemplation, the general turned and stared at Bourke a moment before continuing. "As the plainsmen in these parts say, it appears the only thing these Sioux and Cheyenne understand is war and blood. Well, Mr. Bourke —I'm about to give them just that: a goddamned bellyful of war and blood."

Crook headed back to his table and settled in the creaky chair, where he again studied the stacks of odd-sized paper.

Bourke sipped at his coffee for some time, watching Crook read, repeatedly scratching at his ledger notes with that nub of a pencil he kept licking with the tip of his tongue.

As much as he was uncertain about what the horizon to the north might hold for him, Bourke felt excitement for this challenge. The coming campaign was the bold, final solution to the government's nagging dilemma: the army would drive the hostiles back onto the reservations to Christianize them, thereby opening up that huge tract of unceded territory to white settlement and ending the sporadic conflicts between white man and red in that country of the Bighorn and Tongue and Powder rivers; the army's winter campaign would ultimately bring the railroads and towns and farmers' plows to this land.

Was there any man who could find fault with bringing civilization to this savage land, anything wrong with bringing civilization to the savage peoples who wandered that wilderness with the coming and going of the seasons?

But before the plowshares and the iron rails could be brought to the land of the Powder and the Tongue and the Rosebud, the army would have to cross that wilderness now tracked by only the hoof of the buffalo and the unshod pony.

The general's army would have to find the warrior bands in their winter camps.

And give them Crook's goddamned bellyful of war.

Chapter 5

Late December 1875

"*A* bloody cold time of the year for a man like me to be heading north, Bill," growled Robert Strahorn.

He sat leaning back on his chair, his feet unceremoniously propped up on the desk of his publisher, and the paper's owner, a graying William N. Byers.

"Never known you to duck a good story, Bob."

Strahorn grinned, scratching his clean-shaven cheek, gazing out the smoky window at the bustling Denver street two stories below. Despite the falling snow, life went on at its easy pace beneath the ROCKY MOUNTAIN NEWS, EST. 1859 sign suspended over the muddy boardwalk. "You got me there, you old dog."

"And this is going to be one helluva story."

"I won't argue with you there," Strahorn agreed. "The way Washington has been keeping us supplied with word of what's going since Secretary Delano resigned—I've had a suspicion they're getting us ready to do something for them."

"What with the way that bunch fluttering around Sam Grant has no love lost for journalists—they'll tell us only what they want us to print. And just like an owl is mostly head and bone—what the government's dishing out is mostly lies."

"So you want me to go north to sniff around and see what's happening with the army—why they're of a sudden leaving the roads north to the Hills all clear, eh?"

"Seems they've gotten instructions from Washington to

leave the miners go to the Black Hills, Bob," replied Byers. "There's something afoot—perhaps something that will be brought to a boil by spring."

"A summer campaign."

Byers ran a single finger over his tobacco-stained lips thoughtfully, then aimed for the nearby brass spittoon in the corner. "Yeah. Don't you know I want to be the very first to tell our readers about it."

"I'll need a horse and some gear."

"What sort of gear, Strahorn?" Byers asked as he pulled open a drawer and brought out a small ledger he opened atop the mound of paper littering his desk.

"It's getting cold out there, Bill," Stahorn moaned theatrically, clutching both arms around himself and shivering. "A new coat and a couple pair of underwear. Some new boots and gloves, and I'll need some winter mittens and hat. Tell me where'm I going to get a reliable animal too?"

Byers waved that off. "I'll see you're sent to a good man to get your trustworthy steed, Strahorn."

"You really didn't have anybody else to do this for you, did you, Bill?"

Byers gazed up from his ledger. "We understand one another, don't we, Bob?"

"Yeah, we do. And you realize I'm the one who can make sense out of all the rumors leaking out of Fort Russell and up to Laramie. All the whispers of meetings and conferences and the hush-hush back in Washington City going on right now."

Byers tapped the end of his pencil against those browned teeth. "You've got the nose for it, Strahorn. Saw that right off when you first came to work here. It's you I want there when they make it official and start to march come spring."

"Spring?" he snorted. "You want me to hang around up there until spring?"

"And be with the first outfit into the field." Byers grinned. "Won't be so bad."

"Bad?" Strahorn groaned, acting as if he were going to gag. "Stringy steaks and saddle varnish for whiskey."

"Shit," Byers replied, having none of the reporter's complaints. "I hear they've got some good saloons up in Cheyenne City. Lots of action with the miners moving through there. Why, even up there at Laramie there's some good watering holes I've heard of just across the river from the post."

Strahorn pointed to the ledger sheet Byers worked over. "Just make sure you put me down for plenty of drinking money."

"Like any good Irishman needs. Right, Strahorn?"

"Ouch!" He feigned mock hurt. "How the hell do you expect me to grease the wheels of journalism if I can't offer me own sources a bit of the potheen now?"

"You'll have a little extra—but nowhere near what you're expecting."

"Ah, Bill, c'mon now. And what about the girls? You know how I love the women. How you expect me to stay up there as celibate as a parish priest all the way till spring?"

"Your nocturnal habits are none of my concern, Strahorn. Only that you get the story I know you're capable of —the story that's brewing up there right now." Byers tore the sheet from the ledger, hurriedly copied it onto the next page, then handed the loose paper across the desk to Strahorn.

The reporter in his mid-twenties quickly studied the figures. "You expect this pittance to last me?"

"It will, until after New Year's—so there's no use in begging. No use in groveling either. That voucher holds you until the first of January. Then I'll be able to deposit some more in an account you can draw on by wire when you need it." The publisher leaned back as Strahorn stuffed the page in his coat pocket. "Eighteen seventy-five has been a quiet year, Bob. Too damned quiet for all the prodding and goading the army's done to the Indians . . . along with those miners traveling to the Hills."

"It all might make a man think the Sioux and Cheyenne intend to hand over the Black Hills to the army and those gold-seekers."

Byers snorted. "Doubt it. For some reason, the tribes have been moving farther and farther away from contact this last year."

"But it won't always be that way, will it, Bill?"

"No, Strahorn. The army's going to war. That much is plain as paint. Grant can't get the Indians to sell us the Hills. And he can't keep shooing the miners off the road and settlers out of that part of the country. Poor Sam Grant —hopping from one horn of his dilemma to the other. Sooner or later he had to land, and land hard."

"I figure you think the President's landed, Bill." Strahorn slapped one palm down on top of the other, making a resounding echo in the small office.

The folds of skin between Byer's eyes deepened. "Damn right he's landed. It's 'Old Unconditional Surrender' Grant all over again, I'll lay my reputation on it, Strahorn. But this time the Federal government's not declaring war on the Confederate states. This time Grant's declared unconditional war on Sitting Bull and Crazy Horse."

The days of winter-coming passed slowly for He Dog. Here now in the Moon of Seven Cold Nights. The winds out of the north, spurred on by *Wanitu,* the Winter Giant, blew dry for the most part. But still He Dog felt the coming cold seep deep in his marrow.

This would no doubt be a winter like few could remember.

Already the ponies they rode, the game they killed to eat, all the animals had put on a thick coat for the coming time of great cold. The oldest ones shuddered most. No man, no woman, could remember such a time when all the omens told them to lay in the firewood and dry their meat, then stay close by their lodge fires.

And now the runners from the white man's agency had come to tell Crazy Horse's band of Hunkpatila Oglalla that they were being ordered to return immediately, or the pony soldiers would come looking.

Most of the young Lakota warriors had laughed at that milky threat. Laughed all the harder at the two riders who brought the ultimatum from Red Cloud's reservation people. He Dog himself had given the men a place to sleep that night, and filled their bellies twice before they left long before sunup the next morning. He Dog knew Red Cloud's emissaries did not want to hear any more laughter.

No man wanted to be called an old woman.

So this was to be a hard thing for He Dog, who for many winters had fought shoulder to shoulder with Crazy Horse. Harder still to look at the faces of his wives and children, at the faces of the old ones who for just as many winters had depended upon him to provide for them. There was no other to feed these old ones, the ones who no longer had family of their own. So it was that He Dog and a handful of Hunkpatila hunted not only for their own families, but for the growing number of old ones, sick ones, the lame and the blind and the toothless whose day of glory had gone the way of sunset.

Deep in his marrow He Dog sensed the sun setting on the Hunkpatila of Crazy Horse.

His old friend was not the same young man he had come to know in their youth. No rawhide shield made from the neck of a young bull could have turned the arrows of tragedy from the Horse's life across these last nine winters. First the loss of Lone Bear at the Battle of a Hundred in the Hand. Then four summers later to lose Hump, his childhood *kola*. The next autumn he had brazenly pursued Black Buffalo Woman and nearly caused war among his own people.

Then only a few moons later the brother of Crazy Horse was killed in making an attack on some Snakes. Among the enemy had been some white miners with many repeating rifles. Even braver, perhaps crazier, than his older brother, Little Hawk charged and charged again, and finally fell. This terrible death blow to the spirit of Crazy Horse! First his *kola*. And now to lose his brother.

Later that same year, Crazy Horse had returned to camp after raiding into the land of the Sparrow Hawks to learn that his daughter had died of the white man's whooping cough. Learning where the body had been left, the Horse rode back with He Dog to the scaffold. While his friend spent three days and nights atop that tree, clutching the blanket-shrouded body of his tiny daughter, He Dog stood a sleepless vigil below, his eyes forever scanning the horizon for enemy.

Scared more than he had ever been in his life. For this

time the white man had killed without coming close like an honorable enemy. The white man had killed with his evil spirits, taking the youngest, the weakest and the most helpless among the Lakota.

"Do you want more stew?" asked Lame Dog Woman.

He Dog looked up at his first wife and shook his head, then went back to staring at the flames of the lodge fire. His belly was not really that hungry these days. He too seemed to sense some of the emptiness, the gnawing despair that must be eating Crazy Horse alive.

Two summers ago they had fought the Long Hair's pony soldiers along the Elk River.*

The following summer they had watched the Long Hair's winding blue columns of horsemen and wagons penetrate the sacred Paha Sapa, knowing the day was drawing nigh when the Lakota and the Shahiyena would have to do more than kill small groups of white miners and wagon men as Crazy Horse did in his wild, random attacks, leaving the enemy dead with their scalps untouched.

But ever since last winter, all had been very quiet. For the most part the warrior bands stayed away from the white man. And the soldiers had hung close to their forts, making little trouble in this great hunting ground given them not by the white man, but by the Grandfather Above. So quiet had it been that by the end of this past summer, the white man had called the bands together near Fort Robinson to discuss selling the Black Hills back to the government. This so enraged Crazy Horse and He Dog, Little Big Man and so many others, that they threatened to kill the treaty-talkers and their guard of pony soldiers right on the spot. The white men had hurried away.

After that there were no good omens last autumn.

So it bothered He Dog when Red Cloud's messengers came from the agency with word that the army would soon be marching. There had been no attacks on white settlements for many moons. Not like that time they had raided and killed and burned and mutilated in the moons immedi-

* Yellowstone River

ately following the white man's massacre of Black Kettle's camp on the Little Dried River.*

Many days after Red Cloud's emissaries rode out of camp, carrying their message on north, Hunkpapa riders showed up, coming down from Sitting Bull's camp some eight suns to the north. The Bull was calling the faithful to come join him, to resist. Those Hunkpapas left too, riding south for the agencies, to call the people away from the flour and the bacon the white man used to keep the Indians on the reservations. Sitting Bull was calling the people to make a decision on how they would live.

Fat buffalo or *kukuse*, the white man's moldy bacon. Antelope and elk and deer, or weevil-infested flour. To wear feathers of the great war bird *wanbli* in their hair and feel the free wind in their faces, or to live in one place as the white man did, and smell the stench of too much offal, unable to move on and let the seasons reclaim the land.

Sitting Bull was calling the Lakota to make their decision. It was time for He Dog to make up his mind.

Red Cloud's messengers explained that life on the reservations that winter was hard—there wasn't enough to eat. What food there was had arrived late, and there was precious little of the white man's skinny spotted buffalo to butcher. Famine appeared on the horizon, and the little ones were already crying pitifully with empty bellies. And then the final blow came when Spotted Tail's Platte River Brule were ordered east to a new agency along the Great Muddy River, to save the white man the cost of shipping his food and beef to the starving Sioux.

Here in the Crazy Horse camp on the East Fork of the Little Powder, He Dog watched the flames dance in the fire pit. He felt like a Ready-to-Die staked out and facing his many onrushing enemies, but not knowing which one of the enemy would kill him first.

Here he stood now, faced with the dilemma of staying with his old friend and their band of Hunkpatila, depending on finding game to make it through the winter, just as their

* Sand Creek Massacre, November 28, 1864

people had since time began . . . waiting too for the pony soldiers to attack.

Or He Dog could take his family and relatives in to Red Cloud's agency, where the little ones and the old ones and the sick ones would all be safe from soldier bullets—and pray they got enough to eat and stayed warm enough wrapped in the white agent's thin blankets to make it through the coming time of hard cold.

Like he was being choked by that Ready-to-Die sash looped around his neck and staked to the ground at his feet with a lance, He Dog grappled with self-doubts, struggling to make a decision like a man fought to catch his breath at the bottom of a deep, black pool.

"I must go tell the Horse," he said quietly as he rose, dragging the heavy buffalo robe with him, wrapping it around his shoulders.

Lame Dog Woman did not say a word. She did not have to. Instead she gazed around the lodge at the children and the old ones they had taken in. And in that silence, they both listened to the wheezing and coughing of the sick ones. She nodded, her eyes falling to the marrow bones she was cracking open with a stone mallet.

As he stood for a moment outside his lodge door, he knew she realized this would be one of the hardest things he had ever had to do. With a slashing gust, the cold wind cruelly slapped against the warmth of his cheeks. One of the braids nuzzled below his chin was tormented by that same north wind which carried the smell of snow strong in its nostrils. Much snow. *Waniyetu,* the time of much snow falling.

How to explain to an old friend that you are going to do what the white man asks? How to find the words, when you and that old friend have stood back to back and fought Scalped-Head Pawnee and Sparrow Hawk Crow, white wagon men and pony soldiers too? And gloried in the scalps taken. Laughed over the many ponies stolen. Then cried over the deaths of friends the white man's bullets have claimed across the seasons.

How would he explain to Crazy Horse that he was taking his relatives to the safety of Red Cloud's reservation? To face starvation rather than the bullets and knives of the pony soldiers. Deciding to do this for the ones who stood no chance of fighting the soldiers who would be coming.

That was the one certainty above all others, he knew.

If one thing was true, if there was one thing He Dog could count on—the white man would come. And it was always the weak ones, the small ones who could not run fast enough, the sick ones too lame to run at all . . . these were the ones to die in the bloodstained snow.

Standing here outside the lodge of Crazy Horse now, He Dog felt his throat go dry. What he had to do was like no other trial he had faced in more than three decades of life. This struggle like no other enemy he had faced ever before.

For now He Dog had to deny his warrior spirit. Realizing that this was just what the white man wanted to do to the Lakota warrior was like a cold stone in his belly.

Nervous, his gut filled with the flapping of unseen wings, he scratched on the frozen lodge cover beside the door flap.

"Who is there?"

It was Black Shawl's voice. Maybe, he prayed, she would understand.

"He Dog," he said quietly. "Is Crazy Horse with you?"

"I am here, my old friend."

A heartbeat more and the Horse's head appeared through the lodge door, smiling. "It is good that you come, He Dog. Come in, we have soup on the fire. Sit. Eat."

He Dog swallowed hard, then watched the smile slowly drain from the lips, seep from the eyes of his old friend.

"Crazy Horse . . . I have come to talk."

Eventually the war chief nodded, his moistening eyes saying he knew already. Crazy Horse flipped aside the elk-hide door flap for his old friend.

"Yes, He Dog. Come in. We . . . we must talk."

Chapter 6

Late February 1876

"Sorry to tell you, but all travel north from here is restricted."

Seamus Donegan stared disbelieving at the commander of Fort Laramie. "Colonel, I thought I'd made it clear: I'm not intending to take my wife to the Black Hills. I know your sojurs been doing their best to keep everyone off that road to Deadwood."

"A damned thankless job it is," replied Henry E. Maynadier with exasperation. The colonel's eyes squinted and he shoved the smoky oil lamp across the desk toward the tall Irishman standing on the far side of the disarray of papers and maps in the cramped, cold office. He studied his uninvited guest more carefully for a long moment, then said, "We've met, Mister . . . ?"

"Donegan," Seamus replied. "Yes. Almost ten years ago, Colonel."

"Good Lord, yes!" the colonel said, seeming to sink more deeply into his cracked leather chair. "Someone else to remind me how long I've been stationed here."

"Waiting for promotion, I take it," Donegan replied.

"A field command is the only path to promotion, Mr. Donegan. When was it we met?"

"Eighteen sixty-six.* July, as I remember. I was part of a small bunch that tagged along with a couple young lieuten-

---

* The Plainsmen Series, vol. 1, *Sioux Dawn*

ants of yours, headed for reassignment up at Carrington's new fort."

Maynadier's head nodded as he stared at someplace in the mid distance. "Then you were with that detail when they were struck by the Sioux."

"At the Crazy Woman. Yes, a hot afternoon of it." Seamus inched right to the edge of the desk, peering down at the top of the colonel's balding head. "So now you know I'm not some ignorant civilian."

"No," Maynadier agreed with a bit of a twinkle in his eye, "just a stupid one. Wanting to push north. Across that piece of bloody country." He rose slowly from the horsehide chair permanently wilted with a depression.

"I know the country, Colonel."

"I'll just bet you do. But still you're wanting to head north with winter ready to set down hard on us."

"I was up there on the Montana Road for one winter already. Even carried dispatches and letters from Carrington's post up to the one on the Bighorn."

"Smith?"

"I was there the next summer. August."

"Lord, man!" Maynadier exclaimed with a gleam of admiration in his eyes. "You were there at the Fort C. F. Smith when the Cheyenne tore into those hayfield workers a few miles from the post?"

Seamus snorted, wagging his head. "Not exactly at the post, Colonel. You see—I was one of those stupid civilians: in the wrong place at just the right time."*

The colonel wagged a finger at the younger man. "See there? You've just proved my point, Mr. Donegan."

Then they both laughed. Together. And Seamus felt some of the tension ease as the post adjutant and the two privates at the door laughed with them.

"I can make it, Colonel. You must believe me."

"I won't allow it." Maynadier sounded firm. "Why don't you take your wife back to Cheyenne City. Maybe even on south to Denver City and wait out the winter."

"I need work."

* The Plainsmen Series, vol. 2, *Red Cloud's Revenge*

The colonel nodded, appraising the tall Irishman once again. "I see. Run out of funds and you figured to find work here?"

"No. Nor would I find the work I want to do in Cheyenne. Not in Denver neither. You're right, though—I'm near busted. Just about run out of the money I earned scouting Comanche and Kiowa for Mackenzie down in Texas."†

"Jesus Christ!" the adjutant blurted. "Excuse me, Colonel." Then he turned back to the Irishman. "Why the hell didn't you stay down there, mister—where the army's finally got things settled down."

Donegan turned back to Maynadier. "I want to get to Helena. An old friend of mine's up there."

"Not this winter, you can't."

"What if I ride out on my own? Make arrangements for my wife until I can come back for her."

The colonel's lips drew into a tight line. "Then you do just that—ride out on your own, Mr. Donegan. But I'm putting your wife under house arrest. If you want to ride off and kill yourself—getting scalped, maybe freezing to death too . . . then that's your business. But I'll not have you dragging your woman one more foot farther north. Not with Sitting Bull and Crazy Horse on the rampage."

Donegan felt something burn inside him. Deep. "Crazy . . . Crazy Horse?"

Maynadier whirled and jabbed a finger at the yellowed map nailed to the wall behind his desk. "They're up there. All of them, so the scouting reports have it. Sitting Bull's Unkpapas. Crazy Horse's Oglallas. He's got the remnants of old Red Cloud's Bad Faces with him, don't you know? The ones who hit you and Carrington's fort, carrying on that bloody war of attrition for more than a year of death and destruction—until the army finally pulled off the Bozeman Road."

"Then there's bound to be some Northern Cheyenne up there too," Donegan said, staring at that map laced with the known creeks and streams and mountain chains,

† The Plainsmen Series, vol. 7, *Dying Thunder*

pocked with the fords and crossings and bridges and ferries. "Mayhaps, a few loose Arapaho too."

"Appears you know a little more about that country than you're telling me, Mr. Donegan."

He gazed back at Maynadier, a flicker of pride burning in his breast. "I learned a little from Jim Bridger back in 'sixty-six. Enough to pay attention to most everything around me."

"And then you dug for gold and retired to Texas where you hunted Comanche for Mackenzie."

Seamus grinned. "After I'd fought Roman Nose's Northern Cheyenne with Major Sandy Forsyth. Out to the Arickaree in 'sixty-eight."*

Maynadier didn't say a thing, but immediately sank to that rickety horsehide chair, reaching for his ink quill. He tried it across a piece of paper repeatedly, then cursed, "Damn things don't work in this cold." Tossing the quill aside, he grabbed up a long lead pencil and set to work over the page.

Finished, the colonel folded the page twice and held it up, waving for one of the two soldiers at the door to come forward. "Private. Take this to my missus. But take Mrs. Donegan with you when you do."

Donegan wheeled. "What the hell are you—"

"It will be just fine." Maynadier waved a hand to shut the Irishman off. "Go on now, private."

"You're having my wife imprisoned in your quarters, Colonel?"

"No. But that is where she can stay for her own welfare."

"That mean you're putting her under your custody?"

He interlaced his fingers on the desk before him. "Yes—"

"Goddamn you!"

"Custody, but not in the way you think, Mr. Donegan. She probably needs a good, hot, home-cooked meal. And a tub of hot water. Women have this thing about lots of soapy water."

Seamus felt the sudden fire of his anger and indignation

* The Plainsmen Series, vol. 3, *The Stalkers*

exhaust itself, like a thin soup seeping from a cracked china bowl. "That's all, Colonel? You aren't kidnapping her from me?"

"No. But I do want her to stay with my wife and me for a little while. I will have to meet her myself this evening, when I can apologize for the cramped quarters at the moment. None of us had expected the buildup for this campaign to put the strain it has on all of us." He dragged out another sheet of the paper and put the pencil back to work.

"For a while, you say," Seamus repeated, then leaned over, curious, attempting to make sense of some of the colonel's scrawl.

"You can read this soon enough, Mr. Donegan," Maynadier said, without raising his eyes from his work. "It has to do with you."

"Orders for my detention, no doubt," he snarled.

Now the colonel gazed up at the Irishman. "You do have an odd sense of humor, don't you? It has served you well fighting Indians, I take it. But, no: these are not orders for your detention." He finished, set the pencil aside and folded the page as he had the first, into a neat square which he handed to the civilian. "These are instead . . . orders for you to report to the general commanding, Big Horn Expedition."

"Who'd that be, me asking?"

"Crook. General George C. Crook."

Donegan cocked his head, suspicious. "And where'd I be finding this general?"

"Up the road a ways. Ninety miles. Place called Fetterman. Heard of it?"

"The man. Not the place."

Maynadier rose, nodding. "Yes. I figure you knew William Judd Fetterman. A good soldier he was."

"What he had in courage, he lacked in horse sense," Seamus said quietly.

"Well, now . . . yes. A shame, but the army names its forts after its dead heroes."

"Like Colonel Carrington found out."

"Exactly."

"This Fort Fetterman is less than a hundred miles away? North?"

"North by west." The colonel nodded his head as he came around the desk. "You'll follow the North Platte all the way."

"And when do you figure I'll be going there, with this letter you've written to General Crook for me?"

"As soon as you've had supper with us and filled your belly proper, and had one last night alone with your wife, Mr. Donegan. You need to provide for your woman—and scouting is the only game in these parts . . . unless you'd like taking chances digging for gold in the Black Hills, perhaps playing cards at the tables in Deadwood."

Seamus cleared his throat. The realization suddenly struck him like a Pittsburgh freight wagon and rolled on over him. He almost reeled from the impact. "So, this is it. I go on by myself and hire out to Crook for this Big Horn campaign of his. Or I take my wife back south to Cheyenne or Denver."

Maynadier nodded, his eyes half lidded, as if hiding a deep personal hurt. "I won't have the blood of another woman on my hands, Donegan."

Angrily, Seamus chewed on the inside of his cheek, staring at the aging colonel—knowing that Maynadier already lived with the blood of many women, women the colonel likely figured he could have saved during the fiery years on the Bozeman Road.

"You're going to care for Mrs. Donegan until I get back?"

"Yes. My Lucy will." Then he glanced quickly at his adjutant, who just as quickly put his eyes on the floor. "And if you don't make it back, I'll personally see that your missus receives your back pay and a travel voucher to get her back home to her family."

Donegan swallowed hard then. Never before had he had to worry about anyone but himself. This was something entirely new, and completely foreign. And more than a little frightening.

He took a deep breath, fingering the folded paper. "All right. Samantha . . . my missus—she's gonna be seen to by you and your wife. That much is settled in my mind. So, what is it that this Crook and his sojurs are gonna be doing in the middle of this godforsaken country, with winter about to come roaring out of the north?"

"Why, Mr. Donegan—I figured an old plainsman like yourself would have put that together."

Seamus leaned back a bit, straightening. "Yes. All right," he said finally. "I figure you think I can help this general look for Sioux and Cheyenne."

"Exactly," Maynadier replied. Then he stared evenly at the tall, gray-eyed civilian. "Doesn't that fit into your plans, Mr. Donegan?"

"I suppose it does at that," he sighed heavily. "Was looking, I was, for a chance to hunt down that Injin called Crazy Horse."

"You left me once already, Seamus Donegan," Samantha said as bravely as she could make it sound.

"And I came back to you."

Samantha pressed her cheek against his chest, wanting to feel his arms around her, sheltering her, protecting her as they had protected her from so much. Not wanting him to see her eyes.

He mustn't see this lower lip of mine, she thought, until I get control of it.

She grasped that full lower lip between her teeth and clamped hard, angry at herself for coming close to losing control.

Months ago when she took those wedding vows, Samantha had also vowed never to let him out of her sight. Never to let him go again—as she had once, watching him march off to fight the Comanche and Kiowa.* She had taken him for better or worse, and if that meant a miserably cold ride into the maw of winter through the homeland of some savage redskinned Indians, then so be it. Whatever he asked of her to do, she would do for Seamus Donegan.

But his asking her in the cold winter light of this midafternoon *not* to do something had been something alto-

* The Plainsmen Series, vol. 6, *Shadow Riders*

gether different. Not to come with him. Not to ride into the face of danger as they had talked of doing on that long trail north from Texas, through the Indian Nations and across the reservations, up through the endless rolling plains of eastern Colorado Territory. And now into a desolate, high and windy country they called Wyoming. A place Seamus nonetheless still preferred to call Dakota Territory. He always explained his mistake to every listener—apologizing by saying he knew this country ten years ago, when there were fewer white men, likely fewer Indians as well in all its great expanse.

She could feel his steady breathing on her scalp where he rested his chin, gently stroking one of those big hands of his up and down the small of her back. And she could hear the rhythmic plodding of his heart where her ear lay against the solid muscle of his chest. How she wanted him to undress her slowly right this minute, to kiss up the length of her legs, slowly spreading her thighs the way he did, then mount her as his fury built when she pleaded with him to place his flesh inside her.

How she always told him exactly what she wanted, not waiting for him to figure it out. But instead telling him how he felt in her deepest region, moving above her. How it made her feel when she sat astride him, looking down on him, her long, sun-kissed hair unfurled where he could grip it and pull her full mouth down on his while she rocked atop him.

So it was that Samantha slowly brought one hand from his waist and sought that flesh a man used to bring both himself and a woman such pleasure. Softly rubbing against his britches at first, her ear still against his chest, she sensed her husband's breathing grow more shallow, his heart beat a shade faster. And once she felt that flesh of him stirring beneath her gentle touch, Seamus brought a hand to one of her breasts, kneading it in agreement that this is what they both wanted most now.

Pulling away from him a moment, Samantha crossed the tiny room and shut the door fully. There was no lock to throw on any of these doors here in the officers' quarters. She prayed they would have the privacy they deserved this cold winter afternoon, the gray light made all the more opaque through the single, small windowpane, smoky from all too many lamplit winter nights gone before their arrival here at this lonely outpost on the high plains.

They would be her endless winter nights now—alone. Waiting for her husband to return to her here at this edge of the cold, forbidding wilderness.

Lifting her face to him, he met her mouth with his as she closed her eyes, not surprised as he raised her in his arms and flung her to the bed. There, in the gray shadows, they tore at one another's clothing, running hands and tongues over flesh growing heated and more demanding of satisfaction. She shivered from time to time, not from the cold of the tiny room where she would wait out his journey into the land of the valley of death. No, Samantha shivered more from what her husband did to her, and what pleasure she knew she was bringing to him this, their last night together.

And when he rolled her over and pulled her up on her knees, positioning himself behind her as he never had before, she grew a little frightened—unsure and afraid of just what it was Seamus was about to do.

"Take me in your hand," he whispered against the reddish-blond hair at her ear. "Put me inside you, Sam."

Reaching between her thighs, she found his rigid, quivering flesh, feeling it throb at her touch, knowing he was not far from expending himself in her. And as he had instructed, she took his heated lance and placed it inside her waiting portal.

Driven by such consuming fury, Seamus flung himself the rest of the way, seating himself before he began to rock back and forth, side to side, his hands grasping at her suspended breasts with such immediacy that it made the breath seize in her chest.

It was as if he had never been deeper, more a part of her, than at this moment.

And it seemed that she had never felt more free in making love to her man—in this way like the animals of this farflung wilderness. Answering his need of her, Samantha drove herself back against him, pinning his flesh all the deeper within her with every savage thrust, listening to him moan each time, sensing the guttural growl growing deep within her own throat.

Then she felt him swell and begin exploding, each hot crescendo bringing her closer to her own, until she was whimpering, falling, and wetting the pillow below her cheek with hot tears, feeling his short, raspy breath against the back of her neck where her hair lay damp and matted.

It was sometime later that she was awakened by the soft rapping at the door. Blinking her eyes, Samantha glanced at the window, finding it nearly dark there, the first stars of this winter evening winking into a silky brilliance, one by one by one. At the bottom of the door, she saw the lamplight seep almost a foot into the room. A second light rapping came at the door. Nowhere insistent was it. Then the saffron light disappeared from the crack at the bottom of the door, and she listened as soft footsteps disappeared down the hallway.

Time enough to get up and dressed for supper. And if they did not budge from this room tonight, it did not matter to her. Time enough to eat tomorrow morning after he had left at first light. If . . . if she had an appetite.

But for now, she would do as Seamus had asked, and let him go without making a scene, without clinging too close to him like a lost child all alone in a world she did not know, nor understand. She would do what he asked of her —and not tell him that she had missed another of her monthly troubles.

No sense, she decided laying there now in the inky, cold light of winter's night coming down on the central plains, no sense in giving him something more to worry about before he went riding off to find Indians for the army.

As if the army couldn't find the Indians by themselves. What with the Indians always ready to find the soldiers, Seamus had told her.

She giggled a little, in spite of the sinking feeling in her heart, feeling mischievous. Perhaps it was the fact that she had really begun to feel a part of his life at long last. Perhaps it was for the fact that she believed she carried his child inside her now. Perhaps it was for her hope that they had no need to stir from this room the rest of the night

. . . that she gently reached back and grasped his limp flesh with her fingers.

It responded with a small quake as he moaned like a great tom awakening from a long nap in the sun. His flesh aroused to her touch as well, growing, swelling in her hand until he moved atop her, rolled her onto her back and kissed her hard and long.

Then said to Samantha, "Let me say good-bye to you one more time before I have to go."

Chapter 7

Late February 1876

"*W*e've been wondering when you'd show up."

Frank Grouard impassively eyed the graying soldier who was rising behind the desk, holding out his hand.

"I'm Brevet Major Thaddeus Stanton. I'll be in charge of General Crook's scouts."

He didn't take the soldier's hand. Only looked at it once, then peered back into the officer's face with its gaunt cheeks and scoop jaw. Frank decided he had an Adam's apple the size of a turkey egg.

Stanton took his hand back self-consciously. Swallowed, then continued by gesturing to the civilian standing at the corner of the desk. "This is Ben Clark. Our chief of scouts."

Grouard measured the tall, whipcord-lean scout with a quick appraisal. He found nothing there to dislike. His dark brown eyes went back to Stanton. "Who I work for? You?" He threw a nod at Clark. "Him?"

"Yes."

Wagging his head in doleful confusion, the dark-skinned, twenty-five-year-old scout said, "Came here to work for Crook."

Stanton scratched his leathery cheek, which had the appearance of waxed paper many times wadded up and then smoothed out. "Yes. Well, yes—you are."

Clark leaned forward. "General Crook heard of you from Captain Egan of the Second Cavalry."

"I know Egan."

"Well, Captain Egan and Johnny Deere, trader down at

the Red Cloud Agency—they both said you're a man knows the country where Crook has us marching."

"You going north to the Tongue and Rosebud?"

Clark nodded.

"I know that country."

"That's why Crook wants you," Clark replied. "I hear you spent some time with Sitting Bull's and Crazy Horse's bands." When Grouard didn't answer, the white scout continued. "No wonder you know that country up there— prime hunting ground. Stands to reason we'll find the warrior bands up there."

Despite himself, Grouard was starting to like this man Clark. "You let me lead you there—we'll find 'em both."

"You're hired," Stanton said. "Louie, you and Bat come over here."

Two dark-skinned men emerged from the morning shadows of the tiny office steamy with the smoke of pipes and cheroots, fragrant with the smell of horsemen. Grouard did not like the close feeling this place gave him. Better outside, where the wind always moved. In here the smell of men and their crusted britches and sweat gone cold was enough to make anyone who had spent the last half dozen years of his life on the open plains with the nomadic warrior bands turn up his nose.

These two who strode into the winter light shooting through one of the room's windows were swarthy, every bit as dark-skinned as was Grouard. The bigger man was also the older one, the short one no more than seventeen, maybe eighteen winters, Frank calculated. For the last half-dozen years, he had been in the company of young warriors —enough to know that this half-breed clearly had a chip on his young shoulder. For a moment Frank wondered what tribe, then gradually remembered hearing about both of these trackers of a time.

"These two boys going with us too," Stanton explained enthusiastically. "They've done some scouting for the army before. This is Louie Reshaw."*

The young one nodded at Grouard, his flinty eyes mea-

---

* Louis Richaud, also known as Louie Richard

suring Frank haughtily. But his arms remained locked across his chest.

"And this here's Baptiste Pourier."

"You're the one called the Big Bat," Frank commented.

He smiled back at Grouard, happy at the recognition. "You hear of me?" then presented his hand.

"Yes. You, and the one called the Little Bat."

"Garnier ain't my brother," Pourier said, holding a hand out at shoulder level. "Just that he's shorter'n me."

Grouard nodded. "They say you and Mitch Bouyer are half brothers."

"You know Mitch?" Big Bat asked.

"Met him more than once."

"He's a good man," Bat replied. "We had the same father."

"Bouyer is a good man. I think I'll like working with his brother."

No doubt these two standing before him were half-bloods, Grouard figured. For a moment Grouard's eyes played over more of the civilians in long muddy coats hanging back in the corners, or seated on the floor, perhaps leaning against the wall, unfamiliar faces filled with eyes that measured and appraised him from afar. Some of them were light-skinned, bearded, hard-edged men. And the rest were swarthy, their copper hides betraying their native ancestry. Fur traders or buffalo-hide men, some French or English or Scottish or by-damned American who slipped a hard one to a willing squaw, then maybe run off leaving the woman with a little half-breed swelling in her belly. A child born and reared among the constantly moving villages, now back to trying things among their father's people once the peaceful tribes had been herded onto the reservations.

He felt Reshaw's eyes on him and turned back to the young tracker. There was a smirk there on the youngster's face. He turned away to find Clark's eyes amused with it all.

But Grouard did not like Louie Reshaw. Right from the start. Reshaw looked like he wanted to yank out his knife and gut him right there on this pine-plank floor of the fort the soldiers called Laramie.

"I knowed your father." Grouard said the words first,

then finally let his eyes come to rest on Reshaw. He was rewarded with a flicker of something on the half-blood's face, less hatred, and something more kin to downright suspicion simmering in his eyes.

"How you know my father?" Reshaw demanded, making it come out like a clear challenge.

"John Reshaw. Knows that Bighorn country of the Sparrow Hawks."

"They're Crow."

"Sparrow Hawks," Grouard repeated calmly. "You got your father's blood and some Sparrow Hawk."

"And what you got in you? Nigger blood?" Reshaw growled, his crossed arms coming away from his chest.

Rolling his lips against his teeth to disguise their size, Grouard struggled with the impulse to choke the youngster, tear off his head and shit down his windpipe. Time was, he would have, and said to hell with this job for Crook. He didn't need the work that bad to have to ride alongside stupid youngsters like this.

"Reshaw," Clark said, emerging from behind the table and quickly edging between the two. He nodded that he wanted the youth to move off.

With a shrug, Reshaw reluctantly trudged back into the shadows, his hand still fingering the handle to his knife.

"I'll kill him, Clark," Grouard said quietly. "You tell him he ever talks about nigger blood to my face, behind my back—I'll kill him and take his scalp to his father."

Clark stood in front of the man. "No need, Grouard. No need. I'll tell him. Lord, but you're stout as a nail keg."

"I want to talk to Crook. Now."

"General Crook?" asked Stanton, and he wagged his head. "I don't know."

"He's the one wanted me," Grouard continued. "I want him to tell me I'm working for him."

Grouard watched Clark and Stanton eye one another furtively, then Clark shrugged a shoulder.

"All right," Stanton said finally. "I'll take you to see the general right now."

Grouard kept his eyes on that place back in the corner shadows where he knew Reshaw stood, those hate-filled eyes boring a hot bullet hole between his shoulder blades until Grouard stepped through the door into the shocking winter cold of this late morning.

Frank Grouard had been a long way getting here. His father had been black-skinned, an escaped slave with a gift for talk and a knack with weapons in the early part of the century. A fur trapper in those first days in the far West. One of the handful who came west as freedmen, like James Beckwourth and Edward Rose.

Frank's mother was a Gros Ventre living with the Shoshone. She had been captured as a child and grew up with the Snakes, where the coffee-skinned trapper made her his wife. He later took his family south toward the land of Brigham Young's Saints.

But in Mormon Country, growing up a half-breed nigger-Injun opened no doors. It wasn't long before Frank invented his own family tree, and found at least one good Mormon family who would take him in there in the land pacified by the Saints.

As a dirty, wretched orphan dressed in rags when first he showed up afoot in Beaver, Utah, Grouard convinced the Addison Pratt family that his own father had been a Mormon missionary out to California who had gone on God's call to the South Pacific, where he married an island woman and sired three children before returning his new family to San Bernadino. As events turned out, young Frank explained to the Pratts, his mother took her two youngest back to the islands and left him with his white father. The two soon became separated tragically, and Frank made his way east to the kingdom of Brigham Young his father had so often spoken of in gilded terms.

Without hesitation the prominent Pratts took him in, educated him with the finest of books and the strictest of their spiritual teaching, then tearfully let Grouard go when it came time for the young man of fifteen to make a way for himself. Frank began by finding work hauling freight north into the gold diggings in Idaho and Montana territories, a fitting occupation for a youth who stood six feet tall and had two hundred pounds of iron-strap muscle on his frame by the time he turned fifteen. He could read and write, handle animals and a gun with equal proficiency, and kept to himself—which meant he kept out of trouble. In 1865 this was a sought-after combination in a mule skinner who could haul trade goods all the way from the coast of California to the diggings in the northern Rockies.

After a time, Frank took to hauling C. C. Huntley's contract mail between the upriver posts and the gold diggings in Montana Territory, across the Little Belts, along the Musselshell and Judith to the upper Missouri. It was during one of his long treks as a mail courier in 1869 that Grouard was captured by the Blackfeet near Judith Spring. Stripping him of all his clothing, beating him, then driving him into that high wilderness of sage and cactus and forbidding silence, the Blackfeet rode off, laughing, and leaving Grouard to his fate.

Seventy miles lay between him and Fort Hawley on the Missouri—the closest thing to civilization the country offered to the nineteen-year-old mule skinner. Frank had no real recollection of just how long that trek took him, but the journey drained enough from his strength that Grouard's convalescence lasted three long months.

Later that year Frank again found himself hiring out to carry mail from Fort Hawley to Fort Peck at the mouth of the Milk River. It was good money. No one else wanted the route because the Sioux were raiding and stealing and killing all through that country. So it was that in January of 1870 Grouard's adventure of a lifetime began.

Bundled in a heavy buffalo coat, a big bandanna lashed over his nose and mouth, Grouard pointed his horse into the wind-driven snow that shrouded most everything from view and muffled most every sound in that big bend country of the Milk River. Just as his horse snorted its warning, Frank was flung to the ground, the wind knocked out of him. By the time he gathered his senses, the enemy had his rifle and pistol stripped from him, his two horses tied off, and were yanking on that big buffalo coat of his. Shaking with fear as much as the cold, Frank watched one of the Sioux warriors lower the muzzle of his rifle and point it at the captive's chest.

Then a big warrior rode up in a swirl of snow, leaped

from his pony and knocked the brash gunman on the shoulder repeatedly with his bow, driving him back. They argued, the big warrior standing off the rest. Then all thirteen in the war party held a conference—which made Frank recall how the Blackfeet had put their heads together a few months before and decided to make their prisoner run for it. After due deliberation and a pipe smoke, the big warrior came up to the prisoner, announced his name in sign, then motioned Frank onto his horse. The party then set off for the mouth of the Milk River.

At the time, Grouard had no idea just how important a man his captor was. But, in a convoluted way, Frank figured he in some way owed his life to this big warrior who called himself Sitting Bull.

For the next two years, Grouard traveled the high plains with Sitting Bull's Hunkpapas, coming and going with the seasons, while someone watched his every move, still distrustful of their captive, who was learning all he could of the language and tribal traditions, the ways of the hunt and the ways of a warrior. It was then that Sitting Bull decided the time had arrived for Grouard's ordeal. As a measure of their captive's stoic resolve, tribal shamans painfully removed 480 pieces of flesh from each of his arms, from shoulder to wrist. By the time the ordeal was over, Grouard was bathed in crimson that splattered the dry, yellow dust beneath the stump upon which he sat, dazed from the heat and the loss of blood.

Yet the Hunkpapa shamans were still not done with him. One at a time Grouard's eyelashes and eyebrows were plucked, along with all facial whiskers. Burning sunflower stalks were put on the swooning captive's wrists until they burnt out—a final test of Grouard's manhood. After a celebratory sweat with the tribal elders, Sitting Bull announced that he would adopt the dark-skinned Grouard as his own son. One of the shamans stood and pantomimed a grizzly, its arms outstretched, reaching for its victim. This was to be the captive's new Lakota name.

"The Grabber."

At long last Frank was treated with some measure of respect, and for the next year rode proudly at Sitting Bull's side in all wanderings of the mighty Hunkpapa. But Frank Grouard's high station was not to last.

For many seasons Sitting Bull had refused to trade with the white man, especially the post trader at Fort Peck on the Missouri. Instead the Bull preferred to deal through the Red River Metis, those half-bloods from up north who brought the Hunkpapa everything from tobacco and coffee to guns and powder. And whiskey.

Back in the white man's world it was illegal to trade whiskey to the Indians. The Americans wanted the Red River Indians stopped.

When the Fort Peck trader and army officers asked Grouard to lead them to the Metis camp, he agreed. After sneaking away from the Hunkpapa camp, telling Sitting Bull that he was going off alone to hunt for a few days, he led the soldiers to Frenchman's Creek to arrest the whiskey traders. But in that Metis camp were three visiting Santee Sioux.

Warriors who recognized Sitting Bull's adopted son. And promptly went to tell the chief about Grouard's complicity with the white man.

When the Bull heard the story, he grew angry enough to kill. The only thing that saved Grouard's life was being in the lodge of Sitting Bull's mother at the time, then always staying close beside and traveling with the woman even Sitting Bull dared not cross. Still, it wasn't long before the Grabber decided it best that he move on, figuring he would live with Crazy Horse's Oglallas—about the time the Sioux harassed the Long Hair's Seventh Cavalry during their summer of 1873 while surveying along the Elk River.*

It was with Crazy Horse, his brother Little Hawk and his best friend He Dog that the Grabber roamed and raided, made war and stole ponies, courted women and danced and sang among the Oglalla for the better part of the next three years. Grouard even took a wife and settled down in a lodge for a domestic life with the woman.

It was times just like these when he had looked at the hate-filled eyes of Louie Reshaw that Grouard remem-

* Yellowstone River

bered that woman, the feel and smell and taste of her skin as she grew damp when he had mated with her. And Frank always remembered the hate-filled eyes of his wife's brother—a man never quite reconciled to his sister's marriage to the Grabber. So much hate in one man, Grouard had never known.

Until the day the brother's anger boiled over like a kettle set too near the flames . . .

"General, I knew you've been wanting to meet this man —so I brought him to you," said Thaddeus Stanton.

Grouard measured the cut of the man who turned slowly and inched out of the shadows at the back of the cold office. His close-cropped hair was far different from Grouard's long, flowing black locks. And George Crook favored a long, bushy beard that spilled over the open flaps of his unbuttoned tunic. Beneath it the general wore the bloodred long-handles that complimented his hair color.

He held out his hand to Grouard. "Your name, sir?"

They shook as Frank replied, "Grouard."

The general's eyes brightened and a smile creased the thick, unkempt beard. "Frank Grouard. Damn to hell, you don't say. Good to meet you at last."

Turning, Crook motioned to a few chairs in the room where a man's breath was easily seen at his face despite the sheet-iron stove in the corner. "There, you both take a seat. We have much to talk about, Frank. You . . . you don't mind me calling you Frank, do you?"

Grouard settled in a chair, his back rigid. "No. Frank is all right."

"I heard you were learned, Grouard. Read and write."

"Some."

Crook nodded. "Yes." He cleared his throat, never taking his eyes off Grouard. "How long were you with the Sioux?"

"It would be six winters, this one, General," he answered, his hands in his pockets.

"Hmmm. Well—now why don't you tell me just why in the goddamned blazes you ended up leaving the blanket and coming back among white folks, Frank."

"You're suspicious of me?"

Crook leaned back, disturbed at first. "Wouldn't you be, Frank?" Then he smiled and rocked back toward Grouard. "No. Never found myself suspicious of a man I could look in the eye when I asked him a troubling question—and he could look me right back in the eye when he answered."

Grouard never took his eyes off the general's as he began to explain why he had left Crazy Horse's Hunkpatila. About a woman, and her crazy brother named He Dog.

To tell Crook why he would now guide for the general, and take Crook's soldiers north to hunt down the warrior band of Crazy Horse.

Chapter 8

Moon of the Frost in the Lodge, 1876

Seasons ago she had come north, far from the land of her people, hoping to find her man.

And brought her two young sons with her. One, the son of a Southern Cheyenne warrior. Her firstborn was named Sees Red.

Her youngest was born son of the man she now sought to find. His father was white. A soldier chief. The Shahiyena called the soldier Hiestzi—the "Yellow Hair." Because the young boy had his father's hair, she had named her youngest Yellow Bird.

The beautiful Monaseetah had for one long winter eight years before been the left-hand wife of the one the white men called George Armstrong Custer.

Two winters behind her now, scout Ben Clark had told the young Cheyenne woman that the husband she sought had gone north with his soldiers. It was his trail that called Monaseetah north herself, forsaking the reservation for the free, nomadic life of her Northern Cheyenne cousins. For all this time spent roaming, wandering through season after season with Old Bear's village, she had hoped for word of her Hiestzi.

A boy, she believed, needed to know his father. And Hiestzi should know of his son.

Last autumn, in the first days of the Second Summer, just after a hard frost had begun to turn the leaves to brilliant oranges and fire-kissed reds, the fifty-five lodges of Old Bear and Little Wolf had abandoned the Red Cloud

Agency to hunt the buffalo for food and clothing. With them, the people brought some forty new canvas lodges, along with a good supply of new guns and bullets traded from the white man. Wandering across the hunting grounds throughout that autumn, the Shahiyena had been joined from time to time by the Oglalla, close friends and tribal allies since the days following the Battle of the Hundred in the Hand.

This was to have been their second camp of the winter, here on Tongue River. They had come west, over from Otter Creek to escape some of the cold winds slashing down from the north. But instead of staying here until spring, chiefs Old Bear and Two Moon had decided they would move on, in order to avoid danger. As quickly as they could, the village was inching south by east through the snow, back toward the reservation ever since the runners had come.

How she yearned for the old way of things—making only two winter camps, settling in for the season. Not this moving day after day as the weather permitted, scouts out and ranging far, on the prowl for the soldiers everyone feared would be coming. The messengers had brought the frightening warning.

So one of their old habits was broken this winter, the Northern Cheyenne had explained to her. Their habit of making two winter camps. The first they stayed at until that first thaw, sometime after the end of the Seven Cold Nights. Then the village had a chance to put the old camp behind them, find a new location, again in a sheltered river valley, out of the wind—a place where they would likely sit out the rest of the winter. Until spring came to warm the earth, melt the snow, and bring the short grass to feed the ponies of the young men who would go raiding once more.

An ancient cycle.

Monaseetah wondered if her life would truly flow in a circle, praying it would carry her back to the yellow-haired soldier chief. As much as she had prayed for the healing of that circle, the young woman still waited for it season after season, hunt after hunt, with a heart growing heavier with every sunset.

It had been that way for the past seven summers, since the time Hiestzi had sent her and the rest of the prisoners from Black Kettle's village back to Indian Territory. She had already known that her belly would grow great with Yellow Hair's child. For three times in a row that spring she had missed her time of the moon bleeding.

Yellow Bird had been growing as a little life within her belly.

And ever since the day he was born, the boy had been a reminder of his father. Of the man who had promised one day to return to Monaseetah.

Too well the Shahiyena and their Oglalla cousins had been able to avoid the white man. Only the young warriors had any contact with the enemy, usually in raids on supply trains or a small group of soldiers. Yes, Crazy Horse's Oglalla, Sitting Bull's Hunkpapa, and the mighty Miniconjou as well were in the surrounding countryside, each band spending the winter in some sheltered valley, waiting for spring, when the elders would meet once more and decide on when and where to hunt, when and where to raid. And with the new grass of spring would come the swelling of the numbers of lodges raised in each village as those who had wintered at the agencies left the reservations and their bacon and flour for the free life and the taste of buffalo on their tongues.

She wanted her sons to know the free life—for one day soon, she feared, there would be no free life to pass on to the young ones. One day the might of the white man would crush them all.

There had been some fights with the soldiers that first summer she brought her boys north to live. The army had been escorting some white wagon men along the Elk River not far to the north of where Old Bear and Two Moon had chosen this very camp. Word had it that the white man was marking the ground, planning to return later, when he would lay the iron track for his smoking horse—that final insult to penetrate this, the last great hunting ground of the northern tribes.

The following summer, the Lakota said the soldier chief they called the Long Hair brought his soldiers to profane the land of their sacred Paha Sapa. Yet those soldiers hadn't searched for villages, nor did it appear they had come to make war. Still, it had become confusing, mystifying, and ultimately baffling—for ever since that summer, growing numbers of white men had been flooding to the Paha Sapa, land clearly granted the Shahiyena and Lakota on the white man's talking paper. Warriors who had gone alone or in small groups to the sacred land to see for themselves had come back with a scalp or two, returned as well with stories others listened to around the lodge fires at night—tales of these white men, acting as if they were possessed to dig at the ground, crazed for the little yellow rocks they ofttimes found. There were stories of others who did not do the digging—those who raised their stinking and profane towns within shooting distance of the Shahiyena's sacred Bear Butte. There the women danced and the men drank their whiskey, and some men shot others of their own kind dead, just for fun or just to hear the sound of their big guns echo from their wooden buildings.

Those places of the white men were evil, some shamans like Ice were saying. So more young men went out, riding into the sacred hills in small war parties, hunting to kill as many of the white men as they could, in hopes of driving out the rest. Instead only more came: from the south along the Geese River,* and down from the north, along the Great Muddy River in an endless stream. Some came on horseback. Many more journeyed in on foot. At first the soldiers had tried to keep the white men away from the Indian land. But of late the soldiers did not leave their forts to stop the white men going to the Paha Sapa. Rumor had it that the soldiers were staying at their posts, readying themselves for war against the Shahiyena and Lakota.

Sitting Bull had laughed in his camp not far to the north. He laughed and invited the soldiers to come make war on him and the wild tribes.

But Two Moon and Old Bear had seen so much misery in their winters that they just wanted to be left alone by the white man and his soldiers. When the runners had come

* Platte River

from the agencies, saying the agents wanted the roving bands to come in or the soldiers would be sent to stalk them down—Monaseetah grew certain the soldiers would come.

War was one promise the white man never broke.

So even with the threat of great cold and snow that hovered on the horizon, the village had decided to go in to the reservation. Last night there had been a great discussion of it. Too many children and old ones to take the chance of soldiers catching them out here in this broken country with nowhere to run, nowhere to hide from the soldier guns.

Monaseetah knew about soldier guns. When she was but a child of thirteen summers at the Little Dried River,* she had seen her mother killed, her still-warm body defiled by the soldiers. Then at the Washita four winters later her father, Little Rock, had been killed by Hiestzi's own soldiers.

So it gave her heart a small measure of relief to know they would be slowly moving toward the reservation now, away from danger when the soldiers came marching.

Monaseetah heard the sound of hooves crunching over the old snow, coming slowly toward her small lodge. Straightening and turning from the dried limbs she was cracking over one knee, she shielded her eyes against the afternoon sun and found the young warrior approaching on horseback.

"You have no man to hunt for you, Monaseetah," Wooden Leg said, drawing his young frame as tall as it would go, backlit with the falling sun.

"Yes, but Rolls Down hunts for us," she replied, looking up at the handsome youth of eighteen summers. "There is enough to eat."

"Here, then," Wooden Leg said, one hand holding down half of an antelope buck to her. "Be sure this does not go to waste filling the bellies of your children. One day they both will be strong warriors."

His words sounded more haughty than she had ever heard the young warrior talk. Monaseetah was sure he was

---

* Sand Creek

trying hard to act like a man—tough and hard, just at the verge of making an insult. But that would be where Wooden Leg would stop, she figured—as good a young man as there was in Old Bear's clan. An honorable man, even if he was like a young bull with her heavy, fertile scent strong in his nostrils.

Monaseetah was without a man—so many of the young men called upon her lodge at night, playing their flutes, calling her out with soft voices to stand with them in their blankets, some perhaps preparing to offer Rolls Down some ponies and robes and maybe a gun for her if she would only be their wife.

But her friend Rolls Down explained to each one who came to buy her, as she explained to each one who came to court her, that she waited for another, a man who had promised to return.

One cold evening soon, very likely before spring brought the young grass to this broken, scarred prairie, Monaseetah was certain she would find Wooden Leg calling at her door, calling her forth with his love flute, beckoning her to his blanket where young lovers stood and talked of many tomorrows.

But for now all her tomorrows were wrapped up in Hiestzi. Wrapped up in waiting for the Yellow Hair to come looking for her and his young son. Until then she would be faithful to her husband, the soldier chief who stalked this north country where the winters were cold and long in going.

Perhaps one more summer, Monaseetah decided as she laid the antelope flanks atop some of her skimpy baggage. She knelt to take her fire makings from a belt pouch, flint and steel and tinder.

One more summer, she promised herself. Hiestzi had vowed to return in the Moon of Fat Horses. It was not that long to wait, really.

Perhaps he would come to her this summer.

Lord, but he hated this cold.

Every endless day, each endless night of it, reminded him of the soul-numbing cold at the Battle of Stones River.

Young Anson Mills had lost his blanket, lost it somewhere during the tumult of man tearing his fellow man apart in those very first days of 1863.

It had only been a saddle blanket, yet still something thick enough to keep the chill of the frozen earth from seeping too deeply into his bones. He yearned for it at the end of the day, when the battle guns quieted their roar and the screams of the wounded faded with the coming of twilight.

But when he returned to camp, the blanket was gone from where Mills had left it. He asked his good friend and companion, Captain R. L. Morris—but his comrade knew nothing of it.

That night had been another of those endless nights like this one, Mills recalled. And in the morning, he discovered that Morris had taken his blanket and had slept doubly warm before they prepared to move off to battle the Johnnies once more. Cold to his marrow, Mills had challenged Morris for the blanket, angrily turning it over to show his initials, *AM,* sewn into one corner with some yarn.

"Well, Mills, I give it up," Morris had said, nonplussed. "That's your blanket. Take it."

Mills had, angrily. Not knowing if he should turn and walk away, or punch that silly look off Morris's face. A friend.

"I stole it, Mills, knowing government blankets were as alike as two peas," Morris explained. "I wouldn't steal under ordinary circumstances, but such a night as these last few would justify a man in doing anything to keep warm."

Ever since, Anson Mills had been wary of friends and what they wanted of him. And ever since that long night near the banks of Stones River, he had never quite gotten warm enough when the sun began to set. Especially out here on these infernal high plains where the sky itself seemed to suck every bit of warmth right out of the land once the sun disappeared far to the west.

But he was a soldier, having tried his hand at surveying. Making the decision to forge his way as a soldier in this life, even after Stones River, Chickamauga, Missionary Ridge and Jonesboro in Sherman's siege of Atlanta. Anson Mills had decided the place to be a soldier was out here, fighting the red man.

How he wished Nannie were here with him. She was about the only thing that kept him warm, truly warm. But as much as any officer with a wife would have wanted his helpmate there with him, at Fort Fetterman there were few wives. This winter it was to be a gathering of eagles, the chaplain was wont to say. Warriors preparing to carry the last and final strike into the ancient land of the red man. There were no women in war.

Just man's muscle and might, skill and cunning—pitched one against the other.

His heart ached. Oh, Nannie—how I miss you so.

"More coffee, Captain?"

Mills looked up at Lorenzo Ayers, the young private who carried the steaming pot clutched in rags around the circle, men huddling around the blazing fire, one of several along company row. Third Cavalry, Company M.

He nodded. Better than trying to talk, what with his teeth chattering, and lips gone nearly numb enough.

Nannie would be safe, and warm, back at D. A. Russell, the post near Cheyenne City.

How he longed to pull her warmth close to him, smell the perfume of her naked flesh beside him as he ran his fingers along her taut body.

Mills pushed the haunting vision of her away and drank at the scalding coffee. So hot that it hurt going down, pushing away for the moment that heat the merest thought of Nannie brought his loins.

No sense in dwelling on that, he had told himself many times since leaving Fort Russell. It would be a long while before he would be back in that small bed with his wife. And until then there was a campaign to begin, and a war to end.

The Sioux and the Cheyenne were up north in the land of the Bighorn, the Tongue, the Rosebud and the Powder. And General Crook was the one to smite them, drive them once and for all back to their reservations, opening the land up for white settlement.

Six months before, on the last day of August, Anson had

celebrated his forty-first birthday with his wife and children at D. A. Russell. For some time now he had reconciled himself to the fact that he was not a youngster anymore— blood thick and hide like rawhide, able to take this goddamned cold night after night without respite. Nonetheless, he had come from a stoic heritage, born of Quaker stock, his ancestors come to the colonies with Sir William Penn to settle in the new township of Philadelphia. He became the firstborn of nine, growing up at a time when every boy became a marksman, and was soon apprenticed to a local carpenter. The death of his mother when Anson was barely fourteen ended that apprenticeship, and left him, along with his two oldest sisters, in charge of those duties of home and raising the six youngest children.

It was a lesson in taking personal responsibility that Anson was never to forget.

"Captain Mills?"

He turned, finding Crook's aide-de-camp, John Bourke, striding up, the heavy buffalo coat like a dark wave swirling about his ankles.

"Yes, Mr. Bourke?" he replied, standing, his nearly empty cup still steaming in his hand.

"The general is gathering his officers, sir."

"When, Lieutenant?"

"He's calling his meeting now, Captain." Bourke smiled in that dark beard of his he had begun growing.

"I take it we're finally going to embark on this campaign?" Mills inquired. He already knew.

"Yes, sir!" Bourke answered with energy. "Day after tomorrow."

"The second of March?"

"No, the first of March—it's a leap year." Bourke rubbed his furred gloves together over the fire. "Captain Mills, we're now on the eve of the bloodiest Indian war the government has ever been called to wage. The war with a tribe that has waxed fat and insolent on government bounty and has been armed and equipped with the most improved weapons by the peace commissioners or through the carelessness of the Indian agent. By God—this column of ours will crush them!"

He snorted at Bourke's enthusiasm, taking as well some dubious pleasure in that extra day February had presented them, a day devoted to campaign preparations and more freezing. Mills gazed at the sky clouding over, the stars having disappeared far to the west, the heavens growing murky overhead.

"Something's blowing in, Mr. Bourke."

"Yes, sir," the young lieutenant replied, also regarding the inky dome overhead where the night fires shot their exploding sparks. "It's absolutely perfect: here on the eve of General Crook's march to the Bighorn."

Mills watched Bourke as the lieutenant turned and disappeared down company row, searching out more of the company commanders, both cavalry and infantry. Then his eyes once more sought the heavens.

"Yes," he said quietly to himself. "General Crook is about to march us into the jaws of winter itself, and who knows what else."

Chapter 9

1 March 1876

"*Y*ou're lucky the general doesn't leave you locked in the guardhouse till he gets back!"

Seamus peered up at the general's chief of scouts.

"Ben Clark, is it?"

"Look at him, will you?" said Captain Thaddeus Stanton, his leathery neck looking like creased waxed paper many times crumpled.

"You'll damn well keep me away from the whiskey this trip out, won't you, Major Stanton?" Donegan said, his lips puffy, one side of his jaw not working as well as it should.

"Get him out of here, Ben," Stanton growled, his big Adam's apple bobbing as he flung an arm in the direction he wanted the two civilians to take—out.

"Gladly," the loose-shouldered Clark replied, stomping into the tiny guardhouse cell, sweeping up Donegan's big hat and coat as the Irishman turned to gather up his blankets.

"I'll see you two at the head of the column in an hour," Stanton reminded and turned away. Out the door and into the blackness that had swallowed this high land.

"Holy Mither of God," Donegan said not quite under his breath, which steamed from a man's lips with the frightening temperature. He wobbled a little unsteadily.

"Like winter suddenly decided to pay us a visit, eh, Seamus?" Clark asked. "Wait till you get outside. See what's on the ground."

"Snow?"

"Not like you never saw any before, you cup-hugging Irishman."

He snorted, then smiled at Clark. Seamus liked the man. No nonsense when it came to his work, but still, Clark realized that life was more than work.

Seamus ran his tongue quickly around the inside of his pasty mouth, his tongue furry with last night's indiscretions. With a throbbing head, his aging body complaining in more places than he cared to count, Seamus replied, "Aye. And I've spent me one winter up there in that country where George Crook wants us to lead him."*

"That's why you're here," Clark said, nudging the Irishman's bulk from the tiny cell. "It's you and fellas like that Frank Grouard who are going to show us where Crook can find Crazy Horse."

"Right now, all I want to find is a cup of coffee," Seamus grumbled sourly.

They emerged from the tiny guardhouse and stopped for a moment, taking in the bustling scene throbbing about them, men and animals in motion across the snowy parade of this fort, its buildings bunched along the edge of the bluff above the icy North Platte. Behind them in the bottomland the beef herd could already be heard lowing as they were driven toward the crossing.

"Stanton's an old fire-eater from the Omaha office," Clark explained. "A paymaster by trade. And he's going along as a campaign correspondent for the New York *Tribune.*"

"Heaven protect us!" Seamus growled as he rammed an arm down the sleeve of his blanket-lined canvas mackinaw, popularly known as a St. Paul coat.

"You should see the way he's turned up his nose at the scouts I've hired."

"He doesn't take much to a man drinking whiskey, I take it?"

Clark laughed. "You? Why you're the least of Stanton's worries. No, the captain says the thirty-one of you I've hired is as sweet a bunch of cutthroats as ever scuttled a

* The Plainsmen Series, vol. 2, *Red Cloud's Revenge*

ship. Half-breeds, squaw men like myself. Bounty jumpers he called some, thieves and desperadoes from various agencies he names the rest."

Seamus grinned slightly, only that much for it hurt the whole side of his face. "Ben, you and me . . . and Crook too—we know it takes fire to fight fire. He sent Apaches after Apaches down south. Makes sense to me that Crook's hired him a bunch of bad characters to track down these bleeming hostiles—"

"Donegan!" a voice called out across the snowpacked darkness scoured with yellow lamplit streaks below every smoky window surrounding the parade.

"Strahorn?"

As the lowing from the nearby beef herd grew in volume, the reporter strode into the light, looking far more bulky in his blanket mackinaw than he had last night. He stopped before Clark and Donegan.

"You do look the sight. I heard about your little . . . difficulty."

Seamus tried to smile at Strahorn's judicious choice of words, but that smile stretched the puffy, cracked lips. He felt one of the dried wounds once more seep some blood into the groomed chin whiskers. "Damn your worthless carcass anyway, Strahorn. Disappearing on me like that."

Strahorn held up his hands in defense. "It seemed a good night to get myself wet. So I was long gone before you started your argument."

"Yes, you were long gone at that," Seamus responded. "When it came to blows, I looked around . . . and glory be! You were but nowhere to be seen."

Beneath his cat's draggle of a black mustache Strahorn chuckled, swinging a fist at the Irishman. "I get paid good money by my publisher to figure out what's going to happen before it happens. That way he'll scoop all the competition back east."

"And last night you figured out that Donegan was going to get himself into trouble?" Clark asked.

Strahorn nodded, his eyes flicking to the tall, rail-thin scout. "Yeah. I see a man going at the whiskey that hard and heavy, playing some slick cards with a bunch of soldiers who just got their hands on a little pay—doesn't take a schoolteacher to see the writing on the wall."

"I'll make you pay for deserting me soon enough, Strahorn," Donegan grumbled. "But for right now, one of you just find me some bleeming coffee!"

Strahorn grinned impishly. "Can I interest you in a little whiskey with your coffee—cut the bloody chill from this bloody hour—"

"Whiskey?" Donegan roared, startling some mules nearby. As their packers sought to bring them back under control, Seamus continued, his head throbbing all the more just for the mention of the evil elixir. "I'll not be wanting whiskey for some time to come, you bloody rut! Coffee, it is! And now!"

The three set off to the east, toward the corrals where the scouts had erected their camp across the past few days. Most of the thirty-one were already in and accounted for. The last few would join the column at a rendezvous not far to the north.

All about that trio the parade of Fort Fetterman teemed with life: curses of soldiers and teamsters, the whinny of cavalry mounts and the bray of Crook's mule teams. Twelve full company of troops had been here assembled through the final days of February, and it seemed every one of them was on the move at this moment. Here on the south bank of the North Platte River, at the mouth of LaPrelle Creek, Crook had gathered those units from nearby posts he found in the best of fighting trim: five companies of the Second Cavalry; another five from the Third. Along with two companies of the Fourth Infantry to guard the wagon train, it all accounted for some 692 officers and enlisted under the immediate command of Colonel Joseph J. Reynolds, Third Cavalry. Word was that Crook was riding along merely as an observer.

Rumor had it the general had awarded this campaign to an old associate in hopes that, with a resounding victory, Reynolds could clear his tarnished record following some bribery scandal down in Texas years before.

Still, there were many of the line officers and noncoms who were damned happy to have George Crook along just the same. It wasn't that they didn't trust Reynolds to get the job done—it was just that Crook was a fighting man's general.

Night before last, Colonel Reynolds had established his orders of the march, dividing his command into battalions of two companies, each under a handpicked captain. In addition to a surgeon and medical staff riding in five ambulances, the column would be augmented by eighty-six freight wagons hauling coffee and rations for forty days—two-thirds of that, beef on the hoof, the rest in salt pork—along with 200,000 pounds of grain for the stock, tents and blankets for the command, all pulled by mules and driven by eighty-four civilian teamsters.

But the noisiest component of Crook's plunge into Indian country was his now-famous mule train, divided into six divisions of fifty mules apiece, all under the command of Thomas Moore, who had honchoed Crook's mule trains down in Apache country and been brought in especially for this difficult campaign. To each of the divisions, Moore had assigned a civilian leader. Those sixty-two civilian mule skinners who had been hired for this march north were being paid good money for their talents. To George Crook, the fortunes of this Big Horn campaign could well rise or fall on the strength of his mule train—able to march where wagons could not; able to sure-foot it through an impossible night march; able to pop up when and where the enemy least expected his troops to appear.

Even before the eighth of February, when Sheridan had wired Crook that operations were to commence against the hostiles who had not complied with the government directive and returned to their reservations, the general had been making preparations for his column to fight in the worst of conditions the northern plains could throw at warriors, both white and red.

And in the waning days of that month, Crook had learned that he would likely be taking the field alone—to be the first to move against the hostiles of Crazy Horse, perhaps even the Hunkpapa of Sitting Bull. Yet it appeared that Colonel John Gibbon up in northern Montana was not yet ready to march. And General Alfred Terry would not have his column of infantry and Custer's Seventh Cavalry ready to plunge into the field for some time. Custer had gotten himself bogged down in some damnable congressional investigation of graft and corruption involving the traders licensed onto the Indian agencies.

With what he was calling his "Big Horn Expedition," Crook would be the first to take the field.

But to get Reynolds's soldiers to the Indian country where intelligence and the bands of friendlies had said Crook was to find the hostiles, the general first had to assure that his troops would arrive there protected from the cold just then squeezing down on the high plains. Especially Crook's cavalry—his first strike force. While an infantryman could stamp his feet and beat his arms to stay warm, a cavalryman must of necessity sit still in the saddle, where his knees and wrists, ears and hands, could fall prey to frostbite.

Long underwear went on first, the preferred made of merino wool and perforated buckskin that would allow a man's skin to breathe, followed by the standard issue blue flannel shirt and layers of socks, some of lamb's wool reaching clear to the knee. Over them went the boots of most, tall moccasins chosen by those veterans of prairie winter campaigns. Buffalo-fur outer moccasins went over those for warmth and durability, the hair turned inward all the way to the knee. A double-breasted blouse made of a heavy blanket material was then pulled on, followed by a buffalo or bearskin overcoat, or one made of Saint Paul canvas lined with more blanket and complete with fur collar.

Atop their heads, Crook's motley army wore wool hats trimmed with fur mufflers that could be turned down to protect their ears. On their hands they wore the standard-issue wool army gloves or mittens, over which the men pulled long gauntlets of horsehide, or beaver and muskrat fur. In the next three weeks, frostbite would become every bit as serious an enemy as would the elusive warriors they were stalking.

The winds blew here on this bleak hilltop where Reynolds prepared to move out his attack column this morning at dawn. Those winds would blow all the more cruelly as the army marched mile after mile to the north.

Seamus gazed at the thirty-six lodges of Black Crow's Arapahos pitched just beyond the corrals. "How many you think we'll find, Ben?" he asked after he had more than a half pint of steaming coffee down his gullet beside the scout's fire.

"Warriors? From everything I can put together," Clark replied, watching Strahorn lean in closer so that he would not miss a word, "maybe a thousand."

"If they're all together in one place, right?" Strahorn asked.

Clark nodded. "That's the hostile villages—the ones what'll never come in to the agencies. Less'n four thousand all told: women and children, and men of fighting age."

"It ain't the numbers what really scares a man," Donegan said quietly, almost speaking into his tin coffee cup at the fire where Stanton was calling together his thirty-one civilian scouts. "What worries me is that the bands we're going after are more than ready to fight."

Clark nodded, his eyes on the flames. "That's the bloody truth, Seamus. The ones we're tracking would rather starve than come in and eat handouts."

Seamus looked at Clark and Strahorn, shaking his head. "No, Ben. The ones we're looking for would rather die in battle than die of starvation. There's a big, big difference."

Clark nodded. "Black Crow, the Arapaho chief hanging around Fetterman now that war's coming—he says that a few of his young hotbloods already took off."

"Heading north?" Strahorn asked.

The lean scout nodded.

"Going to tell the warrior bands we're on our way, eh?" Seamus commented.

"Damn if they're not," Strahorn added. "Crazy Horse will know Crook is coming in a handful of days. It'll take this outfit twice that to get anywhere close."

"This isn't your first campaign, I know," said Clark, his eyes still on the steam rising from his tin of coffee. "From what I hear—the soldiers like you."

"They do now?" Seamus asked, slapping Strahorn on the back.

"I'm proud to say that, yes," the reporter replied.

"Knew there was something worthwhile about you," Seamus added. "A man well-liked by the common sojur is sure to—"

The sudden shrill notes of assembly rang through the cold, predawn air.

"They're playing our song, boys," Clark announced.

All three chugged back the last of their coffee, dropping the tins where they had been sitting, and moved off at a trot to the picket line.

"I saw to your horse, Donegan."

He nodded to the chief of scouts. "You have my eternal thanks, Ben Clark."

"One of these days, we'll have to sit and have ourselves a long talk, Seamus."

"Saints preserve me—you're not trying to mend my wicked ways, are you now?"

"No." Clark shook his head, then took up the reins to his horse and vaulted into the saddle. "Talk about someone we both knew of a time."

"Who would that be?" Seamus asked, freeing the ground hobble from his mount.

"Liam O'Roarke."

The name caught Seamus flat-footed. For a moment he just stared at Clark's back when the scout reined his mount off the picket line, away into the darkness bustling with horses and men moving into company order.

"Liam O'Roarke." He whispered his uncle's name here in this killing cold darkness, for but a moment recalling the suffocating heat of those summer days almost eight years gone, days spent huddled within a stinking barricade of bloating horse carcasses.* And remembering the tragic, needless death of that sturdy, laughing plainsman whose blood flowed in the veins of Seamus Donegan.

---

* The Plainsmen Series, vol. 3, *The Stalkers*

Chapter 10

2 March 1876

"Strahorn! Throw some more of that greasewood on that fire!"

As if he had been interrupted from something far more important, Robert Strahorn glanced at Lieutenant John Bourke, nodded, and threw two more limbs of sagebrush on their evening cookfire, just for good measure. Then he went back to his writing. Too cold for his ink and pen, the *Rocky Mountain News* reporter used pencils he sharpened from time to time with a small penknife Strahorn tucked away in his vest pocket.

There amid the snow-covered scrub cedar, sage and bunchgrass, miles and miles of desolate red-clay country stretching beyond him on every side, he was rereading his original copy of the dispatch he had sent down to Denver, back on the twenty-third of February.

Lying north and northwest of Fort Fetterman is a vast scope of country known as the "unceded lands," to which the Indians have no right or title, but in which the most warlike of them have sought refuge, rest, and succor ever since the general abandonment of that region by the military and settlers during the massacre of 1866. Since that date, those bands of Sioux who bid defiance to our attempts at reconciliation, have marauded north, south and east of this, their natural stronghold . . .

This, then, is one of the secrets of Gen. Crook's movements. The reason given for the hasty and quiet manner in which he has thus far proceeded, are simply, first, that he is determined to strike a blow at once which will demoralize the savages from the start; second, that a winter campaign, although terribly arduous in that region, will have thrice the terror of one two months later; third, because everything points to a general Indian war in that section adjacent to the Black Hills, even in the advance of the advent of spring, and to make the small force at his command adequate to the demands of next summer's tasks, Gen. Crook sees the prime necessity of immediately crushing out the more western tribes, at the same time showing all others that the Black Hills and Powder River regions are not to be made the hiding place of the whole Sioux nation, in case of its general defeat.

Strahorn leafed through a few more pages of his notes, looking for something. Just what, he wasn't sure of, then found his dispatch of the twenty-seventh.

About noon the third day out [from Cheyenne] we commenced overtaking the long column of picked cavalry headed by the gallant officer whose hardships and duty we were to share in the very near future. Men they looked and men of the best stamp they are, whom General Crook has detailed for this difficult undertaking. Rank and file are in excellent trim, mounted upon the best horses the Department affords, and everything in their appearance betokened "business," from the start . . .

We rode in the face of one of the most severe storms of the season until 2 PM today, when we reached this post [Fort Fetterman] . . . having accomplished 170 miles in less than four days . . . Long lines of tents are pitched on the banks of the quiet and peaceful La Prelle nearby; hundreds of men are crowding around the campfires—which tonight lead me in fancy back to

Denver's lamplit streets—cleaning their arms, looking
up the few necessities that a soldier is allowed to pos-
sess, and speculating, as a soldier will, upon the campaign and its results; horses, mules, and pack animals, to
the number of a thousand or more, are pawing and
neighing a loud refrain to the hum of masters' voices;
the fort is flooded with commissary supplies, arms, ammunition, etc., and officers are galloping back and forth
with the orders that bring system out of all this din and
chaos.

ALTER EGO

"Mind sharing your fire?"

Strahorn looked up to find the tall Irishman leading his
horse in from the tangle of tents, wagons, and cookfires
dotting a military camp going about its evening chores.

"Tie your animal there and dust off a chunk of ground
for your ass, Donegan."

"You're busy, I see," Seamus said as he kicked snow from
a small circle of the flinty earth, then rubbed his thighs
slowly in the fashion of a horseman taking his ease.

"Sit. Share some coffee and what little warmth we can
squeeze from this puny greasewood fire."

"That's right, Mr. Donegan," said John Bourke as he
strode back into the light carrying a coffeepot sloshing with
water taken from a pool in the frozen creekbed. "Perhaps a
man of your talents can get us a proper supper fire going.
Seems Strahorn here is more interested in his papers than
in his belly."

"Straightaway," Donegan answered, crouching at the
side of the small fire, poking the burning limbs, blowing on
some of the coals to give punch to the fire's warmth.

That morning at dawn, Colonel Joseph Reynolds had
given the command to move out to his restive men and
their anxious animals ready for the trail. But rather than
marching north on the road toward the Hog Ranch, nothing more than a gathering of sod and clapboard shanties
housing a nondescript saloon and whorehouse, the scouts

were directed to lead the command west across LaPrelle Creek for a couple of miles. It was there they made their crossing of the North Platte at a shallow ford. A handful of miles beyond the river, the column struck the old Bozeman Trail, where the battalions ultimately closed up ranks for the first day's march. From point riders far in the advance, breaking through the new snow still falling, to the beef herd bringing up the rear, the entire command was strung out for something close to three miles as Crook and Reynolds inched their army toward the land of the Sioux and Northern Cheyenne.

Nearing mid-afternoon, after making a scant fifteen miles through the icy snowdrifts that short winter day, a halt was called on the north side of Sage Creek, where Donegan and the other scouts had found a good supply of grass for the most part blown free of new snow. What water was to be found they drew from small pools down in the creekbed, their surfaces thickly crusted with rippled layers of ice.

After marching a dozen miles the following morning, the command was given a splendid view in the pristine prairie air: not only the Black Hills shouldering the sky some seventy miles to the northeast, but the Pumpkin Buttes as well, four large ocher outcrops that resembled pumpkins squatting about forty miles almost due north. Shortly after noon, upon reaching Brown Springs, the scouts turned the column east by north, angling away from the Montana Road, following the valley to the Dry Fork of the Cheyenne River, where camp was made on a long tongue of land where an easy crossing for the wagons could be made come morning.

Strahorn peered north into the growing darkness—at least what he took to be north, as the stars whirled in the western sky. "We're in Indian country now, aren't we, Seamus?"

Donegan paused at his work by the fire, warming his one bare hand over the flames, and grew pensive as he stared back at the reporter. "A man crosses anywhere this side of the North Platte—from here on out, he's in Injin country."

Strahorn smiled. He liked the Irishman and his no-nonsense approach to life. "You'd rather be at the Hog Ranch now, wouldn't you, my friend?"

"No." Donegan shrugged. "Had my wish, I'd be with my wife, back at Laramie." Then his eyes came up to Strahorn's. "You got yourself a poke at the Hog Ranch that last night before leaving Fetterman, didn't you?"

He started to deny it when Donegan interrupted.

"That's it—that's why you wasn't there when all the ruckus started on me."

"How was I to know you'd get in a fight over cards while I was enjoying a ride on a big-breasted pony?"

"Was a place, that Hog Ranch was, Strahorn."

"If wishes came true, I'd like to have me a piece of that place's business," the reported replied.

The Hog Ranch was well-known in that part of the northern plains, for it served not only Fort Fetterman's soldiers, situated only a mile north of the post, but civilian travelers along the Great Platte River Road, those cowboys and ranch owners in the surrounding countryside, and an occasional argonaut going to or from the Black Hills. With a saloon and dance hall, a small hotel and low-roofed restaurant, all owned and run by Kid Slaymaker, the Hog Ranch took a considerable piece of the whiskey trade from Eugene Tillottson, contract sutler at Fetterman.

Strahorn stood, stretching the kinks come to plague his muscles in the short time he'd squatted on a saddle blanket thrown on the frozen ground. Dragging over his nearby bedding, the reporter unrolled the heavy canvas wrapper. Inside it was stretched one heavy plaid blanket, a thick comforter, a pair of buffalo robes, a large wolf robe, along with a thin prairie tick mattress filled with fresh straw, while some officers had filled their ticks with crushed cork, in addition to a pillow and case, with a large rubber poncho capable of covering it all.

As Strahorn plopped down in the middle of his bedroll, Bourke came back to the fire, another coffeepot sloshing at the end of his arm. "Pull out the grounds, Donegan," he said, pointing to the waxed leather satchels near the Irishman. "The general's going to want some coffee when he gets back from his talk with Reynolds."

"Crook's made him a real study of this mule train thing, ain't he now?" Donegan asked.

"I should say," Bourke replied. "To him, it's the only way to wage war on these wild, hostile tribes. He knows every one of Moore's packers by name, and most of the names of Moore's favorite mules—at least the bell mares. Why, Crook'll even dismiss a packer who he finds beating his mule unmercifully. There's no room for cruelty. And there's enough experienced packers on the plains that the general doesn't have a man working for him he doesn't like."

"How's the general for taking care of his men?"

Bourke looked up from across the fire as Donegan handed him the waxed satchel filled with coffee grounds. "General Crook is admired by every man who serves under him, Seamus. They don't question his orders, because they know he'll back them all the way."

Strahorn said, "Good to be riding with that sort, ain't it, Seamus?"

"He's a rare breed, if he does, Strahorn. A rare breed in this army."

"Just count your blessings, Seamus," Bourke replied. "While we've got the wagons along—we'll all sleep in the lap of luxury."

"And once we have to leave the wagons behind?"

"Then say good-bye to the dog tents," Bourke answered, one arm sweeping in an arc to indicate the A tents popping up all through the camp. "Which means our reporter friend here will be kissing his cushy army bedroll a fond farewell too."

Strahorn didn't like the sound of that. He grumbled, "Let's all join in prayer then, Lieutenant: that General Crook finds his hostile Indians right where he can take his wagons!"

"Just makes me cold thinking on it," Donegan said. "Having to think about you, Strahorn—riding that beast with two backs in some chippie's crib at the Hog Ranch . . . nice and warm you were, weren't you?"

"Plenty warm," Strahorn answered, a big smile on his

face as he pushed one of the coffeepots toward the flames to boil.

"Aye. But plenty cold you'll be soon enough."

"What you mean?"

Looking from lieutenant to Irishman, both wearing their most knowing of smiles, then back again to Bourke, Strahorn didn't like the sounds of it.

"So, if we don't have the wagons, we don't have these big bedrolls." He shrugged. "What is it we'll have to sleep in?"

"Likely a couple of those gum ponchos and your blanket, Bob," answered John Bourke.

Strahorn blinked and wagged his head. "God bless us all then, if that's the case—for the general will be lucky to get any of these soldiers to Crazy Horse country in shape to fight. Shit, to my way of figuring, the Sioux won't have to worry about firing a shot at this goddamned army, will they?"

With a doleful wag of his head, he added, "What Crazy Horse's warriors can't kill—it's for sure this bloody cold will!"

After a supper of thick steaks sliced fresh from the loin of one of the cattle butchered that nightfall, along with fluffy biscuits and coffee, and followed by a dessert of canned peaches, Seamus Donegan strode over to the picket lines where he had tied his horse. Kicking at some of the deep snow that had fallen yesterday, he tore at some of the tall, brittle bunchgrass dried with autumn's winds. With it the Irishman brushed the animal a second time since the soldiers had gone into camp for the night.

It was more an exercise in futility—this trying to find something to keep his mind off her. The smell of her, the taste and feel and . . . hell, just how she made him feel. More alive than he had in so, so long.

"Jesus Christ!"

Seamus whirled suddenly at the words flung against his back, his hand dropping to the pistol hung at his waist.

"Didn't see you standing there," the stranger said, nervousness in his voice as moved closer now, crunching across the icy snow.

Donegan's own heart throbbed in his throat. "By the saints, don't come up on a man like that."

"Had no intention, mister," the civilian replied, lowering his carbine. "Just passing this way, going out to stand my watch with the herd. Surprised me as bad as I surprised you to find anybody here."

He took a deep breath and ripped off a glove, presenting it to the miserable, mud-homely boy as lean as a weather-split hickory fence post. "Everyone's a little jumpy, I suppose—it being our first night out. Name's Seamus Donegan."

"Jim Wright," the young herder answered, grasping the Irishman's big paw in a gloved hand that was hard of knuckle. "Best get your mitt back on."

"And my arse back to my bedroll," he said, starting to shake a little with the dropping temperature. Seamus glanced at the sky to the west, stars winking into view as the heavens cleared on the far horizon.

"Yeah," Wright replied. "It clears off like it's threatening to, be damned cold by dawn when we get rolled out."

He studied the youth a moment, that freckled face clean-shaven, his hair a flaxen blond, hung straight and greasy. "You got your night cut in half, taking this middle watch, Jim."

Wright shrugged. "I don't mind, really." The herder patted the front of his blanket coat. "Got me a mess of them biscuits, tucked away right in here—keep 'em warm. Gimme something to do besides—keep my mouth working and my belly full."

"Good meeting you, Jim Wright. Likely see you a time or two over the next few weeks of this cold march."

"Likely. Share a cup of coffee with me sometime, Seamus."

"That I'll do."

When Donegan had wound his way through the maze of dog tents pitched by the soldiers and the picket lines strung up by the mule packers, on past the teamsters' wagon yard, Seamus kicked his bedroll out flat, plopped down on its blessed softness and yanked off his boots. Almost as quickly his damp feet grew chilled, and stayed just that cold for some time after he had buried them at the bottom of his bedroll. Pulling his head in as well, Seamus let out a sigh, made a notch for his shoulder in the prairie tick, his mind immediately drifting to the warmth and fragrance of Samantha.

She was likely finishing her supper about this time of a winter night, he brooded unhappily. Warm, well-fed . . . and hopefully just as lonely as he.

The growing warmth began to cradle him, like a thick molasses poured over corn hoecakes. And he knew he was dreaming already. Feeling her wrapped around his flesh like an oozy warmth . . . it made his loins ache for her. His groin tingled, flesh going taut, and he realized he was growing hard just from this dream of her.

Then of a sudden he wasn't so sure, down there in that murky half sleep. Not so sure it was a dream of her . . . more like he was really blinking his eyes—watching her come quickly toward him through the cold mist rising from off the freezing rivers. Strange as it was, he could hear no sound as she came to him across the icy ground. Samantha was not touching the snow, merely floating, her arms outstretched, calling to him. Calling him to her beckoning warmth . . .

She was screaming—

Reaching for her, he found himself bundled, lashed down, unable to move to her rescue.

Now Samantha was shrieking, hideously, beckoning for him.

Then the ground beneath him began to rumble with the dull thunder of distant hooves, drawing closer, ever closer, close enough for the Irishman to feel the terrifying quake of it.

"Stampede!"

At the horrified cry of a nearby picket, Seamus was shucking his bedroll and pulling on his cold boots—

"Indians!"

—yanking down his wolf-hide hat and sweeping up the seventeen-shot Henry into his mittens.

Still asleep. But moving just the same.

Chapter 11

2 March 1876

"*S*tampede!"

At the high-pitched cry from a nearby picket, Seamus was shucking his bedroll and muscling on his cold boots, yanking down his wolf-hide hat over his long, unkempt hair, then by groggy instinct sweeping up the seventeen-shot Henry into his mittens.

"By God—they're Indians!"

Along the company rows men were shouting, high voices and low, every one of them trying for command. To Donegan's right the horses were crying out, whinnying in fear and pulling at their picket ropes, rearing clumsily in their hobbles, fighting the efforts of the young soldiers who were suddenly in among them, struggling to keep the whole remuda from escaping. And off to his left the teamsters and Moore's packers had their own hands full, soothing, whipping, beating, cursing in among the hee-hawing mules. A matter of yards away the thunder grew deafening as the bawling cattle began to lumber up and out of the creek valley.

For a man in the dead of sleep but a few seconds before, it had to be the din of Hell itself.

But, behind it all, a plainsman could clearly make out the banshee cry not quite drowned out by all the nearby clamor. Behind it all, sweeping down along the creek bottom, came the unmistakable sound of Cheyenne war cries.

And then the thought struck Seamus, more something

that roared right through him like grapeshot—had they dogged Crook's column for the past two days? Had they been shadowed since leaving Fetterman? Were the warriors to the north aware the army was coming, and had they decided to tease and lure, seduce and entice this army farther and farther north? Just like those dozen horsemen had lured Captain Fetterman and eighty soldiers to their deaths almost ten years before?*

Suddenly come awake, Seamus was off like there were a fire beneath his tall boots, glancing quickly at the sky to find the moon already setting in the west, guessing it to be sometime after two o'clock this late in the winter.

Then the first shots raised the hair on the back of his cold, cold neck, causing him to realize he had lost the wolfskin cap. Those sharp cracks of smaller weapons, perhaps the Colt revolvers, .45 caliber, maybe a .44-caliber Winchester or two. And the solid, reassuring boom, boom of the 1873 Springfields, .45 caliber as well.

A man yelped in pain. It was the voice of a white man, not the bowel-puckering cry of those brown-skinned banshees who had come riding down on this camp of soldiers, brazen and bold, sassy as could be.

"There they go!" a new voice shouted.

Several were standing, pointing up the gentle slope of the creek valley as a hundred more soldiers and civilians tore up and came to a ragged stop. The cattle, half-a-hundred in all, were lumbering off at a gallop, tails high behind, urged on by the redskinned drovers who reined their darting ponies in and among the frightened herd that scattered this way then that—like some thick, flowing beast without a head or any real sense of direction.

"Someone—get the doc!"

Seamus turned with many of the others, yet he was one of the few who went to the sound of the voice, the rest choosing to mill about and mull over what had happened in less time than it would take to tell in a hundred years of campfire stories.

* The Plainsmen Series, vol. 1, *Sioux Dawn*

"You a doctor?" the man asked as he leaned over a body stretched akimbo across the snow.

"No," Seamus answered, going down on one knee beside the wounded civilian.

The eyes rolled open, blinked once and seemed to come to focus on the Irishman. They were hollow eyes, sick-looking as a wet dog with distemper.

"I know you," the youth said, a little dark fluid oozing out from his lips beneath the pale starshine that gave a silver luster to this snow-smitten tableland.

"Yeah, it's me," Donegan said quietly as he gazed down at the young herder. He put his hand on the greasy splotch just spreading across the blanket coat.

Setting the Henry aside, Seamus quickly unbuttoned the front of the herder's coat.

Shot in the lights, he thought. Right through the upper chest. "How'd you get yourself in this fix, young Jim?"

Trying to smile, Jim Wright coughed. "Always was the lucky sort, you know?"

"Just be quiet now," the other civilian said. He raised his head and flung his voice into the dark. "By damn, hasn't somebody gone to get that doctor yet?"

"Donegan," the young man whispered, his voice growing faint.

Seamus put his ear down closer as more men moved close about them.

"Am I . . . am I dying?"

Seamus straightened, looking at the spreading blood on the herder's shirt, gazing up a moment at the bystanders—anywhere to look but at Wright's eyes.

"The surgeon's coming, John. You'll be fine, he gets here."

"I saw 'em coming," Wright whispered, his voice phlegmy. "Half dozen . . . maybe more."

"Save your strength."

"Over here!"

Seamus twisted about at the shout, others giving directions in the dark.

"He's over here!" Another, closer this time, shouting.

Hoping it was the surgeon.

"I yelled, Donegan," Wright said, his voice rattled with bubbling liquid.

"It's fine—you done just fine—"

"That's when they saw me," and he broke off in a coughing fit.

"By God, you're clear across this goddamned camp," growled a man tromping up behind Donegan.

Seamus turned as the graying soldier crouched beside Wright. A young soldier knelt at the surgeon's side. The doctor placed his hand over the growing stain on the herder's chest.

"I'm Dr. Munn. Chief medical officer for this campaign," he told his patient quietly, his tone suddenly soothing where a moment before it had been gruff and demanding of all the rest. "I've brought Steward Bryan with me. We're going to take a quick look at your wound—to decide on how to move you to one of the ambulances."

Wright's eyes seemed to implore Donegan.

"It's all right, young Jim. You're in good hands now," Seamus cooed.

"Jim, is it?" Munn asked as Donegan rose to stand.

"Don . . . Donegan!"

He looked down at the herder, Wright's face even more pasty-white in the pale starshine.

The herder said, "Don't let anyone sneak up on you—hear?"

Forcing a grin, Seamus answered, "No one gonna sneak up on me now, young Jim."

Seamus turned and shouldered his way through the crowd. All around him company captains and lieutenants were shouting, spreading Crook's and Reynolds's orders: doubling the pickets on the perimeter; doubling the guard around the mule and horse herds for what remained of the short winter night.

"Get what rest you can now, fellas. Sergeant—we'll be rolling the men out early!"

Some officer bellowing.

"We'll be drinking coffee at five. In the saddle at six."

Another farther down the line giving more hope of little or no sleep for the rest of the night.

At the first pink telltale hint of dawn, Crook had a half dozen of Clark's scouts heading south, following the tracks of the runaway cattle herd.

"That was our rations," grumped Speed Stagner at the tiny fire where two dozen more of the civilian scouts drank coffee and waited for the return of Ben Clark and the rest.

"Don't take it so hard," Louis Shangrau said. "It's turned out just the way old Crook wanted it to."

"How you figure that?" asked Jules Ecofee.

Shangrau looked over the attentive group, grown quiet and respectful, waiting for his reply. "You really think an old war horse like Crook wanted to have that beef herd tagging along, slow as molasses in January on an aspen stump? Hell no. I'll bet Crook figures it ain't no great shakes, no loss to us. Now we don't have to play cowboy to no beef on the hoof."

"Louie's right," agreed Charlie Jennesse. "Now that we ain't cowboys, we can get down to business."

"Damn right," Buckskin Jack Russell said. "Find the Injuns then get back to someplace with a stove."

"Hog Ranch got a nice stove," Joe Eldridge said.

"And whiskey," added Mitch Shimmeno.

"Women. Good, sweet-smelling women," replied Tom Reed.

"Hell." John Provost laughed. "A fresh-laid cow pie be sweet-smelling to you, boyo! Bad as you smell yourself!"

They laughed together, and that laughing together brought most of them more together than they had been so far. Yet Seamus noticed that there were two who did not laugh, two who did not even smile, much less join in on the good-natured ribbing over the hot coffee and the warm coals as they waited for Crook's campaign to get rolling once more.

Two who did not laugh, with hard eyes for each other. Both half-breeds, with some secret burr down deep in their craws. Frank Grouard, who kept to himself for the most part. And the younger one who seemed to follow Grouard around a lot, as if stalking him, making Grouard always feel the presence of his shadow. That one, the half-breed named Reshaw.*

"Irishman!"

Seamus turned to find Bob Strahorn striding up, his long coat slurring the trampled snow. Beyond him, on the far side of camp, there came a flurry of activity as one by one the companies were interrupting their camp-breaking to watch the return of the detail sent out to follow the cattle thieves.

"You hear about the herder shot last night?" Strahorn asked as he came to a halt.

Seamus nodded his head. "Youngster named Jim Wright. Yeah. Took a bad one in the lungs."

"Yeah," Strahorn replied, mystified. "How you know already?"

"I was there just after it—"

"Stands to reason you would be," the reporter said sourly with a wag of his head. "There comes Clark now. Suppose he's already reported in to Crook."

"Man like Ben Clark would do that, Bob. Before he came to warm up, get his hands around a mug of coffee."

There wasn't much for the chief of scouts to report to his men, telling them they had followed the tracks far enough to see that the cattle were heading south.

"Our goddamned beef rations running right back to Fort Fetterman!" someone growled.

"Fellas, let's get mounted up and back out on the flanks," Clark ordered. "You know where you're riding today." He took another long sip of the coffee that would have no chance to go cold in his cup. Over the rim of the tin, he caught and held the Irishman's gray eyes.

"Those cattle won't make it back to Fetterman, Ben."

Clark glanced about him quickly, waiting a moment while the rest of the civilians, scouts and reporter Strahorn, all moved off.

Clark nodded once. "No one can be sure. It's for certain those Injuns aren't drovers."

"Don't have to be good at working cows to get some

* Louis Richaud/Richard

dumb cattle herded into a box canyon, maybe a narrow coulee someplace. Keep 'em there until they're ready to butcher 'em."

"The white man's spotted buffalo, eh?"

Seamus nodded, a grin on his dry, cracked lips. "Yeah. General George Crook is providing better rations to the hostiles than all those agents down at Spotted Tail's or Red Cloud's agencies."

"C'mon, Irishman. Let's mount up," Clark said with a smile. "Get your mind off cattle and back on finding warrior villages."

"Get my mind off cattle? You daft, Clark?" he chided. "By bloody damned, without that beef, we all can forget about eating good on this bone-killing march of Crook's! Why, looks to me like it's back to biscuits and beans, bacon and bullets! Ben Clark, you and mother Donegan's boy are back in the goddamned army!"

"Each man must follow his own heart, He Dog," said Old Bear.

The Oglalla warrior nodded, not taking his red-rimmed eyes off the yellow and blue flames licking their way along the limbs in the fire pit.

"Crazy Horse follows his heart on the Little Powder," added Two Moon.

He looked up at the old Northern Cheyenne chief. Two Moon's face appeared all the more seamed in the flickering firelight of the lodge this winter night.

"You follow your heart, bringing your old ones, the little ones who do not have long legs to run through the deep snow when the soldiers come," Old Bear continued. "It is good. No man can shame you."

"No." He Dog finally spoke. "No man can ever shame a Lakota warrior. I am the only one who can bring myself shame."

"There is no dishonor in feeding your people," Two Moon said. "Was there ever a warrior as honorable as you, or Crazy Horse, the summer when you both took vows to be shirt-wearers of the Hunkpatila?"

That summer long ago swam before his misting eyes.

Inside he cried out for his old friend. Yet the Crazy Horse he had left behind on the Little Powder was not the Crazy Horse of winters gone the way of their youth together.

"Yes, I took a solemn vow."

"It is that way with the Oglalla, I know," Old Bear said. "You took a vow to protect your people first."

"And this you do," Two Moon added. "You add your lodges to our circle. Together, we travel the same trail to the White Rock agency."*

He Dog went back to staring at the flames. He did not really hear the wheezing of the old men in the lodge, nor the shuffling feet of the others. The council was packed, more than two dozen crowded into this tiny lodge, deliberating on the route to take back south to the reservation. Skirting the fringe of their sacred Black Hills, then pointing their noses almost due south to the land of summer—until they reached the place of safety.

"There are times my heart still hungers for the excitement," He Dog tried to explain in a soft voice that brought the others quiet. "Yes, there are times my heart still dreams of counting coup."

"You have been in many battles, He Dog," Two Moon said. "You carry your scars with honor."

"He Dog," Old Bear began, his rheumy eyes watering more from age than lodge smoke, "you have proved yourself. No man could question your courage."

"No man would question mine," Two Moon added.

"You have no need of proving your courage," Old Bear continued.

He Dog considered, thinking on his children, on the younger ones, those who could not yet walk, but were carried on their mothers' backs or on the travois. There were ten lodges of Hunkpatila Oglalla who had followed him and his wives out of Crazy Horse's camp in a tearful parting. Families leaving friends behind, warriors bidding farewell to their comrades and warrior societies, children parting from their dearest playmates. Then, after days of travel,

---

* Red Cloud Reservation

this afternoon they had seen the two riders crest the hill ahead of them. Cheyenne hunters.

Old Bear's clan, camped with Two Moon's village, welcomed the ten lodges of Oglalla like lost cousins. Together they would do what was best for the old ones, and the little ones too young to fight pony soldiers in the deep snow.

Tomorrow with the rising of the sun, He Dog and the rest would begin to make their way to the White Rock agency.

Tomorrow they would begin the long, painful journey south to the prison that had no iron bars.

Chapter 12

5 March 1876

"*I*n no way is this a question of who is going to win this war, gentlemen," George Crook told the officers he had assembled as the cold seemed to seep right down out of the high places with the sinking of the winter sun. "Nor is who will ultimately stand as the victor of this campaign in question either."

Here at sunset as a slashing, voracious wind picked up force, viciously snapping the guidons outside the tent Crook called headquarters, a wind so cold it brought tears to the general's eyes, he let those eyes touch some of the younger ones—captains and lieutenants—those officers he realized who did not have all that much field experience against the hostile warrior bands of the northern plains. Especially under these cruel weather conditions.

In the last three days, he had driven them more than sixty miles.

"No," he continued, his words falling about him like hammer strikes, yet gently stroking one of the two long sweeps of the beard he kept parted at the middle of his chin. "The only two questions in my mind yet to be determined by history are: just when the red man will finally surrender to the dominant white race . . . and just what it is going to cost us to finally drive these warriors back to their agencies."

"We can begin that drive with this very march," declared Colonel Joseph J. Reynolds, nominal commander of this Big Horn Expedition.

Crook nodded once, glancing quickly at the white-headed officer whose white muttonchops rustled against the upturned wolf-fur collar of his wool coat in the cruel wind. He had sensed some pangs of sympathy for Reynolds last fall when plans for this campaign were coming together. A solid, proven commanding officer during the Civil War, the colonel had in the end stained his own career down in Reconstruction Texas, forever tainted with rumors of taking bribes from private contractors and sutlers, both in the form of money and in a private home constructed for his family. Crook had wrestled with the dilemma of completely turning this march over to Reynolds—doing so only when at last he decided to come along as an observer. It was a decision Crook could stand behind—in this way giving the aging Reynolds a way to repair his tottering career, this late in his life.

"General," Crook addressed Reynolds by the colonel's brevet rank, won during distinguished service in the Civil War, "while I agree that this expedition could ultimately drive the hostiles in to their reservations forthwith, I want to be realistic about the situation of things here in my department. More than anything over the next few weeks, I see our march more in terms of accomplishing two goals: first, to determine once and for all the ability of men and animals to campaign under arduous conditions; and second, our march truly serves as a scout for the forthcoming summer campaign."

"You don't believe we will find the hostiles' camps, General?" Reynolds asked the question likely on many a man's lips.

Crook nodded. "I hope to hell we do." He waited for some of the approbation to grow quiet. "But if we don't, and aren't able to smite the warrior bands—we will have learned some valuable lessons nonetheless."

Just before sundown Crook had called Ben Clark and Frank Grouard together, asking his chief of scouts to select five of his men to accompany Grouard, the man who best knew this Powder River country. The general instructed Clark to have the half dozen ride unshod ponies, so as to leave an Indian backtrail on their three-day scout north by west toward the Tongue. Riding with Grouard were Big Bat, Charlie Jennesse, Little Bat, John Shangrau, and Louie Reshaw. In the meantime the column would continue along the abandoned Montana Road toward the Crazy Woman Fork, where Crook planned to rendezvous with the half-dozen forward scouts if they had not found any villages.

"By God, General," John Bourke began, already clearly worked up, "forget the lessons we're going to learn. If I'm asked to campaign in damnable weather like this—I sure as hell want to smite these wild bands, and give them some instruction they'll not soon forget!" A smattering of agreeable laughter echoed from the group as the lieutenant continued. "If we can only find their village, there will be another Black Kettle affair, I promise you. Riding about in this godforsaken weather would almost make a man want to find himself a civilian job!"

Most of the others laughed easily, a little louder now as they shifted about, stamping their boots in the soul-robbing cold.

"You may yet have your chance, Mr. Bourke," he cheered, then let the smile drain from his face. "But mark my words, this cycle of attack and revenge, attack and revenge—this must stop. And we—no matter what camp our scouts find for us—we are the beginning of the end."

"Lord help us if this campaign turns out to be a long one, sir," commented Anson Mills.

"Lord help us all, Captain," Crook replied. "While I'm not a particularly religious man—those of you who know me, served with me before—I feel as if a prayer would be in order this evening before this meeting is adjourned and you return to your outfits. Captain Moore, would you lead us in prayer, that we may see through our objectives with the minimum loss of human life?"

Alex Moore eagerly launched into a prayer, then, before the rest could turn to disperse into the growing twilight, the captain launched into singing the "Old Hundredth." Only after its last chorus echoed off the brittle alkali ice of the lazy Powder did the officers' assembly break up, leaving

Crook alone with his aide, Lieutenant Bourke; his adjutant, Charles Morton; and his striker, Andrew Peiser.

As Private Peiser punched up the fire and Bourke busied himself inside the headquarters tent with the general's adjutant, Crook settled as close to the flames as he dared. Seemed a man had to roast on one side, freeze on the other.

It was damnable country, this, although the desert of southern Arizona and New Mexico grew surprisingly cold at night this time of year. These plains, high and every bit as arid as that in Apacheria, he considered a desert as well. But something more brutal in that cold rushing down off the high peaks to the west of them, that spine of a great continent the white society back east was anxious to subdue and husband and bring to fruition. But first there was work for the martial arm of that society—a job for military men like himself.

Society would always have need of men like him, Crook mused as he stared into the flames.

Without children of his own, over the years he had come to regard many of the young officers who served under him as the sons he had never sired with wife Mary Tapscott Dailey. He an Ohio Yankee, she a daughter of old Virginia —theirs had been a spirited alliance at the time of the Rebellion in the South, especially when he was assigned to the eastern theater to serve in Sheridan's Shenandoah campaign and the Union's final push for Richmond. Early on, both he and Mary had decided to have her remain behind, not to follow him from assignment to assignment. Instead she maintained the family estate, Crook Crest, outside of Oakland, Maryland. While some would likely call theirs a disappointing marriage, one of convenience—Crook would argue with this, deeply hurt at such a characterization, saying he and Mary truly loved one another, that theirs was a relationship of two truly strong people: she to manage a great estate and build her own fortunes; he to manage a sizable piece of the frontier army of the West and to possibly seize a political fortune of his own.

Snugging down the black-furred Kossuth hat bare of insignia more securely over his ears in the driving wind that rawhided his ruddy face, Crook stroked his beard thoughtfully, then shifted himself. The flint arrow tip in his right hip gave him trouble of times, an unwanted souvenir from his campaign against the Pitt River Indians of the Northwest back in '57.

Nearly twenty years now, he brooded, watching the sparks roar and scatter along the ground as the wind slashed and gusted painfully. Reshifting the wide leather belt where better than fifty brass cartridges were snugly ensconced in their loops at his waist, again Crook yanked up the wolf-hide collar that trimmed his coat, the skin from an animal he had shot himself years before in one of those Indian campaigns before the southern states attempted rebellion.

"I've seen to Apache, picketed and hobbled securely, General," declared John Bourke as the lieutenant came back into the light.

"Thank you, John," Crook replied. It was always one of the last duties of his aide, this securing of the general's beloved mule, an animal that had carried him into battle across the years, from Apacheria to a cozy stall in Omaha. Apache was once more on the campaign trail with George Crook.

"Are you warm enough here, General?"

Crook nodded at Bourke as the lieutenant dragged out his bedroll. The general slept outdoors these bitter nights, when he could easily have slept inside the headquarters tent with Bourke, Morton and Peiser, a collapsible sheet-iron stove glowing fervently to cut the chill. Instead the general was the sort of man who asked no more of the lowest of his privates than he would demand of himself. The frozen, flinty ground of this wild country for a bed, the cold blackness of the diamond-flecked heavens for his canopy, George Crook slept in the subzero cold.

When he could sleep. More and more over the past years, Crook had found himself afflicted with bouts of insomnia. And even when he could get to sleep, he would often awaken early, in the middle of the night, unable to relax enough to fall back asleep. It seemed his agile, ever-busy mind often gave him no rest.

He pulled the flaps of his long wool army coat, itself lined with red flannel, over his tall government boots and the trousers of brown wide-wale corduroy he had cut to length himself then burned at the ends to prevent the cuffs from unraveling.

"We were certainly watched today, General," Bourke commented as he came out of the tent and stopped near Crook.

He did not take his eyes off the fire. "Plenty of mirrors flashing, John. Yes, has been a lot of that the last few days. Yesterday I spotted my first bit of smoke to the northeast. They're talking to each other."

"So they know we're coming."

"They'll likely know where we are every step of the way."

"But we still have to find out where they are," Bourke said, squatting on the hard ground brushed clear of most of its snow. "Just how can we hope to keep them from running, hope to find a village long enough to attack if they know our every move?"

"We may not ever find a village," Crook said, repeating his belief. "But if we are lucky enough to catch them napping—then we just have to do something unpredictable . . . keep them guessing . . . show up where we aren't supposed to be."

"Time and again, sir, we've done it before."

"With an enemy like the Apache, or these Sioux and Cheyenne—you have to fight their kind of war, John."

"You've engraved that in my mind, sir."

He smiled at Bourke, then gazed across the quiet, milky river at the shadowy ruins of old Fort Reno. Back in '65 General Patrick Connor had built the post during his Powder River expedition to subdue Red Cloud's Bad Face band of Oglallas. The army brass quickly renamed the post after a fallen hero of the Civil War, and Connor went back to Utah, to watch over Brigham Young's Mormons. The following year, Reno was again posted, becoming the southernmost of three forts the army established along the Bozeman Trail to protect traffic heading north to the Montana goldfields. When the government signed the paper-thin treaty made with Red Cloud and the Northern Cheyenne in '68, all three Montana Road forts were abandoned. Here at Reno the Sioux had rushed in to burn down everything they could before the army was even out of sight on the southbound trail that fateful summer.

All that remained along the banks of the sluggish, yellow-tainted Powder River were the remnants of a few earthen walls, their charred timbers protruding like blackened bones from the snow-covered earth, and a few ten-foot-tall chimneys standing like sentinels of a bygone era when soldiers sought to protect this road.

And now the army was back.

On this their fifth day out, they had marched fifteen miles, angling down the valley of the Dry Fork until they struck the Powder itself. Deciding to make camp there, Crook had Stanton dispatch some of his scouts to look for signs of Indian villages in the surrounding country. Besides the flashing mirrors and an occasional column of smoke, Little Bat had even been the first to sight a large distant column of dust. Crook and the others surmised it could be nothing else but a sizable village on the move, being herded away from the army's line of march. After all, for the previous three days, the column had been crossing and recrossing an increasing number of travois tracks, accompanied by the prints of a large number of unshod pony hooves.

With the snow-mantled Big Horn Mountains rising sharply to their left, Crook's column was in enemy territory, make no mistake.

And this afternoon the advance had actually spotted a half-dozen or so horsemen in the distance. Crook had given strict orders that these luring decoys were not to be pursued, when he knew the only aim of the seductive warriors was to wear down the horses of their pursuers plodding through the white-shrouded, broken country slashed by coulees and sharp-lipped draws, a seemingly endless horizon rising and falling in a monotony of crumbling sandstone and slate, from one yellow-tinged creek drainage to the next.

Lord, how he missed Rex.

His black and white border collie, a gift from an officer's wife down at a post in Arizona; Camp Grant it was. Rex.

A damned good dog, more suited to the campaign than some of these soldiers. But damnable weather like it was, the icy snow would turn the collie's paws to bloody ribbons —and it was for certain Rex would not be content to ride along in one of the wagons, much less slung atop Apache with Crook himself.

The general sighed at the growing darkness, the growing cold, and the coming loneliness that night and inactivity always brought him.

A sad parting from Rex—in some ways harder than the good-byes he allowed himself with Mary. Perhaps because Mary was not at his side night and day as was that faithful animal. Maybe because Rex was always there to count on in the middle of the night, warm and affectionate and trusting. A true friend. How hard it had been to tie Rex to the porch outside Major Alex Chambers's quarters, watching the collie gnaw at his rope then lunge from the porch to the full extent of his tether. Whining and howling, yipping pitifully in frustration and perhaps even some primitive anger at this insult—not allowed to leave with its master.

"Oh, Rex . . ." he said quietly.

"Sir?" Bourke asked.

"Nothing—"

But his answer was interrupted from the near side of camp: shots and shouts.

"They're coming across the goddamned river!"

Down along the riverbank he could hear the soldiers hollering, ordering, working themselves up after the first rattle of gunfire. The loud boom of the infantry Springfield, called a "Long Tom" because its barrel was indeed longer than the shorter Springfield cavalry carbine. That boom followed by the sharp crack of smaller weapons. Indian guns no doubt.

All through their bivouac the tent lanterns were going out and the campfires were being doused as quickly as the frightened men could extinguish all back-lighting—with no way to know how many warriors were attacking camp. Others ran to guard the horses along the picket lines. Teamsters hunkered down after pulling mules inside the protective cordon of their wagons.

"Only three spotted for sure, General," rasped Captain Anson Mills as he hurried up in a crouch to report a short time later.

For more than thirty minutes the hostiles fired into the soldier camp from the north side of the river, having gotten their range before the hapless troops were able to douse their fires. Here and there a soldier cursed at his unseen enemy, able to fire only when he spotted a muzzle flash across the icy Powder.

"Casualties?"

"One, sir," Mills replied. "Corporal Slavey—a ball passed through his cheek, sir."

"Much of a wound?"

Mills shook his head in the inky darkness. "A lot of blood for all of it, and three teeth he had to spit out."

"Damn," Crook muttered as he leaned back again at last on his bedroll. He placed his hands behind his head and regarded the constellations in the great black dome of the heavens. "Dismissed, Captain."

He listened to the fading of the officer's footsteps on the new snow as Mills scurried off, back to his battalion.

The enemy had tried—however few there were—young bucks most likely. Attempting once more to run off the horses and mules.

Put us afoot, Crook brooded. That would end this campaign far short of our goal.

"I know you're up here . . . out there somewhere . . . maybe even close," he said quietly, as if by whispering he could actually talk to his enemy, warriors and chiefs. "You know I'm coming, but you're powerless to stop me."

Chapter 13

6 March 1876

*G*rouard's scouting party hadn't made it all that far in the growing darkness before the silence of the snowy land brought to them the sounds of gunfire on the dry, prairie air.

Donegan watched the six return from his side of camp.

After a rousing half hour of shooting back and forth between the soldiers and their unseen enemy across the Powder, things had begun to quiet down. Colonel Reynolds saw to it that each company was well-represented among the double pickets he ordered to surround the nervous bivouac. The sky was clearing a little to the west of its dusting of clouds as the half-dozen scouts rode back in, telling Crook they likely made it five miles before they turned around, figuring they would be needed if the camp were under attack.

In the predawn cold that sixth morning of the march, the men enjoyed about the best breakfast of the whole campaign. Plenty of coffee to wash down biscuits lathered with plenty of butter; slabs of beef served up with chopped potatoes and eggs; and even some stewed apples for a tasty dessert before breaking camp.

After crossing the ice at a shallow ford, the command climbed the north bank of the Powder to pass by the ruins of Fort Reno, littered with the charred stumps of construction timbers like blackened, broken bones protruding from a gaping wound, and the crumbling adobe walls that could not hide the rusting debris of iron stoves and broken wagon wheels, a solitary broken-down wagon box and a half-burnt artillery carriage for a mountain howitzer.

"Eyes right!" came the cry at the head of the column.

"Eyes right!" echoed the call again and again, up and down the line of march as Crook's command plodded in silence past the tiny graveyard some two hundred yards north of the abandoned remnants of the army's brief stay beside the silent, milky Powder. About a dozen busted, dry-split headboards with wind-scoured, unreadable names leaned precariously at their last stations above the gallant roll call of those who had given their all to this high and forbidding land.

Even the Sioux and Cheyenne leave a place like this alone, Seamus thought as the advance of scouts approached the bare slope of windblown hill given over to this final resting place.

Like a few others riding the point this subzero morning, Seamus bared his head to the cold wind sweeping down out of the far reaches of the Bighorns. He found his thoughts yanked back to a much different morning nearly six years before . . . a hot summer dawn, taking leave of Fort Reno, the small command of soldiers he and old Sam Marr rode with being begged by the post's commander not to go on one last time—for God's sake, the man had pleaded, most certainly they should leave the woman and her nursing infant behind.

The soldiers and civilians went on, despite the warnings.*

He remembered the soldiers, young—at least younger than he then—a decade gone now. And the older ones, who had seen their way through the war back east, four long years of bloody hell, come to the West to soldier, and to die. There were already far too many of those nameless ones who lay in unmarked graves.

"Eyes right!" came the faint cry way down the column.

It was for those who laid on the unmarked, uncharted wastes, as much as for these who were at their final rest beneath this flaky, yellow soil beside an abandoned post on the banks of the Powder River, for all who had faces and

---

* The Plainsmen Series, vol. 1, *Sioux Dawn*

dreams and families—for them Seamus uncovered his head and silently mumbled one of the childhood prayers Mother Donegan had taught to her eldest, her firstborn son, so many years before on that faraway green isle of his birth.

Sometimes, like this, his memories of his mother rose in his mind like the coming of a fever. Not really thoughts of her—more just sense memories: the warmth of her hand against the small of his back; the smooth feel of her cheek beneath his tiny fingertips; and the vibration of her throat when she held him at her shoulder and sang softly to him.

Tears froze in his eyes before they could drop to his cheek. And for that he was thankful of the brutal cold that whipped the low clouds overhead into a fury.

"Here. You'll want some of this," Ben Clark said quietly as he brought his mount alongside, slowing to it to a walk.

Donegan looked at the small amber jar the scout held in the palm of his glove. Pulling the frost-crusted bandanna down from his nose, he asked, "What's this?"

"Tallow. Get some fresh every morning at breakfast. Beef or bacon—makes me no never mind."

Donegan studied the lean scout dubiously. "What you want me to do with it?"

"Your lips." Beneath one arm, Clark yanked off one of his horsehide mittens, then dipped a finger in the amber jar and smeared the tallow liberally over his lips. "You use it through the day—lips won't get in the bad shape yours are in now."

Looking at the rendered tallow, he licked his lips unconsciously. Instantly they protested painfully, stung at the touch of his tongue. So he stretched them, which only made the pain worse. He sensed another of the sore cracks had reopened, robbed as his lips were of moisture by the high, dry wind that kept this land a veritable desert. A drop of blood seeped from the old crack on that puffy lower lip.

"Long as I been . . ." he started, then let his tongue dab at that open, oozing lip again.

Clark passed the small jar over to the Irishman. "Lots of men, good at scouting and reading sign—their whole lives they never know some of the little secrets to making themselves comfortable in bad weather like this." He turned his collar up again beneath the big, floppy-brimmed hat.

"Where you learn about this?" Donegan asked as he generously smeared the tallow on his lips and began to work it in.

Clark smiled genuinely. "Indians. Married me a Cheyenne, you know." He took the small jar back from Donegan, replaced the stopper and stuffed it down in his pocket. "Look me up you need some more. I'll keep you with me riding point today."

"Obliged," Seamus replied, pulling the bandanna back over his mouth and nose so that it rested just below his eyes. It helped cut some of the icy sting from the snow that slashed at them with tiny arrow points as the scouts pointed the column straight on into the cruel wind tearing down out of the northwest. They were following the Bozeman Road toward Montana Territory, straight into the teeth of the building storm.

And into a frightening wilderness of monotony.

The wind-whipped, yellow-streaked ridges and coulees passed by at an agonizing slowness, all of it smeared with yesterday's fresh snow, which clung in icy ribbons to every rock outcrop, encircled every tuft of bunchgrass like a frozen lace doily, and lay forbidding in every wrinkled crevice of this land chopped and tormented for countless eons. Yet, of all things, the land had survived.

"Halt!"

Donegan heard the distant call behind him and twisted in the saddle, watching the long blue line of motley cavalry rattle to a ragged stop. In their bulky, disparate winter dress, they looked more like an advancing column of Mongolian hordes. Raiders and pillagers, come to scorch this high wilderness. Brigands and highwaymen all—little distinction could he make at this distance between officers and their enlisted.

"Dismount!"

The weary troopers made no attempt to climb from their saddles as one man. Slowly they dropped to the frozen snow.

"We'll walk for fifteen minutes!" came the command. The order was sent back along the column.

Seamus glanced at Clark with that question in his eyes. Clark shook his head. They would stay in their saddle. With only a wave of his arm, the leathery old scout motioned off Speed Stagner to the right flank, out of sight in the broken, vaulting land of arroyo and ridge top, to bring in anything to report from Big Bat's scouts continuing to push a mile or more to the east by north.

So they would not walk like the cavalry. The greatest bane of horse soldiers was to be asked to walk like those miserable foot-sloggers of the Fourth Infantry. Yet Seamus had heard few complaints from them, a hearty bunch for the most part. Seamus knew when it came down to the nut-cutting of this campaign, Crook had brought the infantry along to guard his wagons, the life-sustaining wagons, while the cavalry would be his spear and saber, jabbing and slashing at the enemy.

But the enemy knew Crook was coming.

In those broken moments of sunlight that poked through the clouds, the warriors talked across the distance with the mirror flashes. Just as they had that summer and into the fall and winter of 1866 along this same road. Occasionally, when the wind died as well during the day, there would be tall columns of distant smoke rising to speak to others unseen, signals off to the north and east. The land of the Tongue and the Powder.

But for now Crook kept them marching through country that grew increasingly more broken, rougher for the rumbling, noisy wagons to negotiate. Late that afternoon, they climbed a final ridge where Donegan was immediately struck with a sense of reliving real horror, a stark, heart-seizing terror that was calmed only when he laid eyes on the hoary peaks to his left, bared now as the clouds dropped lower along their white summits.

"That's the Crazy Woman," he told Clark.

"You been here." Clark made it a statement, as if there were no question of it as fact.

"Ten years ago," Seamus explained. "Almost ten. Come July."

From the narrow draw they were descending to reach the creek's crossing, Seamus pointed to the left, up the gentle slope of the windswept ridge. "Up there, Ben. For a whole bloody day—hundreds of 'em. The first I'd ever seen. Kept us buried down in rifle pits."

Clark stood in the stirrups, yanking his woolen muffler from his sharp-stitched face to holler back to Charlie Jennesse. "Inform the general we're making camp here for the night."

The half-breed nodded and wheeled away, back to the column, which looked like a many-jointed serpent wending its way through the yellow-white countryside.

"That all right with you, Irishman? Us making camp here for the night?"

With a shrug, Donegan's eyes went back to that bald knob of sagebrush and sand where he and the rest—some soldiers, a few civilians, and that lone young woman nursing her infant daughter through it all—held off the screaming, red-eyed horsemen . . . only by the grace of God and two repeating rifles. Along with the savvy of Jim Bridger, who showed up after dark had settled down like God's own benediction on that weary little band of holdouts.*

"No. No problem, Ben. I think after supper I'll make that climb up yonder." Seamus pointed.

"That where it was?"

He nodded now, once. "Buried more'n one good man here, Ben."

Clark sighed, stuffing his hand in his pocket for the amber jar which he again offered to Donegan. "Just don't get too far down in your thoughts when you go up yonder, Irishman. This place ain't your grave. Never was meant to be neither."

He clamped the glove in his teeth and tore it off his right hand, stuffing the horsehide mitt in an armpit before he swabbed a bare finger in the tallow, smearing his lips thankfully.

"Does a man ever know where his grave's gonna be?" he asked of Clark. "Does a man ever know?"

* The Plainsmen Series, vol. 1, *Sioux Dawn*

* * *

"The evidence is damned well plain enough that I—for one —am firmly convinced the enemy is at hand, gentlemen," Crook told them.

With his own personal double-barrel shotgun laid in the crook of his left arm, Captain Anson Mills stood listening to the general with the other officers who had gathered in a tight semicircle. Crook paced back and forth in front of his headquarters tent.

"Any one of you who hasn't seen the mirror signals flashing like heliographs from the hilltops . . . or those smoke signals they prefer under cloudy conditions—that man would have to be blind, and stupid as well, to know that we aren't closing in on the warrior camps."

Mills shifted his weight to the other foot. Both were just about as cold, numb really, as his feet had been all day through each of the twenty-seven miles up from the ruins at the Powder River as measured by the odometer mounted on the lead wagon. They had stopped here at the Crazy Woman Fork just past four P.M., made camp and started supper fires when Crook sent around word that at seven there would be an officers' meeting. Once again it was more than clear that the general was hardly leaving any of the leadership of this campaign up to Colonel Joseph Reynolds. Crook was in command, make no mistake of that.

"I'm sure that each of you realize that this country is growing rougher with every mile, and how that strain is showing on the wagon train." Crook turned to E. M. Coates. "Therefore, Major, in the morning after breakfast, you are to retrace our tracks back to Fort Reno."

"Sir?"

"From that time on, the train will be under your command, and under the protection of your two companies of infantry."

"Yes, sir."

"I have informed Dr. Munn, and his steward, along with Dr. Stevens, that they will be coming with us while Dr. Ridgely will accompany you back to Reno. He is caring for that herder who was wounded the other night. Ridgely tells me the man appears to be doing better. So, with your train and infantry, you are to establish a base camp at Fort Reno, entrench and fortify in the event of attack on your camp, then await our return," Crook went on to explain, a chestnut burr to his words.

"Ridgely is to make ready a field hospital for the casualties—in the event we encounter the enemy. Now, either we will rendezvous with you there after fifteen days, or I will send you word of where to meet us, and by what route. In that event, a scout will be sent to guide you."

"Fifteen days—yes, General," Major Coates repeated as Crook turned on his heel and strode away a few steps.

The cavalry will go on, Mills thought. Say farewell to our cork mattresses.

"I'm issuing light marching orders to the battalion commanders at this time,". Crook continued, turning back to the entire officers' assembly. "We'll bid farewell to Major Coates and his infantry in the morning, then use tomorrow to recoup the animals—and leave this camp ourselves at sundown for a night march."

"A night march, sir?" asked Henry E. Noyes of the Second Cavalry.

"Yes, Captain. As much as possible I want to elude the watchful eyes of the enemy's scouts. Under cover of darkness we will move after sending the wagons back."

"We hope to fool the enemy, confuse him at the least," Bourke explained.

For a moment Mills thought it strange that a lieutenant would be explaining the order of the march to this assembly. But then, Bourke was aide-de-camp to no ordinary general. Mills glanced at Reynolds, finding the colonel's eyes riveted to the ground, not daring to rise and meet the questioning glances of the rest of the command, especially those of his own Third Cavalry.

"I am sure you are all aware that dividing from the wagons will mean we'll have to travel lean, gentlemen. The clothes on your back, and no more. Company commanders have the duty of personally inspecting each man's baggage to see what might be left behind to lighten the load on these mounts."

Crook sighed a moment, looking quickly at the fire before he continued. "I figure all of you knew this time would come. Fifteen days of half-rations: hardtack, bacon and coffee. Sugar if you like. But we will not unnecessarily burden Mr. Moore's pack train with impedimenta, as I'm ordering Tom to have an extra hundred rounds of ammunition for each one of your men packed on his mules."

Mills didn't know what that meant, only that the final outcome of carrying extra ammunition would mean sleeping cold and eating far less. What they would eat at half-rations for the next two weeks would be standard army fare, and hardly much of that at all. Good-bye wagons, farewell cork mattresses, so long beans and biscuits and pork gravy.

Crook was getting serious about finding him a village, quick as he could, and striking it hard.

"Inform your companies that each man has his choice of bedding," Crook explained with iron in his voice. "A single buffalo robe or two blankets. I don't want to wear down our mounts over the next two weeks. They must be fit and ready when we call upon them for their utmost."

"The mules will carry our rations and extra ammunition?" asked Captain James Egan, better known among his fellow officers as Irish "Teddy."

"Yes. That and the extra forage. Moore has already set his packers to work, gentlemen. Twenty-six thousand pounds of that forage will be carried by the mule train from here on out. I don't want to depend a wit upon grazing in this frozen country. We must take what we need into that . . . that forbidding land."

Mills followed Crook's arm as it pointed north by east. "Sir, are we leaving all tents behind?" he asked.

Crook stepped behind the fire, then put both balled fists on his hips. "No tents."

There were a few groans, whispered comments from the crescent of officers.

"I'll suffer the cold as much as the next man," the general continued. "But I will allow each of your men to carry a shelter half, in the event of a driving storm pinning us down. And you officers—for every two of you—a tent fly can be taken along. Bunkie up, men. Like the old days! Bunkie up."

They laughed easily now, what with Crook smiling in that two-tailed beard of his. Even Reynolds tried to laugh, glancing at the officers of his Third Cavalry. But the old man's laughter came nowhere as easy as the rest.

"We're down to fighting trim, gentlemen," Crook emphasized. "The only way we can track these warriors and their scouting parties, with any hope of catching one of their villages, is to travel just as lean and fast as does our enemy."

"Sir, may I remind you to explain the mess arrangements?" John Bourke prodded his commanding officer.

"Yes, thank you, Lieutenant. Every one of you line officers will mess in with your troops, rotating from squad to squad, meal to meal. The rest of us," and now his eyes went to Reynolds and the colonel's staff officers, "we will eat with Mr. Moore's packers."

There were some groans and good-natured complaints about mule skinners.

"But, General—you staff officers are getting the long end of the stick in this, I must say," voiced Teddy Egan with good humor. "Everyone knows the packers are the best cooks on this frontier, while we line officers—well, sir— we're left eating with some fellas who can ruin even army food!"

They all laughed again, every one of them together. Egan could do that. Mills felt good for it too. That camaraderie, and the way some of them had laughed earlier that evening when they went down to the bank of the Crazy Woman. They had found the ice a foot thick, so had dared one another to slide their way across, poking fun at those who would not give the surface a try.

Yes, these men, these fellow officers who had for the most part served together on this fringe of the open wilderness, were ready for what the land and the enemy would hand them. And at this moment this officer corps seemed as if they were binding themselves one to the rest for these next fifteen days. Crook's horse soldiers would damn well carry the fight right to the warrior bands.

Nannie, pray for me. Pray for my safety, dear woman, he thought of a sudden as a cold gust of wind slashed through that officers' conference, stirring the fire and scattering sparks and coals along the ground.

Pray that we find them—and quick. Do what we marched here to do, and get back out . . . before this high, cold land claims my bones.

Chapter 14

7–12 March 1876

"Let's pray for bad weather, Bob," young lieutenant Bourke said as he rose to his saddle in the deepening twilight.

Bob Strahorn snorted as he stuffed a boot in his stirrup. "Ain't it cold enough for you, John?"

"Bad weather for the Indians, don't you see? The general hopes for cold and snow to keep the warriors in their village —not out hunting, or scouting for us."

"Bad weather, is it?" Strahorn repeated. "I'll be sure to say a lot of rosaries and a few more Hail Marys over some snow and cold on the general's account." He shivered involuntarily. "It's colder than the hubs of Hell with the axles frozen!"

Just as Crook had said they would, the cavalry bid farewell to the infantry and their wagon train as Major Coates set off to retrace their trail back to the ruins of Fort Reno. Meanwhile that cavalry camp beside the frozen Crazy Woman Fork had gone about repacking the mules, along with stripping down bedding and rations to the barest they would need for the next fifteen days. Around every fire the men had huddled, eating as much as they could, resting, then eating even more through that short winter day. Close to those fires was where a man wanted most to stay.

Although the snow had let up and the sun shone with a dazzling, eye-numbing brilliance throughout the seventh of March, requiring many of the men to wear their "Arizona goggles" to combat sunblindness, the cold never hinted at letting up.

Fact was, the temperature was preparing to drop even further still.

Just after sundown on that seventh day of March, in the inky throes of twilight, the stirring refrain of "Boots and Saddles" had been heard across the cavalry camp, followed quickly by the order to stand to horse. Minutes later, near seven P.M., when all was in order, the command to mount was given the five battalions.

Beneath the rising crescent of a three-quarter moon, the long column of fours crossed the icy creek and began to stretch out at a steady pace. It was not long, however, before the order was given to form a longer column of twos when the country grew even rougher, requiring steeper climbs and descents of both the mounts and pack mules as the command made their way across the frozen landscape toward the divide of the Clear Fork. More than anything else, Ben Clark's scouts were leading them by taking bearings on the heavens above—ever onward toward the North Star.

"Look at that, will you, Strahorn?" gasped John Bourke, who was twisted in his saddle, gazing down the undulating slope at the long column following behind them.

Bob Strahorn rode with the advance party, stirrup to stirrup on the climb beside the lieutenant. He turned now to look at the cavalry and pack train winding its way up the divide below the white-mantled magnificence of the Big Horn Mountains, the entire column dark and glittering against the moonlit snowpack.

"Looks like an enormous bull snake, doesn't it?" Bourke asked, his face aglow with more than the numbing cold.

"It does at that, John," Strahorn replied, struck with the aptness of the lieutenant's analogy.

"A snake whose scales are glittering revolvers and carbines," Bourke continued. "Its steamy breath escaping on its climb."

Above the wriggling column rose the frosty breath of man and laboring beast alike.

"You ought to think about writing, John. More than just your diary. You turn a phrase nicely."

Bourke smiled, still gazing back at the scene. "Others have told me the same thing, Bob. Perhaps, one day, I'll write a book about this campaign. At least about my adventures following the general across the West."

"I'll buy the first copy," Strahorn said, his teeth rattling like dice in a cup. "And we'll drink a toast to your success. Were that I could drink that toast right now."

"Warm the inner man?"

"Damn well warm the outer man," Strahorn replied, shivering with the gusts of chilling cold that swept down off the silent, frozen ice packs high in the Big Horns.

"Quiet in the ranks," growled a voice just ahead of them.

"Yes, General," Bourke replied sheepishly, flicking his eyes over at Strahorn like a schoolboy who had just been caught dipping pigtails in an inkwell at his desk.

"You civilians are under the same orders as my men, Mr. Strahorn."

"I understand, General Crook."

Strahorn snugged the wide wool muffler that wrapped both his ears and covered most of his face back over his nose. At least it was warm breathing and rebreathing in that way. He let himself slip back into thoughtlessness, nothing more taxing than sensing the easy sway of the horse beneath him as it picked its way up the rocky, uneven slope, then felt its way cautiously down the next slope. A rise and fall. Ever upward with the rise and fall, he imagined, like sailing the huge swells of green waves out on the ocean—never seeing your destination beyond the horizon. Just setting out.

The newsman had heard some of the officers talking late that afternoon in camp, discussing the hardships to be encountered with abandoning the wagons. But, to a man, those officers had admitted it had been only a matter of time for leaving the wagons behind when campaigning with George Crook. Already the general had given the men and mounts and mules a week to toughen to the trail, to harden to the cold, each day marching a little more than the last, pushing and prodding the column into this chase. And once that strength and endurance surpassed the capability of the infantry and the wagon train—it was time for the cavalry to strike out on its own.

They had halted only briefly during that night march of the seventh, pressing on into the morning of the eighth, and only that when a mule misfooted and stumbled over the lip of an icy ravine, breaking its back. The packers Moore sent over the side grumbled all the way down. Then a single pistol shot was heard to echo up from below on the damp, chilly air. The civilians cursed all the way back up with the panniers the hapless mule had been carrying. After redistributing that weight among four other animals, Crook's column was back on the march.

Upon reaching the banks of the Clear Fork of the Powder River just past four A.M., Crook ordered a halt. Cinches were to be loosened slightly, a minimum of pickets put out, and the rest of the men were allowed to collapse on the ground, to fall asleep as they could. After the thirty-mile night march they had just endured, fall asleep they did.

But for only on the order of four hours. Just past eight o'clock they were awakened by a pelting popcorn snow, icy pellets of misery and torture raining down on the countryside, whipped into a fury by a powerful wind out of the northwest. When Strahorn pulled back the canvas wrapper of his bedroll to look over the camp, he found the mess cooks struggling to keep their cookfires lit. When bacon, beans and coffee had no hope of being thawed, Crook finally grew disgusted enough to order the troops back into their retightened saddles.

They covered another five miles down the Clear Fork to the mouth of Piney Creek, where the general ordered another halt, Here, in the protection of a wooded copse of trees down in the lee of the wind, the cooks had their second chance to feed the command. The cavalry and packers had gone nearly twenty-four hours without food. And while the fires warmed the rock-solid bacon and beans, bringing coffee water to a boil after chopping through some eighteen inches of ice in the creek, some of the men tried to string blankets to the trees for shelter from the driving snow that continued to batter the high plains. Others attempted to construct shelters of branches and limbs. Crook and chief of scouts Stanton themselves found a cozy den along the creekbank, recently abandoned by a family of beaver. If blankets were available, orders were given to lash them over the mounts and the mules where they stood in picket lines down in the windbreaks along the icy stream, heads bowed and rumps turned to the north.

At a nearby fire, one of more energetic of the many Irish recruits was performing a bit of a jig for his mess mates, a dance that Strahorn realized was bound to keep a man warm if nothing else. And then the soldier stopped to regale his friends with his thick brogue and ready humor in the face of the swirling snow and the dropping temperatures come the return of twilight.

"Och, then by Jesus, sure for didn't I enlist in the Feet! Be once cowl! They have nothing to do but march with the wagons and march back home again. Sure the cavalry does be marching all the time! They takes us across the mountains all night, in a storm of snow, without a bite of grub, be God, and then General Crook will say, 'Now, boys—make yizselves comfartibble as yiz can—throw yizselves down on yer picket pins for a math-thress and cover yizselves with yer lar-rhiat ropes!'"

They laughed, one and all, soldiers and civilians, for it was true. They had marched all night without so much as a look at their rations, and when they halted there wasn't much for a man to roll himself up in to get out of the weather. Yet for all the good-natured fun, there was some real expression of profound respect for Crook too—for the man who had ordered the discomforts upon them was at this moment suffering that same overpowering hunger and soul-numbing cold as they.

"What do you keep looking for out there, Donegan?" asked Strahorn of the scout sitting near the same fire.

The Irishman turned, trying out something on the order of a smile. "I've been in this country before."

"I've heard you say that. Something special you're looking for?"

Donegan shrugged, turning back to squat at the fire, his mustache and much of his chin whiskers coated with icicles and hoarfrost. "Up the Piney—this creek here," and he pointed with his horsehide mitten quickly, "there's an old fort the army thought it wise to build some ten years back."

Strahorn gazed up the Piney toward the beckoning foot-hills of the Big Horns, the entire land mantled in glistening white as the setting sun rendered the land an iridescent rosy orange. "Fort Phil Kearny, was it?"

Donegan nodded.

"What did you think of Captain William Judd Fetterman?"

With a snort, the Irishman held a twig in the fire to light his pipe. "I think he was the sort that wanted to find the Sioux so bad he was bound to get himself and his men killed."

Strahorn studied the older man's face, the clear seams of experience and trackless trails to be read there already crow-footing from the eyes. "So, what do you think of General Crook?"

Donegan glanced up at the reporter, and held Strahorn's gaze. "I think Crook may want to find Crazy Horse pretty bad too."

"Bad enough to get himself and this bunch killed?"

"You never know, Bob. You just never know about a army commander—until it comes down to a fight of it."

They were back in the saddle before daylight on the ninth of March, working their way up that valley of the Piney, then pushed over the low divide to the headwaters of the Prairie Dog, a creek Frank Grouard had told seven of the scouts would feed into the Tongue River. The eight half-breeds had been sent ahead to feel their way down the Tongue, looking for sign.

It was there on the Prairie Dog, after a struggling march of only some twenty miles into the teeth of a driving, day-long snowstorm, that Crook ordered his cavalry into a sheltered ravine to camp. With Surgeon Munn reporting his thermometer reading of minus six degrees and dropping rapidly, the general called Captain Stanton and Ben Clark aside. Together they selected twenty of Clark's scouts to strike out and probe the countryside ahead, leaving when darkness fell to look over the trail north in hopes that the column would find the hostiles before the hostiles knew just where the army was.

"The scouts found some fresh buffalo droppings, Bob," explained John Bourke at their fire with some packers that evening of the ninth.

"Glory be, what I'd give for some fresh buffalo!" Strahorn cheered.

"More Injun sign too," Bourke added.

"That why he sent out the scouts, eh?"

Bourke nodded. "We've got to be getting close. The hostiles were watching us there for a time, and now we haven't seen sign of them for the past few days."

Strahorn laughed. "Shows they're smarter than we are, John. Glory be, but in this weather, no sane man should be out wandering up and down across this country! Tucked away at home I should be, with a whiskey in one hand and a good-smelling wench wrapped in the other!"

Descending the north-flowing Prairie Dog at sunup on the morning of the tenth, the command again marched over twenty miles face-on into the snowstorm that continued to batter the land, turning the trails icy and treacherous to even the sure-footed, mince-stepping mules. During the early afternoon, the mount ridden by a Third Cavalry corporal had slipped and fallen on the soldier, breaking some of the soldier's ribs.

Finally, four miles from where the Prairie Dog tumbles into the Tongue, the order to halt was given and bivouac was made for the night while Crook awaited the return of his scouts.

"But Grouard says the camp sign is old," Stanton argued as he threw the heavy blanket over his mount, which was already showing signs of serious trail wear, gaunt and worn-down from battling the temperatures and lack of graze.

"By damn, that has to be a fresh site," argued John Bourke.

"I figure that half-breed Grouard would know, Johnny boy," Stanton replied with a smile.

Bourke was getting his red worked up. "Stanton saw the place too—ten miles west of here it was, where Goose

Creek joins the Tongue. And Reshaw. Reshaw's a half-breed too. He ought to know as much as Grouard!"

"You don't trust Grouard, do you, John?"

"I suppose I do," Bourke replied after a moment of thought. "But that Reshaw doesn't. And it's for damned sure General Reynolds doesn't trust Grouard. The old man's told Crook, 'That lying snake of a half-breed nigger so much as steps a foot out of line—I'll drop him where he stands.' "

"Sounds like Reynolds has been listening to Reshaw gnash his teeth about Grouard."

"Nearly every day it seems," Bourke agreed. "There's blood in their eyes for each other."

"Plain enough to see there's bad blood there."

On Saturday morning, 11 March, a buttermilk-pale sun surprised the encampment with its appearance at the edge of a clearing sky that nonetheless left the morning even colder still than the last four had been. Still, it was the brightness that pewter sun gave to the virgin, snow-blanketed landscape that did much to raise troopers' spirits as most of the men again pulled on their green "Arizona goggles" to fight the brilliance of the shimmering snow before they climbed into the saddle to march down the Tongue. They were forced to cross and recross the twisting river with its steep-sided banks as many as eighteen times in a day's march, eventually forging their way across the border into Montana Territory. With each new dawn, Crook was constantly probing north and east with his scouts, sticking with the Tongue, where the general's cavalry camped out of the cruel wind on the nights of the eleventh and twelfth as the mercury plummeted all the more.

Ever since bidding the wagons farewell at the Crazy Woman Fork, Strahorn had been taking his mess with a group of Tom Moore's packers. Two of the oldest hands, veterans of Crook's Arizona campaigns, were the German-born Hans and his Irish comrade Pat—the best of friends and trail mates for more than a decade in the far West. Both shared a well-developed sense of humor that had allowed them to deal with what adversity a life outdoors could throw at a man. Fact was, on their first night north from Fort Fetterman, Hans had even gone so far to take a stick charred in the fire pit and used the charcoal "pencil" to boldly write across the canvas face of his personal knapsack the words: "To the Big Horn or Hell!"

That night of the twelfth found Crook's command camped where the Tongue had narrowed itself into a ribbon of gorge bounded on either side by multihued sandstone cliffs of ocher and yellow and bloodreds reaching a height of some two hundred feet. The wind seemed to funnel the cold right down on the cavalry's bivouac with a growing vengeance. Above that camp in the indigo sky the cold pricks of cheerless light swirled ever onward to the west as the men, troopers and packers, paired off to share their blankets and body warmth, feet to the fires they struggled to keep going.

After tugging against one another for more than two hours of bone-numbing misery, an endless nightmare of cold laced with a lot of colorful German and Irish invective, Hans and Pat growled in agreement that after years of their camaraderie they should part before matters of their struggles in the cold came to blows. That agreed, they divided their meager supply of wool blankets, then moved off some twenty paces in either direction, crustily bidding good riddance to the other. As each laid down on the creaking snow in plain view of one another, an amused Bob Strahorn closed his eyes once more to make another attempt at some fitful sleep.

Off and on across the next several hours, the newsman listened as Hans and Pat individually tossed and rolled, grumbled and cursed their lot, attempting to find some solitary warmth and comfort on the frozen ground beneath their skimpy allotment of two blankets.

"What you think's going on?" Bourke grumbled, without sticking his head out into the frosty cold. He and the reporter were bunkies for the campaign, sharing their blankets and body warmth.

Strahorn chuckled quietly. "I figure right about now they both are dwelling on how beautiful it is for brethren to dwell in unity together, especially when it is so unmercifully cold, Johnny!"

"So how long you figure are they going to keep the rest of us awake?" Bourke inquired quietly, his voice muffled down beneath the layers of wool.

"Until one of 'em can grin and bear it no longer, I'll wager."

Strahorn was just finding himself warm enough to doze off again after checking his pocket watch beneath the star-shine, finding it approaching two A.M., when he was aroused by the loudest grunts of the night and the most profane declarations. Pulling back the folds of his blankets from his eyes to peer about, the newsman watched both Hans and Pat sit upright as if on cue, then without a word clamber clumsily to their feet as if the two were but one man. When the packers met on common ground once more, Hans threw down his two blankets upon the frozen soil. Both stretched out on them, whereupon Pat carefully pulled his offering of two blankets over them both.

Back to back, and back together, the two old comrades sighed audibly.

Strahorn pulled the edge of the blankets over his face once more, thankful that their spat had been resolved so that he could once more try for a little sleep. But as he was again making a warm spot for his cheek, he heard the two friends talking in their own muted tones.

"Hans?"

"Vat?"

"It's damned cold, ain't it?"

There came a short pause before Hans said, "Pat?"

"What?"

"Ve been damn't fools, h'ain't we?"

The two trail veterans had a good laugh together before the packers' camp fell quiet once more while the constellations continued to slowly spin across the blackened heavens toward the western horizon.

In the morning, at their breakfast fire, Strahorn watched Hans charring the end of a cottonwood limb to make himself a new "pencil." With it the packer crudely scratched out his old declaration: "To the Big Horn or Hell!"

Then beneath it in big letters he inscribed the words: "Hell Froze Over!"

Chapter 15

13–15 March 1876

*A*t dawn on the thirteenth, another cloudy, gloomy day with a low sky threatening to blanket the land with snow once more, Grouard and some of the scouts were sent north with Crook's order to make a long foray in the direction of the Yellowstone, instructed to rendezvous with the column in two days farther down the Tongue.

Shuddering unconsciously inside his buffalo-hide coat, John Bourke pulled the furry collar up against his wind-chaffed cheek, watching the scouts disappear among the hills to the north as the battalions issued their orders of the march for the day and bellowed their commands to stand to horse as Tom Moore's packers brought their mule train into formation along the east riverbank.

"Lieutenant!"

Bourke turned to find one of Moore's five civilian crew chiefs trotting up to him, his heavy bearskin coat flapping against his calf-high boots. It was Richard "Uncle Dick" Closter, a veteran of Crook's campaigns in Apacheria. His face tanned the color of an old leather valise, as seamed as the prairie itself with the tracks and trails of his thirty years in the West, Closter lumbered to a halt beside Bourke's mount. He spat a stream of brown juice onto the trampled, icy ground at his feet, some of the syrup bleeding another dark lace of brown in the snow-white beard that spilled to the middle of his chest.

"You need anything, Johnny—you come back in column and find me now."

Those eyes, how they sparkle in this cold, Bourke thought as he peered into their clear, icy blue beneath that oversized muskrat hat the old man wore. He patted the mittened hand that Closter had laid upon Bourke's reins. "Don't figure I'll need a thing till we get to camp tonight and I can do with some more of your stories over our supper fire, Uncle Dick."

"General's had us on half-rations from the Crazy Woman, Johnny," the old man said without a hint of complaint. "But we'll feast on what we got us to et!"

With a broad smile that showed two missing teeth he himself had yanked out years before when they had grown troublesome, Closter patted Bourke's leg paternally before he waved and was off again at a lumbering trot, heaving back to his station in the column, cheerfully calling out orders to his dozen packers as he went.

By late morning the command crossed to the west bank of the Tongue, continuing its march north across the broken, rugged country of southern Montana Territory. With each new erosion scar to be crossed on their trail, those sharp-sided coulees and arroyos where, come spring, the rains would begin as a trickle and gather into a torrential flood, the mules and horses had to negotiate down one icy slope and up the frozen next. It had never ceased to amaze Bourke, as many miles and coulees as they put behind them on this march from Fetterman, how the mules adapted to making each descent with their three-hundred-pound packs strapped to the sawbucks cinched around their bellies.

As the lead mule approached the edge of a coulee, the jack or jenny would stop momentarily as the animal shifted its hind feet more closely together, slowly settled to its hind flanks, then slid all the way to the bottom with its fore legs stiffened, thereby keeping its load from shifting. As each mule in turn reached the bottom, the packers brought the next animal to the lip of the coulee, where that mule executed its snowy slide to the bottom. On and on it went at every coulee and arroyo, with each mule in turn making its descent, some with more alacrity than others, some with far more grace.

That difference not only in temperament of the mules,

but in their native savvy to negotiate the difficulties of the trail, had over the last two weeks increasingly led the packers to boast and brag on their favorites, until that subfreezing afternoon of the thirteenth.

Bourke had reined back to the rear of the long column to ride for a few hours with Uncle Dick Closter. Yet now, as the heated intensity of the roughened voices clearly grew in volume, the lieutenant urged his weary mount forward into a trot. He reached the edge of the coulee where the march had halted, mules waiting with their heads hung in weariness as frost rose in steamy wreaths around their pointed ears. More than two dozen of Moore's packers stood milling, shouldering in on one another in a semicircle. And at the middle stood two more of the civilians, cheered on by the gathering as they pummeled one another, stumbling and falling on the icy ground, clutching clumsily at each other's heavy coats, swearing and spitting in their opponent's eye when the chance presented itself.

Dismounting as best he could, Bourke struggled forward on his numbed, creaking legs, stabbing a path for himself through the surging crowd, finding that the last mule to descend the coulee was now on the far side and about to disappear around a twist in the trail. If General Crook found out the line of march was being delayed, there'd be hell to pay in baskets.

"What the devil is going on?" Bourke demanded as he thrust himself right into the impromptu ring.

One of the combatants lurched forward, tearing open his blanket-lined, canvas-wrapped Saint Paul coat, and yanked out a long skinning knife.

"I'll cut your heart out!"

Bourke swung at the packer, catching the civilian's arm. He barked his orders to the rest. "Grab that one! Someone help me hold this one!"

With some grumbling that the lieutenant had spoiled their frolic and likely a good-natured blood-letting, the packers obeyed, firmly separating the two contestants.

"All right," Bourke gasped, ripping the long knife from the dark-skinned packer. "I asked what's going on. Now before I turn you both over to Moore for a horse-whipping, someone tell me!"

The ruddy-skinned packer restrained by the others spat out an oath and swore, "Gimme the chance to carve up that greaser good, Lieutenant. Better me than some Sioux doing it for me!"

"I'll make a coin purse from your ball bag, gringo!"

"Hold them! Hold 'em dammit!" Bourke demanded again. "How'd this start?"

"The mules, Lieutenant," another packer began to explain. "They been at each other for the past three, maybe four days."

"That's right," agreed a new voice. "It was bound to happen."

"What was bound to happen?" Bourke asked.

"The betting."

He was just as confused as when he had loped up to the whole affair. "Betting on what?"

A new packer stepped forward, motioning toward the sharp lip of the icy slope. "On just whose mule makes the prettiest slide going down."

Bourke shook his head in amused frustration. "You fellas mean . . . mean to tell me you were going to carve each other up into bloody pieces over the way your mules slide down the side of this coulee?"

The white packer nodded. "And how my Keno climbs back up the far side."

"My Pinto Jim makes Keno look like burro dung!" the Mexican packer growled.

"You puny sun-grinner! I'll see you in Hell!"

"Hold him!" Bourke shouted again as the white packer lunged for his brown-skinned opponent. "So, you figured you'd fight it out. Just the two of you, eh?"

They both nodded. There was a stillness falling among the rest, along with some growing curiosity, as Bourke strode to the edge of the icy ravine and peered over.

"A pretty bad drop, this one," the lieutenant pronounced. He came back to stand between the two combatants and their holders. "Can't believe you two going to cut into one another, when you should just let Keno and Pinto Jim duel it out themselves."

"What you mean, the mules duel it out?" demanded the white packer.

Bourke's wide face and broad forehead seemed to indicate to the civilians the breadth of his unruly fair-mindedness. "It's those mules you two are fighting over—so let the damned mules show us which one is best."

"How we do that?" asked the Mexican suspiciously. "Pinto Jim show he's the best, no doubt."

"He's trail fodder!" the white packer snarled. "Keno is king of the slide."

"Gentlemen!" Bourke held his arms to silence the surging mob. "We all will be the judge." He swept an arm in an arc to indicate the civilians gathered there. "We'll watch each of you take your favored mule down, then up the far side. That's when we'll vote. The mule wins that has the most votes in this democracy."

Most cheered at Bourke's solution to the impasse.

"I'm game as a gouty rooster! Let's slide!" declared the ruddy-faced packer.

"All right." Bourke turned to the Mexican, handing the man back his skinning knife. "You, with Pinto Jim—you're first."

With it tucked back in his sheath, the packer stepped through the parting crowd to Pinto Jim, the mule he stroked and cooed to, then led to the edge of the coulee. Without hesitation the animal cocked its rear legs together, settled on its haunches, and slid to the bottom where, without a misstep, it dug in with its tiny hooves and climbed up the far side, followed by its Mexican handler. On the north bank of the coulee the swarthy packer raised his arms in the air, prompting a raucous cheer from the audience on the south side.

"Your turn—with Keno," Bourke instructed, without joining in the celebration.

"Awww, mule marbles—that Pinto Jim's not worth a red piss!" grumbled the white packer good-naturedly.

He led his animal to the edge of the coulee, stroked an ear and eased the mule over the side as it settled on its rump for the ride down. But at the bottom, instead of striding right for the far side, Keno raised his tail to deposit a steamy heap on the trampled snow before he trotted skillfully up the north lip.

The packers went wild before Bourke could call for a vote, every man of them jumping and cheering, slapping one another on their backs, throwing hats of wolfskin and muskrat in the air. On the far side, the Mexican packer stood wagging his head as he offered his hand down to his white comrade to help the man up to level ground.

"You win, my friend!" the Mexican shouted so that those on the south lip could hear it on the dry, cold air. "Pinto Jim slides much prettier. But this one, your Keno, is clearly the master when he reaches the bottom!"

"Ain't that the goddamned truth?" roared the white packer. "I figure he told us what he thinks of this bloody cold march, didn't he?"

The civilians were still laughing and pounding one another on the back as Bourke broke them up and got the column moving once more, tramping past Keno's steamy deposit at the bottom of the coulee, continuing their march north. From time to time throughout the rest of the day the civilians regaled themselves with the minutest detail of that squabble and its eventual contest, until late in the afternoon Ben Clark located a spot to camp out of the wind down in some timber along a flat on the west bank of the Tongue.

As Uncle Dick cheerfully busied himself over the cookfire that twilight, Bourke settled back against a pile of packs and *apishamores,* the leather and canvas covers for the pack saddles. He laid out his leather-bound journal so that he could seize the fire's glow on the pages, and began transcribing that day's events to record, as he did each evening. While he was starting to commit the duel between Keno and Pinto Jim to posterity with his pencil clamped tightly in his numbed fingers, Closter hurried over to make the lieutenant more comfortable, piling up a windbreak for his friend from the *aparejos*—saddle pads used beneath the mules' wooden pack frames.

"There, Johnny—now you can stay warm while you write in your book."

"You are something incredible, Uncle Dick," Bourke said as Closter squatted once more at the cookfire and returned to stirring the pot of beans he was cooking.

"You're always writing in your book, Johnny. Every night."

"Every night," Bourke replied, putting his pencil back to work. "Maybe one day I'll make my journal into a real book, Dick."

A long and thoughtful moment later the lieutenant was struck with the wistful sound apparent in the old man's voice as the packer said, "Johnny, I ain't never seen my name writ on nothing but a muster page. Never seen it writ in a book, not proper like that."

Bourke looked up, a smile creasing on his frozen cheeks. "Why, what do you mean?"

"You think you could put me in your book? Put my name right there in your book when you write it, Johnny?"

Bourke's heart leapt at the request. He hurriedly stuck the pencil over his ear beneath the lip of his muskrat hat and flipped back two pages in the journal. "C'mere, Dick. Want you to see something."

Closter hobbled over, his huge iron ladle dripping bean juice on the snow as he came to a stop at Bourke's shoulder. He was smiling like all of sunshine poured forth from his face, the back of one hand stroking his long, tobacco-stained beard.

"Where, Johnny?"

"Right here," Bourke said, pointing with a cold finger to the spot on the page. "That's your name . . . there, and there too. See for yourself."

"It . . . it certainly do look like my letters, by God!" Closter exclaimed. "By cracky—you did put me in your book."

"I wrote about you a lot."

"A lot?"

Bourke nodded. "Yes. All sorts of things you've taught me—not only on this campaign, but down in Arizona too."

With wonder and admiration, as much as deep appreciation, in his blue eyes, Closter stared at the young lieutenant incredulously for a moment, then made his way back to the cookfire, where he squatted among several other packers preparing supper for their mess mates.

"Me and the cap'n there, Johnny Bourke," he began to tell his fellows, pointing the ladle at the lieutenant, "we're getting together a book about the Injuns and most everything on the West, for sure."

The young officer felt warmed inside once more by the friendship he treasured sharing with the old man who had taken a young soldier under his wing and was teaching him most of everything John Bourke would ever know about survival in the wilds of Arizona, or high up on the northern plains.

Later that evening after supper, in a ritual practice every night of this campaign, Closter scraped the snow from a piece of ground several yards from the cookfire, moving the burning limbs to the new spot. That done and their fire banked for the night, the old packer shoveled a thin layer of dirt over the glowing coals he had left behind. Upon that warm, dry spot, Uncle Dick and the other packers spread their canvas bedroll wrappers and quickly laid out the blankets.

"Your bed's ready, Johnny," Closter announced. "Time you and Strahorn pack it in for the night."

Bourke settled in his blankets beside the reporter, watching the old man move about here and there around the night fire, assuring that many of the others would have sufficient warmth across the coming hours before he himself squirmed down into his own buffalo robe with another packer.

"Thank you, Uncle Dick."

"T'weren't nothing, Johnny," Closter said from his bedroll. "Nothing I wouldn't do for the young'un gonna make my name famous."

Bourke closed his eyes, vowing that he would indeed write his book one day, and that the kindnesses shown him by that old white-bearded packer would be known to thousands, perhaps millions of readers who would not otherwise ever have any idea of the struggles endured by the army and its civilian employees, men who obeyed and marched across the face of a trackless wilderness with little complaint, even as winter was squeezing its mighty paw down upon this land with a cruel vengeance.

After a difficult, laborious march of only ten miles on the fourteenth, the deepening cold was such that camp was made at the mouth of Pumpkin Creek, called Red Clay Creek by the Sioux. Without the stars to come out beneath the gray, slattish cloudbanks, and only a watery-pale moon rising low along the southern horizon behind the swollen snowheads, winter's early twilight was crowding the light right out of the eastern sky. The men hurried into their blankets and robes, afraid of another storm born of the northwest.

Those same leaden clouds persisted, suspended low over their camp, the morning of the fifteenth. Yet spirits were raised when the troops were informed Crook had ordered a day of rest, here to await the return of Grouard's scout to the north.

"The general's losing his patience, Bob," John Bourke said quietly as he knelt beside the newsman at that fire Closter and other packers fed throughout that Wednesday.

"Don't blame him," Strahorn replied, pulling the coffee-pot off the flames to pour the lieutenant a cup. "You seen Donegan lately? Or did he go with Grouard?"

Bourke nodded, staring into the flames. "I think the half-breed wanted all the white men along, the ones he could count on. Grouard doesn't trust some of those other half-breeds."

"Bad blood coming," Strahorn said quietly, watching the steam rise from the coffee he poured for Bourke. "Yeah, I agree. Crook appears he's growing anxious. Wants to find the enemy and fast, doesn't he?"

"Don't you?" Bourke blew on his coffee and sipped quickly. "We been out almost a week already and haven't run across anything promising in the way of sign."

"Days back I told you to believe in Grouard—when he tells you a campsite is old, it's old," Strahorn reminded his friend. "Not an oily character like that Reshaw."

Bourke shrugged. "I suppose Reshaw is all full of brag and now ballast."

"Best watch that one, Johnny. Having anything to do with him is like sticking your hand down a gunnysack full of diamondbacks."

"Reshaw puts your hackles up, don't he, Bob?"

He nodded. "With all that talk about old sign, Donegan agreed with Grouard too. So did Ben Clark and Speed Stagner. Charlie Jennesse too. Looks more and more to me like Reshaw really wants to see Grouard cut off at the knees, any way he can."

"He's done a good job of that with Reynolds already." The lieutenant sipped at his coffee a moment, warming his face over his steaming cup before he spoke again. "The colonel's made it clear he'll never turn his back on Grouard."

"Like I said, that buffalo wolf of a half-breed Reshaw has poisoned Reynolds's heart."

There arose some excitement on the far side of camp, downstream, to the north. The ripple of it spread across the army's flat campground there on the west bank of the Tongue as the news spread. Bourke rose stiffly beside the fire with Strahorn, cups in hand, watching for some sign as to the cause and origin of that widening ripple of noise.

The lieutenant turned and looked at the newsman. "Bob, looks like Grouard's back."

Strahorn raised his cup in salute. "Let's pray he and the Irishman brought some news of just where Crook can find the hostiles."

Chapter 16

16 March 1876

*T*he tea not only warmed her hands as she cradled the cup within her palms, the fragrant steam rising from the surface warmed her face. As she drank, Samantha remembered winter days back in Indiana. Bitterly cold winter days, and breakfast in the kitchen with her sister Rebecca, before they would be bundled off to school in the wagon with papa.

How she yearned to be with Seamus now. No matter the cold where he was. No matter the wilderness where he was. How she wanted him with her now, with an ache that had become physical, like something opening up in her a little more every day. And Samantha was afraid if she didn't fill it with him soon, she might never get that wound closed back again.

Samantha so wanted to confide in Lucy Maynadier.

The colonel's wife was a good woman: she knew how to be friendly and hospitable to her guests, but as well how to keep her distance at times. Probably from her years of living on the edge of this wilderness, Samantha thought. Here, halfway between nowhere and beyond again. Year after year of watching folks come and go as easy as you please, traipsing in and out of your life—that would surely make a person learn to back off and give folks lots of room. No sense getting attached when they're bound to just up and go on you.

"That's unfair of you," Samantha scolded herself, whispering into her cup, then sipped at the tea again.

"What, dear?" asked Mrs. Maynadier.

"Nothing, Lucy. Just chattering to myself again."

"Your color is better today. You've been feeling pretty peaked this past week, haven't you?"

Samantha only nodded. Not wanting to admit how her stomach revolted every morning, afraid to say anything about how she came near filling her chamber pot before daring to venture down for coffee, most usually some weak tea, with Lucy. A'times they would be joined by some of the other officers' wives, catching up on this fragment of gossip, or that new dress pattern, or sharing the latest stories in the women's magazines that arrived so infrequently from the East.

Her stomach so sensitive to just about everything she ate or drank, it angered her. She did not want to be soft, unable to stand anything dished out to her. But the warmth of the tea this morning felt good in her stomach's rumbling emptiness.

Dear Lord, how she wished she had Rebecca to ask, frightened as she was with facing this alone right now. But then—Samantha remembered—Becky had never had any children, couldn't have children. Or maybe it was Sharp. One way or the other, her older sister wouldn't really know what to do, what advice to offer, nothing but sympathy. No, she would have to walk through this dark valley on her own.

Even Lucy was childless. Maybe some folks out here made that decision, consciously. Truly, this was not the place for someone sane to want to bring up a daughter. Even a son. She closed her eyes a moment, trying once more to conjure up that vision of the child—the same vision that returned each night to flit quiet as cottonwood down through her dreams.

Just a vision of an infant in a long christening gown, its head crowned with short and very dark and extremely curly hair. Cheeks touched with a blush of crimson—but none of that clue enough as to the sex of the new life blossoming within her belly at this moment.

Samantha felt more hope than anything else as she absently rubbed her abdomen, sipping at the tea.

Maybe in its own way this vision and her concentration on it was a prayer that Seamus would come home safe.

She shuddered now, remembering that try as she might in those dreams of the child, how she watched herself carrying it to the front of the little Jonesboro church where Rebecca and Sharp and all their friends down in Texas had gathered in one loving community of the heart . . . there was yet one person noticeably missing from the dream. In the dream, no one stood at her side where Seamus should be, watching that placing of hands and that blessing of the water with the power of the dear Lord's love.

"Dear God, Samantha!" Lucy exclaimed, setting her needlepoint aside and leaning over to lay a hand on Samantha's knee. "Whatever is the—"

But instead of answering, the young woman spilled her half-filled cup of tea as she vaulted out of her ladderback rocker, lurching across the tiny room for the door that would take her up the narrow stairs to the attic room where she could cry alone.

And Samantha knew she was going to throw up Lucy's tea before she got halfway there.

"They're east of here, General," Seamus Donegan had told Crook.

At first the soldier appeared to disbelieve when Grouard told him.

When the scouts returned to the cavalry camp about four o'clock on the afternoon of the fifteenth, bringing with them a half-dozen deer they had shot along their backtrail, they immediately reported their disappointing news to a clearly unhappy general.

"You rode all the way to the goddamned Yellowstone?" Crook roared. "And still didn't find sign of Crazy Horse? Nothing?"

From the corner of his eye Seamus watched Grouard shake his head. Most of the rest would not even look Crook in the eye. Afraid of those icy, pale eyes. But Grouard did not cower. Donegan admired that in the stocky half-breed, as weathered and dark-skinned as a square of trade plug.

Seamus admitted it, "We didn't get to that far, General."

Immediately Crook tore his eyes off the bare-faced Grouard and strode up before the Irishman. "Did I hear you right, mister? I sent you to probe all the way to the Yellowstone, and you didn't do as you were ordered?"

Donegan sighed. "That's a march something on the order of a hundred fifty miles."

"I was under the impression is was closer to fifty miles," Crook said, his voice expressing less of an edge.

"No, General. That's a long ride in country like this, icy the way it is." Donegan glanced now at the shorter half-breed standing near Clark on the far side of Crook, a smirk on his lips for Grouard—the look on the youth's face black as the belly of coming thunder.

Seamus continued, "For the last two days you've had Reshaw there working the Rosebud country to the west—and you just told us he's come up with no sign at all. So, after Grouard and me didn't find any recent campsites for more than a day's ride up the Tongue, for better than thirty miles, the whole bunch of us came to the same conclusion: the hostiles are east of here."

"You've told me that."

Seamus could see the testiness rise in the man like marrow scum rise in blood soup. Worse still, Crook's patience was plainly growing thin as scraped rawhide, and no man would place money on how much longer the general could be patient.

And no one could blame him. From the moment they had marched away from Fort Fetterman, after all, the column realized it was under almost constant observation by the hostiles. But while the soldiers had seen mirror flashes and smoke signals, and a growing number of travois trails cutting the snow on both sides of the river—for the most part it appeared the Indians were successfully eluding Crook's winter cavalry. Enough to curdle the milk in a fighting man's craw.

And now this outfit had been out in light marching order, suffering the bitter cold for more than a week, with nothing to show for the miles they had put behind them. Nothing to show—except for those two abandoned village sites Seamus and the rest had come across a couple days back.

Both camps pretty old, pocked with the blackened scars of old fire pits and litter of bones, spindly racks used for drying meat, circles of pegs used in staking out a hide to be worked by the women. Buffalo had even been spotted by the scouts every day—this was good country for hunting meat and hides. In those old campsites, even cottonwood still lay stacked by the cord, evidence that the warriors had been peeling the bark to feed their winter-gaunt ponies.

In the first of the two, Frank Grouard had found a young mule still tied in the deserted village, abandoned. As well as a young puppy, strangled and hanging from a tree.

"Sioux delicacy?" Donegan had asked.

Grouard had shaken his head. "No. Not particular. Cheyenne like puppy stew better."

"That mule and the puppy they were fixing for dinner seems to say the Injins left in a hurry, don't it, Frank?"

"Camp's old. They been gone a long time."

"You mean we didn't flush them," Donegan inquired.

"Right. They didn't leave afraid of us."

And in that second campsite they had run across, Donegan had called the rest over to examine what he found: the frozen arm of an Indian. Missing two fingers and riddled up to the elbow by buckshot likely fired from one of the old smoothbore muzzle loaders, the arm had been hacked from a body nowhere to be found.

Grouard guessed it had been a pony-stealing Sparrow Hawk warrior the Sioux had caught, tortured and dismembered. Could only be the Crow, angry that the Sioux were hunting in what had once been Absaroka hunting ground.

"I want you to understand why we're saying it, General," Seamus explained. "Reshaw coming back empty-handed from the Rosebud confirms our hunch."

"Reshaw thinks you're full of air, Grouard," Crook said, looking from the Irishman to the dark half-breed.

His eyes puckering into a cold scrutiny, Grouard stared over the general's shoulder to where Louie Reshaw sat across his horse, wrists crossed on his saddle horn. Donegan knew the two were like some men became to one another, poison that might one day end up killing one, or the other.

Grouard looked back at Crook. "Where Reshaw say you find the villages?"

Crook turned slightly, throwing an arm in the general direction. "Back to the west. Along the Little Horn."

"The Little Horn?" Seamus snorted. "Reshaw didn't come up with any sign on the Rosebud, what makes him think they're farther west, over on the Little Horn? That's really Crow country there."

"Reshaw says the Sioux been raiding the Crows lately. Figures that's where he thinks Crazy Horse's band would go."

"Not to winter," Grouard grumbled.

"What'd you say, Grouard?" Crook demanded sharply, whirling on the half-breed.

"He said just what I was fixing to tell you myself, General," Donegan said firmly. "The Sioux ain't out to raid and steal horses in this kind of weather. They're interested in moving back to their own country, their own hunting ground, until green-up. Then they'll start thinking about ponies, and scalps."

Crook seemed to regard Reshaw for a long moment, staring at the half-breed sitting slack in the saddle on his army mount, his dark face an impassive reflection, entirely void of emotion.

"Why east?" the general asked.

"Those of us with Grouard sat down and decided to come on back and tell you what we figure on before we wasted time going all the way to the Yellowstone. You need to look east of here."

"You sure they're not downstream of here on the Tongue —near the Yellowstone?"

With a shake of his head he answered, "Not downstream neither." The Irishman pointed toward the hills to the southeast. "There, General. Up there: no fresh trails, no signs of villages west and north. Everything, even the game trails—all heading east. The hostiles were flushing everything before them as they pushed over into the next valley."

Crook turned to look in that direction himself now. East. He eventually said it quietly, "Powder River country."

With everything he had been told, with his own hunches

all churning in his mind like a plowshare turning over a curl
of fresh, dark sod, Crook had given the order to his officer
corps that they would remain in camp that night of the
fifteenth, resting the men and horses once more. But he
had them aroused from their bedrolls at five A.M., eating
breakfast in the dark and back in the saddle by eight
o'clock. The cooks had had to chop the frozen bacon with
their camp axes, grumbling that the bacon was so hard it
chipped the brittle edges of their hatchets. Unless a man
guzzled down his coffee, it grew cold on him in his tin cup.
Forks, spoons and knives had to be warmed in the ashes of
the cookfires before a man could put them to use. Otherwise, the frozen metal would rip the flesh from a soldier's
tongue or the inside of his cheek. The same care was shown
by the troopers when saddling their horses. No man went
without warming a bit before slipping into a horse's mouth.

Surgeon and steward alike moved among the companies
as they had every morning in the predawn dark, checking
on the men over breakfast, searching for any new cases of
frostbite the battalion commanders had to report. Their
concern was more than real this morning. Beneath the clear
night sky of the fifteenth, the temperature had dropped
well below minus thirty-nine degrees. Upon arising, Dr.
Munn discovered that the mercury had congealed in a solid
button at the bottom of his bulb thermometer.

It would not begin to rise for many days yet to come.

But no one really had to tell Seamus Donegan it was
cold, and getting colder as the day progressed. He envied
the horses and their winter coats like bunched wool, while
time stiffened and poured like cold molasses.

Grouard and Big Bat led the column up the narrow valley of Pumpkin Creek, while Louie Reshaw and Speed
Stagner were put in charge of the scouts riding the right
and left flanks away from the main line of march as the
column climbed the divide that would take them now toward Otter Creek, a small stream that eventually flowed
into the Tongue farther to the north.

Everywhere Donegan looked, constantly moving his
eyes, the endless, vaulted land shimmered beneath the winter sun. He had resisted the green, slit-eyed goggles worn

by the soldiers, preferring instead to rub a mixture of grease and charcoal beneath his eyes to cut down the sun's painful glare. The landscape wavered more and more as they put mile after mile behind them, leading Crook's troops south by east up the low divide marked by stunted cedar and bunchgrass and gray-bellied sage. Endless monotony of a land rarely broken up by real color.

Even the first-growth pine and braided cedar stood almost colorless, the hue of dark, rich maple syrup on the bare, buzzard-bone ridges and knobby sandstone outcrops dressed in bridal white.

The sun had eased over into the western sky behind a new gathering of storm clouds as gray-gilled as death itself along the horizon. Around them stood the rocky outcrops of ocher and bloodstone that cast shadows on the snow like separate beings themselves. Upon reaching the west slope of the ridge that would take them down into the valley of Otter Creek, Frank Grouard reined up. Donegan drew alongside him.

"We wait for Clark. And the general."

Seamus nodded. Grouard had never been a man to talk a blue streak. There was a reason for his wanting to wait, Donegan figured as he watched the half-breed's eyes, moving like restless beads surrounded by turkey-track wrinkles spread like eroded gullies running down into the coffee-brown riverbeds of the scout's broad face.

There they sat for the next few minutes, watching their backtrail and the long, dark snake climbing up from Pumpkin Creek, horses and mules struggling up the icy, snow-crusted slope, spread out for more than a ragged mile through the ravines and sharp-lipped arroyos and crumbling coulees, their yellow-tinged strata striped with layers of white.

"Something to show us, Frank?" asked Ben Clark as he came to a halt with Crook, their horses' chests heaving, frost rising like thickened, steaming halos in that tight circle of horsemen.

Grouard shrugged. "Blow the horses, maybe." Then he pointed up the ridge of white, etched here and there with darker colors of gray and green bordering the water courses. Alders appeared like blackish-brown veins in the afternoon light, the hue of blood long ago dried. "Cow Creek on other side of divide, there. Flows into Otter Creek. Here on out, we will find sign of Crazy Horse. Much sign of the villages from here on out."

"Go find that sign for us, Grouard," Crook said, sweeping one tail of his long beard across the front of his wool coat.

Seamus watched Grouard lick his swollen, cracked and bloody lips. The half-breed seemed the kind who tasted his words before he gave them voice.

"Keep the scouts back," the half-breed told the general with deadly seriousness. "We get close, I need room to work in on them. Keep scouts back."

"You do your job, Grouard, I'll do mine. And giving orders is my job," Crook said evenly, a polished, honed steel in every word.

The half-breed turned without any more talk, nodding for Donegan to follow as he urged his army mount down toward Cow Creek, down into the valley of the Otter.

The pair moved quickly through the broken country, twice as fast as Crook's column could, even though the load on the mules had been getting lighter and lighter, which meant Tom Moore's train could now keep up with the cavalry without difficulty. Seamus figured the general had this cavalry outfit down to its leanest of fighting trim now, and was ready to do battle.

If only the enemy would cooperate, and tarry long enough for Crook to catch up.

Having ridden southeast just below the crest of the ridge, Grouard signaled a halt. He dropped to the ankle-deep snow crusted with a layer of wind-driven ice, and tied off his mount to some stunted cedar beside Donegan's. The Irishman joined him on the grunting climb those last few yards to the top of the ridge.

There, they dropped on their bellies and crawfished to the crest, quiet as spiders making silk. Both peered over, hanging well against some junipers. For several minutes as their breathing became more relaxed after the cold, difficult climb, both men moved their eyes over the down country, carefully studying everything with their looking glasses.

From the sign below in the creek valley, Donegan could see that herds of elk and deer had been cramped down in this valley when the first of the storms and cold had hit this country. Not only was the earth hoof-scarred and chewed where it was blown free of snow down along the creekbank, but the tree bark showed how close the animals had come to starvation before they had been forced out of the valley. Driven east by something, or someone—moving the game before them in a wide fan.

Grouard tapped the Irishman with his buffalo moccasin. He pointed to the north, up the creek a handful of miles.

Donegan nodded, blinking to clear his eyes so he could better see through his looking glass. Dark objects, two of them, inching across the landscape, slowly winding in and out of the stunted vegetation on horseback, in no apparent hurry, stopping here and there as if stalking a game trail. The pair was headed in their direction.

Seamus gazed over his shoulder at the milky sun behind the high, leaden clouds. It was past the middle of the afternoon.

"I better go warn the column," he said in a whisper.

Grouard held him with a firm hand. "No. They are far behind. We come far. Those warriors will be gone in time soldiers get here. No danger they see us."

So they waited, and watched the two distant forms inching closer and closer with every passing heartbeat. They were horsemen, later clearly becoming warriors wrapped in blankets, their long, unbound hair tormented by the cold wind. The pair drew almost opposite the two scouts on the far side of Cow Creek when they suddenly stopped and appeared to look directly at the clump of juniper where Grouard and Donegan lay in the snow. There the two sat their ponies, staring, as immobile as marble statues in the city park of Boston Towne.

Seamus put his mittens over his mouth to hide the frosty breath smoke his lungs betrayed. But the cold knot in his belly told the Irishman they had been discovered.

Of a sudden that next moment the horsemen whipped

their ponies into a small stand of stunted pines several yards ahead of them, where they too dismounted and crept to the brow of the hill, cautiously peering back to the west side of the valley.

"You think they see us?" Grouard asked.

Seamus had just opened his mouth to reply when they both got their answer.

Less than two miles back along the crest of the very ridge the two scouts lay hidden upon rode fifteen more of Crook's scouts, coming along as easy as you please.

"Like a goddamned Sunday outing," Seamus cursed in a whisper as he looked back across the valley at the two warriors.

Grouard tapped him, pointing. Behind them, off to the left along the ridge now, it seemed the whole of the army column was breaking the skyline, making itself known to the enemy.

Donegan turned back to the two horsemen quickly, seeing only blurs of movement in those stunted pines. The warriors broke from cover, whipping their ponies over the crest of the divide, heading northeast.

"They go to the Powder," Grouard growled, his low voice filled with anger. "Not on their backtrail."

"To the Powder," Seamus echoed. Then, "You have a right to be mad."

They waited until the advance was coming near before getting to their feet and making an appearance against the yawning, shimmering landscape of endless white and dark vegetation.

"Well, Frank," Donegan began, his voice controlled and quiet, knowing how it carried on the cold, dry air of these high plains, "looks like I'm a believer too."

Grouard looked at Donegan quizzically. "You didn't think we'd find them?"

The Irishman shrugged. "Last few hours I've been thinking maybe we wouldn't. All the sign was old. So, I was beginning to figure it was like everyone else was saying: maybe the villages had gone east, already run back to the reservation."

"Hunters," Grouard said as Little Bat and the others drew close, bringing their horses up on a lope.

"Not a scouting party," Donegan replied.

"There's more out. More'n just those two," Grouard said flatly.

Seamus shaded his eyes with a flat hand, slowly moving them from north to south across the horizon, trying to pick something out of the ordinary, something just a dog hair out of place.

Closing in on the top of the slope came the advance party, pushing their mounts a little now, frosty halos rising above the horses's heads.

"Looks like our army boys seen that pair too," Charlie Jennesse said.

Crook, Clark, Stanton and the rest of the general's staff hurried atop the crest then reined up where the pair of dismounted scouts waited in the circle of the rest of the mounted trackers.

"You saw them?" Crook asked as his horse snorted to a halt.

Grouard nodded, his lips a thin line of anger.

Crook yanked off a glove and dragged a hand beneath his red nose. "They see us?"

"Likely, General. But dammit—Grouard asked you to keep the rest back," Donegan answered this time, looking from the Cow Creek side of the valley, across Otter Creek to the eastern ridge. "Likely they did spot the whole bunch of you."

Crook shot both Stanton and Clark a flinty glare. "I gave my orders for the scouts to hang back."

The rest of the trackers looked at the ground, the sky, shifted nervous and chastised in their saddles.

"That pair is off to inform the village then," Stanton said, clearly irritated, that turkey-egg Adam's apple bobbing. A melted, iridescent pearl formed an unpleasant pendant from the end of the garnet cluster that was the man's nose. "Damn their red hides."

It was an irritation shared by Crook and some of the rest. Seamus could tell the endless cold and half-rations of bad food was wearing their patience even more thin than it had been the last few days.

Crook sighed. "It will be all right, Colonel," he said, addressing Stanton by his brevet rank awarded him during the Civil War. "Everything will turn out all right."

The general twisted in the saddle and studied the position of the sun dropping into the western quadrant, brooding on something until he said, "We'll make camp down there. Start our fires. Put out mounted vedettes as we always have. Got to make it look like we're staying the night."

"You're marching at sundown?" Clark asked.

Crook nodded. "I want those two, and any others who spotted us this close to their villages, not to worry tonight. Make them think we're marching for the Yellowstone . . . as if we have no intention of following them."

This hunt was of a sudden causing the Irishman to recall the dogs he had so often noticed around the forts and outposts and frontier towns: Crazy Horse's hostile village was the bitch in heat set upon by all the available males who would fight among themselves for the chance to be the first to crawl atop and hump her. Nerves were jangled, if not stretched taut as spider's silk. What with the brutal cold and the half-rations the general had just cut to quarter, with the endless march and growing fatigue—Seamus figured it wouldn't take much for Crook's officers to snap.

Maybe better to be out and away from this column when things did snap.

Donegan pointed to the ridge on the far eastern side of the Otter Creek valley. "General, you want someone to ride over there and see what kind of trail those two left us to follow?"

"Exactly." He looked at Grouard. "Frank, I must be certain you can take us on their inbound trail, back to their villages. Can you do it?"

The half-breed only nodded and mounted, pulling his horse's head around, then said, "Come on, Irishman." Pointing at Charlie Jennesse and Big Bat, he signaled the pair to join them.

The four urged their weary, heaving mounts on down the slope toward the frozen Otter Creek. They were riding the sun down again—and it appeared Grouard and Donegan would be riding the sun up once more.

"A bleeming god-night-damned march," Seamus swore quietly.

"You afraid of the dark?" Charlie Jennesse asked.

Donegan flared with a flush of anger, but that first blush of heat was gone as quickly when he saw the smiles on Grouard's and Big Bat's faces. It told him he was accepted among them, these plainsmen who could make their way across this high land in the teeth of winter with sundown easing the light quickly out of the day.

"Been eating quarter rations of army hard bread, and chewing on dried meat for better'n four days now. Hardly out of the saddle for the last three, fellas. Yeah, suppose you might say I'm a might touchy right now."

"Me too," said the taciturn half-breed.

But the way Grouard said it, Donegan sensed that the scout was upset for an entirely different reason.

"It's Reshaw, ain't it, Frank?"

Grouard never looked at Donegan or the others when he nodded once. He kept his eyes constantly scanning across the slope ahead of them as they got to the bank of Otter Creek. He stepped out of his stirrup, knelt and dug up enough dirt and sand to fill both his mittens. He flung it across the surface of the frozen creek. Four more times he did the same, until there was enough of it to provide some traction, a little grip on the ice in their crossing.

"Reshaw makes me angry enough to kill him sometimes."

"Bad medicine, Grouard."

"I bite my tongue," the half-breed said as he climbed back into the saddle. "But one day, Louie get in so much trouble with me he can't get Crook to back him out of it."

"Wait till you're not around the army no more, Frank," Jennesse advised.

Grouard grinned, then it was gone as quickly as it had brightened his dark face. "I know."

"Just watch out for yourself," Donegan said.

"I will. You are a friend now. I like you."

"A man needs all the friends he can get."

"Yes, Irishman. Especially when a man has enemies like Louie Reshaw. Him, and a warrior riding with Crazy Horse's band I got a old score to settle with."

Chapter 17

Sore Eye Moon

*H*e felt his insides shrivel up like a gut pile under a summer sun each time he thought about that wide trail of iron-shod hooves that slashed the snowy countryside, going north toward the Elk River.

"Soldiers," He Dog had said as he stared at the wide scar, said it almost in a whisper. "Many pony soldiers."

He and another veteran warrior, both Oglalla from Crazy Horse's Hunkpatila band, had been out hunting three days before when they crossed the wide, torn-up scar of a trail cut by thousands of hooves. They had returned to the Cheyenne camp of Two Moon there on the west bank of the Powder River with the startling news. Late that same afternoon, three more hunting parties returned with the same report: the wide trail of white man's iron-shod horses marching north.

That bit of news was the only hopeful glimmer in the worrisome reports. North.

"You worry too much," chided White Cow Bull with his easy humor as he walked along beside his friend.

Still, He Dog could tell the Bull's thoughts were somewhere else, as were the warrior's eyes. White Cow Bull watched only the Cheyenne woman—the one said to have come north from the reservation where her father had been killed by the soldiers seven winters gone. It was spoken that Monaseetah's mother had been killed by soldiers on a winter day beside the Little Dried River.* People gone now, Shahiyena and Lakota all, people once occupying a place between earth and sky.

Perhaps if he believed hard enough, then it would come true: that this land would always belong to his people as promised. At least in He Dog's warrior heart, he wanted to believe, as his people had believed since time began its journey across the stars.

Good that the Cheyenne mother brought her two young sons north where they would live long enough to grow into young warriors who would in turn protect the old and sick. They could one day take the place of warriors fallen, warriors who once stood between the people and the white soldiers. But for now it was up to men like White Cow Bull and himself to join with Wooden Leg and warriors of the Northern Cheyenne in herding Two Moon's village south, away from the path of the pony soldiers, south to the White Rock agency where their people would be safe for the rest of the winter.

Each time he thought on the taste of *kukuse,* the white man's pig meat, his stomach lurched. True enough, the grease on his tongue tasted good on occasions, he had to admit. And he did like the bread the women fried in their pans from the flour given them at the reservations. But the pig meat did not sit well in his belly. Not like wild meat: deer and elk, antelope and buffalo. Lean and red. If a man grew hungry for grease—he could slice off some of the rich fleece from the hump ribs of a tender cow. Now, that was eating, He Dog thought with yearning. Or, better yet, roast some marrow bones in the ashes of the lodge fire as he smoked and talked of old pony raids with friends. Crack those bones open with a rock and lick out the thick, creamy-yellow marrow, rich and warm on the tip of his tongue. The last drops he could trickle to the back of his throat, head tilted back, some of it dribbling off his lower lip onto his chin. Marrow butter, they called it.

He would eat almost anything before he would eat the white man's pig meat. Maybe even a ground squirrel or

* Sand Creek

prairie dog, as the Hunkpapa Sitting Bull had declared he would. Yes, even a skinny ground squirrel before he would eat more pig meat. Maybe even the *kangi,* the dreaded black crow, harbinger of death, messenger of *Yunke Lo.*

"Do you worry about anything?" He Dog asked his bachelor friend.

"Yes," answered White Cow Bull as he came to an abrupt stop. "I worry that I will always sleep cold. Alone and cold in my robes."

Surprised, He Dog stopped, turned and followed the warrior's eyes, finding the Bull staring, fixed on the slim Cheyenne woman from the south. "She does not want you."

White Cow Bull shook his head. "No, she does not know what she wants. Instead, she waits for the one she calls her husband."

"Find yourself another. There are many among the Lakota, even a few among Old Bear's band of Shahiyena, women who would be proud to be the wife of a great warrior of many coups like White Cow Bull."

"I want only her."

He Dog wagged his head. "She has two sons. Each by a different father."

The sudden fire in the eyes of White Cow Bull as the warrior wheeled on him frightened He Dog.

"She needs a man to stay with her. It is none of your business if you do not want happiness for me."

He Dog nodded sadly. "Yes, my friend. It is none of my business. But I do want happiness for you. That is all I was thinking of. The Shahiyena warrior, Rolls Down, he hunts for her. They say Wooden Leg has eyes for her as well."

"I bring in meat for the woman and her boys."

"Let your eyes wander a little. It is winter: the nights are long and very cold."

The Bull sighed, gazing up at the pewter sky, a dull, abalone sun behind the heavy clouds that were bringing an early sunset to this river valley. These last few rays of the sun touched the snow with glints of gold.

"I want to care for someone," he said to He Dog. "It has . . . been so long."

He Dog put his blanket mitten on his friend's shoulder. "Have supper with us. Sleep again in my lodge tonight. We have room for you."

White Cow Bull agreed with a single nod. "Perhaps she will see me one day."

"Yes. How could she miss you, White Cow Bull? As handsome a man as ever rode a war pony across this land, a free man—able to provide for her and her sons!"

"Until then I will have to provide for the sick ones, as you do, He Dog. To hunt and help the old ones."

He Dog tied off his pony on one of the wooden pegs securing the buffalo-hide lodge cover to the ground, and brought the animal some cottonwood bark he had peeled from limbs piled nearby. After some reflection he said to his friend, "I want to send out some scouts to track these pony soldiers."

White Cow Bull grinned. "It is too cold to work so hard finding something to do, my friend. Hunters go out every day we are in a new camp. Others have seen the wide, deep trail of iron-shod hooves as we have. The soldiers are going north to the Elk River.* There is no need to worry."

He Dog shook his head with uncertainty. "I am not as sure as you. We need scouts to watch the soldiers, not just their trail."

White Cow Bull seemed to consider that as he tied his pony off to a peg at the back of the lodge. "You will feel better if scouts go out to find the soldiers?"

"Yes. The army comes to make war on us. Why shouldn't we prepare for them to attack us? Why shouldn't we know if they are drawing close to our camp? Why shouldn't we do all that we can to protect ourselves from the pony soldiers, from the mixed-bloods who lead them like wolves down on our villages?"

"You have been a warrior long enough, and fought these soldiers many years, to know there is plenty of time: we will talk with the others tomorrow," White Cow Bull replied, dropping some peeled bark for his ribby, winter-gaunt pony to gnaw on.

---

* Yellowstone River

"Tonight," He Dog pressed.

The Bull wagged his head and grinned sympathetically at his friend. "Tomorrow is soon enough, my friend. The army is far, far to the north, with the smell of the Elk River in their nostrils."

It was not an easy thing for Donegan to admire Frank Grouard, what with the way the sullen half-breed kept to himself, never making much attempt at being friendly, to join in with the rest at the cookfires. But admire Grouard he did nonetheless.

Not only did the man know the country like the inside of his eyelids, even in this gathering gloom of this sixteenth day of March—but Frank Grouard had shown day in and day out an uncanny insight into the habits of the warriors he was stalking. How they would hunt, or camp, or move their villages, all of that here in the throes of winter.

And if he didn't know any better, Seamus would have bet good money—army scrip to boot—that Frank Grouard was pitting himself against his old friends, those Lakota warriors in the camps of Sitting Bull and Crazy Horse, as if those old friends had now become new enemies.

Enemies Grouard was stalking with a vengeance. As if some furious flame of revenge kept him warm as the sun sat and the wind howled and the icy snow blew like tiny lance points against a man's bare skin.

Winter's early twilight was crowding the light right out of the eastern sky as Seamus adjusted the wide woolen scarf he had tied under his neck, the loose ends tucked within the upturned collar of his blanket-lined Saint Paul coat that turned most of the wind. The scarf held the heavy wolfskin hat down on his brow and over his ears, even as the wind picked up.

It always did that, the wind—prowling among the higher places like this, making no attempt to hide along the bare slopes of these ridges. Whistling hollow-boned, swinging down on them at times like guffaws of raw laughter. Then dropping to a muttering whisper. Down below them the slopes dropped away into the steep ravines where stunted pine and second-growth cedar stood out like black lace on a woman's petticoat.

His mount fought the bit, pulling away, wanting to quarter around away from the wind that came up again with a wiry whine at his left shoulder as they climbed up the narrow ribbon of frozen streambed from Otter Creek. Due east, with the wind keening down right out of the north on them, with nothing to stop it on this bare land but some stunted cedar and junipers and clumps of buffalo grass dried long ago by autumn's winds, along with a profusion of gray-bellied sage, each one crusted in its own icy pot of dirty snow.

From time to time they would pass a buffalo skull, laying akimbo, half in and half out of a skiff of snow. Tracks of an occasional coyote or deer or antelope crisscrossed the wind-scoured icing spread over the rumbling land they climbed and fell with. Very rarely did a prairie dog poke its head up from its dark hole in the midst of all the cold and white, to bark a solitary protest before ducking back into the darkness and the warmth of its burrow before the big four-legged creatures drew near.

A rosy glaze of hoarfrost clung to his mustache and chin whiskers as the sun settled in the west below the coming storm. Seamus found himself having to breathe more and more through his mouth. In this endless cold, his sore, stopped-up nose didn't stand a chance of running.

Yesterday they had come upon that abandoned village after crossing the Tongue to the east, to begin their march up the divide. Big Bat and some others had spotted a small hunting party in the distance, but Big Bat Pourrier had decided not to give chase, choosing instead to report their discovery to Crook.

And now, the closer they marched to the Powder, the better the sign. It wasn't that he had the same hunger in his craw that drove a suffering Grouard, even the driving need that Crook had—Donegan's was more of a curiosity to see for once and for all time the great war chief of the wild Lakota bands, Crazy Horse.

That, and his homesickness. His loneliness for the smell of her, the feel of her warm flesh beside his, the way Sam kneaded the worry right out of him. She had that wild-soft, unnerving kind of beauty that grew in him every day he was without her.

And of a sudden he sensed a hurt in his yearning for Samantha, like the cold wind was blowing through the very soul of him. How he wished to again hear her laughter floating on the air like long streamers of sparkling, many-colored ribbons of pure joy.

But he was alone for all the good it did him to miss her now, and he was damned near half froze despite the layers upon layers and the way they rode quartered out of the wind—and he was worried about her. Knowing that when a man let his mind wander, as his was wandering back to Fort Laramie—that's when a man failed to pay attention and made mistakes.

Seamus blinked his eyes several times, turning his face directly into the icy wind to startle himself into obedience. His life might well depend right now on not thinking of anything but finding that enemy camp.

Finding Crazy Horse.

The aroma of coffee was strong in the air. The way the wind whined and keened along the ridge tops far above them, John Bourke was surprised to find this campsite somewhat protected. A little warmer here, down in the lee of Otter Creek.

He glanced over his shoulder, yearning for a cup, his mouth watering as he glanced over the twinkling string of glowing campfires like red fireflies against the deepening dusk of late afternoon.

Sixteen March, ye year of our Lord, eighteen and seventy-six, he thought.

Bourke reminded himself to take his journal along for the coming attack. If unable tonight to write down his notes from this meeting with the general, at least he might be able to catch up tomorrow when all the excitement had died down. When the fight was over.

And Crook had defeated Crazy Horse or Sitting Bull or whoever it was they had found over on the Powder.

Grouard and his scouts were stalking the backtrail of those two Indian hunters right now.

"My greatest fear is that the village will know we are coming, and drawing close—then bolt on us," Crook declared, continuing his officers' meeting there beside Otter Creek. "That's why I'm making it appear that we are going into camp. But a night march is clearly in order.

"So, as soon as we have a better idea just where the village is, gentlemen," Crook went on explaining to his officers, "General Reynolds can march out at twilight and take the fight right to them."

Bourke supposed he was as surprised as the rest, seeing the looks on most of the faces in that tight crescent, the two horns of which stopped some five feet from Crook and Reynolds, allowing the two leaders a due amount of space. For the first time in more than two weeks, Crook had begun his officers' meeting by calling Reynolds forward to stand beside him before the command. Then Crook had startled them even more by announcing that Reynolds himself was to lead the attack.

Bourke worked to get his mind off the cold, off the aroma of that hot coffee, off the fragrance that bubbling brew lent to the air.

Perhaps, he thought, the general truly does want Sam Grant's old classmate from academy days to have this chance to clear himself of the stain, his reputation sullied, tarnished as it was down in Reconstruction Texas when Reynolds accepted that land and the house from those Texas Confederates. Taking such a rich bribe is a curse, Bourke brooded. Something few men could really refuse. Fewer still could ever hope to get away with.

"Yes, gentlemen," Crook said, glancing quickly at Reynolds. The colonel stood straighter than he had in the past sixteen days, some of his military bearing redeemed here on the eve of attack. An old war horse once more. "I have chosen to remain behind with the second and fourth battalions, Captain Hawley and Major Dewees commanding. They will provide escort for Mr. Moore's pack train and the equipment the cavalry will be leaving behind at this point."

There arose some nervous, unsettled shifting of feet. But

none of the men made the mistake of talking among themselves, for fear of missing the import of Crook's instructions. The general explained he was sending some fifteen officers and 359 men into battle against the enemy, along with as many as fifteen of the scouts to go with Reynolds. Crook continued.

"Captains Moore, Noyes and Mills will report the readiness and fighting status of their battalions to General Reynolds immediately upon the conclusion of this meeting. Remember, gentlemen: you must not break down our stock. These mounts must be ready for use in this summer's campaign as we finish what we will shortly be starting."

For a moment Crook regarded that pewter globe easing down toward the Bighorns to the west. "The cavalry will march at sundown—in light marching order."

"General?"

Bourke turned to find that the bland, flavorless, strap-thin man had taken a step forward to ask his question.

"Captain Noyes?"

That thick broom bristle of a mustache upturned at the corners but hardly worth cultivating beneath the captain's nose quivered nervously. The cut of his mouth and how he formed his words clearly told Bourke that Noyes was a man much too taken with himself.

"Sir—light marching order? Begging your understanding —in this weather?" he asked in his clip-tongued way.

"Captain," Crook replied, toying with one half of his long beard, "with Teddy Egan making the point of the charge, I want your horse into that village by daybreak, crush the enemy, and back here before your men even have time to worry about the cold or their bellies."

"Yes, sir." Noyes edged back among his peers, his skin pale as a quality-folk bed sheet, fresh-washed and line-dried.

Crook continued without pause, "The cavalry will carry nothing but their weapons, extra horseshoes, an additional one hundred rounds for carbines, and field rations of hard-tack for one day, the seventeenth—enough to tide the men over until you rendezvous with us up the Powder."

"Am I to stay with the pack train?" asked Captain Stanton.

"You're asking to go with General Reynolds?"

"Sir, I'm requesting to go with the attack, General."

"Of course," answered Crook. "You are in command of the scouts. I will keep Clark, Reshaw too . . . and about half of them with me. The rest you will divide off and take with General Reynolds. Grouard is to lead you to the village upon his return from his scout and making his report."

"Thank you, sir," replied Stanton, clearly pleased. "Tomorrow's action will make a hell of a story for the *Tribune*."

"General Crook, will you want me to remain with you?" asked Curtis E. Munn.

"No. I am assigning you to go with General Reynolds," he answered. "Dr. Stevens will remain with me, to stay with the pack train."

"We will rendezvous with you following our capture of the enemy camp?" inquired Anson Mills, his hard glare feeling like the slap of a heavy hand. He was standing at attention, stiff-backed and braced as a toy tin soldier.

Bourke thought he read some concern on the faces of some of the other cavalry commanders. Then he guessed the mood of that anxiety: riding into battle with an aging colonel who had not enjoyed field experience in more than a decade.

For a moment the young lieutenant glanced over at the frost-browed old man. A walking barrel of a man seemingly supported on toothpicks for legs.

Crook swiped the back of a furry mitten beneath his red nose. "I have instructed General Reynolds to rendezvous with me at the mouth of Lodgepole Creek."* He pointed in a southerly direction. "Farther up the Powder. At the consolidation of his victory over the hostiles. Whoever arrives first at that junction will await the other."

Many of the eyes were on Crook. But to Bourke it appeared that just as many of the officers were steadily regarding Reynolds as Crook continued.

"I want the enemy village captured. You are instructed to

---

* present-day Clear Fork (of the Powder River)

kill or capture as many of the hostiles as possible. If the scouts do not do so, you are to run off the pony herd." He drove one fist into the other palm. "Do them some damage, goddammit! Hurt them! Hurt them bad!"

"Here! Here!" came the sudden, surprising cheer raised from a few throats.

"Washington has turned us loose, gentlemen," Crook said as the officers grew quiet after their rousing display of enthusiasm. "We are the first in the field of what has the makings of a great campaign, here on the verge of our grand republic's centennial celebration."

The general held out an open palm to them now, taking a moment to move slowly, dramatically, from one horn of the crescent around to the other side. "We alone can bring this campaign to a conclusion before the other columns ever get into the field. By God—Gibbon can't move out of Fort Ellis or Fort Shaw for the weather! And Terry can't leave Abraham Lincoln without Custer. While Custer himself is tied down testifying in Washington. They're all three stymied."

"It's up to us then, General!" rallied Teddy Egan.

"As well it should be, Captain." He nodded. "Gentlemen —heed my words. By Providence, we alone are handed this opportunity." He flung an arm out, pointing at Reynolds. "The general will lead you to victory and renown. The Big Horn Expedition will live on in the annals of military history as the opening and perhaps even the *closing* act of the great Sioux campaign!"

Lord, does he ever know how to stir men into a martial furor, Bourke thought, sensing a burning fire searing in his own breast as he responded with the others.

"If there are no further questions," Crook concluded, "you are dismissed. Report your readiness immediately to General Reynolds and receive your disposition for the attack."

Crook saluted the assembly, then turned on his heel, striding off quickly. "Mr. Bourke!"

John caught up with him in three long strides. "General?"

"You'll be wanting to go with Reynolds?"

"H-How did you know?"

Crook stopped, turned, and smiled at his aide. "We've been fighters together long enough, John." Then he uncharacteristically held out his mittened hand to the lieutenant. "Go, go as my representative—and with my good wishes." They shook, Crook holding Bourke's mitten between his two. "And bloody well do them some damage!"

Chapter 18

17 March 1876

"*T*he trail leads down Indian Creek." Frank Grouard had returned to tell Crook and Reynolds more than nine hours ago. "It's an old way through this country. Used for many years."

"But, it's a fresh trail?" Crook asked, his eyes flicking between Grouard and those of the tall Irishman.

Seamus Donegan nodded. "We followed the tracks far enough to know before it got dark."

"The village isn't far," Grouard snapped, almost cutting Donegan off.

"On the Powder? No farther?" Crook had pressed.

"It's there." Then Grouard had added, "Crazy Horse is there."

Donegan thought on that again now, as he had over the slow parade of passing miles and hours, through the bitter, stinging cold of that night of broken clouds and patches of icy, diamond light raining down on the rolling tableland. A night as black as a bear's winter den.

Not long after he and Grouard had started out, the winter darkness had thickened above him like a blood soup coming quickly to a boil.

Straining to keep himself awake, to keep himself in the saddle with legs numbing, muscles like cramped charley horses, feeling more like chunks of wood that might fail him once he got down out of the saddle . . . yes, it had been a fight all night long. Struggling to keep his mind off Samantha, wondering if she missed him as much as he did her. Feeling about as lonely as a solitary wolf crying the sun down back of the Bighorns.

It was just too damned easy to think on her—his memories of Sam slipping effortlessly through his mind like spring runoff over mossy stones. Too damned easy . . .

Upon their return to Otter Creek, Grouard's scouts had been given a few minutes at the fires with the soldiers as they wolfed down some supper, guzzling the hot coffee that steamed around the men's faces with their breath smoke. Crook had ordered fresher mounts saddled for the five scouts, horses already fed their scanty quarter rations of grain. It was tough for the men breaking through the thick ice covering the creek, but break it they must. Their mounts had not had a decent drink for the better part of a day and a half. And this might well be the last water before those big, brave animals would be asked to carry their riders into battle.

The stock must be ready, the general reminded the men, ready to attack with every advantage possible. And, Crook added, he would not spare his scouts the same—or any advantage as well. Those half-dozen civilians were his eyes and ears, maybe even his nose. Crook was hot on the trail like a baying hound: tail up, and nose down thick in the scent.

During the last day-long scout, Seamus hadn't liked the way they had failed to spook up any game. Strange, it was— not busting up a bunch of antelope, rarer still not scaring a herd of startled deer out of the coulees here and there. Likely there were elk, though. They would hang back into the timber and merely watch horsemen pass them by.

But this country had all but been driven clear of game. That much was for damned certain.

Bob Strahorn had come up during those few precious minutes before departure and gently nudged the tall Irishman away from the bulky assembly in the fire's light. Pulling a German silver flask from his campaign coat and yanking out the cork-wrapped stopper, the newsman presented it to Donegan.

"Here. You'll want some of this, if I know you."

Seamus had taken only a heartbeat to sniff at the neck before tossing back a healthy swallow.

Mother of God, how he wished he had another long pull on Strahorn's flask right now. Hours gone, and the glow of that whiskey fading with them. But still a remembrance of the taste lingered on his tongue, and for that he thought he should at least say a rosary. The whiskey, and the cold, metallic taste of uncertainty, like sucking on the Henry's brass cartridges. Not really fear—but uncertainty just the same. It had been there through every battle of the war, charging in to the attack, or riding out to turn back an attack. That same cold, metallic taste on the back of his tongue had stayed with him after the skirmishes in Appomattox Wood—whether it was a hot summer day on the Crazy Woman Fork, or an unnamed island in the middle of the Arickaree Fork of the Republican.*

Damn, but this was a new thing, making war in the bitter, subzero cold. Even when he had crossed the snowy, wind-swept Lodge Trail Ridge with Ten Eyck and looked down on that field of Fetterman's carnage. Seemed as hard as he tried to remember, Seamus could only recall fighting in the heat: that day-long battle in the hayfield†, Carr's attack on Tall Bull's Dog Soldiers at Summit Springs^, or that time he almost died in the shadow of that black, lava-strewn mesa . . . for some reason he might never know, left alive as the Modoc warriors withdrew without killing every last man of them.#

So rare was it that he had fought in the cold, as he had grown accustomed to month in and month out during the Rebellion, forced to stay in the saddle through the cold and the rain, so much that he had almost welcomed the warmth he could count on when he finally journeyed to look up an old friend on the southern plains in '73. And ended up staring down the barrel of his Henry at the Comanche and

---

* The Plainsmen Series, vol. 3, *The Stalkers*
† The Plainsmen Series, vol. 2, *Red Cloud's Revenge*
^ The Plainsmen Series, vol. 4, *Black Sun*
# The Plainsmen Series, vol. 5, *Devil's Backbone*

Kiowa charging down on that June-cured meadow at the Adobe Walls.*

Now he had made the mistake of trying to go north to look for another old friend up Helena way, and had to leave Samantha behind—

"Got to stop that," he scolded himself in a whisper.

"Quiet," someone snarled behind him.

Had to be one of those bleeming soldiers, Seamus thought. None of the scouts would have said something like that—ordering him to be quiet in the ranks.

So he sucked on his tongue as they inched forward, drawing as much memory of the whiskey as he could.

Reynolds had been ready to move out about half past five, the last of the pale winter light loosening from the eastern sky like a shopkeeper's sign hung on a hinge swinging lower and lower. For a time the silver of the rising sliver of moon limned the crest of the far hills against the lighter sky.

From what calculation of distance Donegan could make of Grouard's estimate of time, the cavalry had something on the order of thirty miles to climb and fall, climb and fall through the black of night. Hard work beneath those patches of stars in that crooked strip of sky and that icy-blue quarter moon sailing behind them toward the Big Horns.

If he wasn't seeing it with his own eyes, Seamus would not have believed it. Grouard was doing the unthinkable, the impossible: following the tracks of those two unshod ponies across the silvery countryside, holding ever to the southeast as the darkness swallowed them like coal cotton. Into the land of the Powder. The half-breed was amazing. Little matter that Grouard wasn't the sort Donegan wanted as a friend, standoffish as he was. The half-breed was next to a bleeming miracle as he took the point, followed the trail, stopping here and there to get down on the snow, then remount to move the long, squeaking, jingling column forward a bit farther through this countryside of aching silence, like a great bird's wing folding.

* The Plainsmen Series, vol. 7, *Dying Thunder*

There had been a few times that the half-breed had held them up for some long minutes that had made Donegan begin to doubt Grouard could do it in this blackness as dark as the snout of a coal scuttle—places where the trail had become obliterated altogether. But in the end Grouard alone had traipsed left, then right: sweeping the country in a wide arc until he cut the warriors' trail, hurrying back to Reynolds and setting the hot-blooded hounds back to their chase.

The horses were weary. Pushing them into this night march had been a calculated proposition by Crook and Reynolds, he thought. A little grain, a little rest, and a mouthful or two of water before asking the mounts to climb and stumble and slide their way across the icy hillsides in the black of winter's night. With the way this country was slashed in every direction by shallow, eroded ravines that turkey-tracked every few hundred yards, there were countless times the entire column ground to a halt while the scouts investigated the ravine to determine its width and depth in the black of night, ultimately to find a crossing for their played-out horses.

As the buzzard blackness of that endless night finally grew old, Donegan realized the trail was not getting harder to follow. Perhaps easier—for the pair of riders had been joining up with other hunters until there was a wide, well-beaten path returning to the Powder to follow: thirty or more Indian ponies making their way back home to the shelter of the river valley.

Then, sometime after three o'clock, Grouard rode back to the colonel, requesting that the soldiers remain behind for a time—until he and a handful could locate the village itself. There were six the half-breed pointed to, silently signaling them to join him on his lonely mission.

In this first gray light of false dawn, no man could mistake the hammered trail beaten by those unshod hooves. There was no delay now. Grouard moved out at an increasing pace now, leading the half-dozen scouts almost at a trot, all that the horses could give, their breath coming in shots like ragged, gauzy ribbons in the gray light, the paunch-water belly sounds hammering against heaving ribs as those animals struggled to give these seven men their last ounce of effort.

The Irishman knew why Grouard was hurrying. Day was coming. And with first light, the wary, warned village would likely be on the move—to flee, to escape the approaching soldiers.

Grouard was hurrying to catch Crazy Horse. For some reason, the half-breed had something to settle with the camp of that Oglalla war chief. Something perhaps too private even to put to words.

Then the half-breed was reining up, his arm raised. The others came to a halt on either side of Grouard, the late winter air a full-bodied wine sap with pinion pine and cedar. Below them, almost at the fetlocks of their horses, lay the valley of the Powder. Totally shrouded in a fog the color of old fire-pit ash. They could not see a damned, bloody thing down there below the steep river bluffs sliced and layered in garlands of red and yellow rimrock.

Grouard sighed. A look of disappointment, more so anger on his face, Donegan thought. Nothing to find. Nothing to see—

Then the bell.

He sensed his own heart leap like a flapping of wings. Saw the grin cross Grouard's full, sassy lips as he turned. The rest, half-breeds too, they were grinning, nodding knowingly, moving their lips wordlessly in some invocation of spirit, a medicine call, a prayer for power bestowed from the all-powerful. Perhaps giving thanks to the One Above who had helped bring them here.

Helped bring Frank Grouard to this slope overlooking the Powder, there to hear that pony bell.

A herd was just below them, off to the right.

"Stay here," Grouard whispered to them. "Wait for me."

No one said a word as the half-breed turned away on foot to be absorbed by the inky, cold fog that gave the deepening cold all the more of an edge. From time to time Seamus heard the faint tinkle of that bell, but little else save for the soft snorting, impatient, weary pawing of their thirsty horses, which were smelling the distant water in the river valley.

Then Grouard was back, seeming to draw himself out of the fog as a ghost would appear from a solid wall.

"I got down under the fog," the half-breed announced, a wide smile on his oak-brown face, fires of revenge burning in his eyes. "Oglalla ponies down there."

The rest grunted with approval.

"I know those ponies," Grouard continued. "You know what that means."

All the rest nodded their heads. Only Donegan did not, for he knew not the import of those ponies Grouard found familiar.

"I counted on this village being here," Grouard said, clearly smiling now in the gray light of predawn. The sun would be up soon, and he suddenly seemed concerned about the coming light.

"Buckskin Jack," Grouard said in a rough-edged whisper.

Russell nudged his horse forward, stopping stirrup to stirrup with Grouard.

"You want to ride?"

Russell nodded wordlessly.

"Watch the trail. Bring them here. Come quick. Very quick. Pony herd there," and Grouard pointed. "Village . . . down there." And he pointed again. To the left.

"Jack . . ." Grouard paused a moment. "Tell that old general—Crazy Horse is waiting for him."

As much as any man, Bob Strahorn was amazed at what the scouts had done to bring them here through the black of night to the slopes overlooking the Powder River. Down there lay the enemy camp of Crazy Horse.

It was just too damned good to be true—to be here with the attacking force that would in a matter of minutes be slashing through the Oglalla war chief's village, routing his warriors, driving his people into the cold of the wilderness, burning their lodges and robes and meat, and hopefully capturing that mythical creature whose very name stirred fear in the heart of civilian and soldier alike.

For most of the night as dark as the inside of a smoke-house, he had ridden along blindly, struggling to keep his mind off his legs as they grew increasingly numb. To keep his mind off the growing pain, Strahorn had been composing copy. Trying to commit his brilliant turns of a phrase here and there to memory, for it would still be many, many hours before he enjoyed the luxury of pulling paper and pencil from his saddlebags, writing the most important dispatch of this entire campaign. Perhaps the most important story of his entire career.

CRAZY HORSE CAMP CAPTURED

the wide, bold banner would read across that special edition of the *Rocky Mountain News* publisher William N. Byers would put out on the street as soon as he received the telegraph from Fort Fetterman.

> Famous war chief a prisoner.
> Winter campaign a success.
> Special correspondent rides with attacking
> cavalry charge into hostile village.

As a matter of history [the night march] well deserves a place by the side of any similar incident known to frontier service; and . . . the three hundred gallant and uncomplaining spirits who participated in its thrilling scenes . . .

. . . with darkness already shadowing the gulches, the three squadrons pushed silently forward. A cutting breeze with its usual perversity in these parts, drove the falling snow directly in our faces.

. . . I had, during the night, an excellent opportunity of witnessing the truly remarkable achievement of Frank Grouard, our principal guide and trailer. His knowledge of the country had been noteworthy ever since the opening of the campaign, but the duty he was now called upon to perform was of just the nature that would have bewildered almost any one in broad daylight . . . This he did through the entire night in the face of a storm that was constantly rendering the pony tracks of the two savages less distinct . . . Over rugged bluffs and narrow valleys, through gloomy defiles and down breakneck declivities plunged the indomitable Frank; now down on his hands and knees in the deep snow . . . darting to and fro until it was found, and again following it up with the keenness of a hound . . .

Perhaps this time, he dreamed, he would write his story and sign his name. Although most readers already knew his nom de plume, Alter Ego, was in fact Robert Strahorn . . . he considered signing this first dispatch from the scene of the army's victory by his real name.

Let there be no confusion. Nay, let there be no mistake made in assuming just who it was rode with the cavalry into this Sioux village, facing down the bloodthirsty warriors of none other than Crazy Horse himself!

For more than an hour the column had been ordered to halt along a narrow ravine while Grouard and the scouts he chose to accompany him worked down into the valley. Here it was hardest, so close to the enemy. But the trackers had to be sure: being a mile or more off when they plunged toward the Powder River would make all the difference in severely routing and destroying the enemy, or merely running the village off into the snowy countryside.

"Colder'n a buffalo cow's hind tit dragging through a snowdrift," growled an old veteran in among the waiting files.

Another's teeth clattered like dominoes spilled across the top of an oak table.

"I—I'm shaking worse'n a wet hound in a hailstorm," complained a third as Strahorn crabbed past them, looking for Teddy Egan's company.

"Cold as an open grave."

"Make sure it ain't your grave, bucko."

While the battalions waited, Strahorn moved up and down the icy ravine, talking quietly here and there with some of the officers—Egan, Mills and Stanton. From time to time a man would drop from his horse, so stiffened with the brutalizing cold and lack of movement, sleeplessness and overpowering fatigue, that he could no longer stay in his saddle. They would hit the snow, struggling to rise on unworkable legs. There would be an order given, others clambering out of the saddle on their own shaky legs to help lift the fallen one to his own feet, rising again to their saddles, where they continued their miserable wait.

Up and down the line they fell, struggling back into the saddle to shiver in the interminable cold some more, each and every one reached by Dr. Munn or Steward Will Bryan, who quietly examined the soldiers for frostbite, injury, or the chance that a limb was suffering the first signs of irreparable harm.

Buckskin Jack Russell caused a stir of excitement upon his frightful appearance out of the cold wilderness, gray as it was, a new day coming now, far to the east. As the first pink, then orange-tinged filaments stretched along the horizon, the command was issued back along the narrow ravine. It was "March."

And march on the village of Crazy Horse!

Scouts, Reynolds, and those three battalions of frozen soldiers moved out, coldly boasting of their readiness to pluck the feathers of the Sioux war chief and his bloody henchmen.

"By Jesus, Johnny! At least brother Lo is no longer playing the cat and the rat with us!" Strahorn was grinning at John Bourke as the newsman inched his way back up the column of twos to find Crook's aide-de-camp. "Was that smoke we saw from the village?"

The lieutenant shook his head, feeling the chill of the fog tighten the skin across his cheeks into rawhide when he tried to smile. "Big Bat rode out to investigate it. Just a burning vein of coal. Said it was likely ignited by lightning. But my faint-of-heart friend—we've got word Grouard did find the village farther on."

Strahorn's eyes beamed with excitement. "How many lodges did the half-breed see?"

"A hundred." Bourke felt his mouth go dry. And it was more than the cold, arid air of this high land. He could even smell a hint of wood smoke on the wind now.

After Buckskin Jack brought Grouard's message back to the waiting cavalry, Reynolds had moved his troops forward for the six intervening miles, the first two miles covered on foot to conserve the strength of the horses for the attack as well as to warm the men up after their wait in the ravine. Just past six A.M. the anxious soldiers came upon the half-breed's group of scouts waiting in the broken country above the fog-shrouded Powder.

"Bob, Grouard actually counted the lodges. He told us as the fog lifted he could see the tops of them. A hundred lodges means seven hundred, maybe a thousand Indians down there."

"Damn," Strahorn nodded. "And at least a third of 'em warriors."

The soldier nodded, carefully watching the nearby conference. "He was coming back up from the fogbank when Reynolds got here. Told the colonel he'd been down to the river bottom—heard the warriors talking himself."

"No shit?"

With a wag of his head, Bourke continued, his eyes still on the knot of officers clustered around Colonel Joseph J. Reynolds. "Grouard says he heard them talking about us—the soldiers coming. They sent back some scouts to find us, but Grouard figures they took the lower crossing of the divide—that's why they missed us in the night."

"Reynolds is in the soup now," Strahorn commented.

"Let's go hear how he's going to deploy the battalions," Bourke suggested, moving off toward the tight ring of officers circling the colonel, who was tapping a glove against the chest of Louis Gringos, one of Clark's scouts.

". . . and that nigger half-breed makes the slightest hint of betraying us," Reynolds was saying, his voice a low, ominous grumble as he lowered his head close to the civilian scout, "I want you to drop him in his tracks."

"General—beg pardon," Bourke excused himself, "but I don't think Grouard is going to betray you to that bunch down there."

"Mr. Bourke," Reynolds snapped, whirling about as if surprised. "I'll remind you that you are here as an observer, and as such you will remain here with my command only at my discretion and goodwill."

Bourke knew Crook would not like the sound of that. "Sir, if I may speak frankly. The general respects the job Grouard has done for us, and I know he believes Grouard wants to crush that village as bad as—"

"That will be enough, Mr. Bourke!" Reynolds growled, his disposition suddenly as ragged as a shard of broken glass. "Entirely enough. If you have anything else to disagree with me on, you can make a report upon your return to Fort Fetterman. Otherwise, I will expect your silence while I complete the deployment of my men for the coming battle."

The colonel turned back to the scout as Bourke glanced at Strahorn, finding the newsman rolling his eyes back knowingly.

"You got that, Gringos?"

The short half-breed tapped the big grips on his army pistol, Colt .45, strapped around his waist on the outside of the blanket coat he wore.

"All right, gentlemen," Reynolds said, seeming to rock back on his heels.

Behind them along the plateau about a mile and a half west of the river itself the column had halted. Moore's battalion in the lead, with Mills behind them and Noyes bringing up the rear. For almost as far as Bourke could see, the troops were busying themselves to move into battle: checking their weapons, tightening cinches, digging frozen snow and ice from the hooves of their horses with pocket knives, or with all of that finished, merely standing there, slapping their arms about, stamping their boots to futilely try for some warmth.

"Assemble your men on the breast of this hill by companies," the colonel continued, pointing to his left and right. "Captain Mills, you and Captain Noyes will bring your battalions abreast of Captain Moore's battalion, in column of twos. You have your disposition and route into the village."

Reynolds glanced at Bourke momentarily. The lieutenant shuddered involuntarily with the cold, his breath having rimed the upturned collar of his buffalo coat with layer after layer of frost. Indeed, the fog was rising out of the valley, its frozen crystals stinging the painful, red rawhide of a man's bare face.

Wheeling to look back at his cadre of officers, the colonel asked of a sudden, "Are there any further questions?"

Waiting a moment to clumsily pull his watch from the pocket of his bearskin coat, Reynolds looked at the time. "It is but minutes until seven. Gentlemen, get your men into position for the attack."

Strahorn turned to the young officer, smiling. "Let's go, Johnny me boy. Oh, by the way—happy Saint Paddy's Day to ye!"

Bourke grinned back at the newsman, then slapped Strahorn on the back as a surge of adrenaline warmed his blood. "Luck o' the Irish, i'tis, i'tis, boyo! C'mon—let's catch up our mounts before these soldiers leave us behind!"

And for the moment, Lieutenant John Bourke no longer seemed to notice the damnable cold.

Chapter 19

17 March 1876

"Pistols? You're going to initiate a charge on that village of hostiles down there with pistols?" Captain Anson Mills asked in complete and utter disbelief, his eyes darting like spider bugs on a summer water.

Then he realized his mistake as a look of gray, simmering rage crossed the countenance of Colonel Joseph J. Reynolds. All too well Mills knew his own anger had once again blazed up like a fire in a dry pine woods. Better to apologize and get down to cases . . . "Excuse me—begging the general's pardon, sir. I respectfully request a clarification—"

"Cut the crap, Captain!" Reynolds snapped in the cold gust that nearly stole away with his words. "You heard me."

The colonel's curse had spilled just like winter ice down the rigid channel of the captain's spine. "With your consideration," Mills continued, hurrying to keep up beside the colonel as Reynolds stomped away to meet with the rest of his officers, "I'd like it on the record that I take exception to—"

"Exception goddamn well noted!" he growled at Mills as he came to a stop in the snow, his face as white and tight as rawhide drying.

Almost from the moment the column had reached this bare, snowswept bluff a thousand feet above the riverbed, Reynolds had been in consultation with Captain Alex Moore.

After Crook and Reynolds had decided to have all but

one of the cavalry companies leave their Colt's pistols behind with Tom Moore's pack train at the Otter Creek campsite, Captain James Egan's K Company of the Second Cavalry was the only one of the cavalry troops still carrying the regulation weapons. The decision to have the rest of the companies make their march and the forthcoming attack armed only with the Springfield carbines hadn't made much sense to Mills back at the Otter, and it sure as hell seemed all the more dubious a plan in these moments before launching the charge.

But Reynolds wasn't listening to his officers. Perhaps only Moore.

Maybe, if I can get—

"Lieutenant Mason," Mills called out to Reynolds's adjutant, motioning him aside as the rest went through some of the preliminaries of dividing the scouts among the battalions.

"Sir?"

"Will you give my compliments to the general and try to convince him that Egan is just going to scare the hostiles away—without doing a damned bit of damage?"

Mason wagged his head, his eyes rolling over in the direction of Reynolds. "Already tried it. Between you and me, Captain? We both know better. But the *old* man is having his way now—what with Crook back over the hills. This will be Reynolds's show, and his show alone."

Mills gritted his teeth on that, like something sour going down. "Thank you, Lieutenant." He stomped back down the plateau to where the rest of the battalion commanders were gathered.

"Good of you to rejoin us, Captain," hissed Reynolds in a nasty tone.

"We're deploying the troops, Captain Mills," announced Captain Alex Moore. He had that drawn, brittle look that comes of a lifetime doing work one truly doesn't love. "There'll be a blizzard of lead for those Sioux of Crazy Horse this morning, by Lord. And a bucketful of Indian blood in the river before this day is done."

Reynolds turned away from his ebullient battalion commander, his eyes boring into Mills's. "As I was explaining when you got yourself excited, Captain—I am going to open the attack with Egan's pistols charging in from the south. Grouard here has given me to understand the pony herd is south of the village, where he has recognized some of Crazy Horse's ponies. So as Egan's cavalry moves in, and Captain Noyes secures the pony herd, Captain Moore will have his dismounted battalion move down on foot to the north of the tepees. There he will meet with the hostiles as they flee from Egan's charge."

Mills had to agree that the colonel was acting far up in the collar. Reynolds was smiling like he was damned proud of himself—this first chance since the Civil War to draw some enemy blood.

"Captain Noyes," Reynolds turned to the officer, "as you break off from Egan, I want your men to follow your scouts and capture the pony herd. You are to drive it south," he pointed, his arm sweeping along the high bluff, "and hold those ponies."

"We're going to put the enemy afoot, General. Very good!" Henry Noyes commented enthusiastically.

"Exactly. Captain Mills, your battalion will be following Captain Moore's down the slope. I will be with you, however—holding your companies in reserve."

"To be sent into the village at the proper moment," Alex Moore added with a flourish, "to administer the coup d'grace." He said it with that mealy voice some folks used when talking to those they consider below them.

"Sir?" Mills asked of Reynolds, yanking his eyes away from Moore.

"I'm charging you with going in to secure the village behind Egan. Secure, and hold the village, Captain."

"With carbines, General?"

"Damn well you will—with carbines," Reynolds spat, his face screwed into something hard and mean.

Mills turned so that he wouldn't laugh at the man. The horses around them were pawing anxiously, fighting their holders in the cold with their severe thirst. None of the animals had been taken to water for more than a day—everything frozen. But now they smelled the river. Even up here, a thousand feet above the Powder, the creatures smelled the river shrouded in fog down there among the cottonwoods in the valley.

Reynolds pointed down the bluff. "Grouard says there is a ravine not far down the slope." Motioning a little to the right now, he continued, "Noyes and Egan will follow it down to the valley floor."

"General, I'd like to request that Grouard lead my battalion down the ridge," said Noyes.

Reynolds's eyes flicked from Grouard to Moore. Then stepping up to the half-breed, he said, "Would you excuse us a few minutes, Mr. Grouard."

The scout nodded without a word and stepped away, back with Seamus Donegan and a large circle of the rest who squatted out of the cold wind as best they could.

"I don't trust Grouard, Captain," Reynolds explained.

Noyes wagged his head. "You trusted him enough to take his word that the village was down there—"

"Yes, enough to do that," Reynolds said quickly. "But I don't want him guiding you, and more so, don't want Grouard guiding Egan into that Sioux village. If he is going to betray us, he won't get me to help him do it. I want to keep him more in a support position."

Noyes nodded reluctantly. "I understand. May I request Little Bat?"

"Of course. Charlie Jennesse and John Shangrau too. But I'm going to assign Big Bat and Buckskin Jack to Captain Egan here."

Mills set his jaw. "I'm taking that tall civilian over there —the one they call the Irishman."

"Donegan?" asked John Bourke. "He'll do you well."

"Yes," Mills said. "It's him I want with me."

"Very well, Captain," replied Reynolds. He turned and seemed to regard the foggy river valley for a long moment. The wind tugged at his snowy muttonchops.

And for that moment, despite his grave misgivings about the manner of the coming attack, Anson Mills wished Joseph Reynolds well, for the fortunes of them all rested squarely upon the colonel's shoulders at this moment.

"All right, gentlemen," Reynolds declared as he rocked back on his heels, exuding an air of great confidence.

"You've assembled your men on the breast of this hill by companies, off left and right. Captain Mills, you and Captain Noyes are now to bring your battalions abreast of Captain Moore's companies, in column of twos. You have your disposition and route into the village."

In a flurry of motion, the officers broke in as many directions. Ahead of Mills the scouts were clambering to their feet, the reins in their hands. They realized the time had come.

Mills motioned for his lieutenant, August C. Paul, and his six sergeants—his arm straight in the air, waving it in a small circle. As they were hurrying toward him across the fresh snow, Mills next pointed that arm at the tall civilian knocking the snow from the tail of his long canvas coat.

"You there—Irishman!"

Donegan tapped a glove against his breast as if to ask, Me?

Mills nodded. "You, yes."

"Donegan, Captain."

"Mills, Mr. Donegan," the captain replied hastily as he strode right on past the taller man. "You're going with me."

"Captain?"

Mills turned, irritated that the scout was still standing there, some of the half-breeds in a crescent behind him, their dark eyes shaded by fur hats.

"Goddammit, Mr. Donegan—you're going to help me attack and hold that enemy village down there!"

John Bourke had never been on anything so steep, nothing this slick and treacherous combined.

In those minutes before Reynolds called his officers' meeting on the bluff overlooking the river valley, Bourke had made a compact with Robert Strahorn and William C. Bryan, Dr. Munn's trusted hospital steward. The doctor wanted Bryan moving into the village with the initial charge, in the event of casualties taken by Egan's pistoleers. So the three young men had vowed to hang together and cover each other's backsides when the need arose.

But not a man in that Noyes-Egan battalion had spoken

for the last twenty minutes or more. Too damned busy getting themselves down this icy slope.

The entire command had formed up by battalion on top of the ridge, with designated scouts in front of each company, when Reynolds gave the order to move out. In this case, riding with Noyes and Egan, that order meant to move *down*.

They had begun by moving out in concert with Captain Mills's company around a low rise in the plateau. Then Mills took his men off to the left, marching to the north to find his way down to support Egan's charge. A few yards farther on, Noyes and Egan turned sharply to the right, marching south between two tall, flat-topped buttes. They moved south slowly, conserving the strength of their anxious, restive horses, until they reached the steep bank of a shallow ravine. After a moment to talk it over with the scouts, Noyes and Egan decided they should be well south of the village now, so pointed their battalion off to the northeast, marching back toward the river.

"We should have seen it by now," Captain James Egan was grumbling to Noyes as Bourke and Strahorn came up during a second, hastily-called halt.

"How far, Little Bat?" Noyes asked the half-breed.

Garnier looked north. Shrugged. "Not far."

Egan was nettled. "I can't even figure why we haven't found the river yet."

"Only reason can be that it's got to be farther than Reynolds said it was."

"Let's keep moving, Captain." Egan twisted in the saddle to fling an arm forward. "Little Bat—go find us a route to the village."

Noyes turned back to his battalion, waving his arm. "Forward at a walk."

It was far more agonizing minutes before Little Bat and Charlie Jennesse stopped, waving the officers in the advance ahead, motioning toward the dissipating fog. Then Bourke saw, and leaned over to tap Strahorn on the arm.

"Smoke," the newsman replied in a whisper that was being hissed up and down the column of twos. "I see it."

"Village," Little Bat said, pointing out the obvious, the

smudge of hazy wood smoke that lay over the river valley up ahead.

In another two hundred yards Bourke finally saw the copse of cottonwood standing on the west bank of the Powder. And realized that a great error had been committed. At that moment he caught sight of movement on up the gentle slope to the west.

That will be Mills, he thought. With the Irishman in their lead.

Mills's Company M was coming down the bluff, floating in and out of view as the sky awakened with more and more light at every moment, up and down the broken ground along Thompson Creek that fingered its way toward the Powder.

Bourke wagged his head in disgust as Egan and Noyes moved them out once more. "That village is a mile farther east than Reynolds figured it was," he whispered in a growl to Strahorn, riding at his side. "And it's at least a half a mile farther north than Egan planned on."

Bourke stood in the stirrups, straining to see into the foggy haze hugging the river bluffs like cottonwood down. But try as he might, the lieutenant could not see any sign, any flicker of movement of Moore's battalion far up the slope from Mills. Nothing where those companies of dismounted troopers would have to be stationed at the moment of attack—if Moore was to catch and turn the hostiles fleeing from the village.

He was afraid that the colonel's battle plan was already doomed to failure—ruined by misjudging both distance and time to cross the tortured terrain.

But in the next moment, they were moving down into the Thompson Creek drainage themselves, with Mills's men far off to their left, still struggling down the slope, coming east.

"We'll be first," Bourke said, not realizing he had spoken out loud.

"That's the way we planned it, Johnny," replied Bob Strahorn, wisps of his straight black hair blowing across his eyes. He swept them back under his muskrat hat.

And then the lieutenant saw the first of the lodges. Below the smoky haze of early morning breakfast fires. In the midst of those winter-bared skeletons of cottonwoods and plum brush. As the fog was burning off beneath the sun of a new morn.

St. Patrick's Day, by Gor!

"Sleep now, my little one," Monaseetah cooed to Yellow Bird.

She cradled her youngest across her lap, shivering slightly at the great, damp cold of this predawn darkness seeping like blood ooze from an old wound. At last she recognized the calming regularity of his gentle puff of breath smoke. Still she rocked him gently, back and forth, murmuring away his fears and the terrifying nightmare that had thrust the child awake, screaming.

It had taken but a moment for Sees Red to roll over and fall back to sleep, pulling the buffalo robe over his head. Much longer for Monaseetah to calm Yellow Bird enough so that he would curl himself within her blanketed arms beside the feeble light that came from what coals still remained alive in the fire pit, casting faint shadows on the sooted wall skins. Shivering now with the damp freeze that for the last nine suns had not released its grip on this land, the Cheyenne mother raised her eyes to the smoke hole. From the darkness that seeped into a smudgy gray, she could see that dawn would not be long in coming.

Midway through the Sore-Eye Moon. When late winter cold and the life-giver sun battled through each lengthening day to render a paralyzing brightness to the snow that blinded a person.

She welcomed this cold darkness in the lodge here beneath the sliver of moon, her eyes long adjusted now to the lack of light. A pony snorted nearby, answering the faint whicker of one farther away. Soon enough this village camped on the west bank of the upper Powder River would awaken for the coming day. Young boys would take the ponies to water, breaking the ice for the animals as they had their last two mornings camped here.

Here, two camps south from the mouth of the Little Powder.

Two days ago scouts had again brought word of a long

soldier column spotted to the west, toward Hanging Woman Creek, in the country of the Tongue.

Everyone had felt much safer then. Old Bear's band, along with the people of Two Moon, and some Oglalla going to the agency with He Dog—together they vowed to stay out of the way of the soldiers who were marching about this cold winter. All these people wanted was to journey south to the White Rock agency where they would be safe. Then yesterday afternoon, twenty lodges of Miniconjou had come into camp. They too had in their hearts to make the difficult journey to the reservation for their old people, for the little ones who could not run in the snow.

This winter had been colder than normal. Much more snow. Ice burying the creeks and rivers much thicker than she had ever seen. It had become a time of hunger and despair. Most everyone agreed it would be hard on the reservation. But, along both Scabby and Big Head Woman, her best friends among the Northerns, Monaseetah realized the danger in remaining out with the wild tribes of Sitting Bull and Crazy Horse. There would be danger enough for them until they reached the agency.

And the nights had seemed all the longer for it.

Here the buffalo-hide lodges and the canvas lodges sat together in a thickly wooded river bottom, a twenty-foot-high bluff to the west of camp where the river had carved itself in its recent years with the spring runoff from the mountains rising above the buffalo ground. Beyond, the ridges rose more than two hundred feet in layers of yellow and ocher and red earth, scarred with the black stripes of lignite deposits.

One hundred ten lodges came here, all told. Maybe as many as 250 experienced warriors. Men like He Dog, and that friend of his who kept his eyes on Monaseetah all the time. He told her his name was White Cow Bull.

In council late last night the old men had decided to send the Oglalla and some Shahiyena warriors out beneath the cold stars, to find those soldiers the hunters and scouts had seen nearby—to locate the soldier camp and monitor the movements of the white men.

With those scouts sent out to cross the hills to the west by the lower pass, everyone again felt secure. So safe that the old men saw no need to post camp guards around the village, no pickets down among the ponies.

So it was that the fires in their lodges twinkled, then burned low as the Seven Sisters whirled overhead beneath an icy sky, their starry light crawling from west to east.

Like the relentless progression of the seasons.

Come spring, Old Bear's people could once more abandon the reservation for the hunt, for that nomadic wandering that sang in their Shahiyena blood back generations beyond time. Come the new grass time, she would continue her search for her husband. Perhaps he too was looking for her now.

Monaseetah gazed down into the child's face now. Were it not for the high crook to the nose and the gentle swell of his cheekbones, Yellow Bird might remind any white man of his father. The buffalo-blood tints to Yellow Bird's rust-brown hair, his light eyes not quite the color of the summer sky when a thunderstorm brews itself to a boil, not quite the greasy yellow color of old marrow, but more the liquid ooze of a dog's seepy eye—all of that she had long ago accepted would betray the child's mixed blood.

"Hiestzi," she whispered, watching her young son stir restlessly in her arms. "Your son one day demands to know you."

Gently she laid Yellow Bird back among her robes and blankets, tugging the soft, curly warmth beneath his chin as he slept on, more peacefully now.

Monaseetah remembered the terrors of her own nightmares, when she too was a little one. A mother butchered, her bloody body stripped naked in the cold beside the Little Dried River, then that body defiled in the snow by white soldiers. Later she had suffered the agony of belonging to a cruel, vengeful Cheyenne husband who beat and sodomized his young wife. And finally the recurring nightmare of her father's bullet-riddled body lapping against the icy bank of the Washita. That, a winter long ago gone now.

Hiestzi's own soldiers had killed her father that cold morning beside the Washita.

And though she was pregnant with the child of her Cheyenne husband, Hiestzi had claimed her for his own. It had not been long after she had given birth to the dark-haired, black-eyed Sees Red that Monaseetah sensed she was carrying the white soldier chief's child in her belly.

She gazed down at the boy as she crawled beneath the covers with her child. Seeing so much of his father in the boy's peaceful, sleeping face.

Chapter 20

17 March 1876

"Leave your overcoats!" Anson Mills ordered, quickly yanking his own from his arms, dropping it at the side of the ravine Captain Moore had taken with his troops.

"S-Sir?" Lieutenant Paul started, his lips cracked and bleeding. "It's damned cold, Captain."

Mills felt for the men. All those eyes imploring him. But nonetheless . . .

"I'm going to freeze my ass with the rest of you," he explained, trying to get them encouraged a little. "And those heavy coats are just going to slow us as we make our way down." He was pointing off in the direction where Moore's men had disappeared in the broken, snow-covered country like a rumpled bed sheet.

"Mr. Donegan?"

"I'll keep mine, Captain—thank you."

Mills drew his lips into a thin line. "Very well—lead on."

The forty-seven men with Mills did as they were ordered, quickly marching away from their coats and the horse holders, down, down toward the Powder River.

When M Company reached the bare top of a low plateau two more spurs down the slope, the captain spotted Moore and his battalion again. Mills turned, waving for his own men to follow him on. They would join up with Moore for the descent.

But as Mills turned back around, he found the distant captain standing, waving him back with both arms.

"Lieutenant," he said to Paul. "Keep the men here with

Mr. Donegan. Get them down out of sight. I'm going for a conference with Captain Moore."

Ten grueling minutes later Mills was standing with a clearly agitated Alexander Moore, about halfway between their two commands.

"But Captain—the general ordered me to follow you down so that I could be of support in Egan's attack!"

"No—don't bring your companies any closer," Moore told him, his mustache bristling.

"Then what are you going to do, without my support?"

"I'm already in a position that overlooks the village," Moore explained. "About a hundred fifty yards above it. When Egan begins his charge, I will commence firing per the battle plan. We'll stalemate those—"

"Captain," Mills said, exasperated, for with his own eyes he could not see how Moore could possibly believe he was so close to the village. The rising fog was at last exposing the camp. "You're more than a thousand yards away!"

"Dammit, Captain—I've got some sharpshooters up there. We will lay down our covering fire and pick off the Indians. Don't you concern yourself: we'll make the blood flow today," Moore went on nonplussed, then turned, flinging his voice over his shoulder at Mills. "I'm going back to my men."

"Captain—what in the tunkets the matter with you? It's utter folly for you to fire from here. We're supposed to take the village, and not fire until we're in amongst them."

"Of all the rotten cold-decking I've ever run across! Just follow your orders and support Egan, Mills. There's no way possible I can take my men any farther to the left," Moore explained with a snap, growing red with agitation. "And if I move my troops any closer—we'll be discovered and ruin Egan's surprise."

Mills shook his head in consternation, looking down at the village, which seemed to be as far away as El Paso was right now. Bullets from Moore's sharpshooters would never threaten any escaping hostiles. Instead, those army bullets would likely fall among Egan's men at the moment the battle was enjoined.

"I was ordered down in support of you for the attack," Mills repeated.

"Then work your way down that way," and Moore pointed downslope toward the southern end of the village. "Get as far as you can without being discovered, and as soon as Egan begins his charge, get into the village. I'll follow you with my men as quickly as we can move."

Mills nodded, took a couple steps away through the ankle-deep snow, then turned. "Promise me you won't fire until you get near the village."

"Goddammit, you chucklehead! I'm not an idiot, Mills! I won't fire until I can hit something!" Moore roared, then whirled away.

Anson Mills stumbled and clawed his way back down the broken country, returning to his men.

"What're we going to do, sir?" asked Lieutenant Paul.

He looked down at the valley, unable now to see the village from where they stood along the steep-sided creek that flowed into the Powder. "We're going to join in the attack on the village. Let's get the men moving."

"No longer in support of Captain Moore?"

Mills shook his head in disgust. "No," he snapped, gazing back up the slope for a moment. "From the looks of things, I don't think Captain Moore's battalion is even going to be in this fight."

It looked impossible to move their horses down the ravine cluttered with deadfall and brush, big and small boulders lying askew in every direction. A man on foot would have a difficult go of if, much less these tired, cold soldiers leading their weary horses to the river bottom. Yet Egan and Noyes were going to try it.

John Bourke glanced over at Strahorn. The newsman raised an eyebrow and shrugged as the whispered order came back to proceed single file. In a matter of moments the snapping of twigs, snorts of stumbling horses, quiet curses of the soldiers and the tumbling of rocks was reverberating up and down the column.

"We're never going to surprise the savages," Bob Strahorn said, walking in column in front of Bourke.

The line came to a ragged halt, the horses with heads hung, their breath leaving little streamers of mist in the cold air. Then the column began moving again, more slowly now as the leaders had to guide the horses one by one around a difficult stretch of the chosen trail—just enough room to inch past a large boulder jutting out of the side of the hill and the sharp drop into the narrow and deep chasm. They lost one horse, the weary animal misstepping, tumbling to the bottom to break its neck. Noyes sent the dismounted soldier back up the hill to report to one of Reynolds's dismounted companies.

At the bottom of the spur, Egan and Noyes reformed their column of twos behind a low ridge where the soldiers could not be seen. Here they dispatched Pourrier, Garnier, and Jennesse to inspect the ground ahead for the coming charge. During that twenty-minute wait for the scouts, the two companies inspected their horses, tightening cinches and adjusting bridles, examining each iron-shod hoof for ice buildup. After close to a half hour Bourke noticed Little Bat was spurring his horse back to the head of the command, where he reined up in a swirl of snow.

"Charlie and Big Bat stay," Garnier said, pointing over the spur. "The village ahead, across the creek. Camp is waking up." Then he pointed to the west. "Soldiers coming down too soon."

They all looked up the slope together.

"Moore?" Noyes asked.

Egan shook his head. "Doesn't look like his battalion. Mills." He turned to Little Bat. "Get up there and tell him to stay put until we're going into the village. Got it?"

The scout nodded and sawed the reins hard, nearly spilling his mount as he dug his heels into its flanks. Bourke watched Garnier disappear around the low slope of the spur.

Ten yards off to the southwest, the officers saw the dark-skinned half-breed emerge from the broken ground as if he were materializing out of the snow itself.

Egan whispered, "Grouard."

"It's me," the half-breed replied as he came to a halt on foot.

"You were with Moore," Noyes challenged.

Grouard shook his head. "He does not want to fight today. Stays too far away to shoot. I come down to fight Crazy Horse."

"All right," Egan replied with a nod.

"I see his horses, there," and Grouard pointed to the south, where the pony herd would be.

"You want him, don't you?" Egan asked.

The half-breed only nodded, his thin lips a taut line of determination.

"So do I, Grouard," James Egan replied. He turned back to Noyes. "Nothing keeping us, Captain."

"Ready when you are, Captain," Noyes said, looking firmly at Egan. "Great God in the land of Beulah—from here on out, looks like it's your show."

Egan smiled. "Always did like being the opening act."

His fellow captain nodded. "You got balls, Teddy. That show last summer near Fort Robinson, standing firm in front of all those Sioux—moving your company in front of those warriors to protect those peace commissioners."

Slipping a big boot into a stirrup as his horse chuffered in protest, Egan nodded. "Maybe some of them are here to-day."

Noyes swung into the saddle. "Take your men to the front, Teddy. I'll follow and divide off when you're ready to make your charge." He turned and arm-signaled his men to mount.

Egan nodded. "Pull off when it's time for 'front into line.'" The captain then gave the signal to First Sergeant John McGregor and the rest of his noncoms to pull Company K, Second Cavalry, ahead of Noyes's company, taking the point of the attack.

"Boys, this is where we strip for battle," James Egan told them in something that wasn't quite an order. He pulled off his coat, dropping it into the snowy brush, then sat there a moment in the saddle as the rest did the same.

Bourke nodded to Strahorn anxiously as they shed their warm buffalo coats. The time was come.

Together they urged their mounts ahead with Bryan to join Egan at the front of the column.

"On my signal, boys," the captain explained when his men had stripped to fighting trim, "draw your pistols and inspect your arms." He watched as they pulled off their mittens, exposing their bare hands to the bitterly cold air, forcing back the protesting, frozen mule ears on their holsters, dragging out the cold pistols with the creaking racket of worn rawhide buggy springs. Quickly checking their loads.

They brought them up to port when ready, one by one by one down that long line of blue.

Their captain smiled as he stood in the stirrups to address his forty-six riders: tough, hardened, brass-mounted men. "Damn, but I'm proud to lead you hellions in this! Let's ride our bottoms raw, boys!"

Bourke felt a sudden burn of pride himself. He glanced at Strahorn, finding the newsman swallowing in some apprehension, but nonetheless wearing a smile on his handsome face.

"All right, we'll go out at a trot until we're in there . . . or the red bastards see us," Egan explained, settling himself in his saddle, inspecting his forty-three troopers plus the three recruits: Bourke, Strahorn and Bryan.

"Good luck, Teddy," Captain Noyes said, saluting.

Egan nodded, returned the salute, then turned back to his company of pistoleers. "When that door busts open, boys—it's time for O'Fagen's dance. Open up with them yaps of yours too! Let's hear you beller like a flock of the Devil's own!"

Egan reined around to the right, shifting in the saddle with anticipation as he led them out. Noyes's black-horse troop brought up the rear, their captain guiding them off to the right slightly as Egan urged his weary mount into a canter, then a trot.

Jesus, Bourke thought. My heart is beating like a parade drum.

Wind whipping into his face, he glanced beside him at Strahorn. The newsman was intent as a hound on the point, staring to the front of the column easing into a full trot behind Teddy Egan, the hooves hammering across the frozen ground with a sound like handful after handful of pebbles thrown against the rawhide head of a warrior drum. Glancing behind him, Bourke caught sight of Bryan, struggling somewhat with his jaded mount as it fought the bit, head twisted sideways, eyes widened.

Once the shooting starts, John thought, there'll be hell to pay with these goddamned, done-in animals.

Then he heard a change in the hoofbeats up ahead. They had broken onto the flat just southeast of the village. Twisting in the saddle for a moment, Bourke glanced behind him, saw Noyes's company had pulled away sharply to the right to begin their sweep for the pony herd. And then he realized why their hoofbeats sounded different. They were on different ground. Hammering now just above the riverbed itself. The last two hundred yards of it left between them and the enemy.

It was then John Bourke saw the village for the first time —saw it good.

In that grove of cottonwood trees that loomed all the larger now as they drew closer, ever closer. Across the river, past the swamp willow and plum brush, lay an open pasture of riverbank, a flat piece of ground that looked to gently slope away from the Powder for at least a mile.

Quickly he shot a glance at the rising sun over his right shoulder. The sky was lightening, ballooning around him, becoming a shield of pink.

If they did this right, they could trap the Indians between the river and that rumpled land rising in raw ridge after ever higher ridge just west of the Powder. Then Moore could unleash his riflemen on all those who sought to flee. And Reynolds would have his village for the general.

Closing on the lodges, the column came abruptly to a coulee some ten feet deep. Egan, followed by his first sergeant, then Bourke and Strahorn, led the way down into the ravine, reining sharply around to the right—

Bourke saw the teenage herder appear out of the brush, standing off to the side near a cottonwood stump, as still as the poised forefoot of a stalking coyote with prey in sight, wrapped in a greasy blanket, looking all the more forlorn for it. Leveling his pistol at the young Indian, the lieutenant decided the youth was one of those coming out early to water or check on the ponies. Unflinchingly the Indian's dark eyes locked on Bourke. Continued to gaze impassively at the soldier as the lieutenant brought his service pistol down on target.

Then suddenly felt his mount nudged sideways.

Looking up, startled, Bourke found Egan's mount beside his, nudging him again.

"Leave him be, John," Egan said firmly. His squinted eyes gave the words some muscle. "We can't make any noise yet."

Bourke watched the youth stand there as they trotted on past, the Indian motionless as a stone statue—wondering if they dared leave the youngster behind alive. Too late now . . .

He looked forward again, finding the wind cold on his face once more as they burst out of the end of the ravine, back onto the flat—realizing the wind-whipped tears were freezing at the corners of his eyes.

Damn, but it's cold—

"Hepa! Hepa! Heeeyaaaaa!"

That wild, throaty war whoop split the cold, dry air behind them like the sudden blow of a tomahawk.

In the next heartbeat Egan was bellowing, *"Left front into line!"*

That order was heard above it all, the whinnying horses, the hammering hoofbeats, the rattle of bit chains in a cacophony with the squeak and creak of saddletree and leather kept at subzero temperatures days on end. It promised to be one hell of a charge, Bourke decided: all guts and gumption, with a lot of luck thrown in.

Up ahead, dogs were beginning to bark and howl.

Egan was standing in his stirrups once more, a jagged smile slashed across his winter-tanned face.

"Bugler!"

Private Augustus E. Bellows responded, yanking on the gold rope slung over his shoulder, bringing the bright brass horn to his quivering lips.

Twisting a moment in his cold saddle to look behind him, Bourke found the Indian youth lunging toward one of the ponies, grabbing its mane and lunging atop it bareback, continuing to screech his warning to the village.

Then turning back around atop his faltering, weary mount, Bourke saw an old squaw raising her door flap. She stood there for a matter of a breath before the woman's mouth became a black O as she yelled out her warning. Her shrill keening echoed off the nearby ridge, bouncing back at the cavalrymen again and again.

And again.

"Katie bar the door!" Bob Strahorn shouted into the wind, his words yanked behind them, going no farther than the frosty steam issuing from his mouth as Company K, Second U.S. Cavalry, closed on seventy-five yards.

"Mr. Bourke, just stick your horse like bear-grease stink to an Injun," Egan shouted at the young lieutenant with a grim smile before the captain rose in the stirrups, his pistol arm waving, giving his final order to bring up the stragglers on the far flank.

"Left front—NOW!" bellowed Egan.

Without slowing a step, the whole of the company flowed left away from the captain and his bugler until there were forty-seven in a solid front, stirrup to stirrup and knee to knee, urging their weary, protesting, prancing horses into a ragged gallop at last.

Like the belly of summer thunder pounding in his ears, Bourke heard the loud triple clicks of the hammers on those single-action Colt revolvers up and down that long line of blue.

Hell a'mighty, he thought. Here we go!

"Bugler!" Egan shouted into the cold wind. "Sound the *charge!"*

At the crack of the rifle, she wheeled about, knowing.

"The soldiers are charging!" cried an old man's voice from the bluff just above Monaseetah's tiny lodge.

"The soldiers are here!" warned another voice, farther away, to the south end of camp.

A second shot erupted from the village. And then she heard the rattle of weapons firing like winter rain pelting off a lodge cover. First the small sounds. Then the big booms of the soldier guns. She remembered. If any Indian woman knew the sound of soldier guns, it was Yellow Hair's woman.

"Mother?"

She wheeled. Sees Red squirted from his robes. Then her youngest was lunging for the safety of her arms once more.

"Soldiers!" she shouted at them.

The village beyond them was fully awake in those three heartbeats: people screaming, ponies crying out, babies wailing and warriors screeching their war songs. To the south now, the gunfire had grown constant, like the river tumbling over its bed.

"Come now!" she ordered them, yanking Yellow Bird up in an arm, scooping up the buffalo robe that had sheltered them from last night's cold. "Sees Red—bring your robe, your blanket—something!"

When she swept aside the frost-stiffened antelope-hide door flap, Monaseetah found the world outside a swirl of smoke and darting, flitting forms.

Sand Creek. The Washita. And now the Powder River.

Whirling, the woman bumped into her two sons, sending Yellow Bird sprawling over Sees Red with a yelp of pain. They clawed to their hands and knees in the murky darkness of the lodge. Yanking her belt from the dew-cloth rope at the side of the liner, Monaseetah lashed the ends around the blanket she would wear for warmth, then dragged the long butcher knife from its sheath at her hip. She jabbed the point through the frost-stiffened lodge skins and with both hands struggled to work the blade down through the frost- and fog-dampened hides.

Pulling aside the slit in the resisting skins, the woman motioned frantically. "Come!"

She had to grab Sees Red first, shoving him out the hole in the back of their lodge.

"Yellow Bird!"

She hurled her youngest through the stiffened opening, then dove through herself. They had to wait as a half-dozen warriors darted past, heading to the west, toward the bluffs with their rifles and bows. In their wake she was dragging the boys to their feet, when a spotted pony tore by with a long rawhide tether tied to its lower jaw, a picket pin slapping the hard, crusty snow.

"There! Go now!" she ordered, pointing, pulling and pushing at the boys struggling with the bulk and weight of their robes.

The smaller one faltered, looking up at her for help.

"Do not leave your robe, Yellow Bird! You will pray for it soon!"

Sees Red obediently dove into the madness. Monaseetah followed, dragging the small one into the swirling panic. They cried out, all three, as they were hurled to the ground, knocked aside as a pony careened around a lodge and into them. On the pony's back clung a young, half-naked herder, slumped against the animal's neck.

She recognized the stench as she clambered to her feet, watching the pony bolt off with its bloodied rider. The obedient animal was pulling more and more of the steamy gut coil from its bullet-riven body with each prancing step.

From the direction of the gunshots, she knew the soldiers had already reached the flat meadow between the village and the pony herds.

"Toward the river!" she shouted into the bedlam.

The three dove into the snowy willow at the banks of the Powder as the shouts of wounded soldiers and the curses of white men loomed louder, closer still.

"They ride white horses!" Sees Red hollered.

As they raced for the river, all around them arose the babble of Shahiyena mixed with Lakota and an occasional soldier voice. Brass horns blared in the rosy light of the new day, along with the high-pitched, almost human cry of wounded horses crying out in pain and fear.

And for that space it took her heart to leap once in her chest hopefully . . . Monaseetah stared at the oncoming soldiers, looking for their battle flags. Hoping to see the white man's medicine marks that meant these soldiers belonged to Hiestzi.

Then she was falling, sailing, her feet out from under her as the ground scooped her out of the sky.

"Mother!"

Chapter 21

17 March 1876

*I*t was utter chaos. Pandemonium.

Bob Strahorn had caroused and shilly-shallied with the best of the young men in Denver who considered themselves hell-raisers and ladies' men. And when the saloons in that town celebrated St. Patrick's Day, it was something to behold.

But to a twenty-three-year-old reporter, none of that could compare with the din of noise, the fright of this charge, and the swirl of confusion where he now found himself a reluctant participant. More of a prisoner.

If he wasn't hearing it with his own ears, Strahorn thought he wouldn't have believed it. How this company of white men, spurred on to answer the brass throat of the trumpeter's bugle by yelling at the top of their lungs, could sound like a troop of screeching banshees itself winging down on O'Donnell's farm.

Even his friend John Bourke himself was screaming full-throated like a catamount with a muzzle full of porcupine quills.

But, so some of the old cavalry files had told the young newsman, this getting the jump on the enemy, with the immediate fear such bellowing might arouse in the hostile village, just might mean the difference between a man's hair being worn or getting torn.

Of a sudden the company farrier lunged from his horse on the off side of Strahorn. Hit in the belly, the animal threw its rider as it collapsed onto its rear haunches, crying out. Hollering in pain and fear, Patrick Goings found himself pinned beneath the dying animal, its legs still thrashing in the midst of the charge, horsemen plunging past on either side of the downed animal and its helpless blacksmith.

More bullets were singing their way already. The whisper of one at his ear reminded Strahorn to fire his own weapon. The big army .44 he had carried around for years now. A relic compared to Bourke's .45 Colt's pistol using fixed ammunition.

Not so fast, Bobby, he reminded himself. Shoot when you got something to hit.

To his right a soldier's horse lunged forward, vaulting its rider clumsily toward the thick of the fray. Strahorn watched the trooper's muskrat hat suddenly sail into the air. The man reined up savagely, fingers to the top of his head, bringing away a bare hand covered with blood.

"You hurt?" Strahorn hollered out.

The trooper shook his head. "Dam't t'ing yust graz't me."

Bob hollered back, "The luck o' the Irish!"

"Auch-be! I'm German, be God!" he grumbled, and kicked his mount into a lumbering gait once again, back into the smoke and the din of Hell.

Somewhere to the rear, a soldier's horse cried out. Nearby, another snorted. Strahorn heard the familiar smack of lead against flesh and watched a horse go down without a complaint, easing onto its side as the young soldier bolted from his saddle, darting zigzag on foot among the rest of the oncoming chargers.

"They're shooting at the goddamned horses!" Strahorn said to himself aloud, surprised at how loud his voice sounded, even against the steady racket of the guns, the cries of the horses, the shrill war songs and the wails of the wounded.

Egan and Bourke were just ahead of him. Strahorn reined beside Will Bryan. From the left a warrior leaped clear of the morning shadows behind a hide lodge, lowering an old muzzle loader at Egan riding at the far right end of the line. In a move that could only be described as instinctual, Bryan kicked his animal forward.

Seeing the puff of smoke from the old weapon about the same time the blood and gore splattered, Strahorn looked over to find Bryan's horse twisting its head around, bloody pulp where both eyes had been a moment before.

Bryan shouted, "Something's wrong with my—"

As the steward struggled desperately for control, the horse loped blindly onward, already dead. The bullet had gone in one eye, through the brain, then out the other eye as the heart kept beating, carrying its rider another ten yards until the animal pitched forward in a heap, flinging Bryan into the snow.

"Goddamn you, son of a bitch!" the steward cursed as he rolled to his feet and started running after the warrior disappearing behind the lodge.

"Bryan!" Strahorn bellowed, watching the young soldier hurtling headlong for the enemy. "Get back here!"

Suddenly the newsman's horse wrung itself up in fury and fear, arching its back and rearing, throwing its rider free. Strahorn himself landed in a nearby clump of willow, snow cascading down his neck with as cold a shock as any man would wish to have, watching his animal bolt to the rear, where it stumbled at the lip of a shallow ravine and lunged against the far side, breaking its neck.

"Shit!" he murmured under his breath, shaking uncontrollably.

At that same moment, Bryan realized the folly of his one-man assault, racing as he was right into the arms of the enemy.

Skidding, slipping then falling on the ground in a slide, Bryan was clambering back onto his feet and setting off at a gallop without hesitation, this time heading for the soldier lines.

Strahorn saw him coming, ready to cover the young steward. "You're lucky you're so damned quick!" he shouted as Bryan made it back, bullets kicking up skiffs of snow around his feet.

"He's champion foot-racer of the regiment, I hear!" declared John Bourke as the lieutenant ghostily appeared out of the confusion.

"Where's your damned horse, Johnny?" Strahorn demanded.

"I got rid of him. Sent him back with the holders. Took a shot close enough to cut the reins in my bloody hand! I figured the son of a bitch was too big a target!"

"Bourke! Strahorn! Look at that!" Bryan shouted.

As a man they turned to their left to see a warrior emerge slowly, almost haughtily, from the plum brush and willow at the edge of the copse of trees, dressed in full war regalia, including a horned headdress, sitting brazenly astride his snorting pony, its breath rising steamily into the cold morning air. He held a long-handled, stone-studded war club in his right hand, shaking it provocatively at the soldiers as he kicked the snorting pony into a gallop.

"He's coming right for us!" a voice yelled off to their right.

"If he gets through, he'll go for the pony herd!" Bourke shouted.

"Drop him!" came Egan's voice above the noise.

Strahorn was down on one knee with some of the rest, more than a dozen of them, firing slowly, steadily squeezing the trigger as the warrior came on, ever on, cutting an oblique path across their wide front, heading for the pony herd to the soldiers' rear.

"Got the bastard!"

He didn't know who did, nor who had hollered that joyful declaration. There was really no way to know, with the way the bullets had struck both the pony and the warrior like wet hands slapping putty, tumbling the Cheyenne off the animal, the pony going down in a heap a step later, both of them skidding across the ankle-deep snow in a sun-blazing rooster tail of cascading ice crystals turned red with the rising sun.

Those of Egan's troopers still mounted were slashing their way ever deeper into the village, ever on toward the north end of the enemy camp where the river hugged the snowy mesa, driving the hostiles before them.

Before him the entire field was alive with movement now. Most of the enemy was half naked, for all Strahorn could tell. Like shadows, their brown skins glowing copper as new pennies in the newborn light of this Irish holiday, they darted from their lodges half dressed. Women clutching children, herding them north among the shadows of the great, bare-boned cottonwoods. The men cried out to one another, screeching like devils, hurrying to the left against the flow of the charge. They were going for the ridges west of the village. Taking the high ground, the cheeky bastards!

Yet enough were holding their ground behind the trees, hunkering down among clumps of brush, firing their old one-shot, fur-trade fusils or levering rounds repeatedly through their newly-acquired Winchester saddle guns.

Still, Egan's pistols were having their effect. That and the total surprise of their charge were nonetheless pushing those warriors back from the southern fringe of the village to the first real stand of old-growth cottonwoods. Yet even as they were falling back with the steady pressure from Company K, the warriors had already inflicted a toll on the soldiers: three wounded. One with an arm hung useless at his side, bleeding from a fractured elbow. Another suffered a wound high in the chest, the bullet snapping through the collarbone. And the last, lying still, breathing shallow as death coming—a bullet squarely through the lung.

Along with their captain, more and more of Egan's men were going afoot. Their horses going down in a swirl of snow and gun smoke, stumbling blindly or wounded.

"That was Schneider!" Bourke yelled.

Together they had heard the unmistakable smack of a bullet striking bone, watching the young soldier lurch to his feet, hand to his bloody head, then fall facedown into the snow.

And just then things began to stall about halfway into the village. Company K's horsemen were returning from the far end of the camp, roaring back at a gallop, hugging low in their saddles as bullets whined over their heads.

It did not take a military tactician to realize the element of surprise had been wrung for all it was worth—and now it was down to a close, dirty fight of it. Already one in every eight of Egan's men were out of action to the rear: horse holders, dragging behind them the rearing, frightened animals by the link strap, a fifteen-inch-long leather band clipped to the throat latch, four horses led in each hand.

And there were the wounded, some perhaps already dead, down and out of action. Although no one had stopped to take count.

Teddy Egan was among them with orders to hold their ground there along the thick growth of plum brush and swamp willow right at the riverbank, orders to spread out to the left in a long front but hold their ground and not lose an inch to the withering fire now starting to grow ever hotter as the warriors climbing the mesa to their left claimed the high ground and started pouring bullets down on K Company at the edge of the village.

Up there, somewhere, Strahorn wondered—dammit . . . where was Moore?

"Those red bastards are popping at us right from the spot where Moore's men are supposed to be, bottling them up!" Bourke growled as he slid behind some brush nearby.

Egan scooted up, crabbing along on both knees and one hand, pistol in the other. His cheek was scratched from the sharp, icy limbs he plunged through. "Hang on, boys. Reinforcements were promised us, by lord! Hang on till we're delivered!"

Then Egan was pushing on through the brush, cheering those of his men still able-bodied. Rallying those left to fight. Giving orders to the right flank.

"Defensive line—spread it out. Spread it out, by damned! Sergeant Gleuson—get in here with these men and see they don't bunch up!"

"Yes, sir, Cap'n!" answered John Gleuson.

Strahorn admired that man Egan.

"Reinforcements is what we need, and quick," the newsman told Bourke, then pointed at the far hillside. "I thought we watched some outfit moving down as we were getting into position for the charge."

Bourke nodded. "I figure that was Mills."

Strahorn wagged his head, turned around and squatted as he set about reloading the big army revolver.

"If Mills and Donegan don't get here to take some pressure off us," Strahorn grumbled, ramming another load down a cylinder, "we may be pinned down here for some time to come, Johnny."

"Happy Saint Paddy's Day, boyo!" Bourke cheered his friend.

"Happy goddamned Saint Paddy's Day to you too!"

"I am here for you, Tashunka Witko!"

Frank Grouard stood in the tall brush, shouting his challenge at Crazy Horse in Lakota. Flinging his brave words at the village, his voice reverberating from the rough-cut hillside where the warriors were gathering more quickly now that the women were pouring from the north end of the camp, escaping from the river-bottom camp toward the steep bluffs. An icy climb for them.

But that stupid soldier named Moore would not be there to stop their escape.

His enemies were flushing toward the northwest like wing-crippled birds broken from the underbrush and scattering for their lives. Grouard could hear them fleeing, running noisily in their terror—a cacophony of voices like the throaty husks of quail or sage chicken when they mated.

It was good—how badly he wanted to see them run.

Smoke from the morning cookfires mixed with the first stinging strands of burnt gunpowder, to hang in sleazy layers over the river valley.

Frank gazed over his left shoulder again, watching some soldiers descending the rough, brushy slope behind Donegan now. Hurrying in to reinforce the pistol shooters who had first charged the village.

It was good that big Irishman led someone's soldiers into this fight.

Color came to the sky with a white glow in the east, with a transparent opaqueness changing to a salmon-pink hue as he watched, the flesh of its color spreading, brightening, finally breaking forth into an Indian redness. This was a good sign. Turning back to the village, Grouard shouted.

"I see your horses here, Tashunka Witko!"

A bullet sought him out, but only stung the leafless willow at his side.

"Hah! Do not shoot me from hiding! Come out and fight

me like a man, Crazy Horse! Is He Dog with you? Doesn't He Dog want my scalp? It was I—the Grabber—who brought these soldiers here to destroy your village!"

Another bullet brushed his fur cap, knocking it into the brush behind him. He did not stoop to pick it up. Nor did he move to take cover. Instead Grouard stood there, hurling his taunts at his enemy, his eyes burning as bright as a loafer wolf's hunkering down just outside the throw of a night fire.

"Not close enough!" He hurled his words at the hillside where the gray puff spots showed the enemy riflemen.

"Come out, Crazy Horse. Come fight me, He Dog! These soldiers are here to fight the rest. I am here to fight you both myself! Crazy Horse—I stand here! He Dog—the Grabber has come for you!"

"Grouard!"

The voice came from behind him, to the right. As he turned, another bullet whispered by, smacking the bare willow. He ducked reflexively, pulling his head into his shoulders, dropping to his knees.

A soldier appeared from the brush, bent at the waist. "Cap'n Egan wants you to go see what's holding up our reinforcements."

"More soldiers coming, yes." He pointed up the slope, but could not see Donegan and the blue troopers among the broken terrain.

The soldier nodded, swallowing with a gulp, his eyes searching Grouard's for something to carry back to Egan.

"They're already coming," Grouard said calmly. He pointed again, hopeful. It would be a good thing to fight alongside that big Irishman. The two of them more than a match for Crazy Horse and that brother-in-law named He Dog.

For a fraction of a moment the soldier looked, a hand propped on the scout's shoulder as he peered above the willows. "Shit!" was all the soldier hissed as he dropped, wheeled about and crabbed back in the direction he had come.

Grouard smiled. "Shit," he repeated.

Then the half-breed turned back to the hillside on his left

as he heard the first of the soldiers with Donegan coming up behind him, busting through the thick underbrush, struggling across the icy, broken ground, cursing, their breath heaving in fractured, frosty ribbons from their chests.

They work so hard, Grouard thought.

He stood slightly, cupping his two wool-wrapped hands at either side of his mouth, throwing his voice at the far hillside again where the warriors had taken up their positions on the high ground.

"Your time draws close, Tashunka Witko! You and He Dog can die like warriors . . . or die up there in some hole in the rocks, like frightened ground squirrels!"

Another bullet keened past in the dry air.

"I am come for you, Crazy Horse! He Dog—prepare to die!"

"Maiyun, you must help catch this spirit horse!" Wooden Leg screamed to the mysterious ones above the deafening racket as he stared at the lone pony. Slowly he approached the animal, still trying to shake the moss of sleep from his mind.

Eyes wide as silver conchos, its nostrils flaring, yanking back in terror on its rawhide tether where the old chief of the tribe had tied this favorite pony—the horse had been abandoned by Old Bear.

"Wimaca yelo." I am a man, he prayed. *"Nohetto."* That is all—nothing else. "Help me."

As the young Shahiyena warrior of eighteen summers inched forward on his knees through the deep snow, a bow and a half-dozen arrows clamped in one white-knuckled hand, the other outstretched and imploring the animal, Wooden Leg remembered when a good friend of Old Bear's gave the chief this pony. Pipe, it was: the mystical shaman who dressed in the clothing of a woman. He had said the spotted lower legs were believed to give the pony swiftness in the chase. Now it must help Wooden Leg race through the soldier lines and reach the herd before the ponies were all captured for good.

Frightened, pawing and prancing away from the warrior

at the end of its tether, straining against the lodge peg where it was tied, the pony repeatedly tossed its head back. The wind heavy with the sting of burnt gunpowder tormented its mane. A beautiful animal.

"Help me, Everywhere Spirit," he prayed aloud, his voice soft against the steady hammering of riflefire, every single shot echoing against the snowy bluffs, ringing back into the river bottom.

Then he saw it—hanging from a broken branch of the cottonwood a few yards away. A long rawhide rope coiled in a loose loop. His body as lean as a dried navel cord, Wooden Leg lunged to his feet all fire and sinew, took the lariat in his hands, played it out and sent it singing through the air at the instant the pawing, frightened pony tore his picket pin from the ground and wheeled to flee.

In a grand circle the rawhide loop dropped around its twisting neck, the pony's hooves kicking up sprays of snow and gritty sand as it began its run for freedom.

"Ezhesso!" Thus be the way of all things!

The sudden, searing pain surprised Wooden Leg as his arms were immediately yanked at their sockets, the ground gone out from beneath him. No thought of reaching back for the bow and those arrows. Tumbling, the shock of the cold against his iron-earth-colored skin enough to make him cry out—flat on his belly as he twisted, straining to keep hold, he was pulled through the snow in an icy path as the pony tore through the gathering of lodges.

Just behind him arose the voices of white men, the slap of bullets hitting the ground, stiffened hides, poles splintering all around him. The juices of danger squirted through his body.

In a sharply twisting, gut-wrenching turn taken by the pony in its run between the lodges, Wooden Leg flipped over on his back. Blinking his eyes clear of snow and sandy grit, he caught a glimpse of soldiers charging on foot, stopping to kneel and shoot at him, then studying their weapons upon reloading, before shooting again.

Without missing a step, the spirit pony pulled him to safety. Away from the soldiers, farther into the cottonwood grove where this mystical animal suddenly stopped, turned slightly, and looked back at the youth, its head dancing.

As Wooden Leg lay there, catching his breath from the cold and wondering if any of the numbness he felt from chattering chin to frozen toes were a bullet wound, the pony slowly approached him, still wide-eyed in terror. Yet came up to stand beside the young Shahiyena warrior.

Head bobbing anxiously as if to hurry the man, the pony pawed the ground.

His feelings as high as a meadowlark's highest note, Wooden Leg gave thanks as he grabbed hold of the short rawhide tether, pulled himself quickly from the snow and dragged the rawhide lariat from the animal's neck.

"Nitaashema." Let's go, he said as he threw the lariat aside.

With the single rein that was tied to the pony's lower jaw in his hand, the warrior vaulted quickly to the short bare back, immediately digging his heels into its heaving sides. Wooden Leg's heart jumped in his chest like a slippery fish breaking the still surface of a high country pond.

"Now we can free the rest of your brothers," he leaned forward to whisper into the pony's ear, the wind whipping the hair at his face as they took off at a shot. *"Vovehe!"* Run!

"Thank you, Grandfather!" he shouted gloriously at the winter sky.

Chapter 22

17 March 1876

"*M*ove—move—*move!*" Egan was bellowing at them.

John Bourke didn't need the captain to tell him to get out of there.

For a few frantic moments almost the whole of Egan's line was under assault from above. But not from the warriors who had climbed the bluffs to take up positions along the sharp-sided mesas. No, the bullets raining down on Company K were fired by army rifles.

"Goddamn that Moore!" shouted Bob Strahorn.

Here they were, at first pinned down from above by the warriors, prevented from punching on into the village by the ferocity of the warriors' counterattack, then suddenly put in danger by reckless firing from Moore's soldiers higher up along the ridge. Out of sight as that battalion was, all Bourke could see of Moore's men were the gray puffs above each rifle as the weapons were fired in the cold morning air.

Then as suddenly as the torrent of lead had begun, it trickled off into an occasional shot falling among the plum brush. In a minute more the bullets stopped altogether.

"Damn him," Strahorn growled nearby. "I'll see Moore gets a special dispatch written about his utter stupidity—if I get out of here to write it."

"You'll get out," Bourke cheered, not really feeling hopeful himself, his right hand clumsy and unresponsive as he worked open the cylinder door on the Colt .45 and began reloading. His hands just weren't obeying what he wanted them to do. Maybe it was only his mind—growing numb itself and not getting the message down to his fingers.

"Forget your damned pistols. Time to put your carbines to work now, boys!" Egan bellowed his order again, first to one side of the line stretched suicidally thin all the way from the riverbank, then yelled to the left flank.

To Bourke it seemed the captain was everywhere, here and there, adding his cheer up and down that deathly thin skirmish line strung from the river on the east to a position just shy of the bluffs on the west.

Sergeant John McGregor was bellowing at them too. "Use them damned carbines to hold them drammed red bastards back!"

Up where Moore's sharpshooters should have been in position, laying down an infilading fire over the village and pressuring the warriors to fall back . . . there were only warriors and their weapons—keeping things hot on Egan's shrinking company through each and every agonizing minute of that next half hour. Some thirty minutes from the moment they had burst into the southern fringe of the village. A half hour that seemed like an eternity in the raucous bedlam of Hell.

"We aren't going to last here," Will Bryan whispered as he rammed another cartridge into his carbine and slammed down the trapdoor.

As if he had heard the faint of heart, Teddy Egan was beside them, kicking icy snow over Bourke's legs as he came to a halt and crouched among the three. "Pour your fire into those bluffs, boys!"

Then the captain was gone, crawfishing on along the line.

Bourke turned. He could see the sheer terror of it whitening Bryan's eyes. The youth was a physician's helper who had come along on the charge, expecting Reynolds to overrun the village and have a quick victory of it. And instead the boy was seeing the bloody, nasty, dirty war of it grind down on these brass-hardened men. He had been called here, then there, back and forth as each new man was hit in those first frantic moments of Egan's assault. And now with the wounded pulled back to where the horse holders could haul them to the hospital Noyes had established behind the southernmost bluff, Bryan had hurried back to the line.

John Bourke had to give the youngster credit for gumption.

"You could've stayed back there," the lieutenant said as he rolled back onto his belly and sighted along the short carbine barrel.

Bryan shook his head emphatically. "I talked Munn into taking me with him—with Reynolds."

"No, I mean you could have stayed back there with Noyes, where it's a little quieter," Bourke said, jabbing his head to the rear.

This time Bryan just wagged his head dolefully. "No. I'm a soldier after all. In a soldiers' army. I'll fight until someone else needs help."

"And you'll do just fine, Will Bryan," Strahorn said with a grin. "Stick with us and you'll do fine."

"Bryan!"

The shrill voice came from their left, likely where the Indians were laying down a murderous fire from the mesa.

"Steward!"

Immediately the handsome youth began to move off down the line.

"Take your carbine with you, Will," Bourke reminded.

Bryan stopped, snatched up the barrel and dragged it into the brush behind him as he crabbed away.

"I wouldn't have his job for all the money in Deadwood," Strahorn said, huffing warm breath on his numb hands.

"Oh?" Bourke asked. "Just whose job would you have right now? A cushy newspaper reporter's?"

They laughed easily, a little too loud, when suddenly interrupted by Egan again. Hollering from the left side of the skirmish line.

"Lookee, boys! Lookee there!"

And at that moment they saw him pointing at the low spur to their left and a little behind them. Puffs of smoke. Bourke looked to the right along the mesa where the warriors had infiltrated every ravine and crevice. Spurts of dirt and snow were being kicked up, little volcanoes among the enemy. Someone was finally laying down some effective fire. Some outfit was coming down the ridge to open up on the warriors and take the pressure off Company K.

"About goddamned time!" hollered someone far to the right near the riverbank in a high, shrill voice.

Another sang out, not so treble in tone and clearly Irish by the roll of the R's. "Gloreee!"

Soldier rifles, by God!

"We're moving out and now!" the captain shouted above them, waving them up from their cover. Teddy Egan stood among them, at the center front of their line. Urging them, coaxing these frozen soldiers to their feet once more.

"I don't know how long we'll have this cover fire!" He flung his voice above them all as the riflefire echoed from the bluffs, holding down the warriors. "But we're going to use it to take this village, by Jaysus! Follow me!"

They were in a sprint together, as one man behind Teddy Egan, their throats burning with the cold, dry air—more so from the way every last man of them was yelling, hollering back at the Devil as they plunged into the village, dashing among the trees, darting between the lodges, scattering the last of the warriors before them.

"Arrrghghowwww!" Bourke heard the bear growl tremble in his ears, his throat aching from the strain of it. Then felt the cold snow splatter along the side of his face.

Praise God in His heaven, prayed John Bourke as he tripped over something hidden by the snow, pitching headlong into the gritty, sand-streaked white churned by moccasins and unshod hooves . . . lost his footing trying to rise, then got back to his knees, clambering to his feet, and began racing along behind Captain James Egan again.

Praise God in His heaven for Teddy Egan.

And whoever it was who had come to their rescue.

As the first of the bullets from the south began to fall among the warriors, He Dog turned in that direction, not believing. As he squinted, peering at the far ridge, the muscles in his jaw made tiny ripples under the oak-brown skin.

Like the others, the Oglalla saw the puffs of smoke clinging like puffballs in the cold air over the nearby ridge. And some flickering movement of dark forms among the white, broken hillside, moving down, down toward the village. Muffled voices swallowed by the snowy landscape. A soldier chief barking orders to his warriors. Some of the dark forms stopped again. More puffs rose above them.

Bullets landed among the warriors drawn back in the crevices and huddled at the lips of the ravines running like open scars along this icy river-cut bluff.

The white man fought like that, he thought, almost jealously for a moment. Fighting together, taking orders from a soldier chief. While he, and the other Oglalla, Shahiyena, Miniconjou and those two Arapaho—they fought as lone warriors. With their own personal battle to wage against the invaders.

How he wanted to crawl down the slope and find the Grabber who had been calling out for him. The Grabber had brought these soldiers here. It would be a good thing to take that scalp.

He Dog glanced up the ridge for White Cow Bull, finding him rising from the low spot among the tufts of buffalo grass, waving others before him, moving them farther along the ridge to a new position.

"Go north!" He Dog was shouting now. Standing too, signaling the others, the younger men, the ones less tried. Move them north along the face of the mesa as quickly as they could, out of range of the new guns the soldier trained on them.

Down below as he turned back, He Dog watched the thin line of dark forms rising out of the willow and brush at the south end of the village, beginning their push in among the lodges again. He cursed, kneeled, and threw his repeater to his shoulder, shivering. The cold made it difficult to aim.

No warm blanket capote had he taken with him as he plunged out of his lodge at the first shots. Only this new Winchester and the two cap-and-ball revolvers he had traded with the white storekeeper back at the White Rock agency. Dragging up this pouch he had slung over his shoulder as an afterthought. Powder and ball and caps and a little jerked meat bulging from the bag's flap.

He held half his breath and squeezed the trigger, feeling the reassuring nudge of the rifle's explosion. Almost immediately the bullets rained around him, causing him to flinch. He Dog cursed himself again for flinching at the white man's incoming bullets.

With the repeater held at the end of his outstretched arm, He Dog raised his Winchester to the sky, and with it his voice. A war song. His prayer, a plea to the spirit helpers of his people.

"He Dog!"

Jerking around at the call, he found White Cow Bull just above him, stretched flat on his belly, lowering his arm, offering its help.

He took it, clawing his way up the steep side to the icy ledge that offered a path north along the face of the eroded mesa.

"The ponies," he said to his warrior friend as they lay there together a moment, gasping for breath.

Together they stretched on their bellies, looking past the line of soldiers dashing into the village, even beyond the dark forms of thirty or more soldiers punching down onto the flat at that very minute. Beyond all those, across the flat river bottom west of the frozen Powder, they saw part of their great pony herd ringed by the dark horsemen. There, and there—and there too on the east side of the river, upon that wide, flat meadow—other small bands of soldiers were driving more of the ponies toward the great herd.

"We must get them back," White Cow Bull swore quietly, there in the snow and muck of that mesa beside He Dog.

"We will, my friend," He Dog vowed. "Let us go now, so that we can gather the others who will help us. *H'gun,*" he said, the Lakota courage word.

He did not want to say *anpetu sica,* that it might be a bad day. But without those ponies, there could be no escape of the women and children, the old and the sick, and the wounded who were bleeding among the low places of this ridge at this very moment—without their pony herd . . . there would be no escape from the soldiers brought here by the Grabber.

Forget the lodges. And they could forget the kettles and parfleches, blankets and robes and beautiful clothing they would leave behind. They had been forced to abandon their riches countless times before. As long as the Lakota and Shahiyena had their weapons, and could recapture those ponies—they would continue to fight on.

By the dream—all truth is known!

They had their weapons. "Thanks be to the Grandfather!" he prayed to the sky.

All they needed now were their ponies.

He was wet from his ankles to his crotch, but his feet kept churning. Running, leading Anson Mills and his M Company of the Third Cavalry down through the broken country.

Egan's men were getting chewed up down there, and bad.

At seeing the long stretch of snowy, ocher ridge dropping sharply into the river valley, Seamus Donegan stopped a heartbeat, turned and signaled Mills.

"Cap'n! We can take some pressure off the boys in the valley." Seamus pointed to the far ridge where the warriors were pouring down their deadly fire.

Mills halted his men. "Damned fine idea, Irishman."

"By squads, Cap'n."

"You plan on continuing our descent into the valley?" Mills asked breathlessly as the soldiers swirled about them, coming to a halt. "While you're firing at those hostiles?"

Donegan nodded. "Only way I see to get down to help Egan—and make sure Egan's still got him a company to rescue when we reach the river bottom."

The Irishman watched the light of it cross the captain's face like pond water slicking over with ice. "All right. It just might work."

"It's got to work, Cap'n."

Mills nodded. "I brought you along to help get me down. How long has it been since you've commanded men?"

Donegan turned slowly on him. "Where'd you hear?"

"There's talk. Forget that now," Mills said hurriedly. "How long's it been, Sergeant?"

"If you heard anything, then you know it's been a long time."

"Then let's get your feet wet again," Mills replied. He

immediately turned away from Seamus and hollered orders at his men, peering over them for his squad leaders. "We're going to continue down the slope in six squads. Sergeants Rittel, Kaminsky, Erhard, Prescott, Robinson and Ballard —form up!"

As the soldiers obeyed, their sergeants snapped commands to bunch for volley fire, to check their carbines. Mills whirled back on the scout.

"All right, Irishman—it's your show."

Donegan swallowed with a grim smile, looking over the men who would now rely on him to get them down the slope in one piece, then glanced into the river valley at the soldiers who relied on him every bit as much. "Cap'n Mills, let's open the dance!

"First squad!"

"First Sergeant Rittel to the front!" Mills added his command.

"Kneel and fire in volley on my order!" Donegan growled.

He was pointing as the first of them knelt in the snow there among the sage and bunchgrass, some of them quickly ramming down the trapdoor on their Springfields over another cartridge.

"Fire!"

The soldiers sent their bullets raining into the places where Donegan had seen the grayish puffs of rifle smoke along the mesa. It didn't take a veteran plainsman to realize that those weren't Moore's sharpshooters up there. Glancing quickly up the slope of the ridge, he could see a little movement where that battalion of Moore's would be, near where Mills had left them. Maybe Moore was moving them down at last—as Moore promised Mills that he would.

Then there came the whine of bullets going overhead, right over Company M. Those bullets were being hurled down into the southern edge of the village. But instead of doing damage among the warriors still in the hostile camp, they were falling among Teddy's men.

"Jesus H. Christ!" swore Sergeant Frank S. Rittel.

"Who the hell was that firing?" growled an old corporal, John A. Kirkwood.

"Our own bloody men, that's who!" Rittel answered, shaking his fist back up the hill.

"C'mon—move out!" Mills shouted, turning to Donegan.

"First squad reload! Second squad—prepare to fire! The rest of you follow me down the slope," Donegan bellowed, getting those frozen soldiers up and moving down the slippery slope.

To Seamus's way of thinking, Egan had two problems right now: the first was Moore's distant and poorly aimed volleys showering his skirmish line; and when Moore wasn't shooting at Company K, the warriors were taking up all slack. Making things damned hot on Teddy's boys. Weren't Bourke and Strahorn with them?

Then Donegan realized they had gone far enough.

"Halt! Third squad fire on my order!"

"Sergeant Erhard!" Mills shouted.

Donegan pointed, flinging his arm downhill. "The rest of you. Sergeants, lead your men—downhill at the double. Ten yards apart. You too, Cap'n. I'll catch up."

As Mills nodded and took off to lead the rest down the slope, Seamus wheeled back to the third squad. *"Fire!"*

He was off, hurling his voice into the cold air as the riflefire reverberated off the river bluffs. "C'mon, boys—you can bloody well reload on the run!"

The other sergeants and Mills had spread the rest of the squads out along the edge of the ridge. Not far to go now. Seamus thought he could actually make out white faces down there, now in and among the plum brush, peering up at Company M as they came roaring down off this snowy slope. And maybe, yes—maybe that was Bob Strahorn and John Bourke. Standing up, waving their arms?

"Fourth squad—aim and fire at will."

Mills turned toward those men. "Sergeant Prescott—ready your men."

"Fire at will," Seamus repeated, "then reload quickly and follow me downhill!"

As he turned, Henry Prescott issued the order to his troopers. *"Fire!"*

Another volley rocked the ocher mesa. They had the warriors moving back now. Inches at a time, but moving still the same. Like black ants coming out of the low places among the snow and the tufts of grass. Pushing them back, by lord.

"Fifth squad—take position and fire when ready. Then come with me!"

As Donegan turned, Sergeant Franklin B. Robinson's rifles began to spit and spew.

By the saints! Company M was coming on the double. One by one the squads dropped off, aimed their carbines at the distant ridge and fired, then reloaded on the run, laying down an almost incessant fire as he led them ever down toward the village. Toward Company K.

Down to help Teddy's boys.

And then Seamus knew it had to be a bleeming Irishman —that Egan was: standing there among his men like a tall oak, rallying them, waving first one arm, then another, as he got them out of the brush and onto their feet. His mouth like a huge black hole in his face, spewing orders as he flung an arm over his shoulder, taking off at a dead run out of the leafless willows, onto the snowy, open, no-man's land, sprinting into the village on foot.

"*Fire!*" Donegan yelled at his next squad down on their knees, Alexander Ballard's men, their Springfield .45-caliber carbines jammed back into their shivering shoulders, their faces all but hidden by their muskrat hats. Then their heads disappeared in those puffs of steamy, dirty-gray smoke.

"*Fire!*" he hollered at Sergeant Rittel's men.

And Seamus swore as he found he was going to be the first down the last twenty-five feet of ridge as it dropped off sharply.

He vowed that if it was the last thing he was going to do, Seamus Donegan was going to have a drink of Irish whiskey with Teddy Egan.

Back at Fort Fetterman when this hellish campaign was done.

"*Fire!*" he bellowed to Kaminsky's squad as the rest were following him in the maddening rush.

Then of a sudden Donegan was on the flat, scrambling ahead, looking over his shoulder as Mills and the first of them followed out of the brush and into the open. "Form up! Form up!"

"You heard the man! Form up!" Mills was waving his pistol to the left, then right.

Turning around fully as he heard the sudden, rumbling thunder on the wintry air, Donegan saw the shadowy throb of them coming. Out of the south. Where Noyes should have—

"Out of the way!" he screamed at these soldiers in that last moment before the ponies came tearing into Anson Mills's M Company. "Open up and let 'em through! Get out of their way!"

The men of Company M dove this way and that, sprinting, diving, lunging out of the path of the stampeding herd.

Seamus picked himself out of the snow, raised on an elbow, watching the blur of legs and snow and sandy grit fly past, lying only a matter of feet from the edge of that long cavalcade of ponies.

In among them he saw his first warrior and thought to snap off a shot with the Henry. But it was too late. Gone as quick as a man blinked, his ruddy face stinging with the icy snow thrown into the air by the herd. Had to be at least two hundred of them. Among them a half-dozen young warriors, no more than that. Some of them looked to be no older than boys. Frightened for their lives as they rode bareback, gripping pony manes in great vees held in their brown hands.

Seamus thought of his own, back at Laramie at this moment. Maybe having breakfast.

His stomach turned as the last of the reclaimed ponies shot past, leaving in their wake the churned-up ground, the screeches and yells of the young warriors urging them on, and the grumbling curses of his soldiers as they scrambled to their feet, firing a few random shots at the ponies disappearing among the cottonwoods and the lodges. Headed north once more.

"Damn you, Noyes!" Mills growled, hurling a fist to the south where Noyes's men should have held the herd.

"We got 'em, Cap'n—the warriors bolting for certain!"

shouted Sergeant Kaminsky up ahead as he huffed back toward Mills and Donegan.

And as empty as his belly was right now, Seamus wished he had a good swallow of some whiskey on his tongue. Racing into the village, leading these men in support of Egan's Company K, Seamus Donegan almost tasted that whiskey.

Chapter 23

Sore-Eye Moon

*T*he wind sang in his ears, a shrill, keening cry of war as he lay low along the neck of the sacred pony. Old Bear's animal, sent young Wooden Leg by the Everywhere Spirit.

He had raced south, headlong through the all but deserted village on the pony, when he found himself joined by three others. Young warriors who left a group of a dozen or more on horseback behind to join Wooden Leg. Without invitation from him, no words spoken by them. Merely joining when they had seen the young racer riding southeast at a gallop, toward the river and the wide meadow beyond.

It was good, Wooden Leg told himself: four of them, like the sacred winds. Four young warriors joining in the great circle of life. A magical number, adding its blessing to the coming capture of the herd.

Their four ponies went bug-eyed and lock-kneed, frightened at the prospect of crossing the ice—but in the end did as their riders demanded of them this cold winter morning. Turning south to dash down the east bank of the Powder, in and out through the willow and alder, then making another crossing, this time to the west, when the pony herd was sighted.

Again the four young men shared no talk—going at their duty without so much as a thought to act in concert. There was no need of that. Everyone knew his job was to retake the pony herd. Or die trying.

The first soldier bullets sang past.

They were the opening chorus of Wooden Leg's song of

war. He vowed to remember for all time the sound of those bullets that whispered inches over him as his pony lunged through the protective ring of soldiers surrounding the herd, into the midst of the milling, restive animals—each of the four *hepping* and hollering, flapping anything the young men had in hand to get the captured ponies to break free from the cordon of white soldiers.

He did not have time to count the animals now, his heart hammering like small, prairie thunder in his chest.

In their courageous dash among the startled soldiers, the four had not succeeded in getting all the herd started back north. Still—maybe as many as one out of four. Maybe Wooden Leg and the other youngsters drove as many as a third of them before them now. And as the firing intensified around them, the angry shouts of the surprised, chagrined soldiers—the young horsemen worked their own ponies into the middle of the riderless herd.

There to ride for protection, there to spur the rest north along the river bottom. His people needed these animals like they needed breath itself.

He felt the splatter of blood, warm on the side of his face. The young warrior beside him, Jumps Ahead, tumbled forward from his pony and was instantly swallowed by the herd, lost among the slashing hooves.

"Hotoma!" he cried out, calling upon the mysterious medicine spirit of bravery for the Shahiyena. Jumps Ahead had been very brave indeed, barely fifteen summers.

For a heartbeat Wooden Leg thought of returning for the body, then realized he could not. He was part of the wild herd for now. There would be no escaping.

And there would be nothing much left of Jumps Ahead if he did return for the body.

These soldiers would be leaving the battlefield eventually. Then the family of the young warrior could return to mourn and bury what remained of Jumps Ahead among the rocks of the mesa that flew past over Wooden Leg's left shoulder as the herd galloped toward the southern edge of the village.

Then as suddenly as his friend had fallen, the ponies were among a group of soldiers just dropping off the sharp slope onto the river-bottom flats from his left. The racing herd was forcing the white soldiers to dive this way and that to get out of the way of the hammering hooves punishing the frozen, snowy ground. Wooden Leg was past the frightened soldiers and in among the lodges once more before the white men even began shouting, much less shooting. Then that too was behind him.

Slowly the gunfire faded from his ears. Only the high-pitched whistling, the mournful keening of the cold wind caressed his ears as it spread his long hair out from his shoulders in an eagle tail fan. That and the thunder echoing up from the ground from the hooves. And the labored breathing of the bighearted spirit pony beneath him, its sides heaving as it raced among its kind.

Shahiyena ponies. Free again.

"By blue Jesus, I don't believe it!" John Bourke exclaimed.

"It's about goddamned time," swore Bob Strahorn, looking in the same direction as the lieutenant.

After Seamus Donegan had led Captain Mills's M Company down the slope to support Egan's K, Captain Alexander Moore appeared back up the slope, apparently leading his men toward the abandoned village.

"All right, by God!" Teddy Egan was beside them, shouting his orders now. "It looks like we've got their herd—or a good piece of it—and the village is ours."

"As long as we can hold it, sir," commented Bourke.

Egan nodded, grim-lipped. "Right, Lieutenant."

Together they gazed up the side of the mesa where the warriors were regathering to renew their sniping into the village just vacated for that sweep by the soldiers. The captain turned to look at the bluffs to the southwest. "Wonder where the colonel is?"

"Orders, Captain?" Bourke asked.

"We'll hold on as long as we can here. With Mills holding down our left flank, we might just be able to hang on now."

Then Egan set off again amid the crackle of small-arms fire, moving his men here and there along the line stretched thin from the riverbank on the far right, all the way west in a thin, wavering line that extended up the gentle slope, twisting back southwest toward the bluffs.

Bourke's hand was no longer hurting. In fact he hadn't noticed it in some time. Then the lieutenant remembered that he should be all the more worried.

They had left their coats, back there—somewhere. He looked behind them. South, somewhere. No telling how far away now. He stared down at the hand he held in his lap, gripping the wrist as if the hand were something foreign to be studied, not his.

"You all right?" Strahorn asked.

He looked up into the newsman's eyes. "My hand. I . . . I'm afraid I've lost it."

"Frostbite?"

Bourke nodded.

"You feel anything in it?"

Now he shook his head, biting his tongue for fear of crying out for his stupidity.

"Move it for me," Strahorn demanded.

Bourke laughed, hard. He could do that, by Jesus. "Sweet Mother of God," he whispered with a little relief.

"Bryan!" Strahorn bellowed, turning and flinging his voice west along the skirmish line.

"Who wants me?"

"It's Johnny Bourke, Will!" Strahorn replied. "We need you to make a goddamned house call on the lieutenant!"

"Be there when I can—got my hands full at the moment, Bob!"

A strange voice came up behind them, "What'd you freeze?"

Bourke turned, finding Lieutenant Christopher T. Hall crabbing toward them. The Kentuckian from I Company of the Second Cavalry stopped at John's knee. "Where'd you come from? Thought you were with Noyes."

Hall nodded as he knelt beside Bourke. "Was. We got all the ponies rounded up, drove 'em across the river. They got 'em herded south of that knoll back there where Munn's set up his field hospital."

"How many so far, Chris?"

Hall shook his head. "Six . . . was when I left there to

come back up here to the fighting." Hall looked Bourke over quickly. "What you need the steward for? You wounded?"

"My hand."

"Lemme have a look," Hall requested.

He took the mitten off the hand. It looked whitish, spotted, mottled. And icy cold to the touch.

"I got me one to match," Hall admitted, pulling the mitten off his left hand. "But it ain't the first time I've been bit by ol' Jack Frost. This hand, twice't before."

Bourke was amazed. "Two times—the same hand?"

Hall nodded. "Always gets froze now. Got to watch out careful for it. You will too, from here on out."

"I won't lose it then?"

"Not if you don't want to."

"How you get yours froze? When?" Bourke inquired.

The older lieutenant shrugged. "I been out here in Dakota Territory since I graduated in 'sixty-eight. Man's bound to make some stupid mistakes and get some frostbite in this country, John. But if he can't make sure he keeps himself free of ol' Jack Frost, then the next best thing a man needs to know is how to take the cure."

"Cure?" Bourke asked with a nervous swallow.

Rising to a half-crouched position, Hall peered east, toward the river. He looked back at Bourke. "C'mon. We'll save that hand for you."

Bourke glanced apprehensively at Strahorn.

The newsman nodded. "It'll be all right, Johnny. Besides, you need that hand for writing all your wonderful stories in your journal, don't you? And that book you want to do one day on the general."

John agreed reluctantly, and turned back to find Hall scooting away in a crouch toward the Powder. On the way, Hall paused by an old sergeant, John Gleuson, asking for something quietly, then flicked a thumb back at Lieutenant Bourke. Glueson eyed Bourke, then stuffed a hand deep inside his tunic and pulled out a large scrap of coarse, brown cloth, the color of an old walnut. Taking the scrap, Hall went on to the river, moving south along the bank until he found what he needed.

"A air hole, John," Hall said as he knelt among the willows and ice at the edge of the thick ice.

Hall pulled his gloves off, both of them, then stuffed one arm down through the air hole. Bourke watched Hall's face tighten as the soldier winced in pain.

Gritting his words through his chattering teeth, Hall explained, "B-Believe it or not, the w-water is actually w-warmer than the air around us."

Then he pulled his arm from the hole, into the air, immediately rubbing the flesh from wrist down to fingertips with the rough gunnysack material. "This gets the blood going, working up the circulation, you see."

John crouched there among the willows and plum brush, amazed as Hall next performed the ritual on the left hand. When he was finished, he handed the burlap sacking over to Bourke.

"Your turn, Lieutenant. And hurry—I need to get my feet into that air hole soon as you're done with your hand."

Bourke needed no prodding to hurry, none at all. It was something to be endured and gotten over with as quickly as a man could. What sweet, exquisite agony to feel the pain return to his hand once he plunged it beneath the ice, into the gurgling, near freezing water for a few agonizing seconds. Such a splendid torture to rub the hand with the rough scrap of cloth—but likely he was saving that hand, he told himself.

"Move outta my way a minute," Hall said as he rumped forward on his rear, down toward the air hole, where he plunged one of his bare feet, white as a fresh-laundered bed sheet.

Bourke wiggled his toes, of the moment surprised that he could not feel them. Having forgotten all about his feet in his worry about the hand. Hurriedly he pulled off his tall buffalo-hide gaiters, then peeled back the layers of moccasins and stockings. His feet were as white and mottled as his hand had been. When Hall had finished and pushed himself to the side, Bourke plunged his own feet into the icy current of the Powder River.

He leaned back, gritting against the cold, but savoring again that delicious pain as the crackle of gunfire continued unabated behind them, shots and booms echoing against the bluffs and the tall mesa. Occasionally the two lieutenants were forced to duck or hug the frozen ground for a moment or two as a stray bullet smacked into a nearby cottonwood or keened past through the bare willow branches, snapping and whistling in its futile flight.

"Thanks, Hall."

Hall looked at Bourke and smiled as he pulled on his other boot. "Don't mention it, Lieutenant."

As far as He Dog could tell from looking at the village below, there were only soldiers and camp dogs among the lodges now. He watched one of his young Oglallas scrambling up the slippery slope with a handful of Cheyenne warriors in tow. They were the last. Everyone else had escaped to the north now. The men remained behind to cover the retreat of the rest.

"There is one left," White Cow Bull said as he crawled up and came to a stop beside He Dog. He indicated the young warriors who had just come up the slope. "They tell me an old woman is still in the village."

"Shahiyena?"

White Cow Bull nodded.

"Why didn't they help her escape?" He Dog demanded.

"She refused to come. Said the soldiers would not harm her."

He regarded the village below as the soldiers moved back and forth through it cautiously in small knots, poking their heads into a lodge before proceeding.

"I am not so sure she is safe." He looked into the eyes of White Cow Bull. "You know these *nisma wicas,* the hair mouths, will destroy our lodges."

"Yes."

"And they will find the woman."

"She is brave, this one, He Dog."

He nodded, remembering his own mother. She had died three summers ago, bitten by a rattlesnake. Choosing to go into the foothills to die by herself, she told her family to come for her body later. When she was dead, they could bury her in the trees for the birds to pick over her bones.

He remembered that blackened, swollen leg now, how ugly it looked against the yellowed grass of late summer. An old woman, not meant to die such a cruel death.

Nor this Shahiyena grandmother.

"Let us pray the soldiers do not allow their mixed-blood scouts to kill the woman."

"We will wait here," White Cow Bull said. "If we have to wait until the sun is gone from the sky. We will wait here until the soldiers are gone and we can be sure the old woman is not hurt."

"Go gather some of the others. Hunkpatila," He Dog ordered. "Tell them to stay with us. The Shahiyena who want to wait too. We can keep things hot for the soldiers among our lodges while we are waiting. Keep shooting at the soldiers, never making it easy for them."

"You have something in mind, don't you?"

He Dog smiled as he knelt forward in the crevice, making a place for his left elbow in the crusty snow. He sighted along the barrel of his Winchester repeater. "Seems I can keep no secrets from you, old friend."

White Cow Bull waited until his friend had fired before speaking. "You and Crazy Horse have the same heart, He Dog."

"Yes—we are both looking for the Grabber."

"The . . . the Grabber?"

The Oglalla nodded, peering down into the camp as he levered another .44 shell into the Winchester's breech. "Yes, I heard him calling out to Crazy Horse a while ago. He shouted from the bottom of that slope that he was the one who brought these soldiers to attack our village."

"I would like to be the one to cut out his heart, He Dog!" White Cow Bull growled.

"In time, my friend. For now, I have something more for us to do than sitting up here and firing down on these soldiers. We must make it hard enough on them that they will hurry and leave. And when the soldiers do leave the village behind, we will follow them."

"To hurt them back for all the hurt they have brought us," White Cow Bull said, then waited while He Dog fired another shot at the distant soldiers.

Together they chuckled a little as they both watched a small group of soldiers duck out of the way as the bullet struck the side of a lodge, splintering a pole.

"And then?" asked the Bull.

"And then—we go down to the valley at nightfall. To make it hard for those soldiers to escape with our ponies."

White Cow Bull laughed, a good laugh. *"Hoka hey!* The ponies!"

"Captain Mills! Damn, am I glad to see you!"

Mills turned on his heel to find James Egan hurrying up. They shook hands, mittens on. "Got your hands full, Teddy."

Egan nodded. "Where the hell is Moore?"

Anson Mills shook his head, gazing up the slope, shading his eyes with a hand. "No way to know. He didn't want me reinforcing him. And he wasn't going to do a damned thing where he was. So I came on down. But it sounds like he might be on his way down now."

"Thank God you brought your company down when you did."

That made Mills feel immensely better for ignoring Reynolds's orders to bolster Moore's command. Even if he couldn't see a bit of movement far up the butte where the battalion commander was to have been covering the village. "If he'd only put some more pressure on that hillside, Teddy. Hell—Moore was supposed to be exactly where those red bastards are right now, sniping away at our skirmish line."

Looking up the slope again, Mills still couldn't see a flicker of any movement from Moore's troops. "Damn, Moore was right up there a few minutes ago—and now I don't see a sign of his outfit . . ."

"Get your men into some cover and fast, Anson," Egan said. "If Moore's going to shilly-shally getting here—then it's up to your company to hold down my left flank, from here west."

"You got it," Mills replied. "Looks like the far side of the river might be something you'll have to watch."

"I know. Can you believe it? We drove these sonsabitches out into this cold like we did—and they're fighting still. Getting stronger every minute that goes by. God, but you gotta admire 'em."

"They're fighting for their women and children, from what my scout told me."

"Who's that, Mills?"

"The big civilian. Irishman."

"Donegan? Hear he's a hard one."

"He is a hard case—but because of him, I got my outfit down here without a scratch."

"Where's he now?"

"Sent him back up to make contact with Reynolds—got to figure out what we're supposed to do now."

"Goddamned right," Egan grumbled.

"Haven't seen a thing of Moore, or Stanton—much less Reynolds," Mills said, his eyes once more raking over the western slope of the buttes and ridges.

As some voices near the river hollered out in excitement, Egan glanced to the east. "I've got my men on the lookout for the hostiles to come sweeping around from the north, crossing the river and coming up behind me."

"They could flank you easily."

This time Egan smiled. "Not if K Company has anything to say about it. You keep those bastards up on the mesa busy—and I'll keep them off our backs at the river." Then he stopped, looking past Mills to some of the men of M Company. "Your coats. What happened to them?"

Mills gestured up the slope with a thumb. "Took 'em off so we could move easier. Get down here quicker. Where're yours?"

Egan pointed south. "Dropped ours back there before beginning the charge. Going to send some men back for 'em."

"I pray we'll get ours when I send for the horse holders," Mills said. "Once we get hunkered down, trying to take care of those snipers up there—it's going to be damned cold work again."

"Good luck, Anson."

Then Egan was gone, turning and trotting back into the tumble of brush toward the right flank and the river.

Clumsily Mills pulled his pocket watch out and opened it, turning the face out of the shadow into the bright sunlight. Because of its shape, the style of watch was called a "turnip." Just past nine-thirty A.M. The village appeared cleared of the hostiles, although the warriors still deviled the men from those slopes to their left.

"Lieutenant Johnson!" he called out. "Over here!"

"Sir."

Mills crabbed over to the first lieutenant of E Company, J. B. Johnson, serving as the adjutant of the Third Cavalry on the battlefield. "You found General Reynolds for me? Gave him my message—that Egan and I needed his reinforcements, *now?*"

"Yes, sir. Now."

"Well?" Mills's voice cracked like a quirt on still air.

J. B. Johnson swallowed, looking cornered. "The general sends his compliments—"

"The hell with his compliments," Mills snapped, frost on his words, then caught himself with some remorse. "I'm sorry. What did Reynolds tell you?"

"Said to tell you he would be sending Noyes up in a few minutes."

"That's . . . that's it?"

"General Reynolds said I was to inform you that he was having trouble getting the horses down."

"Jesus, Lieutenant!" Mills said just before they both ducked out of the way of sniper fire.

Johnson backed away from Mills like the captain had just dropped a gunnysack of diamondbacks on the snow between them.

Bristling, Mills grabbed hold of the lieutenant's forearm. "Go on back to the general and inform him that our line is under attack on three sides by the enemy. Egan's having the hell hammered out of him and his right is starting to fall back—under severe pressure. We are requesting help and requesting it immediately. Tell him we are going to be overrun if we can't count on help coming soon!"

Johnson saluted. "Yes, Captain."

He watched the lieutenant move off to the southwest

through the brush, scampering on foot toward the low bluff behind which it was said Munn had established his hospital.

"We'll sure as hell need a field hospital," Mills grumbled icily under his breath. "Reynolds doesn't get this fight sewed up and quick—every last one of us is going to be up to our assholes in hostiles before noon."

Chapter 24

17 March 1876

$\mathcal{D}$onegan dropped down the last few yards of the gentle slope onto the flat ground west of the river, finding the gun smoke lying among the frosted cottonwoods like a veil of Irish lace against a bride's dark hair.

Fifty yards away Captain Anson Mills stood waving him on, anxious for word from Moore's outfit farther up the butte.

Here and there as he reentered the village, a soldier darted past, lugging a heavy buffalo robe, perhaps a painted rawhide parfleche under an arm, maybe a bit of captured clothing or a wolf-hide arrow quiver. Souvenirs to be sure, Donegan thought. But more likely the soldiers were setting aside robes and blankets and clothing for later, to keep themselves warm. At times it appeared the men were like of pack of ants working over the captured village as the warriors kept up a steady racket from the bluffs above them.

"Donegan—you get my orders to the horse holders?"

"They're coming," he answered, coming to a stop by the officer and flicking a glance up the slope toward the mesa. "They'll be a while, bringing those animals down, getting across that ravine, Cap'n."

"Captain Mills! I've been looking for you, sir!"

"Lieutenant Johnson, by lord I'm glad to see you get back—but where are your reinforcements? We've had our hands full here! Where is the help I've been promised? We've been in the village helping Egan on his right—"

"General Reynolds sends his compliments."

Johnson's preface brought not only Mills, but Seamus Donegan up short as well.

"You didn't come back to reinforce our skirmish line?" Mills sputtered. "Not long ago you told me the general himself said he would be sending your men down from the captured herd."

Johnson shook his head. "Sir, General Reynolds sent me down to order the destruction of the village."

"The destruction?" Mills looked even more confused, his face going white with rage. "I received word that the general agreed with me that I should have the men pull the food and robes from the lodges—everything valuable that we can pack on the captured ponies and take with us to rejoin Crook."

Johnson wagged his head and shrugged. "I don't know anything about that, Captain. I just came from Reynolds. He's back at the field hospital for a while, where he's waiting until Moore joins up and the rest of our horses are brought down the mountainside. From what I can tell, he evidently has a different idea for the village now, sir. Says we don't have time to wait, with the pressure from the hostiles on our flanks—he wants you to get the destruction started."

"Just a few minutes ago he gave me orders to separate everything out before burning what we couldn't use," Mills answered, his jaw set resolutely, his back stiffening. "So, I'll see that we burn the lodges soon as we empty them of what we can use for our return march. Then we can get the hell out of here. Look up there on that ridge, Lieutenant. They're pounding hell out of us. You damn well know I'm going to need the help of your unit. You know it's going to be tough to hold off those warriors while we get what we need out—"

"Sir?" Johnson started, then swallowed as if the coming words were distasteful. "The general said for me to remind you that *everything* was to be burned. I'm to return word to him that you have begun the destruction, then bring my men down from the hospital and herd, only to help in the destruction."

"Ev-Everything?" Donegan asked, growing hotter than a rope burn. "He's bleeming daft—Reynolds is! This a bunch of hockum and humbug—burning it all when we can salvage some for our own!"

Johnson graced the civilian a disapproving look that would curdle milk, then turned back to Mills. "Yes, sir. Everything is put to the torch. Noyes and I captured the herd, and now Reynolds is following General Crook's orders to destroy everything of value before it can fall back into the hands of the hostiles when we pull out."

Johnson's eyes followed a pair of soldiers hurrying past, their arms cradled around buffalo robes and plunder from the captured camp. "The general's aware of the pilfering going on."

"Damn him!" Donegan snarled at the lieutenant. "These sojurs ain't to blame for wanting something to eat, or keep warm with. By bloody Jesus—the men are freezing, their bellies empty from a scant quarter rations. Besides, the men watched the half-breeds start the stealing. They aren't to blame for carrying on what the scouts started."

The lieutenant gazed back at Mills steadily, almost as if refusing to give Donegan the pleasure of an acknowledgment, much less an answer. Johnson told the captain, "Under the general's orders—nothing must remain behind for these savages. The general wants you to impoverish the enemy. And you are to commence immediately."

"Immediately." Mills repeated the word with something less than total resolve. "You'll be returning to support me soon?"

"As soon as I deliver word to Reynolds, I'll bring my men back, and reserve a detail to help in the destruction."

"There's likely to be powder and weapons in the lodges —it'll be dangerous work, Cap'n," Seamus advised, moving in front of the lieutenant. "Someone—even this bumptious cock-a-hoop of a lieutenant here, needs to tell Reynolds there's enough powder here to last his army through a summer campaign!"

"Yes. It would," Mills replied, considering it thoughtfully, then looked at Johnson. "Report back to the general and ask him for permission to save the meat and robes, and the powder as well, Lieutenant. When I have those items saved, tell him we will begin the destruction as ordered."

Johnson shook his head at Mills. "Sir, the general is . . . is quite agitated right now. I respectfully request that you don't delay the destruction order any longer. Reynolds wants to move and move quick, sir. Get the hell out, I think."

"I would too, Lieutenant. But these men haven't eaten, and most of mine are without heavy clothing—"

Johnson stiffened, his face as impassive as marble. "Sir, I'm merely conveying the general's orders. Am I to understand you are refusing to obey his direct order for you to take charge of the destruction of the captured village?"

Mills's lips drew into a flat line as he regarded the lieutenant. A moment more and he finally drew himself up rigid as a tin soldier, slitted eyes gazing off to the south, in the direction where a man might imagine Reynolds would be at that moment.

"Lieutenant, tell the general I will begin the destruction very shortly."

"Everything, Captain Mills?"

His words came out clipped and precise. "As—the—general—ordered—Lieutenant."

Johnson saluted and turned south once more.

"Mills, you can't be serious about destroying everything. That old Muttonchop's a pompous blackguard—and he'll let these men freeze in their tracks before he'll admit he's got a yellow strip running down his back that's forcing him to turn tail and run."

"I'll remind you that you're talking about our colonel, Mr. Donegan!"

"Damned right I am. From my reading of things, he's going contrary to Crook's orders. Now someone has to do something—"

The captain gritted his teeth, his eyes fired with fury as he whirled on the civilian, arms flailing animatedly. "I have *my* orders, Donegan! So what if they are wrong? So what if we're making a great mistake?"

Donegan wagged his head, once more sensing frustration with the military mind-set of orders above all. "Most of

Egan's men have put their coats back on. And yours are still up that bleeming mountainside—damned well abandoned for all we know."

Mills shook his head furiously. "I've been given an order."

"Your men won't last without some food in their bellies and something to keep the cold from freezing them in the saddle once Reynolds marches us south to join up with Crook."

Mills wheeled on him again, his face volcanic with red fire. "I can't disobey—"

"Then I beg you: just pull a few robes and a little food from the lodges for your men before you destroy them."

"No, I can't," Mills said firmly, a strange look coming over his face. Something close to a peaceful satisfaction with himself. If not ironic resolve to disobey an idiotic command from a questionable commander. "But if I turn my back and you leave—go into the village and tell the others to pull what they can from the lodges before we come to set fire to them . . . what I don't know you're doing isn't going to hurt."

"A most splendid—"

"Dismissed, Donegan," Mills ordered, flicking his hand in dismissal. "I have my work to do, and you're only in my way right now."

Mills turned away, hurrying toward a knot of soldiers, hollering out, "Supporting fire! I need some supporting fire on our left flank!"

Watching the captain disappear to the south, Donegan did not wait to be given permission a second time. Surprised that so many of the camp dogs had remained after the hostiles had abandoned the village, the Irishman hurried among the lodges like a puff of muzzle smoke, grabbing the first pair of soldiers he found. They both looked as hungry as gaunt, winter-starved wolves, each carrying a pair of squawking chickens at the end of their arms.

"Rustle your tails, boys—we been called. Forget the damned chickens."

"Forget?" demanded the older of the two. "Who the hell

are you to tell us to forget our bellies. Why, we ain't et
in—"

"You'll eat plenty soon enough," Seamus interrupted.
"Unless you prefer skinny chicken to fat buffalo. We got
orders."

"Orders?" demanded the second suspiciously, but nonetheless flinging the first of the frightened, cackling birds
into the air, where it fluttered, landed in the snow and
hurried off on its skinny legs, wings flapping.

"We been ordered to pull out all the robes and blankets
you can. If you find any jerked meat—bring all of it too."

"I'll say," the younger soldier said energetically. "We
been expected to eat what little rations I could stick up a
gnat's ass, and now my belly's so hungry I'd even eat Injun
food."

"You're not alone—but chirk up, my friend," Seamus
said. "Now move on it before the rest come through here
with their orders to put everything to the torch."

Immediately the pair of soldiers split, hurrying into two
lodges as Donegan turned to continue his mission. And
then felt the pangs of his own stomach. That peculiar,
rubbed-together sensation, a knotted, oily tightness that
threatened to overpower him for a moment. He could only
relieve it by stooping. As it passed, Seamus attempted to
straighten—but the cramp cried out again. Only after taking a half-dozen deep breaths was he able to calm his protesting belly and stand straight.

A bullet struck a nearby lodgepole, splintering it, compelling him to duck as shards rained down on him like an
explosion of fireworks. It was for certain the hostiles
weren't short on powder, he brooded, dusting himself off.
But the slow, steady rhythm of the hostiles' riflefire told the
Irishman that most of the warriors were armed with muzzle
loaders, requiring a minute or more between shots. However, there was enough of a steady rattle to tell him a few of
the enemy likely had acquired a trapdoor Springfield in
some recent action against the soldiers on the high plains.
Perhaps some of that steady rattle meant a few of the cov-
eted Henry or Winchester repeaters sold by agency traders.

When another shot whistled past like an angry winter

wasp, Seamus reflexively dove into a lodge, almost at once amazed at the warmth put out by the fire. Then that struck him—the fire appeared well-tended. As Seamus stood there gazing about for something to put down his cold, aching belly, he once more admired the industry of the Indian woman. Besides what pig lead and caps and powder there were for a warrior's hunting or warfare, practically everything he laid his eye on here in the lodge had been created by the hand of a woman.

The well-padded beds at the rear, each draped with blankets and soft, luxurious buffalo robes, many of which were painted or beautified with porcupine quills and beads, beckoned seductively to the man who had spent most of the last forty-eight hours in the saddle. From the liner rope and the lodgepoles hung rawhide containers, some painted, others decorated with quill or beadwork. Elk hides, deerskins, even the skin of a pinto pony lay about in a profusion. Rawhide containers filled with kitchen utensils, cooking pots and ladles, tin spoons and those crafted of buffalo horn, lay with small pouches of herbs and seasonings. Feathers cascaded from a buffalo-horn headdress hung on a pole; near it a coyote-skin quiver, complete with a ram's-horn bow. Knives, cups, and even a small water keg completed the woman's kitchen.

As he knelt to get himself a drink, he caught wind of meat. Tearing at the nearby satchels, Seamus found a generous supply of it in a rawhide container. With a cup of cold river water and a band of jerky as wide as his hand, Seamus collapsed to the blankets to enjoy his breakfast. Outside, the racket of gunfire continued as he gazed about the lodge—

—he stopped chewing as his eyes grew twice their size. Quietly, dropped the jerky so he could slowly pull one of the pistols from its holster. The blankets and robes rustled across the fire from where he sat. Likely one of the camp dogs, a creature of some sort—best not take a chance, he thought as he inched forward.

Dragging the hammer back to full cock, Donegan pointed it at the rustling mound of fur and wool, ready for the appearance of the animal. Gray-furred he took it to be as the creature emerged from its hiding place. Poor animal, abandoned by the family of this lodge—

"By the saints!" he whispered.

An old woman. Wrinkled and dried, and as smoked of hide as these lodge skins.

She froze, cocking her head strangely.

It was then he saw the eyes. Both of them milky, nearly white.

She's blind.

"It's all right," he said softly.

The old woman started, jerking about in his direction, a low rumble in her throat.

"Come on out," he said as softly as he could, his own heart hammering. "I know you can't understand a bleeming word I'm saying—but it's all right."

She might well have her a knife, you bloody idiot, Seamus told himself as he scooted around the fire, realizing he still held the tin cup in his left hand. Setting it aside, the Irishman slowly pulled the blankets and robes off the old woman. For a moment she protested, clawing at the air blindly, snarling like a wounded animal. Then, as if assured no harm was meant her, the old woman allowed him to uncover her fully. Now he could see she was unarmed. And wounded.

He looked down at the dried, brownish patch along her thigh. She hadn't bled much. Though in a body so thin and wizened, there likely wasn't all that much blood to spare.

Stuffing his pistol back in its holster, he reached back for the tin cup. Donegan lifted one of her shriveled, veiny hands, placing the cup in it.

"Drink," he said, gently raising her hands toward her face.

After a moment's indecision, as she licked her lips, the old woman brought the cup to her mouth and drank slowly, toothlessly.

As she did, he gently brought a blanket up around her shoulders, to let her know in some way that no harm would come to her. Then he ducked out of the lodge, standing back in the midst of the hubbub, looking for—

"Grouard!"

The half-breed turned about some thirty feet away. "You want me?"

He motioned the scout over. "C'mere. Got something for you to see."

Seamus went back in first, followed by the scout. He watched Grouard's eyes as the half-breed saw the woman.

"You know her?" Donegan asked.

He shook his head. "Did not know everyone with Crazy Horse."

At the new voice, the woman cocked her head again, gazing up at the men with a look on her face that showed she was acutely aware that a second man had arrived.

"You know the Lakota tongue. Talk to her. Find out how she was wounded."

Grouard eventually knelt near the woman's knees. After they conversed a little, the half-breed shook his head and looked up at the Irishman.

"What'd she say to you?"

"Don't understand—she's speaking Shahiyena."

"Cheyenne?"

Grouard nodded, like it wasn't really making sense to him. "Says she was hit at the beginning of the fight—when her husband was shooting from the lodge door."

"If she's Cheyenne—just who the hell bunch is this?"

Grouard shrugged a shoulder in confusion. "Can't make out for sure what she means . . . says her band is with Crazy Horse . . . but then she told me this is Two Moon's village."

"He's damn well Cheyenne."

"Shit, Donegan!" Grouard grumbled in a whisper. "You can't trust any of these old ones."

"What else she tell you?"

"That her nephew is Old Bear. He travels with Two Moon."

"I thought all this time we'd jumped Crazy Horse's village. Ask her about Crazy Horse," Donegan prodded.

When the woman had answered, Grouard looked back at Donegan, anger, great disappointment, even a smoldering rage written plainly on his features. "Seems Crazy Horse is camped north of here. Down the Powder. Over on the East Fork."

"How was we wrong, Grouard?"

The half-breed shrugged. "Don't know that I am wrong. I saw the ponies—Crazy Horse's ponies in the herd this morning. This must be his village."

Seamus thought Grouard said it as if he were trying to convince himself.

"Ain't looking that way now, Frank." Then Donegan snapped his fingers. "Ask her if there was any Lakota lodges in the camp. Lakota warriors."

"Lakota? Why ask her that?" Grouard started to get up, disgust smeared on his face.

Seamus grabbed the half-breed roughly by the shoulders. "Because you and I both know the Northern Cheyenne and the Oglalla run together—they marry. Most of them speak each other's tongue. Now—do what I said. Ask her."

Grouard pulled himself from the Irishman and knelt before the woman. When he had asked the question and she had answered, she finally handed the half-breed the cup, as if begging for more water.

"What she say to that?"

Grouard wagged his head as he rose. "She told me Sitting Bull's camped three days ride down the Powder. Near the Blue Earth Hills."

"Where's that?"

"The white man calls the place Chalk Buttes."

"So?" Donegan asked, shrugging, "I thought we wanted to know something about Crazy Horse?"

Grouard took his eyes off the Irishman and gazed out the lodge door. "Seems some Hunkpatila joined up to go into the agency with these Cheyenne. Some Miniconjou riding in too."

"Hunkpatila? Never heard of them. What's that?"

With his dark eyes again shining in triumph, Grouard finally smiled at Donegan. "Hunkpatila? Why, that's Crazy Horse's band. See—by damn—we did capture the bastard's village!"

Donegan watched as the scout shoved past him, ducking out the lodge door. He was alone with the old woman.

She mumbled something to him, still holding her cup in the air. He took it, refilled the tin from the small keg and set it back in her old hands.

As the woman drank, Donegan listened to the noises of the nearby soldiers beginning the destruction of the village. Shouts and hollers and yelps of white men eager to do anything that would get them out of that camp and fast.

Seamus decided he had to let Mills know, and Egan too. That one lodge was to be saved. Inform the captains that they had an old woman to leave behind as well. Not a prisoner. Just someone who would remind most any man of his own grandmother.

But this old one had mourned many. A ladder of harsh scars knotted the loose flesh of her bony forearms, showing that she had gnashed teeth and lopped off her hair for many a husband, son and grandson lost in battles in those years down and gone.

Seamus knelt before her, laying one of his hands on hers. The back of her grimy, birdlike paw looked like oiled paper many times folded, almost translucent beneath the light coming through the smoke hole. She seemed so old. Perhaps it was only her hands, her cheeks as well, he decided— the way the flesh between the skin and bone had melted away like fat before the fire.

"I'll be back," he said.

Then was gone into the madness.

Chapter 25

17 March 1876

*R*eynolds did have his hands full.

That much was for sure, an unenvious Bob Strahorn thought to himself.

For the moment, the colonel had possession of an enemy village of 105 lodges, complete with furnishings, food and weapons. There was ample evidence among those lodges to show that some of these Indians had recently traded at their agencies. Reynolds himself had grown angry when he came up to the village, anxious and impatient at the rate of destruction, seeing with his own eyes some of the soldiers pilfering from the captured camp.

Back south of Hospital Bluff, Captain Noyes had ordered his men to remove the saddles from their horses, make coffee and have their lunch, within sight of the battlefield after they had secured the pony herd. A few left their lunch fires and had moved into the village with Lieutenant Johnson to help Mills put the hostile camp to the torch.

To the southwest of the village, Moore kept his men all but out of the action as well, safely tucked beneath the edge of a ridge where his troops were in no danger from the warriors firing down on the village, less than 150 yards away.

Here and there along the wrinkled bluffs, the warriors would regather and pour their fire down on those soldiers moving about in the captured village. With every passing minute it seemed the enemy grew more and more bold. So for just a moment Bob Strahorn allowed himself the fright to wonder if Reynolds was going to get his command back out of that village he had plunged into four hours before.

Another lodge hiding a supply of gunpowder went off like a great Roman candle on the last Fourth of July he had celebrated in Denver City. Spewing like rocks from a small volcano, lodgepoles were hurled into the air, showering sparks and cinders and tumbling shards of smoking timber as they came crashing back down among the soldiers.

"C'mon, Donegan!" Strahorn hollered again.

The Irishman was not far behind him.

Reynolds had had enough. They were pulling out. The colonel's order had come so suddenly and with surprising swiftness, everyone was falling back past Noyes, sent up by Reynolds to lay down some covering fire while the rest pulled back. The colonel wanted everyone out of the enemy camp, now that the last of the lodges were going up in flames, most already smoking ruins. It had been tough at first, Strahorn admitted—getting the frost-dampened hides and some of the new canvas lodges to catch fire. But with a little urging and a lot of gunpowder discovered in nearly every one of the lodges, the job was well in hand.

The greasy stench from the burning buffalo-hide lodges made the reporter's nose crinkle, like the thick, oily scent of kerosene. Everything was on fire behind them as he pulled out, smudging the winter-pale blue of the sky with black, obsidian streamers.

Everything, that is, but that one lodge Donegan had seen to it was left standing, the Irishman remaining around to guard it after Little Bat, Charlie Jenness and Jack Russell came and pulled as much information as they could from the old woman. A blind, toothless hag some might say. But wounded and helpless nonetheless.

"Hey—Irishman!" Strahorn bellowed back into the village. "Your life isn't going to be worth a pile of mule shit in a few minutes if you don't get the hell out of here!"

"I'm coming!" Donegan lumbered out of a veil of black smoke, trotting up across the churned snow turning a muddy muck, growling, wincing in pain. "My feet—think my toes are frostbit. Don't feel, not acting right."

"Sorry. We just don't have time to check them now,"

Strahorn said. He pointed south, at the two low bluffs where some of the men were already mounted and moving off. "By Jesus—Reynolds has them forming up already."

Donegan wagged his head, setting off with the newsman. "That gallynipping son of a bitch is in one big hurry."

"There he is right there," Strahorn said, pointing at a knot of soldiers and milling horses they were approaching.

They stopped near the argument: Reynolds rigid in the saddle, Mills on foot and clutching the reins of his skittish mount, the rest of the soldiers clearly anxious and ready to get in the saddle and moving.

"No—and that means the end of it. These hills are filled with hostiles, Captain!" Reynolds shouted down at Anson Mills. "I can't allow you or your men to retrieve the coats you abandoned up there this morning."

"Forget our damned coats, General—my wounded . . . we can't just leave Ayers here!" growled Captain Mills.

"I asked you to find out if he was dead, Captain," Reynolds hissed, his puffed face about ready to sizzle and explode beneath the white muttonchops.

"Blacksmith Glavinski told me Ayers is all but dead—still alive for now—"

"Then leave him!" Reynolds snapped. "Nothing can be done for him. If he's going to die, leave him." The colonel turned away with Captain Noyes and Lieutenant Johnson.

Strahorn could tell that Mills was furious.

The captain whirled on the group, face livid and the color of old liver. "You heard the general!" he ordered the blacksmith and the other soldiers.

Glavinski, along with one of Mills's sergeants and three privates, had been carrying the wounded private Lorenzo Ayers, one of M Company's casualties, back to Munn's field hospital when Reynolds was making one last sweep at the southern end of the village. It was there he came upon them, ordering the mortally wounded soldier be abandoned.

"Damn you, Mills. We can't leave the man like this!" Donegan protested, shoving past the soldiers for the body of the semiconscious Ayers.

"Our orders are to pull out, Irishman," Mills answered,

his face gray with fatigue and anger, putting a hand out to stop the civilian.

"I recall a matter of you and some goddamned orders you didn't heed up that hillside earlier this morning," Donegan snarled at the officer.

"Noyes has come back to guard our left flank only long enough for us to pull back and regroup with the rest of the column. And I know Noyes won't be able to hold the savages off for long." He looked down at Ayers a moment with a wag of his head. "This one . . . he's as good as dead, Irishman. Now, move out with the rest of us as ordered—or you'll be left behind too when those screaming savages come flooding back in here."

"You heard the man," Strahorn said, clamping a hand around the Irishman's arm. "Let's go while the going's good!"

"Just a minute," Donegan protested, stopping, turning from the newsman's grasp to quickly survey the battlefield and the edge of the burning village.

"We're the last!" Mills repeated. "Now, move out or get left behind!"

Donegan looked at Strahorn evenly. "I'll stay behind, Bob," he repeated as his eyes came back to scan the remaining handful of troopers.

"I'll stay too, by God," vowed blacksmith Albert Glavinski.

"Me too," echoed young Private Jeremiah J. Murphy.

The rest looked sheepish, backing slowly with Mills, clearly ready to bolt at any moment.

"C'mon, men. Those of you going can go with me," Mills told them.

"You're a damned fool, Seamus," Strahorn said with clear admiration as he watched Mills and the rest move off into the brush to the south. He looked then at Donegan and the two soldiers kneeling over Ayers.

"His leg's busted good," Donegan declared. "Broke clean through."

"Likely lost a lot of blood from that arm wound too," the blacksmith said quietly, respect in his eyes not only for the young soldier on the ground, but the Irishman as well.

Donegan looked up to say, "G'won, Bob!"

"I'll remember you in my prayers, Donegan!" Strahorn called out as the air around them sang with enemy bullets.

"Get out of here while you can, Bob!"

"You may be a fool, Donegan," Strahorn said as he scampered away across the pockmarked snow, his words spoken quietly amid the rattle of gunfire. "But a damned brave fool at that."

"The way Bob was talking—I was afraid I'd seen the last of you," declared John Bourke as he settled down beside Seamus Donegan.

The Irishman smiled grimly at them both, his face smudged with soot. He took another sip of the weak coffee brewed over the fires the cavalry companies had built here near the mouth of Lodge Pole Creek,* then passed the cup on. Precious little coffee to go around.

Finding that Crook and the pack train hauling their rations had not arrived at the rendezvous, the men of Reynolds's retreating command were having to share what crumbs of hardtack and few coffee grounds they had among the companies.

"By the grace of God and a prayer or two—I made it out of there with Glavinski and Murphy," Seamus said, wishing for another bite of the dried buffalo meat some of the men had spirited away from the burning village; even another bite of the pasty hardtack might do. Anything to put down in his cold, cramping belly, more than two days without food now.

What little there was to eat was being passed among the men. Making the rounds: less than a mouthful for each man who would take a bite, then hand it on to the next beside him. Most every man shivering around the fires, especially Mills's Company M. Without the coats they had left behind on the hillside and weren't able to find when the horses came down, with their blankets still among Crook's pack train somewhere in the nearby countryside, Company M was shivering, every man of them, brooding on the thick

* present day Clear Fork (of the Powder River)

blankets and glossy buffalo robes they had burned among the smoldering lodges beside the Powder River.

Little warmth could be offered the few wounded among the many frostbitten that Dr. Munn and Steward Bryan attended to that night as a sliver of moon as cold and blue as a cake of river ice made its climb out of the east, all light in the sky bleeding away into an aching stillness. Little comfort could they offer their wards, save for the fires that spat glowing fireflies into the growing darkness as the black of night clotted in around their frozen command. Overhead, the storm clouds stretched streamstone smooth out of the west, threatening more snow.

Bourke scraped his bare fingers at the bottom of his haversack, coming up with some cracker crumbs. He sucked at his grimy fingers longingly. "Bob and I have taken to calling this 'Camp Inhospitality.' "

"I think we ought to kill and butcher some of those ponies, don't you, Seamus?" asked Strahorn.

"We damned well risked our necks taking those ponies from the red niggers," grumped a nearby soldier across the fire. "Seems we ought to have some say in what happens to the goddamned Injun ponies."

"Feed us, they should," complained another.

"We could always go find Noyes's outfit," said another disembodied voice. "Those bastards might have some coffee left!"

A crackle of mirthless laughter lifted over their bivouac.

"Not after their little tea party on the battlefield, they won't!"

There arose more humorless laughter at the banter.

Donegan continued to stare at the blue and yellow flames licking along the cottonwood limbs, not really listening at all.

"As much as Mills might appear not to like you, Irishman —the captain is recommending Murphy for a citation," Bourke announced.

"It's well Murphy should have it," Donegan said softly, not taking his eyes off the flames. "The boy has some sand. More than most."

"On the retreat here Murphy told me that you three

were overrun there at the end—when we were getting out," Strahorn said. "That true? Murphy says that's why the three of you ended up pulling out without bringing Ayers. Not that I blame you—from what I saw, Ayers was for sure a dead man anyway."

Donegan took a long, studied look at the newsman before he answered. "We had to leave him. Thirty warriors, maybe more, come busting out of the village as soon as Mills and Noyes pulled back to Egan's position."

"Talk is," said Bourke, "that the red bastards got Ayers alive. Tore the man limb from limb."

"That's as big a scum-bellied lie as I've ever heard." Donegan shook his head. "Maybe someone else. But not Ayers." The Irishman closed his eyes, like he was blotting something out. "He was dead before I left him."

Strahorn crossed himself. "Did he go easy? Ever come to for you?"

"No," Seamus replied, lying through his teeth. "Me and Murphy, we was the last. Down in the brush near the river-bank, it was. So when the red h'athens come at us—I just told Murphy to start running, get the hell out of there when the warriors come screaming right for us."

"You was the last?"

"Yes—so I figured it was up to me not to leave Ayers behind. Not alive."

"It was up to you?" Bourke asked. "I don't understand."

"I made sure Ayers wasn't alive."

The young lieutenant swallowed hard. "You . . . you made sure . . . you finished—"

"I wasn't about to let him fall into their bloody hands alive, now was I?"

Suddenly Donegan stood and pushed himself through a cordon of soldiers sharing the coffee. To escape. Without another word, he left the lieutenant and the newsman behind, hurrying into the welcome darkness.

Seamus doubted he would feel better here, alone. But at least there were none of those noisy voices and the jostling bodies out here where he walked off and away from the edge of Reynolds's camp south along the west bank of the Powder River. Still, Seamus Donegan realized he had to admit he was not alone. Knowing he would likely carry the image of that young soldier's face with him a long, long time.

Recalling the way Ayers's eyes fluttered open there at the last just after he ordered Murphy to make a run for it. And when he had looked back down at the mortally wounded soldier, finding the youngster staring back up at him, the Irishman had been struck with the remembrance of the agony having to leave the wounded behind during the Rebellion. Ordered to abandon a position without taking your men in the haste of retreat. Staring at Ayers, Donegan remembered how back then in the war he had sworn he never would abandon a man again.

Now, beneath the dark sky as black as the inside of a bull's paunch, the young soldier's eyes came swimming back before the Irishman out of the darkness of this winter night. Remembering how they had looked soft, and at peace. Like Ayers understood. The soldier had blinked once, no fear there in them. And said two words.

"Go ahead."

Seamus had choked on the sour ball at the back of his throat. "I can't leave you like this."

"F-Finish it."

Seamus squeezed his own eyes shut, shuddering with the mind-numbing reverberation of that one pistol shot that had followed him all the way across the frozen, trampled ground until he caught up with Captain Noyes's rear guard, just then rising into their saddles, swinging around to abandon the low bluffs south of the village.

Donegan was the last white man to leave that battlefield.

Reynolds was hot-footing it out of there while he still had some shred of a victory to claim as his own.

Maybe it wasn't the easiest decision a commander of cavalry ever had to make, Seamus thought now. Yet, there would be hell to pay when Crook found out.

The colonel had squirmed on the horns of his dilemma for the better part of four hours. His troops already into the village by nine-thirty A.M., Reynolds hadn't ordered his retreat until after one-thirty P.M. By then he had ordered his horses brought down from the mountainside, which took more than two hours, then ultimately tired of wrestling with his options.

Reynolds made his hasty decision.

His first consideration was to follow Captain Anson Mills's suggestion: to consolidate their control of the village and make their camp there among the warmth of the lodges, buffalo robes and the captured meat supplies, then send some of the scouts with word to General Crook that they would rendezvous at the enemy village.

But with the hostile snipers up along the mesa making things hotter than any of them had foreseen, the colonel dismissed this first option as untenable. Utterly impossible for him to ask of his weary battalions to hold the village against an enemy that was surging back to counterattack with more and more resolve as each hour passed, seemingly bolstered by reinforcements.

His second alternative could have been to separate out the supplies of meat, along with as many buffalo robes and blankets as could be packed on the captured ponies, then abandon the destroyed village and rendezvous with Crook at Lodgepole Creek as planned.

But this second option would take time—more time that Reynolds didn't think he had to spare. If he delayed too long loading meat and robes, the warriors would take more soldier casualties. The colonel already had four dead and six wounded. And by the time they made their despair-filled camp that night, Dr. Munn reported at least sixty-six men badly frozen.

Reynolds cheerily informed his officers they had accomplished what Crook had ordered of them, and chose his third option. Getting the hell out while the getting was good. He had destroyed everything he could, then turned tail and pushed his weary, hungry, frozen command south toward the mouth of Lodgepole Creek. Leaving behind the smoking ashes of what had been some eighty lodges and about twenty-five small bowers where the bachelor warriors lived. Only one lodge had been left standing. In it, a wounded old woman.

Hurriedly pushing along the west bank of the Powder as if the Devil himself were on their tails, Reynolds had even neglected to assign troops to act as herders for the captured ponies. Captain Stanton was with five of his scouts among the herd near Hospital Rock as the cavalry column filed past. He sent his orderly to ask the colonel what to do with the ponies. The message came back that Reynolds wanted as many killed as possible. But since Stanton and his few men had little ammunition, the captain decided to drive the herd along at the rear of the column. The captain's six, along with eight men from Lieutenant Rawolle's E Company of the Second Cavalry acting as a dismounted skirmish line to protect the retreat, kept the ponies from straying away from the line of march while some fifty warriors doggedly pursued the troops, firing sporadically from the tree-covered slopes and ravine-scarred ridges immediately to the west.

For more than twenty miles their weary column of twos had plodded south in the light of the falling sun, forced to cross and recross the icy Powder until the fish-bellied gray of winter's twilight overtook them short of the mouth of the Lodgepole, just inside the boundary of Wyoming Territory. In the growing darkness, Reynolds ordered a bivouac made until first light on the bottomland where there appeared to be enough grazing for the trail-hammered animals. What there was of the autumn-dried grass wasn't near enough to go around.

The colonel's battalions had covered more than seventy-three miles of torturous, icy terrain in the last twenty-four hours—marching east from the Tongue, men pushed without sleep for better than a day and a half, soldiers who had engaged a fierce enemy in a battle lasting just shy of five hours. All of that on one meal of hardtack.

So now, rather than inflict any more punishment on his troops, the colonel ordered a skimpy "running guard" put around the camp, but none around the captured herd that came in just after dark, then told his troops to settle in for the night. In this way, Reynolds explained, each man would pull the shortest duty and have the most sleep.

"Gentlemen, this day we've convinced the hostiles that it is folly to live their wandering, nomadic ways," Reynolds announced at his officers' conference after deploying the first guard around their camp that winter evening. "In the end, they will submit to life at their agencies."

With the colonel's pompous declaration, Donegan had wagged his head and turned away from the conference, hoping to find a fire where coffee was on the boil and he might talk someone out of a sip. Perhaps someone would share a bite of hardtack or a strip of the jerked buffalo hump stolen from the lodges. Then he realized—no, just then he really didn't have the stomach for any food. Still, a hot cup of coffee might go a long way to settling his angry, knotted stomach.

In his soul, as well as his muscles, the immense cold was settling—numbing his will with bone-aching fatigue. He wondered if he had any strength left to fight off the cold, to fight off what was even worse.

There wasn't a man in that camp the night of 17 March who found himself immune from despair.

Still, better than most of those cavalry officers, surely better than Colonel Joseph J. Reynolds himself, Donegan remained convinced that the Sioux and Cheyenne warriors would not be driven into their reservations so easily. They would have to be whipped and whipped soundly.

More important perhaps—to the Irishman's way of thinking, that village of warriors had not been whipped. In fact, for the last half of the fight, the hostiles had clearly regrouped, gathering in renewed strength, and were beginning to seriously threaten the whole rest of Reynolds's command: not only Mills, but making things hot for Egan from the riverbank, pinning Moore's troops down below the mesa.

The colonel had been plainly scared of losing what scrap of victory he could clutch in his hand as he turned tail and fled to the south. Not that there was an officer in that camp who would blame him.

Not just yet anyway, Seamus thought.

Every last one of them had wanted out, and quick. What with the way some of those officers had been talking up the fight on the trail south to the mouth of the Lodgepole, how they had been ordered to pitch into a band of Sioux of nearly equal strength—something on the order of 250 to

300 warriors. And with the troops fighting dismounted, which meant that every eighth soldier was not on the skirmish line, the colonel actually had no more than two hundred men to hold onto the captured pony herd, destroy the village, and keep the warriors at bay while he did the rest.

So when he had decided on his course of action, Reynolds had decided quickly, and wanted his battalion commanders to move as rapidly as possible in pulling back, without delay.

There had been some grumbling among the ranks on that march south—many of the line soldiers complaining about serving under officers who would leave the bodies of their dead to the enemy on the abandoned battlefield. Seamus couldn't blame them.

No soldier wanted to serve such a man as Reynolds—the sort who would leave their fellows to the inhuman mutilation of the enraged warriors they had just stung. And if anyone had witnessed what horror an Indian could commit on a white corpse, it was Seamus Donegan.

Few of those men mounted and moving south in column of twos could fail but see the two bodies there beside Reynolds's path down the Powder. Lying side by side beneath a single, thin blanket on what had been Dr. Munn's field hospital, their toes pointed to the cold sky. Blood gone black on the hard, old snow.

The pleading eyes of young Ayers swam back before him now.

"F-Finish it . . . p-please."

Remembering the face gone all fish-gut gray at the end, a blank look of peace spreading like ice scum over the dying soldier's face, Ayers's last words still rang through the empty, gnawing echo of Donegan's mind. Unable to shake the thunder of that pistol shot.

He blinked his own eyes, clearing them, bringing them to focus on the pinpricks of diamond light winking through a open shaft of sky overhead.

And wished all the more he were inside the fortress of Samantha's arms.

Chapter 26

Sore-Eye Moon

*T*he night and the cold and the agonizing journey through
that darkness lit only by a few icy stars peeking through
the gathering snow clouds had finally claimed some victims.

In the murky light of predawn it was evident to
Monaseetah that of all who had begun this march north of
the camp circle among the frozen ridges, some were not
here this morning, huddled out of the wind beneath what
blankets or robes they had thought to carry with them at
the moment of attack.

When everything had been terror and noise and confusion.

A sadness overtook her for a moment, a few tears freezing on her cheeks as she thought on those who were not
here among them. No scaffold, no rock cairn, nothing
would mark the last resting place of their bones. For those
who were no longer here had simply disappeared somewhere in the snowy ridges through that long winter day,
into the black of that freezing night.

A full day gone now since those first shots, a full day
since the growing rattle of soldier guns that followed
Monaseetah as she dragged her two sons from the back of
their lodge into the leaf-bare willows and plum brush, into
the cold-fingered fog where they joined the rest who were
scrambling north while the warriors hollered out and sang
their songs and surged back into the village. Some, like her
Southern Cheyenne friend Rolls Down, had seen to their
duty of helping the small ones escape. Little Wolf too, he

had helped many children flee into the high, dangerous places among the ridges, where the soldiers would not look for them, where the soldier bullets would not find them.

"We will go with the others, staying with Two Moon and Old Bear," Rolls Down had explained there at the north end of the village as he prodded them out of harm's way.

"When will we turn and fight?" Sees Red demanded, flinging his youthful anger over his shoulder at the two adults.

"Come a day . . . soon, little one," the old man answered. "Very soon the Shahiyena and Lakota will turn together and sting the soldiers who poke their sticks into our nests!"

Throughout that gloomy, cold day, stragglers from the camp gathered in the icy, wind-scoured hills. They came in singly, or in pairs, often helping one another struggle through the deep snowdrifts. Others brought in the old and the sick on their backs, or in their arms. Praise be to the Everywhere Spirit, for so few had been struck by soldier bullets.

As they huddled in the snow, freezing toes and hands and noses and ears, the Shahiyena, the Miniconjou and Hunkpatila Sioux watched the dark, antlike soldiers fighting off the warriors while the white men dragged a few things from the lodges then set fire to everything else. Explosions of powder rocked the valley, the echoes eventually disappearing from the river bluffs. Her people had but to watch in frustration and growing despair as the soldiers pulled away to the south, taking with them close to half of their once-great herds.

There were angry recriminations from some who said they should have heeded the warnings brought to their camp, those stories that the soldiers were coming. Words of rage and frustration shouted between the angry men as orange flames cast eerie reflections on the low, gray bellies of the clouds suspended over the valley, oily black smoke climbing the mesa to choke the Shahiyena huddled in the snow among the stunted pine and second-growth cedar.

"Do any of you know who is missing?" Two Moon asked, coming among them, mostly old men and the women now.

"I saw one Cheyenne fall. Eagle, shot from his horse," answered Wooden Leg, his hands on the reins to a weary pony. "Another was Jumps Ahead. A brave herder boy. I know of two more wounded. But now I go join the others who fight from the hillside."

"I cannot find my grandmother," a young woman had complained.

"She is the blind one?" Two Moon asked.

"Yes. I got my children out of the lodge, then returned for her," she wailed. "I could not find my grandmother!"

More loud explosions erupted from the village, like the coming of summer thunder, rattling the trees and rumbling the ground beneath their frozen feet. As she had watched, lodgepoles were flung into the air, tumbling down among the smoky ruins like tiny bits of cottonwood kindling.

Two Moon and Old Bear, Little Wolf and He Dog too—they had decided to assign some of the strong young men to guide the people across the frozen Powder River, to begin heading north by east over the rising land, marching for the village of Crazy Horse on the East Fork of the Little Powder. Many of the war ponies that had been gathered north of the village, or in the meadows east of the river, had not been captured by the soldiers. Now those ponies were given over to the old and the sick. From time to time as well, the warriors came among the fleeing ones with gifts of blankets for the weak, perhaps for the little children who that first night had already huddled two or three within one thin blanket.

Some of the warriors no longer needed their blankets. Somewhere on the hillside, they had come across a great pile of long, blue wool coats. More than three times ten—soldier coats left behind and now worn by the warriors turning about to ride south with He Dog and the rest. They had vowed to bring back the rest of the herd.

As Monaseetah hurried her two sons along with the rest, she would turn from time to time, looking at the low strip of sky stretched over the valley they left behind. With each successive hill put behind them on their freezing march, the pink glow tinting the cloud underbellies and the black smudge staining the southern horizon grew more and more faint.

Later, with the retreat of the soldiers, some of the warriors returned to salvage what they could from the torched village. And found that the white men had left one lodge standing.

"The old blind woman?" Monaseetah asked Scabby, another fugitive from the Southern Cheyenne reservation, as he knelt beside her and the boys in the muddy slush softening the ground, as the sun made its climb this morning, one sunrise after the attack.

"Yes." With hands red and blackened from searching among the smoldering ashes, he handed her a small handful of dried meat. "Divide this among yourselves. It is all I can give you—sharing everything I have between your family and mine. There was so little left among the ashes. And so many to feed."

"The ponies?" asked young Yellow Bird.

Scabby smiled. "It will not be long, little one. And you can ride."

"Our herd no longer belongs to the white man?" Monaseetah asked, her heart taking a leap.

"Yes, a rider just came in. He Dog and the others sent him hurrying back with the good news, coming ahead of them. The soldiers were not careful: did not guard the herd."

"Then we can go after the soldiers now!" Sees Red cheered.

The old warrior shook his head and cupped the youth's chin in his smoke-blackened hand, tender and raw from digging through the smoking heaps that were once their lodges. "We cannot. Instead the chiefs have decided that we will follow He Dog when he returns to the camp of Crazy Horse."

"So we are running from the soldiers now?" asked Yellow Bird.

"No. We are only going to the camp of Crazy Horse, where we can be safe from the cold until we can hunt hides for our own lodges," Scabby explained. "We have our ponies back, and we have saved what we could from the burned lodges." He smiled at the youngster. "The fate of the Shahiyena is now the fate of all free Indians. If the soldiers want to fight us—they will have to fight the Oglalla of Crazy Horse and the Hunkpapa of Sitting Bull."

"And no soldier chief is foolish enough to attack us all," Monaseetah said.

Frank Grouard had shivered most of the night of the seventeenth, like all the rest, so bone-tired and marrow-cold, it was all but impossible to sleep. What little heat his body put out had drawn the frost right up from the ground, right through the saddle blanket he lay on now as the first wink of gray light appeared along the crest of those hilltops to the east. With only his coat and the scrap of a blanket he had captured in the village, Grouard had kept his feet near the fire all night, a fire that a dozen or more of the scouts had fed with cottonwood limbs.

He blinked his gritty eyes in the growing light, making out the restless, shivering lumps on the ground around the fire pit, spread like the spokes of a wagon wheel.

Times like this, he wished he were still hauling freight from California to the land of the Mormons. Warmer work, that was.

Nearby their horses snorted, snuffling for some of the skimpy grass they could paw free of the snow. Complaining for water after all of yesterday's hard use. The animals ridden by the scouts, like those of the soldiers, had been hobbled and picketed last night after Reynolds had asked Grouard's advice.

"We got their ponies, General," Frank had told him at twilight. "They'll be coming for them. You don't want your horses getting run off too—better take care."

"So, we'll keep our horses in camp. All right," Reynolds had said wearily.

Grouard could tell the general was a man worn down to his last fringe. Too old to be leading soldiers after young warriors, that's for sure, he had thought. Yet more than anything, it was how the soldier was treating Grouard now. Whereas before the fight on the Powder, Reynolds had been unable to disguise his distrust, maybe even outright hate, for the half-breed scout, Frank found it gratifying that the general now hung on every one of Grouard's words. Even called him by his first name, as if Reynolds thought they should be friends.

Which was the last thing in the world Grouard wanted.

"Frank, you must tell me what to do with the ponies." Reynolds had searched him out again to ask long after dark, near nine o'clock, when Major Stanton finally brought the herd in.

"I know those ponies, General. Many times they grazed in this valley of the Powder. They know this country." He had pointed up the valley, to the south. "If you take the herd there, a mile or so—you can find them in the morning. They will not wander."

"Will the hostiles come for the herd tonight?" John Bourke had asked.

Shivering as the frosty cold sank down the river valley at twilight, Frank had looked at Crook's aide and said, "Don't think they'll come tonight. Looking after their families now. The cold, no food, with their blankets and robes gone in the fires. The warriors have other things to do tonight."

"Aren't there any trails the herd will use to get past us in the night?" asked Captain Alex Moore.

Grouard had shaken his head, fatigue like a heavy cloak weighing on him. "The only trail the ponies can use will come right through our camp."

John Shangrau stepped forward from the edge of the group listening to the discussion. "General, you want us scouts to put a guard out to night-herd the ponies?"

Reynolds had looked from Grouard to gaze up-valley a moment, then answered, "No. Like Grouard said: drive the herd upriver a mile or so from camp and turn them loose. Then you get your sleep too."

He sniffed at the morning's freezing air. It hinted that more snow would come with the rising of the cold sun. Damn, but he didn't want to move right now. Wondered if he even could—his muscles so weary from the two straight days in the saddle, so that when he finally got a chance to sleep, the cold and dampness drawn from the ground stiffened his body as it had never before. Maybe he was getting too old for this sort of thing.

So he tucked his head back beneath the collar of his coat, brooding on those people of Crazy Horse he had helped cast into the wilderness—without lodges, without blankets and food. But were these goddamned soldiers any better off? Hadn't they driven the Hunkpatila from their village and burned the lodges? So why didn't the victors have it better than the vanquished? he wondered.

Grouard had just fallen back into that restless half sleep, the only kind of rest a man can give himself on the cold ground, when he heard someone call his name. Frank dragged the edge of the blanket scrap back from his eyes and blinked into the coming light of day.

"Is that you, Grouard?"

He recognized Reynolds. The man looked haggard, worn. "Yes."

The colonel tottered over to him, followed by a half dozen of his officers, but he alone knelt beside the scout. "It's getting close to eight o'clock. I want you to have one of your scouts check on the pony herd—but first, we need to talk about resuming the search for General Crook."

Grouard sat up painfully, muscles stiffened. He was reminded that it was like stuffing a foot down into a pair of new boots, the leather resistant, cold—what with the way his joints, his bones, refused his commands. Frank rubbed the grit from his eyes with his fur mittens, slowly coming more awake.

"General—someone gotta find General Crook," he said, discovering all the eyes of the officers staring down at him. "Or this bunch of ours not gonna last."

"He's right, General," agreed Captain Henry Noyes. "We don't meet up with Crook, we damned well better be making for the wagons at Fort Reno ourselves."

"I agree," said Alex Moore quickly.

Reynolds waved a hand, impatient with the captains. "Time enough to discuss that. First, Frank—tell me what you think I ought to do about looking for Crook."

After taking a long moment to look around at the scouts who had rousted themselves from their restless sleep and were listening in on the council, Grouard said, "Suppose I can take some of these men with me. We'll go back toward Otter Creek. See what we can stir up of Crook and his pack train."

"Good," Reynolds said, rubbing the palms of his mittens across the tops of his knees in some display of exuberance.

"I'll go with you, Grouard," volunteered Louis Shangrau.

"Me too," said his brother, John Shangrau.

Jack Russell stood, stomping into his boots like a man with frozen feet. "Might as well have something to do—to move around and keep me warm. I'll ride with you."

"Count me in too, Grouard," Little Bat said. Garnier stepped off a few yards, heading for the bushes as he hurriedly worked at his belt buckle and the buttons at his fly.

Grouard's eyes caught and held on Donegan's. The tall white man nodded to him. "You finish watering them bushes, Little Bat—take this big Irishman with you and check on the ponies," Frank ordered, standing slowly, working what he could of the kinks out of his muscles.

Stretching, he continued, "We'll get this fire built up and get warm a little, General. Then we'll saddle up and move over the divide toward the Otter."

The colonel agreed with a nod, then stuck his nose higher into the wind, sniffing. "Doesn't look like we're going to see much of the sun today, does it, fellas?"

The officers grumbled their private curses at the first flakes of icy snow lancing down out of the low-bellied, slow-moving clouds.

"Only thing good about the snow, General," Frank told him, "good for tracking Crook and his mules."

About twenty minutes later, when Little Bat and Seamus Donegan came back into camp from checking on the ponies, they reported the herd had not wandered and were still on the bottomland, working the snowy ground for what dry grass they could paw up. Grouard sent word with Donegan to Reynolds that the herd was all right, then suggested the four who would be accompanying him to the Otter all take their horses and follow him to the river, to water the animals before the work they would be requiring of the weary beasts.

It was pushing nine o'clock when the five scouts brought their horses back to camp and stopped to warm their hands and rumps over the fire Donegan had kept going for them.

"Suppose it's time we saddled up," Grouard reluctantly told the four.

Yet not one of them grumbled, but instead went to work holding the frost-stiffened saddle blankets near the fire before throwing them onto the horses' back. The animals weren't in the best of humor when they discovered more was expected of them, but in the end appeared too hungry and weary to put up much of a fight or to bloat against the cinches.

"Grouard!"

He turned to find the one called Noyes coming toward him, followed by at least a dozen of the captain's soldiers.

"You want me?" Frank asked.

"The red-bellies got the goddamned herd!" Noyes shrieked, skidding to a stop on the icy snow.

Frank's eyes narrowed as he looked over the dozen or so scouts near the fire; time to think. "Hasn't been long. They didn't get far then."

"Frank! Frank Grouard!"

He turned to find Reynolds and some more officers hurrying up. "General, you hear—"

"I heard, goddammit!" The colonel's face was swollen, a puffy crimson with anger.

"The red sonsabitches hit us!" Moore growled.

"Listen, Frank," Reynolds said, huffing from his double-time through the cold, "I want your bunch to keep an eye out down the valley when you climb up the slopes." He pointed to the hillside.

"The sumbitches couldn't have gotten far," Captain Noyes said.

Reynolds continued, "You see any sign of the herd, send one of your scouting detail back with word—right to me. Understand?"

Frank nodded impassively. Then turned to his four. "Let's go."

As he led the others through the skeleton-bare brush, out of that camp and into the icy, painful snow knifing down from the low clouds, Grouard could feel their white eyes hot as iron fireplace pokers between his shoulder blades.

Frank grinned. He took no small pleasure in knowing those pale-skinned soldiers who distrusted and hated him did not stand a chance now of getting that pony herd back from Crazy Horse.

Chapter 27

Sore-Eye Moon

Like tiny, sharp arrow points, the wind-driven icy snow stung He Dog's raw, oak-brown face.

With more than two dozen others, he was driving the ponies northward through the hills on the east bank of the Powder River.

Through yesterday's wintry afternoon, they had dogged the tail of the soldier column as the white men withdrew from the smoldering village, retreating. A few warriors had dropped off to stay behind when they discovered the bodies the army had left behind near the battlefield. But He Dog did not need to exact revenge on any more white soldiers just now. Enough of that already in his life.

Besides, a scalp already hung red-raw at his belt.

What he had needed was to trouble the rear guard of the soldier column, find out where they would be camping come the darkness of winter night—then at daylight sneak in and drive off the herd. What they needed most right now were those ponies so that more of the stranded people could ride, instead of being forced to walk north through the freezing snow. While most of the war ponies and buffalo runners had been kept in camp or among a herd grazing north of the village that hadn't been captured by the soldiers, what He Dog and the rest had gone after to the south were the brood mares, new colts and yearlings, along with those mules and large American horses stolen in recent raids on settlements, ranches and soldier columns.

In all, the soldiers had succeeded in taking less than half

of the ponies grazing among three herds to the north, two
to the west and one on the east side of that Powder River
campsite. And what the white man got wasn't the best the
tribes owned. Still, it smarted to give up and let the white
man keep what could be easily enough taken back. True
enough, the lodges and robes and blankets, clothing and
green meat, were all gone to ash and soot. But those mares
and colts, those yearlings and mules and captured American horses—those were riches He Dog and the rest could
reclaim.

And take great joy in knowing the white man would be
chagrined to find them missing.

Only now as the sun made its first fiery appearance in the
east did some of the nervous apprehension begin to slip
from him the way water would glide from a teal's wing.
With each new mile the raiding party put behind them, He
Dog felt less fearful that the soldiers had discovered the
loss, less fearful that the white men would follow in deadly
pursuit. With every mile gone beneath his pony's hooves in
their race to the north, He Dog was growing almost giddy
with the realization that the herd was once more theirs and
the soldiers were not so much as going to give chase.

His heart sang to realize that he and the rest of the
Oglalla and Shahiyena warriors were alone, riding the
fringes of the herd of more than seven hundred ponies, not
having to do much to keep the animals pointed north now.
By the time the sun climbed to mid-sky, they would have
the herd back at the site of the destroyed village, more a
collection of charred lodgepoles and black, greasy rings
punctuating the snowy river bottom where they had been
camped on the way to the White Rock agency, on their
journey of peace.

But in last night's darkness after the battle, there on the
ridges above the soldiers' cheerless camp, He Dog and
many of the rest sat huddled in the snowy cold, hate in their
narrowed eyes, their cheekbones still rouged with the flush
of hot blood—yet talking quietly about where their peoples
would go, what they would do now. It was not hard for He
Dog's Hunkpatila to decide they would be turning about
and marching north. To once more rejoin the camp of

Crazy Horse. Perhaps even to let the Hunkpapa of Sitting Bull know the soldiers were on the warpath. Hunting down villages to destroy.

Indeed, the word of this attack would spread like buffalo tallow dropped on the surface of a still prairie pond. More quickly than the white man would ever imagine.

It was a bit harder for the Shahiyena warriors like Wooden Leg, Scabby and Rolls Down to decide that they would abandon the peace chiefs like Old Bear and Two Moon, a struggle to decide on joining the Hunkpatila of Crazy Horse and He Dog . . . if for nothing else than the strength they could assure themselves in numbers.

It was as plain as earth paint that the soldiers were stalking the Shahiyena. The Oglalla were camped far to the north. On the land hunted by the Lakota for many, many winters.

Yes, they had finally decided: it was the Shahiyena the soldiers were seeking to destroy. In the end the warriors of the Shahiyena came to understand their very survival depended upon joining with the Lakotas for the coming spring.

Only by once more joining together with the seven council fires of the mighty Lakota bands would the Shahiyena survive against the onslaught of the white soldiers.

If one thing were as certain as the rising of the sun each morning, as certain as the coming of spring after every long, hard, killing winter: He Dog knew the soldiers would be back. Again and again . . . and again as they stalked and chased, attacked and burned.

Far better that the Shahiyena and Lakota bind themselves one to the other in brotherhood for the coming short-grass time.

For the coming war.

"That's officers' call, isn't it?" asked Bob Strahorn as the echoing notes of the bugle faded from the red bluffs to the west of their bivouac this morning of the eighteenth.

John Bourke nodded, looking up at the newsman from his tending to one of the buffalo-hide leggings. The icy snow beginning to fall all the harder, cold as the blue-ice gut of the Arctic, stung his red, chapped cheeks. One thing good about the snow clouds, he brooded—at least they would not have to worry about the bright sun and snowblindness today. It was going to be tough enough forcing a chase out of their weary, trail-gaunt mounts.

"I'll bet old Thunder Bucket himself is ready to call for one of the companies to pursue that herd," Bourke declared as he rose to his feet, stomping them a few times to stimulate feeling. He raised his right boot as if inspecting it. "Damn, I've been rubbing that big toe and the one next to it with that tincture of iodine Will Bryan gave me for frostbite since yesterday afternoon at the village—but those bloody toes still don't feel right."

"Likely froze 'em good," Strahorn commented sourly with a wag of his head. "Mind if I come along to the meeting?"

"Not at all. Let's see what Reynolds has planned for recapturing that herd."

But Bourke could not have been more wrong. The colonel was in no way planning any pursuit of the enemy's ponies.

"General," protested Captain Anson Mills as Bourke came up, "I want it on the record that I most strongly disagree with your decision."

"The record will show your dissent, Captain," Reynolds replied snappishly, turning from Mills.

"Allow me to make the pursuit. My M Company—"

"No, Captain," Reynolds interrupted, his face clearly showing his displeasure. It was as if he took personal affront to anyone who attempted to corner him, holding his long nose in the air as he did now, as though there were a foul smell about a subordinate's dissension.

The colonel continued, his eyes narrowing, "As I've already told this assembly, gave you my reasoning—those ponies are brood mares and yearlings. Worthless to us. And not that damned valuable to the hostiles either. Besides, as I said when Major Stanton informed me that the herd had been run off: I would rather have one company of strong army mounts than all those grass-fed Indian ponies. Any day."

"With the general's permission," Mills pressed his point, his words coming like the slap of a bare hand against your cheek, "it is my belief that General Crook would believe that if we lost that herd—we lost the battle."

"We did not lose that battle, Captain!" Reynolds shouted, grave face going livid with anger.

"General, you made the comparison about the ponies with our mounts. I think General Crook would likely allow us to lose all the horses of the Third Cavalry sooner than he would want to lose the enemy's herd."

"Just what the hell is your point, Captain?" demanded Alex Moore. The graying bristles of that little gray beard that circumnavigated the edges of his jaw bristled, reminding Bourke of the raised hackles on an angry dog's neck.

Mills looked at his fellow officer, his face sour as clabber, and said icily, "Crook understands that the army can replace their mounts. On the other hand, those hostiles fleeing the village cannot replace their ponies near so easily."

"It's entirely unworkable, Captain," said Reynolds, his eyes on the ground, face gone as dreary as a priest's at a sacrifice when reminded of Crook. "The horses . . . the men are not fit for such an undertaking."

"Sir," Mills pushed the point, his jaw set, determined, "those ponies won't travel as fast as mounted men. Those Indian herders will have their hands full while we go in hot pursuit."

"My men . . . the horses are done in," Reynolds grumbled again, pleading now.

"Just assign me ten men from each company—on the ten strongest horses from each outfit," Mills suggested, pounding a fist into his other palm for emphasis.

"It would work, General," agreed Thaddeus Stanton, his bright, cold face draped with that big nose like three ripe strawberries.

Reynolds seemed to regard it a long moment as he stared thoughtfully at the snowy, trampled ground. Then looked briefly at each of his officers. His eyes came last to Stanton. "Major, how many of the captured ponies do we have left?"

"Something on the order of one hundred seventy-five. Maybe a few more. Less'n two hundred anyway."

"Their value is still overrated, gentlemen," Reynolds finally declared, his words coming out like bullets from a Gatling gun. "The fact that the Indians reclaimed the herd is no great loss to us—because the warriors already had their war ponies as it was."

"I agree with you, General," Moore stated, eyeing Mills. "The men and most certainly the horses are done in."

"Besides, I think splitting our forces right now would not be a wise idea," suggested Lieutenant Rawolle, his eyes flicking over the rest for support. "Those men left behind when Captain Mills goes in pursuit would likely be subject to attack by a large warrior force that had regained its strength."

"We have no way of knowing that," Mills argued, looking like Rawolle had just slapped him in the face.

"My decision is made," Reynolds said firmly. "Return to your companies, make your men subject to morning inspection for injury or illness to Dr. Munn—then report back here at the call of the bugle. We will then decide upon our order of march for the day."

"You won't be waiting for General Crook?" asked Bourke suddenly, shocked by the colonel's declaration.

Reynolds's eyes filled with fire. "I am here: right where the general told us to meet him yesterday evening. And, while I have not yet made my decision—I am leaning toward getting this command back to the wagons at Fort Reno as quickly as possible."

"General?" Bourke begged for another comment, his pulse quickening with the heat of anger.

"That will be all, gentlemen," the colonel cut him off. "Until you hear the bugle." Reynolds turned on his heel and walked off briskly with some of the rest in a narrow wake behind him.

As Frank Grouard had led his four scouts away from that soldier bivouac beside the river, he had made his decision on which trail to take west in the direction they had last seen Crook and the pack train. Easiest to travel was the trail following the Powder northeast for at least a dozen miles before the trail would branch off to the northwest. That would still keep them south of the village they had destroyed yesterday.

Nonetheless, Frank decided on the shorter, although tougher, route leading almost due north as it took them directly over to the Otter Creek drainage. It made sense to him that Crook's scouts would most likely follow the shortest route south from their Otter Creek camp where Louie Reshaw had stayed behind to guide Crook's command. As much as he hated Reshaw for all the poison the half-breed had been spreading to undermine him, Frank nonetheless tried for the moment to put himself into the mind of the other scout.

If Reshaw was as good as the soldiers claimed he was—then he would bring Crook to the Lodgepole Creek rendezvous by the shortest, quickest route open to the mule train.

As the minutes stretched longer and longer in that cold morning, the snow came down all the harder, flakes the size of wood-ash curls piggy-backing into a windy swirl of white-out at times. They landed on his eyelashes where he squinted into the pale light to pick out landmarks, the shadowy depressions, or the dark, emerald-green of treelines surrounding open meadows near the top of the divide— anything that might guide him in making the crossing down to the Otter.

"Lookee there," Jack Russell said, putting out a furry mitten to tap Grouard's arm.

Frank signaled a stop as he peered down the slope to the northeast, making out the pulsating movement of dark forms through the dancing white curtain. "How many riders you make it, Buckskin Jack?"

Russell shrugged. "I can only see two."

"Gotta be more warriors than that," Louis Shangrau offered.

"I can't see no more—only two," offered Louis's brother, John.

"Little Bat?" Grouard asked.

Baptiste Garnier dragged a gloved hand from his brow. "Two riders. Sixty, maybe so seventy ponies."

Grouard smiled. "Let's go get those ponies back."

"Hold it," Garnier said, putting up a hand. Then he pointed to the left, up the drainage where they had been headed over the divide. "General says we go find Three Stars. We don't need ponies to find him."

With a widening grin Grouard said, "Three Stars will want those ponies back, won't he? Now, let's go get 'em before they get any farther away. Then we can drive 'em over the top to find Three Stars."

He nudged his horse away quickly from the rest, trusting that they would all be following. He heard them coming and refused to look back as he worked his way down through the broken timberline toward the river valley. It wasn't many minutes of hanging close to the black line of pine and cedar before the two warriors spotted the five horsemen coming up quickly at an oblique angle on their tails.

The warriors began hollering, at one another, at the horses, slapping rawhide lariats against the rumps of the mares and colts and a few mules. Urging the animals into a ragged lope.

Grouard pulled the big army .44-caliber pistol from his holster lashed around his Saint Paul coat, cocked the hammer and brought the front blade down on the first warrior as he neared the side of the throbbing herd just then crossing a half-mile flat long near the riverbank. Squeezing, he felt the reassuring buck of the weapon in his palm.

As the smoke was stolen from the muzzle by the snowy wind, Frank watched the warrior clutch his arm, his pony veering off suddenly. The Indian kicked the animal with his heels, guiding it with his knees as he made for the timber, yelling something to his only companion on the far side of the small herd. In a heartbeat the second warrior was working his way through the surging animals at the lope, moving northward at a steady, ground-eating pace.

As the pair disappeared into the timber, Frank signaled the four scouts to gather up, and reined his own horse around, prancing a moment. "They're all ours, fellas. Let's go down and turn them ponies around. Head them back uphill." He pointed up the slope with his pistol. "Now we can find what happened to Three Stars."

"General Reynolds, I must take exception, sir," Anson Mills protested in the woolly smother of the falling snow.

"As officer of the day, Captain—I had expected more support from you," replied the colonel. "But it is nonetheless surprising that I don't have your total agreement in moving out: after all, it is your own company that suffers without blankets or coats of any description."

"True, sir—the men are cold—"

"Cold, Captain?" Alex Moore accused. "Freezing to death is more like it."

Mills tried to ignore the officer as he stepped closer to Reynolds. "General Crook gave us specific orders to await the rendezvous here near the Lodgepole."

Reynolds shook his head, his face as pale with worry as the side of a limestone bluff. "I have the welfare of my command to think of first, Captain."

"I want it on the record that I do not agree with disobeying General Crook's orders."

"There is a higher order I am following, Captain," said the colonel. "These men are in need of warmth and food. Our horses require forage and refitting before we can pursue General Crook's objectives. Surely you can see that I have the welfare of my men at heart when I consider marching away from our planned rendezvous."

"I want it known that I differ from the rest of you on this," Mills said.

"So noted," replied Captain Henry Noyes.

Reynolds turned to the captain. "What time is it now?"

Yanking the big pocket watch out of his tunic, Noyes flipped open the cover and replied, "Just past eleven, sir."

Reynolds chewed on a lip for a moment. "We will plan to start out at twelve, gentlemen."

"General, may I ask a question?" inquired Bob Strahorn.

With a deliberate slowness, he turned toward the newsman and answered, "Yes, Mr. Strahorn. The press is always given its due by the army."

Mills watched the young Strahorn almost wince.

"Then you are going to move south to Fort Reno—with or without General Crook?"

He nodded. "Yes. That is where our wagons await our return. Where we can re-outfit with food and blankets and tents. Where these men are in a better situation to await Crook's return. Here—we have nothing."

"Aren't we pushing things a little, sir?" asked John Bourke. "I mean—couldn't we wait awhile longer for General Crook?"

Reynolds turned to the west, studying the hills a moment as he played with one of his long muttonchops, those white whiskers cascading from his jawline. "All right, Mr. Bourke —I'll grant you that. Gentlemen, we will wait until two o'clock for Crook to rejoin this command. Make note of that for the record. At two o'clock you will have your companies ready for the countermarch to Fort Reno."

With a pinched look that seemed as if the colonel would broach no further discussion on the matter, Reynolds said, "There being no more questions—this meeting is dismissed."

Chapter 28

18 March 1876

Little Bat wagged his head at Frank Grouard. "I think Three Stars long gone now."

"Seems so," Grouard said in resignation as they sat atop their horses in the dancing white scurry of the falling snow, looking down into the Otter Creek drainage.

"What you figure to do now?" asked Jack Russell.

Grouard threw a thumb at the seventy horses pawing at the ground in the small upslope meadow behind them. "We take the ponies back to Reynolds. Don't have Three Stars —but we got ponies to make that old White Head happy."

They had pushed north along the divide slashed with sharp slopes, loose scree and talus, all of it covered with old, icy snow from the storms battering this land the last ten days. Today's wind-driven snow felt like tiny cactus needles in Frank's eyes. Gazing a moment to the west and north both, it seemed little chance there would be a letup in the storm.

"All right," Grouard sighed, beginning to rein his big roan around. "Crook's pack track not likely coming this way to the Powder. Maybe we'll cut his trail on the way back to Reynolds."

"Good that we go back now," said Louis Shangrau. "My belly hollering for fodder."

Grouard grinned. "Only thing that Reynolds can feed his men now is these ponies. How your belly feel about horse-meat?"

Shangrau shrugged, glancing at the other three scouts. "Makes me no mind. I et worse before."

John Shangrau, Louis's brother, agreed. "Horse ain't bad."

The horsemen broke apart, spreading out now, pushing, urging, driving the herd before them back up to the top of the divide, where they would then drop over into the valley of the Powder River.

Little Bat flung his voice at the rest, "Horse ain't so bad at all."

"No," Grouard said, remembering his years among the Lakota Sioux. "Not bad at all . . . if you're hungry enough."

Anson Mills walked up to the officers' meeting at the colonel's fire.

Most of the others were already gathered by the time Lieutenant Howard Mason had come around to tell Mills of the session with Reynolds. Captain Alex Moore was center stage, driving home his well-worn point.

"I don't know about the rest of you," Moore said beneath that broom-bristle mustache, "but I got an uncanny feeling Crook has already passed through this country and is headed for the wagons."

"That's bullshit," Mills growled.

Moore whirled on him. "You wind-belly! Just how the hell are you so damned sure?"

The tension, the growing fatigue, the endless hunger and soul-numbing cold was clearly beginning to show, taking its toll. Those little hairline fractures in the solid wall of Reynolds's command that had first opened yesterday morning at the moment of attack were now widening into deep, yawning chasms.

"Where the deuces are their tracks, Captain?" Mills demanded, his face as taut and white as rawhide. "You've got your brain tied in knots if you think Crook and that mule train can pass on through this country without leaving tracks!"

"There," Moore said, pointing west. "Crook was over on that side of the mountains when we last saw him. We haven't seen a damned track over here on the river side of the divide. So it's as plain as the sun that Crook marched past the rendezvous somewhere over there."

"That's the stupidest, pin-titted thing I've ever heard of!" Mills wagged his head. "Why the devil would the general let his scouts take him past the rendezvous point?"

"I don't know," said Lieutenant Rawolle, shaking his head. "But there's some good reason for Crook not meeting us here yesterday—and half of today."

"It's after noon, gentlemen," Reynolds agreed. "I've decided we're not going to wait until two o'clock as I previously agreed to do."

Mills felt the anger searing like a hot poker driven through his chest, sensing it enough that he put off speaking—but for only a few moments while the rest grumbled, murmuring amongst themselves.

"There's nothing strange about this," Mills announced. "He's traveling with the pack train. It's slower than our mounts."

Moore snorted sarcastically, his laughter sounding like river ice breaking up. "We damned well went over that same divide, down to the enemy's village, fought a battle for five hours and then retreated here. Don't tell me Crook's goddamned mule train can't get here by now!"

"That's right!" Lieutenant J. B. Johnson said. "I think the general has gone straight for the wagons!"

"Me too! We're the ones been abandoned!" echoed Lieutenant Rawolle. "We've been left behind."

"I ought to bring the lot of you up on charges!" Mills snapped.

"In a pig's eye!" Moore snarled. "If anyone is guilty of anything here, General Crook is guilty of abandoning his forces in the field without resupply!"

Mills felt like taking the captain's grinning face and using it for punching practice. He wagged his head. "The thought that Crook would leave us behind is so ludicrous. No court-martial in this republic would find him innocent of so clear a crime against his men. Crook's worked long and hard for his reputation—"

"So maybe he figures his reputation will save him now!" Johnson shouted above the growing clamor.

"Gentlemen," cooed Thaddeus Stanton, absently gnawing at a dirty fingernail. "We won't solve anything by arguing. Colonel, what exactly do you have in mind for us to do?"

Reynolds turned to Moore and Rawolle, who stood side by side in the semicircle. "You, Captain Moore, and Lieutenant—I want the two of you to determine the order of march for the day, and when you are ready, Captain Moore can issue the command to move south."

"So," Mills sighed, "you're going to leave, General?"

Reynolds didn't reply to the question. Instead he told Mills, "As officer of the day, it is your responsibility to assign extra men to help Dr. Munn with his wounded on the travois. I can count on you completing this task?"

Fuming, Mills chewed on the inside of his cheek a moment before speaking. "We're ordered to march?"

"Captain Mills—it's imperative that I do something to save my command," Reynolds growled, his eyes narrowing into a scowl, face gone slug-colored as he grew more anxious with each passing moment.

"Permission to be excused, General?" Mills asked, surprising the rest as he saluted.

"Why, Captain?" Reynolds asked.

"This meeting serves no purpose, sir. I am sure Crook will be here shortly."

The colonel shook his head, a benevolent, humorless grin on his lips. "You certainly are a dreamer, Captain."

"May I be excused, General?"

"Permission granted."

Mills strode off angrily, stomping back to M Company's bivouac, where his men stood in knots, not venturing far from the aureole of warmth around their small fires, their thick saddle blankets clutched tightly around their shoulders. Faces liver-colored with fatigue.

"Donegan!" Mills shouted.

"Captain?"

Mills huffed into the bivouac. "Where are those field glasses we've been using?"

"Right over here," answered the Irishman. "You looking for something in particular?"

"Crook?"

The Irishman's face showed interest. "You hear word of him?"

Mills felt the truth of that sink inside him like a stone. "No," he answered. "But I just swore Crook would be here before this outfit moves out."

"So Reynolds is really going to up and bolt, eh?"

Mills nodded at the taller man. "C'mon. Let's go have us a look at what we can see from the top of that hill there."

They grunted and huffed their way up the icy slope in the keening of the wind-driven snow that was just beginning to ease up on the valley of the Powder by the time the two reached the hilltop.

"Wind gets boxy like this here on the northern plains, a man can get buried alive in snow," Donegan told him as they neared the crest. "Pay warning to it, Captain—and you'll survive."

Mills's chest burned with the dry, cold air he was drawing in like life, his legs aching with the climb.

"Here's as good a spot as any," Donegan said as they came to a halt at the top, peering around them in three directions.

"North by west," Mills said to himself absently, swiping the snowflakes from the lenses before he held them at his eyes.

"That's right. If Crook's anywhere down there heading south, he'll be off to the northwest."

"All four ways of Sunday!" Mills exclaimed, feeling the rush of emotion as he brought the distant figures into focus. "There he is, the old Gray Goat himself!" Mills cheered, the joy rising in him like sap in spring.

"No shit?" Donegan asked. "Lemme see!"

Mills handed the Irishman the field glasses and pointed off in the direction where he had spotted the long and winding snake of horsemen and pack mules easing down the last of the rough-hewn slopes toward the valley.

Shading his eyes from the driving snow with a mitten,

Mills asked, "How long you estimate it will take for Crook to get here now?"

The Irishman was a few moments before answering, seeming to scan the country the column had yet to traverse before it could reach Reynolds's camp. Mills shivered in the cold, slashing wind.

"No more than an hour, Cap'n."

"They've gone, Grouard," Jack Russell declared as he rose from the ground, toeing some of the smoldering ashes in one of the fire pits at the Lodgepole Creek campsite.

"I can see that," Frank Grouard replied almost angrily, gazing off to the south. "From the looks of it, Three Stars made it here." He pointed at the smaller prints among the larger ones trampling the snowy, churned ground. "Those are mule tracks."

"Crook come in—means we gotta follow them south now," Louis Shangrau said.

Grouard sighed and twisted in his saddle, eyeing their pony herd, which was nosing around on the river bottom where the weary cavalry mounts had all but eaten every bunch of grass and gnawed at the bark of trees and brush. "Let's get these ponies moving before we're jumped."

John Shangrau approved. "Me too. Don't like waiting around like this. Let's move and quick."

Frank shuddered a little in his coat as the wind picked up again. A wind cold enough that he thought it could cramp a snowshoe hare's hind foot. Grouard squinted at the sky, finding the sun a dull buttermilk color behind the thinning snow clouds just beginning to break up. That disk had started its descent into the west.

"We don't have that much daylight left," Grouard warned them as he put heels to his horse and moved off. "Let's use what we got to catch up with those soldiers. You take the lead, Little Bat. Keep the road clear for us."

Garnier nodded, reined about and headed out. He would ride several hundred yards ahead of the small herd wrangled by the four other scouts.

South along the west bank of the Powder they drove the seventy ponies, then made their first crossing of the frozen river to the east bank. Again and again they were forced to march back and forth across the river as they followed the trail beaten by Reynolds's cavalry and Crook's pack train in those next few hours, until Grouard spotted Little Bat awaiting them in a break among the cottonwood fifty yards ahead.

"You smell something bad?" Grouard asked as he came up, his eyes flicking to the nearby hills.

With a single nod Garnier pointed at the ground. He moved his arm slowly up the slope toward the western ridges.

Bringing his left leg over, Grouard dropped to the off side and studied the prints more closely. He didn't have to look at them long. Unshod.

"How many you make it?" Grouard asked as he rose, dusting the new snow from his canvas britches.

"Half a hundred. Maybe even more," Garnier answered.

"Hasn't been long, has it?" ·

Little Bat shook his head in agreement.

"Looks like they're following the soldiers again, don't it?" asked Jack Russell. "What you figure to do, Grouard?"

Frank took a deep breath, turning to regard the small herd they had driven for most of the day, up the divide then down again before coming south on Crook's trail.

Stuffing a foot in the stirrup, Grouard rose to his saddle and settled himself. "I say we leave these goddamned skinny ponies for the Lakotas, fellas."

"What? We pushed these sonsabitches all day, Grouard!" grumbled John Shangrau. "And Crook said we could have some of the ponies, each of us!"

"Take my share of 'em if you want, Shangrau. I don't care a red piss right now."

"Why you ain't taking 'em along no more?" asked Louis Shangrau, easing over beside his brother.

"These mares and colts will hold us back. I wanna travel fast now." His eyes touched the others. "Rest of you can come with me if you want. We gotta tell Crook he's got trouble coming up behind. That big a war party maybe make problems for Three Stars tonight after the sun's down."

* * *

Bob Strahorn watched a clearly pleased George Crook shake hands with Frank Grouard, pounding the half-breed on the back.

"You go get yourself something hot to eat, Frank," Crook told the scout. "You earned your money today."

The general came back over to the fire as Grouard and his four scouts led their horses off through the command's bivouac here on the west bank of the Powder. "John, I need to give some orders to the officer of the day."

"That'd be Captain Mills, General." Bourke stood beside the cheery fire, pulling on his mittens.

It had begun snowing again at sundown, the fat, fluffy flakes hissing as they struck the flames now, turning to wispy steam while the temperature continued to drop even more.

Crook watched Bourke buttoning his clumsy buffalo coat, then peered down at the fire. "So cold it's begging for a shindy, Mr. Strahorn."

"Yes, General," was all the newsman could reply.

After the rendezvous near the mouth of Lodgepole Creek, Crook had ordered the column to march south another eight miles until they had located better forage for the horses and another supply of firewood for the night. It was as the men were starting supper fires and boiling coffee that Grouard's scouting party had come in with word of picking up the trail of a large war party that followed the soldier trail until just north of the bivouac, where the unshod prints disappeared on the riverbank.

Like the half-breed Grouard, Crook figured the warriors had crossed the Powder to circle well around the camp, to make a try for the soldier horses and mules.

"Very well. Captain Mills it is, Lieutenant." Crook looked up at Bourke. "Tell him I need to see him on the double. From what news Grouard brings me—looks like a sizable war party dogging our backtrail may try to run off some of our stock tonight. I want everything hobbled on company lines, and cross-lined for double measure."

"I'll pass on your order, General—and be back shortly."

After he watched the lieutenant disappear into the

murky light of dusk, Strahorn found Crook gazing at him thoughtfully. Nervously, he asked, "General? Is there something I can do for you?"

Crook shook his head, a bit of a grin inside his double-tailed beard. "No, Mr. Strahorn. Just been thinking of that story you've told me—about the white girl living among Crazy Horse's band. Legend?"

"No legend, General. It's got all the earmarkings of truth," Strahorn replied, the pencil stilled above his writing pad.

With a confirming nod, Crook continued, "A reporter like you seems to keep his nose to the ground—what else have you ever heard about this story?"

Scratching at his dirty, bearded cheek, Strahorn thought a moment. "We heard she was captured when she was only two, maybe three years old."

"Who were her people?"

"Seems they were immigrants on the Mormon Trail, bound for the City of the Saints in Utah when she wandered off from the wagon train's camp and was captured by the Oglalla."

"So, I take it's been some time she's been with that Crazy Horse bunch?"

"That's how the story goes. Twenty years or better now. I got Grouard to tell me a little more about her when he was in a mood to talk."

"A rare occasion, Mr. Strahorn. He's a . . . standoffish sort. Not given to divulging much of anything. I suppose you should consider yourself fortunate he talked to you at all."

"Seems he wanted to talk a little about the girl. Said she's just about the prettiest woman among that band of cutthroats. So pretty and fair of skin—they don't make her do any of the back-breaking work most captives do. Even the labor that makes their own women grow old before their time."

"Did Grouard ever talk with her?"

He shrugged. "I suppose he might have, at least once. But the girl speaks no English. Never did, really. Only Sioux, Grouard tells me."

"A most interesting story, what say, Mr. Strahorn?"

"Interesting indeed, General."

"The stuff of newspaper headlines, eh?" Crook asked, indicating Strahorn's tablet propped on his knees.

"Yes, sir. As always—it seems the truth makes far better reading than anything I could invent out of my own imagination."

Crook chuckled as he turned away and rejoined some of the others from both Reynolds's command and those troops who had remained with the pack train, all regaling one another with stories of the past two days.

Shuddering with the cold, Strahorn gazed back at his tablet where he had been writing by firelight. The newsman went back to composing his dispatch of the eighteenth, describing the reasoning he saw to justify Reynolds's precipitous withdrawal from the battlefield.

The Indians, severely punished . . . took refuge in the mountains thus unguarded . . . and had a positive advantage over the troops. Scattered over this almost impregnable mountainside, and secreted behind the numerous walls of rock, they could pick off our men without running the slightest risk of losing their own lives. Therefore the more the engagement was prolonged, after the prime object of the expedition was accomplished, the more serious and useless were our losses. Realizing this, General Reynolds . . . ordered the command to abandon its position and to at once proceed toward the mouth of the Lodgepole.

"After Reshaw spotted that lone warrior heading upriver along the bank," Crook was explaining to others at fireside, "I ordered a countermarch, and we went into camp about five o'clock on the evening of the seventeenth, after the animals had been watered. All throughout that afternoon, it had become painfully clear to me that Reshaw and the rest of my scouts had no conception of the distance to the mouth of the Lodgepole, no real idea how long it would take us to rendezvous with General Reynolds."

By first light that morning of the eighteenth, Crook had had his column and the pack mules marching south again.

"We hadn't been on the trail all that long," Crook continued, "when Reshaw came riding back from the advance to say that he had spotted a half dozen or so warriors driving eighty or more ponies in our direction. I could only guess that those ponies had been recaptured from Reynolds's column camped somewhere ahead of us. That's when Reshaw and I went to the top of a hill and took a few shots at the horsemen. I knocked one off his pony, but his body was swept up and carried away by his comrades."

"You captured the ponies, sir?" asked Strahorn, paying attention to the talk at the fire once again.

Crook grinned. But it quickly seeped from his face. "We succeeded in getting our hands on only about twenty-five of them. And, in looking at what we did capture, I noticed some cavalry mounts among them. So I surmised at the scene that the hostiles we bumped into had not only stolen back their own, but some of Reynolds's stock as well. After that short delay there, we marched on south until we spotted your camp, Mr. Strahorn."

"I don't think you could have made our bunch any happier than you did when you showed up," said the newsman.

"I suppose you boys were ready for some warm blankets and hot food, eh?"

"Not only that," Thaddeus Stanton replied, recalling for all the universal joy and cheer in Reynolds's camp when the Crook command marched up, "with your fresh companies reinforcing us—we no longer had to fear the savages running up our backside. The hostiles were every bit as strong as we were, General."

Crook's face went grave once more, just as it had from time to time through this evening as more and more of the story of the Reynolds fight started to sink in. George Crook had been clearly overjoyed upon reaching and reuniting with his fighting units, ecstatic to hear Colonel Reynolds's concise report of his destruction of the village. But as more details of the fight were disclosed to the general by Stanton, Bourke, Mills and Egan, among other subordinate officers throughout that cold afternoon—details that gave all the more confirmation of the immobilizing argument and bickering among Reynolds's officers, coupled with reports about the lack of support, how the troops callously abandoned the dead and possibly some wounded on the field of battle, along with that impulsive decision made to burn supplies rather than confiscate them—Crook's first blush of glee had gradually sunk to a morose sadness bordering on melancholy.

Nonetheless, Strahorn realized, General George C. Crook had as yet refused to speak any of his real thoughts. Like the commander he was, this evening the general had instead publicly congratulated before the entire command both Captain Egan for his superior charge on the village that had opened the battle, and Captain Noyes for his company's capture of the pony herd.

Still, the young reporter was newsman enough to see that for Crook the thin luster had worn off what Reynolds had chosen to call his victory over Crazy Horse. Anyone who cared to pay the slightest heed to George Crook would plainly see a department commander troubled by unseen forces, brooding on weighty matters, a man clearly not himself.

Chapter 29

19–20 March 1876

"God curse their red, h'athen hides anyway!" shouted Seamus Donegan as he fired two last shots into the dark, aiming at the disappearing backs of the uncounted warriors who had waited till moondown to make their move on the herd.

All about him was a swirl of motion as soldiers kicked burning limbs from the fire pits to kill the light, officers barked their orders, snappish in frustration, warriors screaming their defiance—while most of the soldiers simply tried to stay out of the way of the pounding hooves that thundered through camp, rattling pieces of rawhide and flapping blankets, screeching or blowing the shrill eagle wing-bone whistles clamped between their lips.

"You think we did any damage?" asked Bob Strahorn as he came huffing up, his breath like filmy gauze draped about his head in the silver starshine of a clearing sky.

It was damned cold, Donegan thought as he turned to the newsman, worse still outside the blankets and robes.

"Not likely, Bob," the Irishman replied. In this deep a cold their voices hung with the breaking cleanness of icicles.

"How about the savages?" Strahorn inquired. "You think they got any of us?"

Pursing his lips, Donegan shook his head. "Not likely—they were after the ponies. But with the way we tied everything down tight . . . what with the pickets rotated out there all night, we had us a pretty good warning when those horsemen started their run through camp. No, Crook did all right taking the precautions he did."

"I'll remember to say something about that in one of my dispatches to the *News*."

"Just don't use my name, Bob."

Strahorn looked at the Irishman strangely. "What—you don't want to be a hero in black and white?"

"No need to." Seamus turned to the reporter and grinned, his face tight in the extreme cold. "But you know, I'm going to look you up when I bring my wife to Denver next."

"You're married? I didn't know."

"Me? Why—don't I look like the kind can be married?"

Strahorn wagged his head with a cat's grin. "Nothing like that at all. Just didn't realize it. Never figured it for a man scouting for this army—I suppose that's it. I look at all the rest of these," and he swung his arm in a small arc around some more of the half-breeds employed as scouts as they headed back to settle at the fire. "I just figured it was a bachelor's occupation."

Donegan's grin flickered out as quickly as a trimmed lamp wick, the loneliness seeming all the more intense as the newsman put words to it for him. "True, my friend. It is just that—a bachelor's occupation. C'mon, Bob—we'll see if anyone's knocked over that coffeepot next to my fire."

Seamus had to move, be doing something, or it would likely overwhelm him. With every passing day of this campaign, the gnawing grew more severe, the yearning and longing something actually tangible. Maybe it was only the endless cold of one day on the end of another, he had told himself after those first few days after leaving her behind at Laramie. But he had not done a damned bit of good at convincing himself that it was the cold.

Not the hunger either—down to half-rations the third day after the beef herd was run off by that bunch of warriors on the trail north. And not far up the Tongue, Crook had put them on quarter rations.

The immense, aching cold and the lack of sleep, besides that yawning belly of his growling in dull protest more and more with each succeeding day—all of it had conspired to make his yearning for her something he had to grapple with physically every waking moment. Not to mention when he at last got a chance to close his eyes beneath the sweat-frozen horse blanket. How those warm, moist dreams of her came back to haunt him night after night, refusing to allow a truly weary man any true rest.

A bugle stuttered its clear notes on the subfreezing air. Officers' call. It was plain that Crook had something of import to discuss with his officers.

"This's going to be one meeting I don't want to miss," Strahorn declared. "C'mon."

In a matter of minutes Crook and Reynolds had the rest gathered in a crescent about them near the fire that John Bourke nursed back to life after the scare for the ponies. The general's young aide had flames leaping some three feet high by the time Crook cleared his throat to dust things off. Donegan could read the burden of something weighing there on George Crook's shoulders, perhaps in the way the man now even refused to make eye contact, much less look in the direction of Reynolds, as well as almost half of the expedition's officer corps.

Clearly, some matter had already been decided between the general and his colonel.

"How many of the enemy's horses do we have in our possession, General Reynolds?"

"I will have to ask Major Stanton, sir," Reynolds replied, turning to Crook's chief of scouts.

Clearing his throat and swiping at his runny nose, Thaddeus Stanton took a couple steps in from the ring around the fire and said, "General Crook brought in approximately thirty ponies he recaptured from the hostiles. That's added to the one hundred and eighty we had in our possession. So we have something on the order of two hundred and ten, General Reynolds."

"Thank you, Major," replied the colonel, who turned to Crook.

Without looking at the colonel for his cue, Crook declared, "In the morning, General Reynolds will order a count taken of just what we need in the way of remounts for our cavalry units. On the trail north, in addition to the brutal action in and around the enemy village, we lost some of our own stock. After we have replaced them, and any needed by the civilian scouts—the general and I agree . . . we are ordering the destruction of the rest."

"D-Destruction?" asked Captain Alex Moore, that one word explosive, like snow falling from a roof.

Crook nodded, toying with one of the tails on his long beard. "We're going to kill them before proceeding on to Reno."

"I heartily agree," said Captain James Egan in that sore-throated, bullfrog colic of a voice he owned. His mouth was more often busy chewing tobacco. "Take what we need and destroy the rest. Keep on teaching the Sioux their lesson."

"Besides," added Captain Anson Mills, "butchering those carcasses will provide this command with as good a meat as we've had on this campaign."

"I'd eat just about anything to get this expedition off of quarter rations, gentlemen," Crook told them.

There arose some uneasy laughter that quickly drained itself as Crook rubbed his horsehide mitts together impatiently.

"So be it. In the morning, General Reynolds may in all likelihood draw men from every company to help in the slaughter. Only when it is complete can we continue our march. This meeting is adjourned."

Crook had the entire command up and finished with breakfast by four o'clock on the morning of the nineteenth. Then the destruction of some fifty colts and brood mares began beneath the fading starlight as dawn gave its first hints of arrival in the east.

Those animals not chosen to replace army stock were herded east across the frozen Powder River, then on south a mile to a little flat near the mouth of Joe Creek. While John Bourke himself had not been near the scene during those two cold, dawn hours it took to complete the bloody task, there was not a man who could not escape the noise of the slaughter.

"It's something you'll never forget, John," said the Irishman quietly as he moved up beside the young soldier standing and gazing off to the east.

"It's . . . eerie—how human the cries can be," Bourke said, feeling more of a chill at the back of his neck. It came not from the cold. "You've heard it before?"

Donegan nodded. "Many times. Had a number of horses go down under me in the war. Had to shoot some myself. But what I was just remembering myself happened a year ago last fall."

"When you were down in Texas with Mackenzie."

"Yes," answered the Irishman. "But what I didn't tell you about was the Injin ponies Mackenzie's troops had to kill— the ones captured from the Kiowas and Comanches."*

"How many?"

"More'n twelve hundred."

The figure shocked Bourke. "And less than fifty are making that much noise?"

"But think how the dying cries of those ponies hurts those warriors up in the hills, John," Donegan told the soldier.

Turning to look west, at the ridges and mesas coming pink and red in the new light of day, he asked, "You really think they're up there, watching us?"

"Make no mistake of it. This wounds those warriors more than anything. More than burning their lodges. More than destroying the meat they've laid in for winter. Those Sioux and Cheyenne are some of the finest cavalry this world has ever seen—likely ever to see."

"An interesting observation, if not conclusion," said George Crook.

With Donegan, Bourke turned at the sound of his voice. "General."

"Only an observation, General," said Donegan.

Crook nodded almost paternally. "Made through a wealth of experience, I presume."

Bourke said, "From the sounds of the Irishman's many travels, I would say Donegan has truly acquired his knowledge through experience."

* The Plainsmen Series, vol. 7, *Dying Thunder*

For a long moment Crook seemed to study Donegan, then eventually moved his eyes across the river.

"I'm beginning to believe I'm going to have to change some of my thinking about warfare with these Indians on the northern plains," declared the general.

That revelation shocked Bourke. "Sir, you learned quite a deal fighting the Apache in Arizona—and taught them some stern lessons as well. More than they ever taught you."

"Perhaps," Crook replied, snapping back as if he had been in a reverie. "But I can't shake the feeling that I'm not through learning all that these plains tribes have to teach me." He turned back to his aide. "We're preparing to get under way, Lieutenant. I'd like you to ride with me on today's march."

"Yes, sir. I'd be happy to."

They watched Crook move off before Donegan asked his question.

"He's picking your brain about the fight, isn't he, John?"

"That he is, Seamus. Trying to sort out for himself what really happened."

"God bless him for that," said the Irishman quietly. "As hard as it will be to separate the wheat from the chaff on this—God bless Crook for trying."

After a march of twenty-one miles south by southwest up the Powder River beneath an increasingly leaden sky, the command went into camp on the nineteenth just above the mouth of the Crazy Woman as the snow returned for an encore. At least here there was some ground blown clear of a lot of the icy crust, so the stock could graze in the bottoms, and there proved to be no shortage of wood for those fires every man not on picket duty huddled around as the light sank from the sky, their faces gone the color of a sick dog's tongue with fatigue.

"I can grumble if I want to, Bob," Bourke said to Strahorn as he chewed on the stringy, half-raw slice of meat.

"A lot of good it'll do you," the newsman replied. "We're lucky to have the horsemeat to supplement what rations we got left."

"Stretching those rations damned thin, aren't we? And this tasteless horsemeat won't last us long."

"Another day or so—we'll get to Reno. And then we'll feast in the land of plenty."

Bourke chuckled at that. "Beans and bacon make for a feast in the land of plenty, is it?"

"At least there will be more than quarter rations and Injun pony steaks."

They were stretching it out to the bitter end. What they had did have to last them until they reached Quartermaster George Drew's wagons. Until then the little bit of fresh horsemeat would have to do, along with a daily ration of five ounces of hardtack and a quarter pound of bacon, a half pint of beans and what little coffee could be spread around among a mess. A lot of the men grumped for a lack of tobacco, smoking or chaw. How such a small thing would have been such a wonderful luxury.

Particles of snow tortured Bourke, too small really to be seen. Only felt against the bare skin of his exposed, raw-hided cheeks as it swirled and danced on the slashing breeze toying with the stiff pages of his journal as he reread some of the sharp denunciation he had for Colonel Reynolds, written at their camp on the eighteenth.

The theft [of the pony herd] was promptly reported to General Reynolds . . . To the surprise of all [he] declined sending any detachments to attempt their recapture. Great dissatisfaction now arose among all: several officers vented their ill feeling in splenetic criticism and openly charged Reynolds with incapacity. This exhibition of incompetency was the last link needed to fasten the chain of popular obloquy to the reputation of our commanding officer . . . in yesterday's fight our troops had been badly handled, the heights overlooking the enemy's position not seized upon . . . [so] that our men were now suffering for food and covering while everything they could desire had been consumed before their eyes in the village and what was the worst shame and disgrace of all, our dead and dying had been aban-

doned like carrion to the torture and mutilation of the
Indian scalping knives. The favorable impression General
Reynolds' affable manners had made upon his subordinates had been very rudely and completely effaced. I
cannot use a better term than to say we look upon him
as a sort of General Braddock, good enough to follow
out instructions in a plan of battle conducted according
to stereotyped rules, but having nothing of originality of
thought, fertility of conception, and promptness of exe-
cution which is characteristic of great military men.
Reynolds' imbecility is a painful revelation to many of
us.

"More coffee, John?" asked Bob Strahorn, who held the
steaming pot in his mittens.

"You tending the fire tonight, Bob?" he replied as he
held up his empty cup.

"A little, between getting my dispatch written. How you
doing with the journal?"

"About to catch up with today's entry."

"Keep at it, Lieutenant," Strahorn cheered as he moved
away with the coffeepot, offering the steaming elixir to others gathered around the fire as the snow drifted down,
dancing from time to time on the stiffening breeze.

Bourke put his pencil to work over the page of his journal.

The Indians hung round our camps every night, occasionally firing a shot at our fires, but more anxious to
steal back their ponies than to fight. To remove all excuse of their presence Crook ordered that the throats of
the captured ponies be cut, and this was done . . . first
some fifty being knocked in the head with axes, or having their throats cut with the sharp knives of the scouts,
and again, another "bunch" of fifty being shot before
sun-down. The throat-cutting was determined upon
when the enemy began firing in upon camp . . . It was
pathetic to hear the dismal trumpeting (I can find no

other word to express my meaning) of the dying creatures, as the breath of life rushed through severed windpipes. The Indians in the bluffs recognized the cry, and were aware of what we were doing, because with one yell of defiance and a parting volley, they left us alone . . .

Steaks were cut from the slaughtered ponies and broiled in the ashes by the scouts; many of the officers and soldiers imitated their example. Prejudice to one side, the meat is sweet and nourishing, not inferior to much of the stringy beef that used to find its way to our markets.

"John, I feel the need to talk. You have some time for me?"

Bourke looked up to find Crook settling beside him. "Very good, General."

"Not here. Let's go for a walk—work up your blood a bit."

"Anything you say. What is it you've got on your mind, sir?"

Crook smiled wanly as he rose, turning up the fur collar against the stinging snow. He waited to speak until they were several yards from the fire, moving in among the horses of one of the cavalry companies.

"Warmer here, John. The heat coming off these big animals, their breath."

"Yes, it is, sir. But I plainly see something is troubling you."

"Damn right, something is. This business with Reynolds. By God, I bent over backward to help him redeem himself."

"That business with the contractor bribes down in Texas, yes."

Crook nodded, stroking the front flank of one of the gray troop's horses. "He had the initiative, the fight was going his way for the most part, from what I can learn."

"Yes, sir."

"And then the son of a bitch let it all slip through his fingers—right down the shithouse hole, John."

"That loss of the ponies was a great demoralizing influence on the men, General."

"I think I could even forgive Reynolds that dunderheaded lapse of military thinking, even destroying the blankets and robes and meat. Maybe forgive him for calling for a retreat so quickly when he was afraid of losing the village he had just captured—all of that . . . if it weren't for leaving the men on the field. An officer must never leave his men behind. *Never.*"

Bourke studied the man in what firelight was being reflected from the underbellies of the low-hung snow clouds. Worry and turmoil lay etched on Crook's every feature.

"General, I don't think there isn't a soldier in this river valley tonight who doesn't know how you feel about the men who serve under you. Why, if they only knew you the way I—"

"Perhaps the blame ultimately lies with me," Crook interrupted, worry carved deeply into his gray features. "I hoped so much to help Reynolds redeem himself among the brass, rebuild his reputation here just before he was to retire. Reynolds is an old friend of Sam Grant's, you know."

Bourke nodded. "You can't be faulted, General."

But Crook shook his head morosely. "No, John. I can, and will be faulted. If not by Washington, then by Reynolds."

"That can't hurt you. Not with what he's done—"

"It always hurts when the men on the line—the common soldiers who make up this army—can't respect and trust their superiors. When that happens, John—every damned officer in the army suffers. All the way up. Which only makes this man's army all the less for it."

Chapter 30

21–24 March 1876

Samantha's soft voice caressed the words of the lament she sang to herself at the window of her cold room, one hand gently pressed against the inside of the frosted glass, the other laid over her abdomen.

> *I'll hang my harp on a willow tree*
> *And off to the wars again;*
> *My peaceful home hath no charm for me*
> *The battlefield no pain.*
>
> *One golden tress of love's hair I'll twine*
> *In my helmet an able plume,*
> *And then on the field of Palestine*
> *I'll seek an early doom.*
>
> *And if by the Saracens' hand I fall*
> *'Midst the noble and the brave;*
> *A tear from my lady love is all*
> *I ask for a warrior's grave.*

How would her warrior take her announcement when he returned from his far-off battlefield?

Would the man flee? Would he change? Would his eyes no longer look at her as lover and woman—from that point on regarding her as something else simply because he would be sharing her with another?

Samantha turned from the window, stepping to the edge of the bed, where she settled slowly. It was cold up here, cold enough to see her breath in the late hours of the afternoon. This far north, March could still be a hard-faced month.

Yet there were moments in the day when she felt the flush of heat radiate through her. No one had to tell her. Samantha Donegan knew what was happening to her body, knew what caused these changes.

Would her news cause him at last to settle down?

Then she laughed at herself. She knew better. It was silly and childish, and above all very selfish to ask that of Seamus Donegan when she knew he could not. It would be her wish that he would find one place and settle down—such a wish would not be his. Again she vowed that she never would ask anything of him that he would not freely volunteer of his own volition.

Hearing the sounds of boots across the old snow outside, she went back to the window, rubbing her bare hand against the thin, crazed frost patterns glazed over it so that she could peer out. A small detail marched across the parade below, their long buffalo coats slurring the snow as they strode purposefully toward the flagpole and the mountain howitzer perched beneath the pole's lofty, regal splendor like a squat, ugly toad. The soldiers stopped, dropped their satchel of powder and wad down the barrel, primed and held the torch, waiting only on the one among them who stared intently into his hand, the glove that cradled the watch set on Chicago time.

Samantha heard his voice give the command, that single word almost smothered by the instantaneous roar of the belching gun that lurched backward.

The soldiers wrestled the howitzer back to its original position, formed up and immediately retraced their steps across the icy snow.

The evening gun already, she thought. This day, how it crawled past. But like so many of the rest she had endured here, waiting at Fort Laramie, it too had grown old. Amazing, but with every last one of those days, she had feared she wouldn't make it through. Although each had come to an end, flowing in some way into the next, and the next and . . .

Then she thought she would have to ask Lucy what day it was. This, the third week of March from what she remembered. More than a month now he had been gone from her. And with each new day she had taken some little, growing pride in surviving. Becoming just a bit stronger each day for that self-reliance. Knowing that Seamus would be all the more proud of her for it too.

But . . . oh, this loneliness.

"Stop that, Samantha!" she scolded herself as she came away from the window once more and went to sit atop the trunk in the corner. It, the small bed and the tiny, wobbly dry sink beside the bed were about all that fit in here. Gazing at the porcelain pitcher and washbowl that sat in front of the tiny mirror on the dry sink, Samantha imagined this to be like a monastic cell for a Catholic monk—and that made her think of him again. Almost everything did.

"You know better, don't you?"

Yes, she did. Samantha Pike had known what Seamus Donegan was even before she had ever laid eyes on him riding into the yard of Sharp and Becky's homestead down near Jacksboro.* Known almost every detail of the man and his life she could drag out of her brother-in-law, every shred worth hanging on to about the tall, gray-eyed stranger who Grover had fought the Indians wars with, then summoned to Texas. It had been clear to see from the look on her brother-in-law's face that Sharp Grover held an immense respect for the younger man, a respect that had likely become fraternal, if not downright paternal in their nine grueling days on Beecher Island, an uncharted speck on these mapless plains almost eight years ago.†

It was sometime after Seamus had come to Texas when sister Becky finally told her that this Irishman was the only man Sharp Grover had met who he would gladly accept into his family. So it was that Sharp's announcement that the stranger was riding into their yard had caused something bordering on awe to stir within her—something closer to terror.

---

* The Plainsmen Series, vol. 6, *Shadow Riders*
† The Plainsmen Series, vol. 3, *The Stalkers*

How she had found herself trembling, heart fluttering like a hummingbird's, upon first laying eyes on that man her brother-in-law loved as much as any man could love another. Sharp loved Seamus every bit as much as he had loved his irascible uncle before him.

And then, remembering it now every bit as clear as the moment it happened, she saw again how the stranger slid wearily out of his saddle, tied the animal off and exchanged hearty embraces with Sharp there in the yard before she ever got a close look at him. And when he finally took his floppy hat from his head, using it to dust himself off from boot to chin, then turned about to approach the porch, Samantha had gasped at the front window, put fingers to her lips to stifle the surprise she felt. And something perhaps a bit more primitive as well.

"He is handsome, isn't he?" sister Rebecca had admitted and asked at the same time from the open doorway as the two men plodded up the steps. "In a rugged, roughly chiseled way."

Yes, she could admit now—there were others who had paid her court in the past who were more handsome. But there were none who were as beautiful as her Seamus. None could come close, none could compare. His rugged, sun-etched, crow-footed look, the way his eyes crinkled at her for no good reason at all, like he was smiling all the way down to the core of him—it made him simply the most beautiful man in the world to her.

And his hair. Oh, his hair.

The way it spilled thick and curly over his collar and onto his shoulders. At first she had thought it odd for a man to wear his hair so long. But that had been before she ever came to Texas, came to buffalo country.

Before she had laid eyes on her Irishman.

How she loved to brush his hair for him, run her fingers through it.

And how she prayed their child would have his thick, curly mane. So leonine, so like the lordly male of the species.

Seamus—in so many ways unlike her brother-in-law. Sharp had settled down; it was understandable, after all, for

Sharp was older when he decided to put down roots with Becky.

Older than when Sam had asked the same of Seamus.

So she had come to understand that if she were to want to be a part of his life, she would have to accept what there was luring him into the next valley, over the next range of hills, far, far to the next sunset and beyond.

Seamus had a wanderlust in his blood that she had vowed she would accept. How Samantha prayed each day for God's help that she would one day come to understand that wanderlust. Understand how that wandering was better than having one place to call their own.

But then it seemed God Himself answered her time and again, reminding her heart that she had Seamus Donegan tied to that porch outside Jacksboro, Texas, long enough to get him to say "I do," there in the summer heat before Sharp and Becky, before that tight-collared minister and a gathering of friends from all over North Texas.

So it was that God's answer gave her some peace each time she forgot and let her heart grow frightened. There was something fearful—yes—in not being tethered to a place and others. Yet Samantha admitted there was something terribly exciting about the life that Seamus Donegan offered her too. And she had vowed many times in the past few weeks that if need be, she would form a family of herself and the baby coming. Learning in those small ways how to make do without a husband.

At least a husband who rode off for long stretches at a time. Tearing her heart from her when he did.

The knock at the door surprised her.

"Samantha?" came the soft question.

"I'm here." It was Lucy.

"It's time for dinner. Everyone is sitting down now."

"I'm not hungry."

"Not again, Samantha. You've got to eat," Lucy Maynadier scolded in that motherly way of hers.

"No. Really. I'll be all right."

"Come sit with us then. If you don't feel like eating—it's all right. But come sit with us. I haven't seen you all day."

She stared out the window at the coming twilight and sighed almost audibly. "Any news from up north, Lucy?"

"No," came the soft answer from the far side of the door. "But soon. We'll hear something soon. Come, Samantha. Please come sit with us."

Through the window she watched the sun inching down off the roof of the building west of them. And the arrival of this golden sunset made her miss him all the more. She rubbed a hand across her belly and smiled. Feeling better and not so alone for the moment.

"All right, Lucy. I'll come sit with you."

"General Crook, may I have a word with you, sir?"

Crook turned to find Dr. Curtis Munn at his tent flaps. Beyond the surgeon the camp was in a state of celebration. Fires leaped into the winter black of night this twenty-first day of March.

"Come in, Doctor."

"I promise not to take up much of your time. I know how busy you must be since we arrived this afternoon—what with preparing to continue our march on to Fort Fetterman."

Smiling, Crook said, "It's fine, Doctor. I've already decided we'll lay over here at Reno through tomorrow. To give you and me time to adequately prepare for the last leg of our journey. And to recoup the stock a bit before pushing on south."

Back on the evening of the twentieth at their camp beside the Powder, the general had written a note he entrusted to scouts Jack Russell and Tom Reed, destined for Major E. M. Coates of the Fourth Infantry, who commanded Crook's base camp of wagons at Fort Reno. In it Crook informed Coates of their impending arrival, saying that he wanted the major's wagon camp moved across the river to the south bank, where the entire expedition could be put to the march without delay.

This morning the column prodded their weary animals for some ten hours across softening ground which grew more slippery every hour as the winds shifted out of the south, bringing in the chinooks to begin eating the snow blanketing that high land.

Then just past four P.M. Crook's advance hove into sight of the ruins of Fort Reno. After crossing on the mushy ice that was beginning to break itself up, Crook and Reynolds encamped as troops under Major Coates, Major Samuel P. Ferris and Lieutenant Colonel John S. Mason set about preparing a hot supper of bacon, beans and hard bread, along with all the hot coffee the cavalry could want. Beyond the expedition's bivouac, infantry herders fed the skinny horses on grain while Thomas Moore's civilian packers tended to their bone-weary mules.

"All the way south, General," began Munn, the army surgeon, "I've attempted to bring some cheer to my wounded."

"*Our* wounded, Doctor," Crook corrected.

Munn nodded, not intending to be thrown off course. "Yes. So, I must tell you I am most disappointed in the lack of preparations for our arrival."

His brow knitted. "I don't understand."

"The only thing Coates and the rest have done for our wounded is to have the hospital tent pitched. The ground inside is still wet. There's no fire inside or anywhere near the tent for warmth, heating water. And the only bed in that tent is where the civilian herder, Wright, lays shivering."

"How is the man?"

"Virtually abandoned." With a wag of his head Munn explained, "I can't believe it's the same man, General. He hasn't been attended to well at all. So skinny I hardly recognize him."

"Have you told Dr. Ridgely about your complaints?"

Straightening, the surgeon took a deep breath before he replied. "I most certainly did. When I asked him why he did nothing when he knew we were coming, and he knew of my previous instructions and orders—all Ridgely had to say was, 'I didn't do this . . .' or, 'I couldn't do that.' "

Crook shook his head. It was all beginning to weigh a little too much on him. Why had all this incompetence, this arrogance, this imbecility decided to raise its hoary head at this moment in his career in the West? Why had the fates chosen him, at this time in his life?

"How do things stand at present, Dr. Munn?"

Grimly, he replied, "I had to do it all on my own, with Steward Bryan's assistance. We located a sheet-iron stove we placed in the tent. Bryan has foraged among the various companies for the food for all our wounded, and any blankets the companies can spare. The ground is drying a bit at last, and Wright seems better just to have some human company. It's disgraceful what hasn't been done, General."

Crook had to agree, but in a much larger context. "I'll second that statement, Doctor. Is there anything else you need to report."

Munn glanced at his boots. "No. Just to see that you were aware of the sorry state of affairs upon our arrival."

"Doctor, I didn't need to get back here to Reno to know that this expedition was in a sorry state of affairs."

Before dawn the following morning, Crook thoughtfully condensed his first report of the Powder River fight in a tersely worded telegram he sent galloping south to Fetterman with a mounted party of scouts and a detail of cavalry.

Western Union Telegraph Co, March 22nd
Dated in the field OLD FORT RENO, WYO. T. 1876
Received at FORT FETTERMAN the 23rd.

TO GENERAL SHERIDAN, CHICAGO.

Cut loose from wagon train on 7th instant. Scouted Tongue and Rosebud rivers until satisfied there were no Indians upon them then struck across country towards Powder River. Gen Reynolds with a part of command was pushed forward on a trail leading to village of Crazy Horse near mouth of Little Powder River. This he attacked and destroyed on the morning of the 17th finding it a perfect magazine of ammunition, war material and general supplies. Crazy Horse had with him the Northern Cheyennes and some of the Minneconjous, probably in all one half of the Indians off the reservation. Every evidence was found to prove these Indians to be in partnership with those at the Red Cloud and Spotted Tail Agencies and that the proceeds of their raids upon the settlements have been taken into those agencies and supplies brought out in return. In this connection I would again urgently recommend the immediate transfer of the Indians of those agencies to the Missouri River.

Am satisfied if Sitting Bull is on this side of the Yellowstone that he camped at mouth of Powder but did not go near there for reason to be given by letter. Had terribly severe weather during absence from wagon train. Snowed every day but one and the mercurial thermometer on several occasions failed to register. Will be at Fetterman 26th inst. and if you desire me to move these Indians please have instructions for me there by that date or else I shall return cavalry to railroad at once for recuperation.

GEORGE CROOK, Brig Gen

Crook had his command rest and recoup that entire day of the twenty-second across the Powder from Fort Reno before resuming their march on the twenty-third.

On that Thursday morning, after the wounded who had been transferred from the travois to the hospital tent were now laid in the springless ambulances, and much of the burdens that had been packed on Moore's mule train were distributed among Quartermaster Drew's wagons, the Big Horn Expedition set out beneath gray skies that threatened a cold spring rain.

That cold, blustery morning, as winter was soaking away into spring, the general sent a second telegram destined for Phil Sheridan's eyes, this one to be taken by more scouts directly to Fort Laramie, where it would be wired to Chicago's Division Headquarters. More than a little concerned now with the way his officers were lining up and taking sides on the Powder River Battle, Crook grappled with how best he should associate himself with the total destruction of the village, including blankets and robes, meat and saddles, while he began to put as much distance as he could between himself and the blunders made by the aging commander of the Third Cavalry.

To that end, he wrote Sheridan:

> . . . We succeeded in breaking up Crazy Horse's band of Cheyenne and Minneconjous, killing more than one hundred Indians and burning their village on Little Powder River. An immense quantity of ammunition, arms and dried meats were stored in their lodges, all of which we destroyed. Our loss was four men killed and eight wounded.

Still, George Crook was plainly grappling with how best to use those powerful and politically potent words: *we* and *our*.

Chapter 31

24–27 March 1876

"*G*eneral Crook—may I have a moment of your time?" asked Anson Mills.

As the captain came to a halt, Seamus Donegan looked up from the fire where he had joined Crook, John Bourke and Bob Strahorn for coffee after supper on that Friday evening, the twenty-fourth. While Thursday's muddy march of fifteen miles to the head of the Dry Fork of the Powder had been extremely hard on the animals, plowing through more than half a foot of melting snow that steadily softened the sandy, arid ground, Friday's twenty-one miles seemed that much tougher: forging on through an intermittent, driving rain that developed into a bone-chilling sleet doing its best to turn the thin topsoil of the high plains into a slick gumbo the soldiers found balled up beneath the hooves of both the horses and mules. Such conditions required frequent stops, while the shivering, grumbling men did what they could to scrape the mud free with their pocketknives.

Without a doubt, those past two days getting here to the head of Wind Creek had taken just about every reserve of strength left in the men and the animals. The Big Horn Expedition had been forced to kill or abandon fifty-eight cavalry horses and thirty-two of Moore's mules on that march south from the village. With every passing hour, more and more of the captured Indian ponies were pressed into army service.

And with each new day following that battle on Powder River, the expedition had continued to tear itself apart with charges and countercharges. Every advance and retreat of the battle was examined and criticized along the trail to Reno, then on south to Fetterman, cussed and argued around the fires every evening.

To the Irishman, tensions were running hot and patience had clearly been stretched about as thin as spider's silk.

"What can I do for you, Captain?"

Mills turned his head to look directly at Reynolds's tent, which stood some fifteen feet off, facing Crook's own headquarters tent. "In private, sir?"

Quickly, Crook glanced over the bunch gathered at his fire. "I see no need for secrets, Captain Mills. We can discuss any concern you have right here."

"Very well, General," Mills replied, then cleared his throat as if working up to start his speech. "You're aware General Reynolds asked each of us to prepare a written report of the fight?"

"What's your question, Captain?" Crook asked impatiently.

To Donegan, the general suddenly seemed edgy. Until Mills had come to the fire, Crook had appeared to be relaxing a bit by the warmth after what Bourke had described as the general's bottling up over the past three days.

"I have asked General Reynolds for permission to list only M Company's casualties in my report, and nothing else."

Crook scratched at one tail of his long beard. "Did Reynolds ask you what your objection was to making a full memorandum report?"

"Yes, sir."

"And you told him what, Captain?"

Mills jutted his chin in that way of his, looking not at Crook but rather staring straight ahead into the growing twilight. "If I made a full report, I would be obliged to reflect upon the conduct of Captain Moore, sir."

Around the fire, Seamus noticed a lot of the others nodding to themselves, perhaps a bit nervously. Crook in turn chose to stare at the flames licking along what dry firewood they had dragged up from the creekbank.

"How did Reynolds receive that, Captain?"

"I have no idea, General. I only followed up my answer by informing General Reynolds that he should take due notice of Moore's conduct on the morning of the battle—for his own protection."

"And?"

Mills coughed nervously before he answered. "General Reynolds laughed at me, sir. Saying that he did not need any extraordinary protection. And he again demanded a full report be filed with him."

Crook seemed to study Mills for a moment, then asked, "Is this the first word given General Reynolds of complaints about the conduct of Captain Moore?"

With a sharp shake of his head Mills replied, "It can't be, sir. Begging pardon—the man's not blind, General. But nonetheless, Reynolds claims this is the first he's heard of any complaints about Moore."

For a few moments Crook used the toe of his boot to gently jab some of the burning limbs farther into the fire pit. When he finally looked up at Mills, he said, "I want you to fulfill the order given you by General Reynolds. A full and complete report on the battle. Full, and *complete,* Captain."

"Then I'm to require the same of Lieutenant Johnson, sir?"

"E Company of the Third?"

"Yes, General."

"Johnson was assigned to coordinate with you in the village."

"Right again, sir."

Crook looked back at the fire, clasping his hands behind his back. "Of course. A full report on his part in the battle, his viewpoint of things, you understand—from Lieutenant Johnson."

"It may be damaging, sir . . ."

Crook put his right hand to his forehead, saluting Mills. "You have your orders, Captain."

"Very good, General." Mills snapped heels together and returned the salute, then quickly whirled on his heel and strode off purposefully.

John Bourke rose slowly at the edge of the fire. "General, you're aware the report Captain Mills is going to write won't be at all flattering to General Reynolds."

"I'm well aware of that," Crook said, a little too evenly, flat as a hammer on a cold anvil. "Gentlemen, the cards will be dealt. I have no way of stopping that. And when it's all said and done, we'll see just how those cards lay, won't we?"

Crook gave none of them time to answer. Instead, Donegan watched the general abruptly push away and disappear through the flaps of his headquarters wall tent.

"They're choosing up sides already," Bob Strahorn said, the first to speak minutes after Crook's leave-taking.

"What do you mean *already?*" Bourke asked him, settling back on a stump at fireside.

Seamus snorted, that burst of a chuckle getting every man's attention. "By the saints—all of you . . . me included, by damned . . . we all had sides chosen in this sad affair before we had marched a mile away from that burned-out village."

Strahorn said, "Well, boys—I don't care what all the Millses or Moores in the world have to say. I'm going to tell the truth of that battle. Crook better get on with a court-martial and get on with it quick. I think the general may be scrounging around to find himself a scapegoat."

Bourke's face went white with disbelief. "So you think Crook's doing this only to find someone to throw to the wolves?"

Strahorn shrugged, looking into the fire. "Johnny, what I think is that Reynolds did what he had to do at the time. Crook wasn't there—but he damned well better get this court-martial going to figure out the truth."

"Just what truth are you talking about now, Bob?" asked Donegan. "Sounds to me like we've got us different opinions of what truth is here."

Bourke nodded, sullenly gazing into the yellow and blue flames. "The Irishman's right, Bob. You're on one side, or another. Every one of us now. And from what Crook's said to me—he sees the failure in this fight as due to poor leadership and downright cowardice."

"Maybe I gave Crook more credit than I should have,"

Donegan said eventually, with a wondering shake of his head. "I figured he would know better."

"What do you mean?" Bourke challenged, bristling like a dog with its guard hair up, with what he took as an attack on Crook.

Donegan stared at him evenly. "That fight didn't go badly for us because of Reynolds's incompetence. Not because of Moore's or Noyes's cowardice. No, we barely got out of that village when we could because we were almost bested by a damned good enemy."

"A damned good enemy?" Bourke asked. "Shit! I'll never buy that."

With a nod, Seamus replied, "No, not yet you won't. I can tell the army is a long way from admitting that it's fighting an enemy that can do a helluva lot more with a helluva lot less. Move faster, eat less, keep moving and attack more in force. But this army's always found it hard to learn its lessons."

"We're going to have to teach these warrior bands a good lesson soon," Bourke said, still a bit upset. "Just as soon as General Crook can re-outfit and put an expedition back into the field, he's vowed to finish this job we got started on Saint Patrick's Day."

"Luck o' the Irish, is it?" Seamus said, forming his words with more of a peaty brogue than he had spoken in many years since coming to Amerikay. "I'm afraid that this whole bleeming army is in for some painful lessons before it learns just what sort of enemy we're fighting . . . and how to defeat him."

"Well, now, gentlemen. Don't take your differences so hard," Strahorn tried to cheer them. "In this, as in everything, it seems there's always two sides."

"Yeah," Donegan replied, swirling the dregs of coffee gone cold at the bottom of his cup. "Always two sides: the right, and the dead wrong."

"General, I'm very much surprised to get this paper," declared a pasty-faced Joseph J. Reynolds as he stood before George Crook's desk at Fort Fetterman early on the morning of 27 March.

The column had continued its bone-numbing descent back to Fetterman for the twenty-fifth, making camp on the South Cheyenne River. They did not see the fort's flagpole in the distance until the sun had begun to sink behind the Rockies late on the afternoon of the twenty-sixth.

After twenty-six days and 485 miles.

As the animals were being tended to and the men were settling around their evening fires to begin some heavy drinking, the threatened storm that had been looming over the past several days finally broke.

Surprising many, Captain James Egan was the first to sign a number of specific charges against Colonel Reynolds, having publicly and repeatedly stated that Reynolds should be held accountable for his shoddy management of the fight, especially in light of the colonel's continued refusal to investigate Captain Moore's behavior on the morning of their attack on the enemy village. Egan was the first to raise in a clear and loud voice what had only been whispered up to that point: Moore had been guilty of nothing less than cowardice.

Late that Sunday evening of the twenty-sixth, Crook had finally drawn up his list of charges against Reynolds. He had then had them delivered to the colonel, just before Crook himself turned in for the night.

Closing his eyes had been a futile effort. Sleep had eluded Crook as he played and replayed every conversation, every order issued, every decision made throughout the expedition. This morning as he pulled on his boots at the edge of his cot, the bleary-eyed general had so looked forward to leaving Fetterman behind, if only for a few weeks while he returned to Omaha to prepare for a spring offensive.

If only to put the debacle on Powder River behind him.

But in the predawn light, Joseph J. Reynolds stood ready to challenge his department commander, clearly as if he were not about to let Crook escape back to Omaha near so easily.

Crook wagged his head in frustration. "Surely you've heard the talk?"

Reynolds nodded, a hand gesturing like a wounded bird

before the old soldier. "Just talk, General. No campaign is without its detractors."

"I think this is a little more serious than that."

"General Crook, I have done my whole duty in this regard—so I'm perfectly surprised to have such a paper as this presented to me," Reynolds declared sadly, in a voice clearly drawn with strain, with the struggle to control his emotions. He held the list of charges out between them. "I would like to have this paper withdrawn, sir."

"I cannot do that," Crook replied, turning away, wishing he were anywhere else but here at this moment. Try as he might, he had found it hard to look into the colonel's eyes. But then he forced himself to.

"I am an old man," Reynolds continued, slowly lowering the list of charges, despair etching his features, deepening a lifetime's wrinkles on his face. "And this is the first time in my career in the military service that I have ever been charged with anything. Can't you see these charges would wipe away the record of a lifetime?"

"General Reynolds—do not forget there was serious question of your conduct in Texas—"

"I damned well know that!" snapped the colonel, his composure cracking. Then the lines on his face softened as he struggled to regain control once more. "Will you withdraw these charges, sir?"

Crook shook his head. "I cannot, General." Now he walked past Reynolds and stopped near the smoky window, gazing out on the muddy, dreary parade of Fort Fetterman beneath dawn's light. "The entire expedition was a failure. In fact, the fruits of the whole campaign were lost when you failed to give chase to the warriors who retook their pony herd."

Reynolds stiffened as if cold water had been thrown on him. "General, I will not presume to take responsibility for the loss of those animals."

Crook whirled. "But it is precisely the loss of that pony herd that clearly makes our expedition a total failure!" he snapped.

"A failure?" Reynolds squeaked, disbelief and anger evident in his rising voice.

"It was through gross misconduct that the expedition failed."

"Granted, General—some mistakes of judgment might have been made . . . but I performed my duty in good faith all the way through—"

"General Reynolds," Crook interrupted. "More than mistakes in judgment were made. So let's not mince words here." He turned fully on the colonel, feeling the heat rising in his neck, and was sure the crimson was beginning to rouge his cheeks above the whiskers. "You clearly disobeyed my orders."

"Sir?"

"First of all you burned the saddles."

"With due respect, I don't recall you saying anything—"

"Secondly, you burned the meat that I ordered you to save—"

"You told me nothing of the sort!" Reynolds's eyes brightened with a sudden glare.

"Dammit! There was enough meat in that village to supply our expedition for a month. And for the good of those men—*your* men, General Reynolds! You should have held onto the blankets and robes as well."

"But *you* told me to destroy everything—"

"General!" Crook seethed as he interrupted Reynolds. "I'll have you know we could have damn held onto that village, used it as a base for our operations. With meat and robes, along with that pony herd, I could have marched the Big Horn Expedition against Sitting Bull himself! But instead—because of your failures on the Powder, I have been prevented from chasing down every last red criminal on the high plains!"

"I repeat," Reynolds replied, his voice an octave higher now, "you yourself told me to—"

"My plan went up in smoke, General," Crook replied, a single finger wagging at the older man.

For a moment it seemed Reynolds refused to take another breath, then suddenly drew in some air with a sharp gasp. "These charges are going to stand?"

Crook turned back to the window, his hands clasped behind his back. Damn, did he despise some of the ground he had to cover in this man's army. Like a first-year plebe forced to run the gauntlet. "I dislike very much having to put these charges against you, General. Truth of it is, I would rather march into a half-dozen battles against an unknown enemy than to prefer that list of specifications against you."

"Then . . . why, General?"

Crook whirled—tired of being questioned, tested, bothered by this man he had sought so hard to uphold, to give the benefit of the doubt to before this expedition had even marched its first mile. Now he was clearly at the end of his string, flaring with anger as his words came out between clenched teeth. "Why? Because it is my duty to prefer those charges against an officer who has disobeyed his commander. I will not withdraw them."

"Can't we just keep this within the expedition command? Have our own inquiry into all these . . . these rumors?"

Shaking his head in frustration, Crook said, "No. It's too late for that now. Things have gone too far. Too many people know. Word is likely spreading around the country already." Throwing up his hands in despair, he added, "I might as well try to smother Vesuvius as cover this up."

"I had no idea this . . . this situation had gone so far."

"It wouldn't have if you had dealt with it earlier. There— on the Powder, the morning of the battle. So now I'm forced to do something about it here—or the matter will be handled in Washington."

Beginning to sway a little, as if he was light-headed and swooning, Reynolds glanced about himself and lurched to a ladderback chair beside the tiny desk. "Tell me your heart, General. Do you believe I disobeyed you—or only exercised poor judgment on the battlefield?"

Crook sighed. "I understand that one of your companies went into camp there within view of the village."

"Captain Noyes—"

"Yes, Noyes. His company unsaddled, built fires and prepared coffee for their goddamned lunch!"

Reynolds swallowed hard and answered, laying an arm on the desk to support himself. "Yes, Noyes's company did just that."

"Good. Good that you admit seeing the malfeasance of Noyes. I'll refer you to Major Stanton, Captain Mills and Lieutenant Bourke for confirmation of the man's misbehavior. Furthermore," Crook continued, "I understand that one of your officers seriously failed to perform his duty in the battle."

Crook waited for a reply. When Reynolds did not utter a sound, Crook turned to find the colonel staring dumbly ahead, face ashen, a blank gaze in his eyes. The look of someone in shock.

"General Reynolds?"

Reynolds shook his head, coming to. "I have heard nothing of that charge until this moment, sir."

"Perhaps the most galling to me—personally speaking, General Reynolds—was when I learned that it was your intentions after the battle to take your command and march straight for Reno."

"No, sir—nothing of the sort. I only decided—"

"Which would have left me with four companies and all the impedimenta of the command while you were fleeing to Reno!"

"As God is my witness: nothing of the kind had entered my head!"

"I have it on good report that you were preparing to leave the site of our rendezvous!"

In frustration, Reynolds shook his head repeatedly. "My men were in dire need of both food and warmth, General! Good God—I would rather have put my own hand in the fire and burned it off before thinking such a thing as abandoning your support column."

Crook turned back to the window, sensing the burn of adrenaline through his veins. Better than caffeine to wake a man, he thought, then considered that thought strange. "After I have tried to do so much for you, Colonel Reynolds. And still you were going to abandon me in your haste to retreat."

The tiny room fell quiet, a few morning sounds slipping in past the ill-fitting door and window, through the clapboard walls. Fort Fetterman preparing for another day of duty on the central plains.

"So, General Crook," Reynolds said when he noisily rose from his chair after some agonizing minutes, "I ask you one last time to withdraw these spurious charges."

That only made Crook angrier at the colonel. Still he refused to turn around and face Reynolds as he spat the words out like bullets from a Gatling gun, "They are not spurious charges. I have enough to make me believe in their validity."

"Who is poisoning your mind against me?"

Crook wagged his head, weary of this confrontation. "General, our meeting is over. We have nothing more to discuss." He watched Reynolds's face seize with a painful despair, his eyes filled with the fright of a wounded, dying animal caught in an iron trap.

It took Reynolds some effort to get his words out. "W-Will you at least give me the courtesy of withholding your charges for a few days?"

With a sigh, Crook nodded and returned to the small desk. "Yes. I can hold the charges for a little time."

Reynolds's reply came weakly, as if his words were rising from the bottom of a deep, and empty, well. "Thank . . . thank you, General."

Crook began, "Where things will go from here—"

A knock at the door interrupted them. "Yes?"

"Lieutenant Bourke, sir." The aide-de-camp opened the door, allowing in the cold of the morning as rays of sunlight made their appearance on the parade. "Our escort to Laramie is saddled and present."

Reynolds asked, "You're leaving Fetterman, General?"

"Yes—returning to Omaha. To prepare for another campaign against the warrior bands."

"Another campaign, yes."

Crook took up his coat, slipping his arms in the sleeves as he said, "Colonel Reynolds. Likely you will not be accompanying that spring expedition. These . . . legal matters will change the command structure here—for a time."

"Not going. Yes, I understand," he replied thoughtfully. "Then, you yourself will lead the spring expedition against the Sioux and Cheyenne."

Crook thought that a needless question. He bristled as he

stuffed his last arm into his coat and dug a glove from the pocket. "Of course I'll be leading that expedition. And this time, as God is my witness—I'll have the victory this army needs so desperately to bring this bloody war to an end."

Epilogue

8 April 1876

*H*e hadn't believed holding another human being could feel so good. Nor had Seamus believed he could have missed Sam the way he had.

It hadn't been just the cold, nor the quarter rations, nor that long march. Not even the things Reynolds's soldiers had done to one another as that Big Horn Expedition tore itself apart at the seams from within.

Crook had sent the wrong man against the Sioux and Cheyenne—to do the wrong job. And now in Omaha, Chicago and Washington City itself, they were figuring out what to do next trip out. Talking again about three columns to converge on the Powder River country. By that time, come spring, the enemy would be west—nearer the Tongue, maybe even on the Rosebud itself.

And Seamus would go, asked as a personal favor by the old, red-bearded soldier who had taken a liking to the gray-eyed Irishman. But first he had to explain it to Sam.

"Are you asleep?" he asked her.

Samantha gave him a throaty answer.

She was asleep, he decided. So Seamus tucked his nose into the nape of her neck as they lay cuddled in this warm bed taking up most of the space in their tiny room at Fort Laramie. He breathed deep of her fragrance. Kissed her, then gently slipped out from beneath the sheets, blankets and the comforter Lucy Maynadier had loaned Samantha back in February.

Quickly stuffing his legs down his long-handles, pulling

the sleeves over his arms and buttoning them clear up to the neck, Seamus put on the wool shirt and canvas britches Samantha had hung over the chair back after she had washed and dried them yesterday. Friday. When he had come riding back to her.

Sam had met him, eyes wide, as he was halfway up the stairs.

Her arms about him in the next heartbeat, legs akimbo, as they stood locked into one another there in the narrow stairwell.

She had whispered into his ear, "Oh, God—Seamus. I thought those steps sounded like yours. I've been praying to hear your boots climb these stairs."

Seamus had sensed a burning high in his chest, his eyes smarting, about to give him away. "I've been waiting . . . waiting to climb these stairs to you, Sam."

Then she had suddenly stood back from him at arm's length on the step above his, looking him up and down. "You . . . you're not hurt?"

"No," and he had smiled. "Still strong as an ox."

And that's when he had swung her into his arms and carried her up the rest of the stairs as she looked over her shoulder at the landing below, where Lucy Maynadier had stood, arms across her chest, grinning.

They had not left their room for supper, nor for anything else, that Friday evening as the fort moved through its own routine of bugle calls and assorted guns near the flagpole at parade center. Two people lost in one another.

How she had clung to him, like never before. Making desperate, hurried love there at the first. Gasping at the end with his ferocity, then quickly falling asleep with him. Later, Sam had aroused Seamus with her fingers and her lips moving up and down the length of him. There was no way a man could have refused Samantha Donegan, as insistent as she was to call her soldier to attention.

For but a moment Seamus had worried about his need of a bath—to scour away those heady fragrances of cold sweat, leather and gun oil, the stench of horse and nights wrapped in not much more than his fevered dreams of her. But Sam hadn't seemed to mind the earthy odor of him in the least. And for more than the last fifteen hours, he had clearly enjoyed her enjoyment of him.

That morning of 27 March when General Crook and his escort had marched south away from Fort Fetterman, the short respite of warming temperatures come to visit those last few days became nothing more than a memory. With the wind angling back out of the north, spitting lances of driving snow, another blizzard closed its icy, subzero jaws down on the central plains. It would have been clear to a blind man that March was going out the way it had come in: with the roar of a lion.

For a half-dozen days Donegan had been forced to linger at Fetterman as the troops were mustered out, sent back to their duty stations to recuperate while awaiting new orders that rumor had it would arrive before the middle of April. Crook had made it as clear as mountain sunshine that he was going back to Sioux country again as soon as his men and animals had regained their strength and he had enough war materiel shipped to the Fetterman staging arena.

Major Thaddeus Stanton had temporarily mustered out his civilian scouts, informing them that they were to keep their ears open and to check back with this person or that post before the end of April. There would likely be work for every last one of them who wanted to ride again in search of the hostile warrior bands.

"Who'll lead the march this time?" Frank Grouard had asked Stanton in that sullen ring of half-breeds gathered in Fetterman's mess hall.

Seamus had watched, seeing how Grouard's eyes flicked for a moment at Louis Reshaw, accusations in their dark, shining depths.

"General Crook says he will lead the coming expedition," Stanton had told them.

"Then I'll ride for him," Grouard declared.

There had been many others who vowed the same before they broke up and went their separate ways—some heading back to family in western Nebraska; others riding south to the Laramie or Russell posts; a few returning to their ranches or cabins along the North Platte. To wait for the call from Department Commander George C. Crook.

"And what of you, Mr. Donegan?" Stanton had asked that freezing morning at Fetterman.

"Yes, what of you, Irishman?"

Seamus had turned to find Anson Mills moving close. He regarded both soldiers for a moment longer, already holding his answer in his heart.

"I suppose it's useless for a man—especially a man with a wife—to try to climb the Bozeman Road to Montana now that Reynolds botched things up on the Powder."

Stanton grinned that knowing smile of his below the red nose. "Things a might stirred up, don't you say, Captain Mills?"

Mills nodded, grinning himself. "You've got far worse things to do next month than sign on to guide for George Crook when he goes looking for Crazy Horse again."

"Maybe even Sitting Bull this time," Stanton had cheered.

"I'll know for sure what I'll do after I return to Laramie."

"Your wife?" Stanton asked.

"Yes."

"I heard you left her in their care," Stanton said approvingly. "She'll fare well when we go to finish the job we started."

Seamus had stared to the southeast a moment before he answered, "It's a wee bit different now, having someone else to worry on . . . instead worrying only on meself."

"I've a wife of my own," Mills had told him. "Not a minute goes by but that I don't miss her—the children."

This ache for my Samantha, thought Seamus at that moment.

"Your pocket filled with army scrip," Stanton said, closing the leather-bound ledger he had used, old paymaster that he was, in paying and mustering out his band of Clark's scouts. "Go celebrate your reunion. Buy her some pretty things. Then, when you hear George Crook's call—come riding."

"It ought to be pretty this time out, Irishman," Mills declared. "We know where they are, and how to fight them now. They don't stand a chance."

Donegan had studied their faces a little longer, then replied, "We'll see, gentlemen."

"Come back for the spring ride," Mills reminded him as Donegan had turned to go.

Perhaps, he had told himself every hour on that miserably cold ride south, knowing there was no *perhaps* to it. It might prove far more fun this time, what with a different, warmer twist to the weather. Even Bob Strahorn thought he might be able to talk his publisher into sending him out again once all his dispatches were edited and he could get back north from Denver City.

But besides, there was that young newspaperman who had shown up at Fetterman just days ago. A fellow Patlander, that one named Finerty. And a whiskey-loving one he was too; Seamus recalled their meeting a few days before. Maybe with friends and enough whiskey and bullets along too, they could all march north again for another try to whip the Sioux.

But as cold as it had been on that ride south from Fetterman, Crook's spring campaign seemed about as far away as the South Pole to him.

In stockinged feet he crept to the small window and rubbed a circle free of its frost glazing. Below lay a fresh layer of snow on the parade, all but untracked. Only a few footprints and hooves had pocked its pristine tablecloth surface. Far to the east the sun had already risen beneath the storm clouds, hung as it was pale as a buttermilk button behind the gray gauze that spat out a flake or two now and then. The storm was passing. This blizzard was over.

How he wanted to walk with her down by the river, to show her the shady grove where he and Sam Marr, where Reverend White* had camped that summer not quite ten years before. How he yearned to hold her hand in his, and stop her beneath those leafy cottonwoods, to take Samantha into the corral of his arms and tell her that he would be going back to scout for George Crook.

To greedily share what he could of their days, these next few weeks together . . . before he would ride off again.

* The Plainsmen Series, vol. 1, *Sioux Dawn*

She would understand, wouldn't she? Sam had known what he was before he asked her to marry him—so she would realize that he had to go. Nothing to do with the Indians, much less anything to do with the army itself. This scouting was not just something he did to earn money to support them now. No, scouting was what he was. *Who* he was. He was a plainsman.

No shavetail recruit. Not a saddle-galled rummy cavalryman. Nor was he like any of these half-drunk half-breeds the army relied on so.

There were few of his kind now that so many of the old ones had gone back east, or lay in lonely graves. No more was there a Jim Bridger to lead the army north on the Montana Road into the jaws of danger. No more was there a Liam O'Roarke—God and the Virgin Mary bless his wandering soul. And these days there wasn't even the like of a Sharp Grover—horse breeder now that he was. Only a few of them left after Bill Cody turned showman back east among all the perfumed men and women in stiffened crinoline dresses and starched shirtfronts.

Rumor even had it that Hickok himself was sitting out this dirty little war, playing cards up in Deadwood.

So more and more the army here sought to use men from the warrior tribes themselves to track down the other wandering wild bands. And when the army could not find any of those to do its work, men like George Crook hired on half-breeds. The closest thing to the brown-skinned horsemen the army could come.

Except for those the likes of Seamus Donegan.

As she stirred restlessly, he turned to gaze in her direction. Slowly Sam opened her eyes, then rubbed one eye with a set of knuckles, followed by rubbing the other with the same hand.

"Aren't you cold?" she asked as he came over to sit on the edge of the bed.

"Didn't notice it before," he replied, only then seeing a wisp of his breath in the cold room.

Patting the pillow beside hers, Samantha said, "Come back to bed, Seamus."

He smiled at her. Lord, how could he keep from smiling

—she was such a joy to his life. So much what he had always hoped for: a woman who knew how to go after what she wanted when it was a man that she desired most. How she sheltered him, cared for him, came into him so fiercely it had scared him more times than he cared to dwell on. Scaring him so with what she gave that he wondered would he be able to return what she had given him.

And knowing that he must, and would—with every day they had together. Every hour and moment they shared. Seamus vowed he would give back his all, gazing down into her red, sleepy eyes . . . vowed he would return in kind what security, what joy, what blessing she had brought to his lonely heart, his empty soul.

When he had knelt to kiss her on the lips, finding them warm and so soft as they opened for him, Seamus stroked her cheek with two fingertips. "I'm hungry, woman."

"Hungry for what?" she asked, that look of devilment like a fire flickering in her eyes of a sudden.

He laughed. "You'll wear me down to nothing—and I'll be no good to you if I don't get fed least once a day."

With one hand squeezing, teasing along one of his arms, she said, "It's true—those few meals you had on that march of yours clearly weren't enough, dear man."

"Like I told you—I must be fed," he replied, knelt to kiss her forehead. "I'll see what I can scare up downstairs in the kitchen. Smells of someone cooking," he replied, taking another whiff of the rainbow of aromas beckoning to him from below.

"Bring back a little something for me," Sam said.

Smiling, he pulled on one boot. "Feeling you again after so long, I'd say you haven't missed a meal nor had to do with quarter rations, Samantha Donegan."

At his words, he watched her blush, turning her eyes away from his for that moment. With one hand she lightly stroked her belly. Seamus reached for the second boot.

"Perhaps, when you come back with something to eat— we can have us a picnic right here, Seamus," she said softly, patting the comforter beside her. "And then you can tell me about when next you will leave."

His breath caught in his chest as he pulled the boot half on. "How . . . how did you know?"

"That you'd be leaving?" she asked, bringing herself up on an elbow, baring a freckled shoulder. "We've heard rumors ever since General Crook passed through here better than a week ago. Talk is common on a frontier army post, so I've learned."

"Yes—but those might well be nothing more than rumors—"

"All right. I knew it when I looked into your eyes last night in the moonlight, Seamus. Knew you'd be leaving again."

"I was waiting to tell—"

"And it's all right," she said to him, rising a bit more, clutching the blankets to her breasts, both shoulders bare.

He glanced at the soft swell of the tops of those breasts, remembering how kissing and caressing them brought him such pleasure as he moved within her heated moistness. "Then, we will have us a picnic, here. And stay with one another every last minute we have until I go back to ride with Crook."

She nodded, her eyes moistening, a look on her face as if she were angry with herself for that—not having intended to cry. "Go, get us something to eat. Seems I'm so very hungry these days, dear husband. So, when you return, I have something of a little secret to tell you of my own."

"You? Why, you never struck me as the sort to keep a secret, Sam," he said as he swept up her hand and kissed her palm once, twice and a third time before setting it back atop the comforter.

"That's why I'm going to tell you when you come back from the kitchen," she answered. "I can't keep a secret . . . and I'm dying to tell you before I burst."

"I'll be back. And then you can tell me what it is you can't hold a secret any longer," he said as he turned and strode across the room.

When he had closed the door behind him and stood in the hallway at the top of the stairs, Seamus paused for a moment with his back against the narrow door, his hand still on the brass knob. Of a sudden, the lance stab of sadness pierced the heart of him.

But why? he chided himself. She understood, didn't she? From the sound and the look of things—Sam showed him she understood his going.

And their time together in the next few weeks would be all the more special for the time they would be apart. So why . . . why did he feel this way, when everything seemed in order, everything in its place?

Near the foot of the stairway someone opened the front door, allowing the early morning its cold entrance. He shuddered, with more than that frigid draft. Deciding when to dare drop into the cold.

What of the brutal storm that Crook and Reynolds had just stirred up and turned loose to batter the northern plains? That blizzard on Powder River was clearly far from over.

And the red blizzard was only beginning.

Afterword

While it was probable that a big showdown between the whites and the hostile Sioux and Cheyenne was inevitable, it was undoubtedly triggered by the Reynolds fight on Powder River.

This statement by J. W. Vaughn, author of *The Reynolds Campaign on Powder River*—the most complete book dealing with the battle—has long formed the framework for my understanding of not only this isolated fight in southeastern Montana, but of the subsequent actions taken, and mistakes made, by the various army commanders in the Great Sioux War of 1876.

For too long too many people have believed that Custer's defeat at the Battle of the Little Bighorn existed in its own vacuum. They have been shortsighted, if not outright wrong. The Sioux War started when Sherman, Sheridan and Crook talked President Grant into reversing his policies, breaking the law and initiating hostilities against the free-roamers. The bloody cycle of events they put in motion would last well beyond the confines of the white man's calender of 1876.

What I've hoped to accomplish in *Blood Song* is to give you, my reader, a grasp of how these events began to hurtle headlong toward a compelling destiny, sweeping up so many in its frightful journey into history. In addition, I have wanted to give you an idea of the simmering controversy revolving around Colonel Joseph J. Reynolds and the rest whose personalities severely limited the ability of the Big

Horn Expedition to accomplish its stated goal of driving the hostiles back to their reservations.

Once again the pride and egos of a few threatened the safety, the very lives, of the many.

In this rare case, the final chapter of this odyssey is far different than we normally read: for in the case of Reynolds, Moore and Noyes, we find that charges were brought against them for the incompetence or cowardice shown in the face of the enemy.

Even more compelling to me is that in his handling of this single event and its seamy, divisive aftermath, I came to see more of George C. Crook than I could learn through a reading of his own autobiography, or in biographical treatments on the man. Here was a commander who clearly saw himself as culpable after the debacle on Powder River, and quickly seized the moment to amass enough testimony from the legions of disgruntled officers so he could assure that the failure of his Big Horn Expedition would not seriously reflect upon his own career and military reputation.

In the end, Crook made as many mistakes as anyone. Errors in judgment and personnel selection, if you will. Try as he might to focus the blame on others—George Crook would live out the remaining years of his illustrious career with that one stain: his choice of Joseph J. Reynolds to lead the expedition would, to many of his peers, show Crook's own lack of sound judgment.

I am also indebted to author Vaughn for making sense of this battle that had no clear front and many differing accounts. Yet when one finally dismisses the self-serving testimony of all witnesses before the military courts-martial of Reynolds, Moore and Noyes—paying heed to that testimony that is corroborated by others—then a clear pattern of the action taken by the various units that plunged into battle begins to emerge. From Vaughn's work among the Records of the War Department, Office of the Judge Advocate General, I was actually able to find spoken dialogue between the principals, words I could put into the mouths of these historical characters. The courts-martial are enlightening reading for their drama, exposing the interpersonal conflicts between the major characters of this sordid tale.

On March 28, the day after his confrontation with General Crook (and the day after Crook hurried back to Omaha), a clearly worried Colonel Reynolds applied to the War Department for an official inquiry whose sole purpose would be to investigate his conduct during the battle, and therefore clear his name. Again on April 5 he applied to the Adjutant General for such an inquiry, but none was ever held.

The army's wheels of justice were already in motion.

At Fort D. A. Russell, near Cheyenne City, Captain Noyes was the first to come to trial on April 24, the charges against him changed from neglect to the more serious one of neglect of duty before the enemy. Noyes, it must be remembered, had always freely admitted that he dismounted his troops and ordered them to unsaddle, allowing them to make coffee and have lunch during the battle. It was the sort of thing that made great grist for the papers both West and East, which repeatedly referred to the battle of March 17 as "the St. Patrick's Day Celebration on the Powder."

When the charges of "conduct to the prejudice of good order and military discipline" were read to the captain, Noyes pleaded not guilty, and the trial had barely begun when it screeched to an unexpected halt. The Fort Russell commander had been unable to locate a suitable enlisted man to act as clerk to the court (since the soldier named Cook was "unavailable"), so the post commandant sent a note to the tribunal: "Cook will be at your service if sober. In case Cook's spree continues, and to save time, the General thinks it would be well for you to look up a citizen clerk."

Accordingly, the court moved to Cheyenne City itself and resumed the trial five days later. Noyes never took the stand in his own defense. Instead, he submitted a written statement where he admitted unsaddling and allowing his men to boil coffee, but he claimed those were not grievous errors, as the fight was a small skirmish and nothing that could be dignified as a "battle."

In the end, Noyes was found guilty as charged, sentenced to be reprimanded by Department Commander Crook. He was immediately released from arrest and returned to duty in time to be given command of a battalion of five companies of the Second Cavalry as part of Crook's fateful summer campaign marching back into the land of the Sioux and Cheyenne.

It is a story I will tell in the forthcoming ninth volume in the Plainsmen Series.

Anxious to have his trial over and done with as well, Captain Moore filed a request to stand before the court immediately following Captain Noyes. However, Moore was not near as fortunate. While awaiting the wheels of justice to slowly grind, Reynolds proceeded under his orders at Fort D. A. Russell to prepare his Third Cavalry for that next expedition Crook was planning to take the field by the end of May. But neither he nor Moore would leave with their units to take part in the famous Rosebud campaign. In fact, by the time the next courts-martial convened on January 6, 1877, not only had the battle of the Rosebud taken place, but the summer and fall campaigns, with their battles of the Little Bighorn and Slim Buttes, the Dull Knife fight and the battle at Wolf Mountain, had become military history.

When at last the charges were read to Reynolds before the military court at the Inter-Ocean Hotel in Cheyenne City, the colonel pleaded not guilty.

The first charge lodged against him by Crook was, of course, disobedience of orders. Included was the first specification that Reynolds had issued orders to march away from the camp at Lodgepole Creek, which would have prevented the ordered rendezvous with Crook's column of packers. The second specification listed the burning of the saddles, meat and robes in the village.

A grave and hushed court heard the reading the second charge, that of abandoning not only the battlefield, but abandoning the wounded and dead to the enemy as well.

The third charge was the eternal catchall: conduct to the prejudice of good order and military discipline. In specifications, Reynolds was charged with allowing the enemy to recapture their pony herd, as well as not giving pursuit to the escaping herd. In addition he was charged with not adequately supporting Captain Egan's pistol charge, and permitting Noyes's company to unsaddle when it was desperately needed on the skirmish line.

As well, the fourth charge—of conduct unbecoming an officer and gentleman—did little to bring credit to the frontier army. These specifications were more a bickering over niggling points brought to light between Crook and Reynolds during their testimony at the Noyes' trial.

The Reynolds case clearly shaped up to be a bitter and heated struggle. There were angry exchanges between Reynolds and practically every witness on the stand. In fact, Reynolds himself stated for the record that Crook had been well-satisfied with the outcome of the campaign until the controversy reached the newspapers.

Reynolds next delivered a sharp attack on Crook for dividing the command at Otter Creek and for failing to cooperate with him in the actual attack. In conclusion, the colonel angrily asserted that Crook was attempting to thwart criticism from himself by bringing charges against his leading subordinate. In short, Reynolds claimed his Department Commander was making a scapegoat of him.

Crook was the first to testify, stating that he had specifically given Reynolds orders to save saddles, meat and robes from the village, in addition to stressing the importance of the captured ponies, which would be carrying the plunder from the village. He then went on to illuminate his thinking, claiming that he was hopeful that the colonel would hang on to those provisions so that the expedition could march farther down the Powder and surprise more hostile villages.

As Vaughn so aptly writes, "This statement must have sounded rather hollow to the court, since the evidence showed that it was all the command could do to get back to its base."

After Private Jeremiah Murphy and Blacksmith Albert Glavinski testified that the column abandoned the dead and wounded on the battlefield, the army rested its case.

When Reynolds began his defense, he again criticized Crook for dividing the command and stated that the Department Commander had never issued specific orders regarding the captured village, that he was instead left to his own discretion. Under enemy fire, he told the judges, he decided that he could not bring anything away from the village without further endangering the lives of his men, so had destroyed the enemy camp as completely as possible.

Catching and loading the hostiles' ponies was totally unpracticable, for it would have taken too many men from their duties at the skirmish line—Egan, Mills and Noyes were just barely holding back the enraged warriors as it was. In the end of his denunciations for just about all his subordinates, Reynolds claimed he had given no orders to abandon the dead on the field, stating that such responsibility rested with the company commanders.

What proves most enlightening to me are those questions the colonel raised during the days of testimony. Questions that went to the heart of the controversy:

"If Crook wanted the provisions hauled away from the village, why did he not furnish some pack mules (at the outset)?

"If Crook wanted the ponies recaptured on the eighteenth, why did he not do it when he arrived at Lodgepole Creek with fresh troops?

"Why did Crook not take the trail agreed upon in going to Lodgepole Creek?

"Why did Crook abandon Reynolds's trail to turn south at the Lodgepole (instead of following in the colonel's wake to possibly assist him in any mopping up of the enemy village)?"

Yet as bitter as were his denunciations of Crook for his lack of support, Reynolds saved his most vitriolic attacks for Major Thaddeus Stanton:

The United States Army is entitled to know whether a non-combatant paymaster can be taken from his legiti-

mate duties, to act as a newspaper correspondent on an
Indian campaign, and giving strength to his statements
by his official position, can, under the smiles and encour-
agement of the Dept Commander denounce in public
print, as cowards and imbeciles his fellow officers, both
his superiors and inferiors in rank, and not even have his
conduct inquired into.

Try as he might with his energetic defense, Reynolds did
not stand a chance. Make no mistake—this was Crook's
court.

The conclusions of that court-martial were that Colonel
Joseph J. Reynolds was guilty of burning the saddles, meat
and equipment in violation of direct orders, and guilty of
abandoning the dead on the field. In addition, he was found
guilty of not ordering the recapture of the pony herd. In the
end, guilty on all counts and specifications.

Reynolds won a small victory when that same court reprimanded Crook for allowing regimental paymaster Stanton
to accompany the Big Horn Expedition as a newspaper
correspondent in violation of long-standing orders and reg-
ulations. The judges concluded: "This Court cannot but
regard such a practice as pernicious in the extreme and
condemns it as unsoldierly and detrimental to the efficiency
and the best interests of the service."

One has only to remember George Armstrong Custer's
long and close relationship with the eastern press, as well as
his decision to ignore Sheridan's directive not to take reporters along when he had welcomed Mark Kellogg to join
the Seventh Cavalry on their ill-fated march to the Greasy
Grass . . . already history by the time the Reynolds court
sat in judgment of the aging colonel of the Third Cavalry.

And, as we will see in the ninth volume of this ongoing
series, there were again newsmen along for Crook's next
"defeat" at the Battle of the Rosebud, barely a week before
Custer and five companies fell beside the Little Bighorn.

Reynolds was suspended from rank and command for a
period of one year, findings that were approved by the Secretary of War.

At that point, however, Reynolds's old classmate at the Academy, U.S. Grant, stepped into the fray. "In view of the long distinguished and faithful service of Col Reynolds the President has been pleased to remit the sentence."

Still, the damage had been done. Unlike the charges of bribery and kickbacks that had haunted Reynolds from his days in Reconstruction Texas, this was something that would not possibly be wiped clean. Grant's own remission of the sentence was clearly a confirmation of the widely held opinion that the colonel was indeed guilty. Dishonored before his peers, disgraced before the nation he had served for most of his lifetime, Joseph J. Reynolds retired on disability from the army one year to the day after Custer's defeat, June 25, 1877.

It was a sad ending to a sadder affair. True, as author Vaughn states, there can be no defense offered for abandoning the dead to the enemy, bodies that could have easily been lashed to horses or strapped on the backs of a handful of captured ponies before retreating to the south.

And this matter of just what orders were or were not given by Crook at that Otter Creek camp? Vaughn succinctly states:

> The charges relating to the giving of oral orders depended upon one man's word against another's. During the stress and strain of the campaign there was every possibility of misunderstanding. It would seem that if Colonel Reynolds committed any errors, they were errors of judgment which were made during the heat of battle, when instant decisions were required.

Indeed, it seems to me that the severe criticisms most historians have leveled at Colonel Joseph Reynolds are entirely unwarranted. And by extension, I have to agree that the findings of the court-martial, with the exception of that matter of abandoning the dead on the battlefield, were not only unjust, but perhaps capricious (as if the judges were totally cognizant of the desires of the Department Commander, George C. Crook).

It was not until January 16, 1877, that the trial of Brevet Major Alexander Moore began, charged with failing to cooperate with his fellow officers or to attack the village as ordered, as well as an infraction of the forty-second article in "misbehaving before the enemy." The main specification stated that the captain did "tardily, timorously [and cowardly fail to] cooperate in said attack ordered and instructed, and did remain so far from said point of attack . . . as to render the service of his command of little or no service . . ."

In addition, another specification noted that Moore had withdrawn his command from the mountainside to a more concealed position of safety down under the mesa, where he failed to resume his former position, nor did he come to the aid of those companies requesting reinforcement in the village.

Both John Bourke in his various writings, and newsman Bob Strahorn in his scathing dispatches for the *Rocky Mountain News,* were quite vocal in their denunciations of Moore for what they described as his cowardly acts, as well as his lack of action in support of other companies in the face of enemy fire.

However, the most intriguing crumb of controversy had already occurred the previous summer of 1876, when Moore signed a sworn statement that had in fact been written by Major Stanton for one reason and one reason only: to be signed by Moore and therefore implicate himself beyond repair. One has to ask why would Moore have done such a thing? Was he threatened with something far more serious if he did not agree to sign the Stanton transcript? And, if he was threatened, who threatened him? Moore would surely not be intimidated by Stanton himself.

One must remember that Thaddeus Stanton was the assigned paymaster at Omaha department headquarters, working directly with General Crook's Department of the Platte.

While some things become more clear from a careful study of these written statements, other matters grow more muddied, fuzzy and impossible of understanding—for this begins to read like a prime-time soap opera with all the principals choosing sides, firing salvos of recrimination after salvos of intimidation at one another.

Ultimately, from my reading of the testimony and documentation of the action in and around the village during the battle, I found it very strange that the court rendered a verdict of not guilty of disobeying orders and of withdrawing his command after the flank attack by the warriors. However, Moore was found guilty of conduct prejudicial to good order and military discipline in failing to cooperate fully in Reynolds's attack. At the same time, he was again found not guilty of misconduct before the enemy and of "cowardly failing to" cooperate with his fellow officers.

Moore was sentenced to be suspended from his command for six months and confined to the limits of his post for that period of time. As light as was his sentence, Moore never recovered from the dishonor. He resigned from the service two years later in 1879.

These officers of the Big Horn Expedition, many of whom had amassed a noteworthy battle record during the Civil War, were seemingly reduced to mealy-mouthed carping at one another in an attempt to save their own rear ends. While those of us today will likely never truly know just what suffering those officers and men endured hundreds of miles from their posts, many, many miles from their tents and extra blankets, as far away as summer must have seemed from their rations on that pack train—most might find it hard to comprehend what that much sustained cold, that much bone-numbing fatigue, and that much soul-robbing hunger can do to a man's faculties to reason, cooperate, work for the common good.

Clearly, the bodies and the minds of that command led by Crook into the wilderness, and especially that cavalry command led by Reynolds into the valley of the Powder River, were starving for proper nourishment, warmth and rest. These were men operating at the far extent of their ropes, expected to fight seasoned warriors under the most miserable conditions the northern plains are known to hand out. While it is clear that the warriors fought bravely and with savvy, making courageous charges and forays into the soldier lines, it is just as clear that it would have been suicidal for Reynolds to do as the second-guessing historians wanted him to have done: to hold that village.

In light of all of those negative factors, it is amazing to me that Reynolds's cavalry didn't take more casualties during the battle and while it was retreating to Lodgepole Creek. Just as was to happen to five companies of cavalry some three months later beside the Greasy Grass, that cavalry column of the Big Horn Expedition might easily have even found itself fully surrounded and nearly annihilated that St. Patrick's Day. Few could dispute the fact that the possibilities of disaster did exist on the morning of March 17, 1876.

For those of you who would like to read more about this little-known and little-read battle that proved to be the opening salvo of the Great Sioux War, as well as its unseemly aftermath of recrimination and courts-martial, I would like to suggest the following titles:

Battle of the Rosebud—Prelude to the Little Bighorn, by Neil C. Mangum

Campaigning with King—Charles King, Chronicler of the Old Army, edited by Paul L. Hedren

Centennial Campaign—The Sioux War of 1876, by John S. Gray

Crazy Horse, by John R. Milton

Crazy Horse and Custer—The Parallel Lives of Two American Warriors, by Stephen E. Ambrose

Crazy Horse—The Strange Man of the Oglalas, by Mari Sandoz

Custer's Luck, by Edgar I. Stewart

Death on the Prairie—The Thirty Years' Struggle for the Western Plains, by Paul I. Wellman

"Debacle on Powder River," by Wayne R. Austerman, *Wild West* magazine, December, 1991

The Eleanor H. Hinman Interviews on the Life and Death of Crazy Horse, edited by John M. Carroll

Fighting Indian Warriors—True Tales of the Wild Frontiers, by E. A. Brininstool

Fort Laramie and the Pageant of the West, 1834–1890, by LeRoy R. Hafen and Francis Marion Young

Frank Grouard, Army Scout, edited by Margaret Brock Hanson

Frontier Regulars: The United States Army, 1866–1891, by Robert M. Utley

General George Crook, His Autobiography, edited by Martin F. Schmitt

The Great Sioux War, 1876–77 (The Best from Montana, the Magazine of Western History), edited by Paul L. Hedren

Great Upon the Mountain—The Story of Crazy Horse, Legendary Mystic and Warrior, by Vinson Brown

Indian Campaigns—Sketches of Cavalry Service in Arizona and on the North Plains, by Captain Charles King

Indian-Fighting Army, by Fairfax Downey

Life and Adventures of Frank Grouard, by Joe DeBarthe

My Story, by Anson Mills, Brigadier General, U.S. Army

The Oglala Lakota Crazy Horse—A Preliminary Genealogical Study and an Annotated Listing of Primary Sources, by Richard G. Hardoff

On the Border with Crook, by John G. Bourke

The Plainsmen of the Yellowstone, by Mark H. Brown

The Reynolds Campaign on Powder River, by J. W. Vaughn

The Snowblind Moon, by John Byrne Cooke

"The Soldiers are Coming!", by Fred H. Werner

Soldiers West—Biographies from the Military Frontier, edited by Paul Andrew Hutton

Warpath—The True Story of the Fighting Sioux Told in a Biography of Chief White Bull, by Stanley Vestal

War-Path and Bivouac, or, The Conquest of the Sioux, by John F. Finerty

With Crook at the Rosebud, by J. W. Vaughn

Wooden Leg, A Warrior Who Fought Custer, by Thomas B. Marquis

In closing, I want to thank those kind folks in and around the friendly community of Broadus, Montana, who helped me learn all the more by walking the land where the Reynolds's fight took place. Bob and Ann Carroll helped steer me on the right track to getting in contact with those who could aid me in my firsthand research. They put me in touch with Jean Sterling, owner of the land, who kindly gave me permission to walk the property and hills west of the Powder River. Mrs. Sterling, in turn, put me in touch with George Fulton, the stockman who is currently leasing the battle site, a man who is as well a student of the Reynolds fight, a gentleman who kindly benefited this author with the wealth of his knowledge.

Yesterday, the 116th anniversary of that cold winter night march up and over the divide from Otter Creek, I spent the afternoon and early evening four-wheeling back and forth along the narrow, rutted, dusty roads that crisscross their way east toward the Powder River from the country of the Tongue. It has been a most unusual winter this year in Montana: unseasonably warm and with little snow—whereas 116 years ago it was brutally cold for that intrepid band of cavalry seeking the village of war chief Crazy Horse. I drove most of the day through those meadows and timbered hills, down the creek drainages, rolling along with the windows rolled down and my shirtsleeves rolled up.

But early this morning, anniversary of the battle, the fickle bitch of weather on these high plains had turned her face against us once more and I awoke in my small motel room in Broadus to find it raining.

And, as they say out here, this is no Presbyterian sprinkle —it's an outright Baptist deluge!

South of town, I cover thirty-five miles to the white-draped battle site on a muddy road turned to gumbo, just as this snow-covered countryside must have done for the hooves and wagon wheels in those days following the battle in 1876.

In the end on this cold, bitter, blustery morning, I have a better feel for what those soldiers and warriors endured during that hard-fought battle here on this ground where I sit huddled out of the wind in the lee of a cedar tree, writing my final notes before I, unlike those cavalry troopers, can escape back to the warmth of my truck and hurry north to town, where I'll find warm food and blankets awaiting me after my muddy, subfreezing journey.

I would like to leave my readers with the following, quoted from J. W. Vaughn's incomparable book, *The Reynolds Campaign on Powder River:*

The warriors, fortified by the consciousness of right, were fighting for their homes and families on land set apart for them by the treaty of 1868. Treaties of the United States, made by the president with the concurrence of two-thirds of the senators present, were the "supreme law of the land." The solemn treaty with the Indian tribes certainly could not have been revoked by a mere departmental order or the Indian Bureau directing them to return to the reservations. The Indians had a right to ignore it. Neither did the army have the right to send the expedition against the roving tribes, because the power to declare war was vested in Congress, which had not acted. The whole campaign was a violation of the treaty and of the Constitution of the United States. There was no more legal right to attack this village than there was to attack a Canadian village across the border. While the troopers were simply acting under orders, the campaign had been carefully planned and executed under the direction of General Sheridan and General Sherman, with the blessings of President Grant. This flagrant action reflected the temper of the American people, who were incensed with the failure of the Indian tribes to surrender the Black Hills. The only regret was that the little band [of Cheyenne] had not been completely annihilated.

The net result of the campaign was the Sioux war. The Indians were enraged at the unprovoked attack. They had withdrawn far from the most advanced white settlements. The Cheyennes had long been at peace with the Great White Father, but now they joined with the Sioux tribes under Sitting Bull and the war chief, Crazy Horse, for mutual protection against the soldiers.

. . . While it was probable that a big showdown between the whites and the hostile Sioux and Cheyennes was inevitable, it was undoubtedly triggered by the Reynolds fight on Powder River.

The rest, as they say . . . is history.

Terry C. Johnston
Powder River Battlefield
Montana Territory
17 March 1992

TERRY C. JOHNSTON
THE PLAINSMEN

THE BOLD WESTERN SERIES FROM
ST. MARTIN'S PAPERBACKS

COLLECT THE ENTIRE SERIES!

SIOUX DAWN (Book 1)
92732-0 _____ $5.99 U.S. _____ $6.99 CAN.

RED CLOUD'S REVENGE (Book 2)
92733-9 _____ $5.99 U.S. _____ $6.99 CAN.

THE STALKERS (Book 3)
92963-3 _____ $5.99 U.S. _____ $6.99 CAN.

BLACK SUN (Book 4)
92465-8 _____ $5.99 U.S. _____ $6.99 CAN.

DEVIL'S BACKBONE (Book 5)
92574-3 _____ $5.99 U.S. _____ $6.99 CAN.

SHADOW RIDERS (Book 6)
92597-2 _____ $5.99 U.S. _____ $6.99 CAN.

DYING THUNDER (Book 7)
92834-3 _____ $5.99 U.S. _____ $6.99 CAN.

BLOOD SONG (Book 8)
92921-8 _____ $5.99 U.S. _____ $6.99 CAN.